In Defense of Eve

A Tale of Yore

by Richard R. Kennedy

Publisher
Richard R. Kennedy

First printing

(© 2002, Unpublished. Revised for publication: © 2006

ISBN: 978-0-6151-6963-7

Published by
Richard R. Kennedy,
Boynton Beach, FL 33436-2081

Printed in the United States

In Defense of Eve

Prologue

Long ago was an unrecorded distant land by the sea. Its southern terrain was mostly rolling hills and dales while a smaller section to the north was mountainous. The tallest mountain loomed high above a cliff along the shore. On the other side it faced a vast valley rich with vegetation. At the base of this mountain, the top of which was partially blown off before the dawn of man, there had been built a millennium ago an enormous castle. Behind this fortress—even long before—slanting off and up was a long, twisting narrow passage with steps ascending and then descending into a wide cavern.

There under poised stalactites high above dozed an ancient, wizened man in a gold and white robe sitting at the edge of a pit raging with fiery lava. On the opposite side, imbedded into the cavern wall was a fossilized tree. Strangely, an offshoot protruded from where its roots once were. An ionic jade-like glow shot up from the lava and shaped a figure of a beautiful dark-haired woman clad in a red and gold linen tunica, laced with a gold belt. She wore a headband of gold with ruby inlay. The old man stirred, then popped his eyes in disbelief and fright. He raised himself up, then fell to his knees in prayer as the glowing figure ascended rapidly up into the cavern heights and streamed through the volcanic aperture into the night air above the land of Lodeston.

The same evening far to the south in the flat lands of Quandron a sultry raven haired young woman danced impassionedly but gracefully in the lambent light of a gypsy campfire circled by wagons and—to the vexation of the women present—the men clapped and ogled, some of whom could not control reaching out for her to touch and pinch her flimsily attired, tawny body. She would look askant, smile coquettishly and nimbly swirl off and glide toward the center near the fire. In exhaustion she finally—to the relief of the women—glided over to a young man and fell into his arms. He carried her off to his hoop cart, covered carelessly with motley cloth, where they engaged in passionate foreplay. As the young man raised himself to spread open her legs, the jade green glow of the north immersed into the girl's body. She sighed and wrapped her legs around the bronze haunches of her mate.

A golden, diaphanous cloud centrifuged tiny, scowling cherubs above the cart, and then illuminated a gorgeous golden haired woman in an elegant white and gold robe. She extended her arm downward and the greenish yellow glow burned through the covering and restored the image of the dark-haired lady from the cave. The two images, enveloped in white and green light, rose up high into the black sky while the golden one with a smirk upon her face commented, "I see, Lilith, that you are up to your perverse sense of good as usual."

"Humph, *usual!*" the dark haired lady blurted, "I shouldn't think after a five thousand year respite, that I'm guilty of a repetitious act!...Besides, how dare you accuse me of mischief after what *you* did!"

The golden one laughed to the stars and glanced at her chuckling cherubs. "Nevertheless, that is the way of the Creation now, and you must return to your fiery grave." A fire bolt launched from her finger and Lilith was jolted and flung, howling all across Quandron, and sucked into the boiling rock of Lodeston.

The old man terminated his praying to the howling plunge of Lilith. Beside him stood the stern countenance of the golden haired beauty. He kneeled before her and bowed his head, nervously tugging on his long beard. Her expression softened with a mild smile as she forewarned him, "Ethan, you must stay alert; the balance of creation hinges on your sounding the alarm when she gets restive. Without the boiling purification and her continuous confinement here, the freedom of the human race will be returned to its spineless origin. It was fortunate that I myself was in Quandron to tend to a precautionary measure—call it intuition."

"Ah, yea, Lady Eve, always the cunning one!"

"And aware," she added, eying the shoot across the pit. "Keep the pruning axe by your side."

Nine months later a baby girl was born. The gypsy woman, holding the child close in her arms, was in awe as she gazed upon the infant shrouded in the mysterious glow of jade.

1. Manor of Mari

Out of a grim but final victorious battle a fortnight ago in the eastern inlands of Quandron, a young leader and his knights on war-worn horseback loped through the silence of their thoughts while winding through a path in a thicket. As the column of horsemen emerged from the dark forest into broad light of a meadow, the leader ordered the men to dismount. The men looked surprised; some grunted and groaned mild protest, now that they tasted the appetizer of home. He smiled and yelled laughingly as he got down from his spotted gray destrier—forbear of the Percheron—several hands above and infinitely sleeker than a generic draft. "I know, my stout hearted, you need no rest in spite of our long journey from our battle....Still, pity your loyal mounts; in truth, they do need a rest; thus let them pasture awhile so at least they will look fresh when we enter my father's castle."

While the knights dispersed to care for their war-mounts, another rode up to the leader. With tempered agony in his voice this heavy set rider said, "My Lord Protector, are you not anxious to arrive at the castle? In truth, your father impatiently awaits details of battle."

The lord shrugged in response. "Oh, much of it has been dispatched—barely worthy of the town-crier anymore."

"Still, the cry of distant victory is not sufficient to curb the appetite of curiosity," said the knight, with light annoyance. "Not only the lord master but the people must be eager to see you in all your glory to believe it."

The lord chuckled. "Seems to me it is you, baron, who are eager—perhaps anxious for a wench, eh?"

The burly knight laughed. A graying goatee and mustache framed big yellow teeth. "Well, yea, I suppose, there is one aching my groins."

The lord chuckled again while he patted Baron Bennet's mount. "It is your steed that aches. Remove its mail and yours and pause awhile." The lord-protector turned away to tend to his own steed, then looked back up with a broad grin and added, "Trust me, you will look more regal to your lady in your homecoming mounted on a steed reborn," he offered as he started to peel off his armor. He was a powerfully built six-footer—unusual for the times but not so among knights. His tabard bore a different coat of arms from Bennet's.

The stocky knight, Bennet, laughed again, wheeling his black charger round toward the other men and cantered off to rejoin the battalion under his ensign.

A long, lean but broad shouldered youth who had just peeled off his own breastplate, revealing the same coat of arms as the lord-protector's—a white eagle with a scroll in its talons across a field of purple, dared to speak: "My lord, the baron's castle is but a two hour ride." He removed his mail headpiece and a thick shock of flaxen hair leaped free.

" 'Tis true, lad, but the horses don't know that," the lord said calmly. "They have served us well."

"Aye, they have, my lord," the lad agreed, nodding with a smile.

"Besides..." the lord knight pointed to the bloody bandage round his horse's once powerful foreleg, and grimly observed, "he's been limping and the leg is swelling."

The youth inspected the leg closer and dourly shook his head. "The lady Rhonda will have our heads for this." He lightly tapped the warhorse's muzzle.

The lord-protector laughed. "Aye, on the mark, honest Bryan, you know well my sister's mettle."

Then Bryan removed the heavy saddle and slid off the unwieldy blanket of mail. The mighty horse trotted off, favoring its foreleg to graze as the youthful knight set the saddle down by the tree and glanced at his master and said with a sigh, "If only people were as loyal."

The older knight chuckled. "In truth, Bryan; still, you are as loyal; but..."

"Thank you, my lord, for your faith in me." The youth cut in as he began to spread out the mail blanket to wipe away the dust.

The protector grinned and shook his head. "Because you've only recently been dubbed a knight on the battlefield, you find it hard to give up your squire habits—you should be tending to your own, *Sir* Bryan."

He spread a shy smile, "Still, a strange ring to it....I shall;...still, there is no one as loyal and faithful as Lady Rhonda, I trust still."

The lord chuckled. "Too many stills may put her in frightful flight! Suffice that she's been waiting starry-eyed these months."

"Amazing how an experienced warlord can turn years into months." The youth chuckled, though suspecting Lance's confusion was his mother's recent demise.

The lord laughed, then tufted his trim beard over the battle scar on his chin. "How long then?—surely not two years yet."

"Two months over it," the youth said, knees in the heavily linked blanket, then returned to his previous thought, "Sti...*Though* I have faith, I shall still my breath, till I'm sure!"

The lord shook his head, then looked amicably upon the youth, "Good, lad—that is, good sir—with your polishing and his well deserved rest, my old gray will look refreshed and invigorated rather than a weakened nag when we march into the shadows of my father's castle. Poor old Stars, he more than I, deserves the honor....But tend to your own faithful steed, the blanket can wait." The lord knight sat down and rested against the trunk of a tree; his eyes followed his *great horse* with silvery starry spots gleaming under the sun as it grazed. He added wistfully to the youth, who was uncinching his own dark brown steed, "Without the great loyalty and endurance of the likes of Stars there would be no honor, no knighthood." He gave a forlorn sigh, knowing his lame horse could serve no more in noble combat.

The former squire scratched his head and asked belatedly, "No knighthood, my lord?—surely, an animal is not cause for such an honored station."

The lord knight laughed. "Oh, but it is; for the finest, and most powerful horses in the land are saddled by knights. That is what separates us from the ordinary fighter who still mounts the imported breed of the traditional past."

"How very odd, my Lord Lance," the youth said as he scratched his flaxen shock; "surely you have heard of the home-grown steeds of the mountain borough. Yet I have heard there are no knights there."

"Indeed, and why they are not in need of ours; for there is no substitute for the likes of old Stars," Lord Lance, said dejectedly as he thrust his chin to the meadow. "Still, I, too have heard of them: beauties, they say."

Bryan, brushing his steed, waxed, "And more,... it is said that the horses there are so swift of hoof, they more than compensate for the heavy protection we require."

"Aye, Bryan," the lord agreed, "there is a point to that. I've often thought myself that the paraphernalia of knighthood might well be counter-productive."

Bryan laughed. "With your war record, I wouldn't go so far as to say that!"

Somewhat phlegmatically, Lance said, removing his riding duster. "We must see for ourselves someday." Silence spread over them, and the lord knight nodded off to dream the dream that he could not escape, nor did he want to.

The Lord-Protector sighed in seeing the *Mari* colors flying from the tower top. The castle would be forever in the name of his mother's maiden name; her grandfather had built it, and her father established the Order, still blazoned on Lance's tabard and escutcheon. Seldom did he flaunt the shield of the king's. On the towering parapet serfs and guards alike poked their faces through the crenelated battlement as the drawbridge creaked in descent. All eyes were on the young but seasoned Lord-Protector as the battle-weary knights thundered across the bridge on rejuvenated horses into the bailey. Serfs like a receding wave reversed themselves and popped their eyes down upon the knights merging with the cheering crowd of the castle's outer ward of commerce. Knights and squires leaned from their steeds to touch the up-reaching hands of admiring marketplace women and peasant girls alike skipping along the column of warriors.

Only the Lord-Protector seemed distant, waving but mildly; only his young knight and former squire fixed his eyes to the donjon window high above when the column passed through the gate to the inner ward of nobles. Lord Lance noticed the young knight's attention elsewhere. He said laughingly, "Eyes only for my sister, eh, Bryan?" as he gestured to the window whence appeared his sister, waving. He beamed up a smile framed by an untrimmed, dusty beard and waved back. He looked over at his squire. "Ah, there she is! Off with you, Bryan, and with Cupid's blessing!"

Eying the quick jerk of the rein by Bryan, cried out a middle-aged knight, "Ah, if only I had his youth!" He pulled along side the protector's hobbling horse.

The protector laughed, turning to his lord captain. "When you had your youth, John, you didn't know how to use it in affairs of love."

"Precisely! Now I would know," he quipped. He looked down at a bosomy matron tugging on the chausses at the calf. "Ah, sweet thing, you want me, do you?...Well, wily woo-ess, meet me at the alehouse in a quarter sand."

She slid her hand up and clinked a cheap ring on the knee armor. She winked and, above the din of the crowd chanting *Lord Lance the Liquidator*, croaked, "Yea, my heroic deary, I'll be there but I warn you I can quaff with the best of them."

"And the other talent, too, I trust?" He sniggered. He glanced over at his lord commander and winked. He heeled his huge destrier, then tugged the checkrein to ask, "Care to join us, Lance?"

Lance chortled. "I thought you were just pining that you were too old for that?"

"Oh, never too old, but I *would* like to enjoy it more."

"Anyway, you go ahead, I must report to the manor lord, you know."

"Naturally,...tell the old sire I was detained." He cantered, dispersing the crowd.

The freshly knighted youth spurred off to the inner steps leading to the keep, dismounted before the tower and bolted through the massive opened door and up the twisting stairs. Reaching the second landing, he knocked on the heavy door—disappointed that she had not been there at open door and open arms greeting him. A sweet voice ordered him to enter. He swung in the door, gazed upon the vision that had been at the window. Then he dropped to his knee, cordially tapped the mail hood, then moved his hand to his heart and bowed his head.

"My, dear Bryan, such a cold greeting after so long an absence. I had rather hoped you'd come to sweep me off my feet," she chaffed with tender sarcasm.

He rose up and momentarily drank in the vision so grandly adorned, highlighted by ravishing red braids adorning the front of her dark green velvet dress. Though two years older now, to him she was still the delicate fifteen year old he had departed from to go off to war as a squire for the mightiest warlord in the land. Nevertheless, he noticed the round, rosy cheeks had thinned to a maturity of supple beauty. He leaped across the room, bowed, took her slim, smooth hand and kissed it. He raised himself up and his dark brown eyes melted into her sparkling blue. He hugged her, released her, nervously toyed with one of her braids, then kissed her on her lips. Her eyes popped, then slowly the lids lowered and she melted in his arms. His mouth slid to her ear and she heard, "Oh Rhonda, my love, how I missed you these years."

She squirmed from his arms and asked coyly, "Empty were they?...Even though my brother's conquests were heralded throughout the kingdom!"

"What good are conquests elsewhere?" He reached for her hands and urged her toward him. "The conquest that counts is here."

"Oh?" she said with a derisive snarl, "You think me a conquest, a trophy from the war?"

"Oh, Rhonda, not thirty grains of sand am I with you and already you lash me with your quipping tongue!" he cried as he released her hand and tugged on his shaggy hair. "You know full well I mean it is you who are the conquistadoress!"

"I see, thus, I command you to kiss me again." she giggled.

In a large room adjacent to the grand dining hall, the lord master of the manor slouched in a giant chair behind a huge table-desk as he pondered Lord Lance's report of the army's exploits. "You have done well, my son; these conquests added to our possessions' tallies to over half the kingdom." He rubbed his hands greedily, then reached for a goatskin bag and poured wine into a horn mounted on a silver stand.

The young lord's brows arched and then he paced the flagstone near the blackened hearth, subsequently backing away from the nauseous dank smell of charred scraps of wood left over the summer months. He approached the table and said jokingly, "Aye, my father, meaning that now you pay over half the taxes to the crown."

The father choked on the wine and let out a guffaw. "Oh, but not for very long, lad. Just think of the manpower we now control. Why, surely in the thousands."

"Aye,...so?" he asked as he sat down.

The father replenished the horn and said slyly, "It seems clear that one who lords over half the population directly should be king."

The young lord reached for the goatskin, grabbed and poured himself a drink into a horn, saying lightly, "Hardly directly, my lord, since you seldom leave the castle even to oversee our own Marian serfs let alone half the kingdom's. Why, the king's men tour the Mari more."

He slammed the horn onto the cradle, "I put a stop to that! I shall decide what the tithe shall be, not the king....Besides, as king I too would tour the land."

The young man laughed. "Only for the glory of worship the masses would extend you."

" Nay, rather for the tithes; I'd need no thieving tax-collectors. Aye, that would be my purpose. Can there be any greater purpose in life than the legacy of a dynasty?"

"There *is*, my lord and father."

"Don't forget eventually you would be king." He grinned and twinkled his eyes and snickered, "Aye, I see what you mean, but I am too old for youth's pursuits of women."

The young lord vaguely shook his head and smiled. "Tales told of you deny that. But I meant there comes a time when war should end, and justice begin."

"I haven't raised you to become a politician, young warrior. There are riches in sacking a manor; nothing but frustration in politics by trying to please everyone. Nay, respect is gotten from taking, not mollycoddling."

"Ah, but justice is stern, even though tempered with under-standing...my mother and my grandfather taught me that....Surely, you haven't forgotten the marriage contract."

"Bah, don't bring that up! You are a Kalab, not a Mari. I am your sire, don't you forget that! Both your grandfather and my wife were too heady, meddling intellects that eat away at power." The lord master looked to the vaulted ceiling momentarily, uttering, "In spite of your glorious victories, from my groins I wormed a bookish warlord, it appears!" He glanced at his son, "Is this the fate of nobility's future?—to be educated by milk-sopping monks and women that attempt to sheathe the power of the sword!"

"I am not a warlord, as you were in your youth, father. I do battle only when the defenseless calls upon me. We are, after all, a Christian nation, my lord; and need I remind you after centuries of travail bordering on barbarism that it is now a nation and thus we owe allegiance to the king."

"Aye, but to a king, which I intend to be. A king who intends to develop a nation of strength. I still hold your grandfather responsible for advocating a central government; yet ironically it now fits my purpose."

"Fie, father, you dare not march against the crown! You can't be serious!" The young lord grated as he leaned forward in his chair.

"And pray why not?" He said slamming his vessel of wine to the desk, spilling some of its contents.

"Why, Divine Right, my lord," he said more calmly.

Lord Kalab replenished his wine, held the horn before his lips and growled, "Bah, Church ceremony and fantasy—nothing more!" He drank some wine down and added, "What the Church and Lord Mari can grant to Henry, it can grant to me!"

"Call it ceremony and fantasy if you wish, but one need not believe, to accept its solemn reasoning on the temporal side of the coin."

"Poppycock! You grant that oaf of a king reason!" With anger he finished off his wine, then his rotund trunk flopped back in the huge chair fit for a throne.

"It is not Henry the man that is at issue, but the idea behind the stability of the crown," his son offered. "That was my grandfather's point."

"I need not your tutoring, my son—nor your ghost dredging. Stability stems from power and that I have more of than anyone else in the kingdom and thus I aim our crossbows to that end and your sword to point."

"Not this time, father."

"What's this? After having conquered the countryside on my behalf you concern yourself with the existing crown?" He quizzed, leaning forward again to refill his cup. "Why, that sop paid the church for the so-called divine right!"

"It is more than the crown I'm thinking of. Till now your wish was my command, but I cannot jeopardize unification of a nation because you have a dream to become king. I know well that you resent the Mari legacy."

"How dare you!"

"Oh, my father, be reasonable. It is not for you that I conquered, but rather to end the petty conflicts among the barons and to bring lasting peace to a young nation. And since you appear to lay claim to half the kingdom, are you telling me that you still haven't turned over the land from the previous exploits to the King's surveyors?—why, that is outrageous! You mentioned *sacking* before. I should not have to remind you that the Mari does not indulge in sacking but rather to protect the defenseless against tyrannical barons!"

"Do I hear right? Not for your own flesh and blood you risked your life and my men; but for some brainless purpose? Why I'd rather you did it for a woman than for this!"

The young lord could not restrain a smile. "Oh as in the war of Troy, I suppose?...Well, schoolmen say that war was for the idea of beauty rather than for Helen herself" Lance smiled and added, "I must confess, I did it in the past for my mother...and now in her memory."

"Bah, you and your ghostly past!" The lord master wriggled his nostrils, grunted, while jerking his frosty beard, "And what do the bookish Churchmen know about war! Warriors need the thrust of boiling loins of appetite to reach their end."

"Such as treason, I imagine. For what you ask of me is just that. True, I did purge the land of monstrous manor lords; but, remember, it was with the king's blessing as well as yours," he reminded him. "Surely, there was the need to defeat the warring boroughs that brought destruction to the people caught in between. Good riddance to that riffraff of monstrous leaders! The king already has sent his envoys to oversee the castles and relieve my contingent forces."

The father slumped heavily in his chair as he laughed raucously. "By God's blood you are a monkish knight! You actually believed I would allow that! Why, my own envoys already occupy those castles and rather than relieve, they now command *our* occupational forces. Since you're so monkish, you should appreciate that charity begins at home."

"Fie, for shame!" the young defender yelped, popped up from the chair to pound a fist on his father's desk. He stared down to the smug, pocked face. "Home is now the state, father. We cannot continue to fight among ourselves, lest forces from beyond the borders see us vulnerable. Defense of a nation is what matters now."

The heavy set lord master looked fiercely into his son's eyes and said in a grave tone, "If this castle in truth is not your home—for that is what you mean—then, you are not my son and must leave these battlements."

The young lord's jaw dropped in disbelief while he looked at his father and dropped back into his chair, shaking his head.

The door swung open and Rhonda dashed across the room and landed in her brother's lap and smothered him in kisses as she squealed in between, "Shame,... shame,...my unkind brother, ...Shame on you!" Her father laid on the scene a wistful eye of better times. She leaned back in his arms and chided, "You've been home for two tumbles of the glass and I have had to search every cranny of the castle for you! Why, my darling Lance, did you not impatiently search me out?"

Lovingly he smiled and gazed at his little sister's pixy expression, then swept her up in his arms and danced and swirled her about the room, she giggling and he laughing heartily. He dropped her gently in the chair, pecked her on the cheek, kissed her on the lips, took her braid and tickled her nose, chuckling, "Don't toy with me, sweet, little Rhonda; for well I know you were these two hours occupied by coyly dodging Cupid's darts of pup's love with Bryan." He tickled her nose again.

She giggled, then squeaked, "Heaven's, Lance, hardly could I trust myself for such a length of time. Besides, Bryan was not with me more than paltry grains and off he rushed to the stable to see to your dear, crippled horse."

His glee turned to momentary sadness, "Aye, I believe you—so concerned and loyal is my once devoted squire."

"What's this? Has Bryan fallen out of favor?"

He chuckled and lightly pinched her cheeks. "No, little sister, I dubbed him after our final battle."

She pressed her cheeks into his chest. "Oh, such good news! He never told me! Oh so gallant he is in modesty! Surely, he is most deserving, though still so young to be a knight."

"Young in years, but not when measured in battle experience," he noted.

"Oh, but such sad tidings in the health of your loyal mount!...Is there no hope for stout Stars?" she asked sadly.

"It's a wonder he survived a blow of a flying chain to bear me home. Nay, never will he be the same to take the brunt of battle."

"Poor Stars...how well, as a little girl, I remember him. So spirited a colt he was, and such pleasure did he give me at play. Now I swear I shall give him comfort while he heals. Though he may never be the same, I promise to tend to him and each day set him to pasture."

The father shook his head and said, "Oh, and are we in the business of extending charity to our horses, like a loyal and devoted serf too sick to perform his duties to the castle? Nay, the cost of feed is too great to retain a useless steed."

She wrinkled her pearly forehead and scowled. "And why not? Truly, one as gallant as Stars deserves our kindness. Oh, father, you cruelly jest to even think to send a proud and loyal steed to the tanner!"

The sparkle in her sky blue eyes faded and Lance eyed her with his own unhappy hazels. "I fear," he said gravely as he glanced down at his father, "our father has lost his sense of loyalty."

The father leered at him. "No more from you, especially to speak of loyalty to a horse when out the window flies loyalty to your blood."

Rhonda gripped the arms of the chair and thrust forward and said with puzzlement, "Pray, my ears deceive! Surely, I do not hear my father chide my hero-brother fresh home from marvelous battles."

Sadly her father looked into her puzzled eyes and said dejectedly, "There is no marvel to victorious battle when its purpose is misconstrued." He leered up at his son.

Rhonda waved him off. "Oh, father, such mystery is unbecoming—there is no other purpose than to win in behalf of good. Truly, our Lance has shown this....Now, stop this, you two....Must I be as our dear departed mother and stand between this boredom of father-son scraps?" She leapt from the chair and tipped the goatskin vessel into her father's horn, and another into her brother's. In handing them the drinking vessels, she said maturely, "Enough now, my men, clink the horns of wine in preparation for tonight's festivities in honor of our knighted warriors who bring honor to our land!"

Lance entered his room; so seldom home, he had to note details. He was grateful for the tub of tepid water drawn for him by Rhonda's handmaiden and other servants. An old man entered and hobbled over to him with greetings: "Young Lord, what a sight for these tired old eyes!"

Lance's eyes lit up. "Ah, my loyal Elm, how wonderful to see you again! Your eyes might not be what they used to be, but your attentive spirit as our loyal castellan, I see, is the same!" He gestured to the bath and fresh clothing laid out for him. "And the room has been sweetened...my nose tells me."

"Oh, yes, but that was Tracy's idea," he corrected his master and glancing over at the pretty dark-haired girl rubbing tallow to lather for the tub. "You do remember Tracy, don't you?"

"Why, of course, how could I forget the curly headed tot who was more a playmate to my sister than a servant girl." Tracy turned round from the tub and smiled reservedly. He walked over to her and picked her up in his arms, much as he had his sister and then pecked her on the cheek. "My between you and Rhonda I can't tell who has grown faster! You're both beautiful young ladies now!"

He let her down, and she looked up at him mildly embarrassed, but then stood on her toes and threw her arms round his neck. With an endearing look, she said, "Oh, my lord, it is so good to have you home and most of all safe....I could never stop worrying about you. I sometimes envied my Lady Rhonda for having such confidence that nothing terrible could ever happen to you."

"Ah, that's sweet of you, my dear." He pecked her on the ringlets over her cheek, then withdrew her arms. Patting her head, he said, "Now go and play with my sister, little one, I have to take a bath." He reached in and tested it. "My, it's just perfect—almost a shame to dirty it with over a fortnight of travel dust. Thank you, Tracy."

"Oh, my lord, dear me, we don't play anymore, except cards! We mostly talk now."

He laughed. "Aye, that's the proof in the plum pudding that you two are grown up women now!"

She curtsied, throwing him an innocent little kiss by the door way and ran out giggling.

He still had a smile on his face while turning to Elm to say, "What a lovely girl! It makes fighting all worth the pain when you see that you are protecting the likes of her."

"Oh, yea, lovely indeed—and worth the waiting too, eh?" Elm chuckled.

Lance shook his head and grinned. "Still have a little of the devil in you, eh?"

"Oh, young lord, it is not a fork, but rather a bow and arrow I carry, you know?" He arched his bushy white brows and tapped his heart. Lance mocked a poke in his face and laughed. Elm went on, "But really, sir, isn't it about time? And since none of the noble ladies have seemed to meet your fancy since you were a raw young lad of fifteen...I thought perhaps, you might be interested in an uncommon commoner."

"You're right in one respect, you honeyed meddling fool, the kind of blood does not concern me, he asserted. "But to suggest Tracy...well, simply ridiculous. Why, I think of her as another Rhonda under the roof."

"Oh, my, what a shame. Yea, we cannot have any of that," Elm laughed. The nation's hero courting a sister! We simply have to change your perspective of her—to ward off scandal to the Mari name."

Lance dropped the last of his raiment and immersed his rump in the tub, laughing. "Mari, eh?...Not Kalab?" He looked at the old meddler gathering up his clothing and then hanging his sword and baldric on a wall hook. "If it will make you feel any better, loyal Elm, you remind me of my mother always chiding me for my bachelor ways...."

The old castellan blessed himself at the mention of his adored former Lady of the Castle Mari, and sighed. "Ah, your dear mother, how I miss her graciousness and beauty!" He crossed himself again.

"But I have been thinking about it, said Lance, diverting the conversation about his mother."

"Tracy,?" the old man jumped, grinning from ear to ear.

Lance laughed. "No, not Tracy, you incorrigible mirth-sayer. I mean, I'm tired of the Order."

"Oh, bless my heart!—the very Order founded by your mother's father!"

"Aye, ironic isn't it that the Order of Governance should devolve upon my father!"

"Ah, but you have reinstated your grandfather's purpose!"

"In any case, I feel something is missing. Oh, I admit, it is gratifying to do good unto others. And the aspect of chivalry is romantic when you're young and you relish the pride when one benefits from your prowess. But I am not a monk; it is not personal enough. There is a big difference between the notion of love and the actual experience, I should imagine."

"Oh, yes, my lord, that's a very clean fact—no vagueness there." Then Elm got a twinkle in his eye. "But you said before that it was all worth the fighting for the likes of Tracy—surely, that's personal."

"Why you codger, you never give up, do you? Among other reasons she is still a baby. At least that is how I perceive her and probably always shall. And I still have enough knighthood in me to be a bit of a romantic—but the errant drive for a love that will totally and completely enchant me."

"I see,...yea, the errant quality of knighthood perceives enchantment residing at another place....Forgive me, young lord, but you still have some growing up to do." He smiled and left a towel within reach, and left his master speechless as he left the room.

Lance did not make the alehouse, but he did summon Sir John to his room before the banquet began at the castle. Sir Charles, a giant red bearded knight and third in command, accompanied John. "Good, Charles, that you are here, for I summoned John to detail a plan that you will be in charge of carrying out. To begin with, have the scribe duplicate this." He held up a parchment. "It seems my father is getting senile and cantankerous." He handed the scroll to Sir John, who appeared inattentive. "I really don't know if I can believe him, but it's too important to the crown for us to ignore. So I want you in the morning to arrange a rapid messenger network to deliver these countermanding orders to the relief guards sent to the manors we occupy."

Sir Charles scratched his shaggy beard and asked, "Countermand what, Lord Lance?" Sir John plopped in a chair.

"My fool father claims he preëmpted the king by sending his own relief guards with orders to subsume our men of the Mari for the purpose of holding the castles for his own designs!"

Sir John's face was in his hands which were rubbing his eyes and then he yawned. "Oh, my, forgive me, Lord Lance. But that wench was true to her word. She almost drank me under the table."

Charles laughed. "Not into bed, I gather, then?"

John shook his head. "Even if she had, with the condition she and I were in, we couldn't have done much." Lance and Charles laughed. John stretched his eyes and said, "But, now that I have gathered my faculties, Lance, it seems to me that old Kalab could be serious. Why, even in the old fighting days, he used to talk about setting up his own kingdom in direct violation of our Order."

"Well, I hope you're wrong, but we can't chance it; so see that the messengers are dispatched first thing in the morning. Our troops, though, I'm sure, have already resisted the old man's order."

The three men rose to their feet. Charles took the message from John: "While you two attend the banquet, I shall take this to the scribe. Those heading to the farthest points should leave tonight."

2. Erinysia

The great dining hall was cast in torchlight fixed to the gloomy walls and by candlelight on the long tables. The minstrel introduced the occasion with soft folk ballads as the knights reacquainted themselves with their wives or lady-friends. Successful merchants and guildsmen within the castle's wards and from nearby villages attended, bearing many gifts for the men of war and their ladies. The continuous flow of wine and ale raised the din of happy times and increased the tempo of song and rhythm. Servants bustled in and out under the arcade that crossed the bailey to the kitchen. Great platters of swine, venison, pheasant, and fruit cluttered the massive bench-tables and the bones and cores strewn the floor to the delight of hungry hunting hounds as the battle-worn men gorged themselves on such food they had not had in two years except, though not as elaborate, in the interims of securing rebellious manors.

At the center of the dais was the Lord Master Kalab, and apparently by design several chairs on his left were vacant. The sundry chairs on his right were reserved for the king and his entourage, even though he knew the king declined. The manor lord was busy gorging himself with a whole bird—though not without frequent glances at the low-profile dancing girl of the minstrel. On Rhonda's insistence, Bryan and Tracy were included at the left end. Rhonda and Tracy had not yet arrived. Lord Lance sat next and up from Rhonda's vacant chair. Nearest Kalab was Bennet, then Sir John between his comrades in arms. Sir John seemed in high spirits again for the festivity—keeping the cup-bearer busy.

Bryan was drumming his fingers on the table impatiently waiting for Rhonda.

Tracy finally entered looking ravishing in one of Rhonda's dresses and sat down next to him, touched his shoulder and asked, "Do you remember me, once-Squire Bryan, now the grand *Sir* Bryan?"

He dropped his jaw in surprise. "No, I can't believe it is little Tracy!...Amazing what two years can do!...And, of course, how could I ever forget you...always so close to Rhonda."

She giggled, then touched the lean knight's nervous hand: "Yea, but even then, speaking of closeness, you barely knew me, so taken up you were with Lady Rhonda."

"That's not true. I remember well how I used to think that nowhere in the world could there be two lovelier girls living under the same roof." He took her hand to kiss.

"My, until this day I've never had my hand kissed before," she said, feeling both embarrassed and proud, "and now this is the second time! The great Lord-Protector honored me with one too!"

"Evidently,... it is so difficult to think of you as a grown lady. I couldn't believe my eyes when I saw Rhonda either."

"Nor we of you!—leaving as a boy and returning a heroic knight! Rhonda and I are so proud of you!"

"Speaking of whom—what is detaining Rhonda?"

Tracy's eyes twinkled. "She wanted to dazzle you with her mother's necklace; but we couldn't find the jewel box. She is now trying to decide from her own jewels what to wear. She sent me down so you wouldn't feel awkward sitting alone."

"Hearken, she doesn't need jewels—why, she's a gem herself!"

"I would agree," Tracy said, "except I cannot think of my soft, gentle lady as a hard, cold stone!"

"Aye, you have a point," he yielded.

Rhonda finally arrived and before sitting down she boldly kissed him on the cheek. A Mari ivory medallion dangling conspicuously.

"Ah, yea, how well I remember that medallion your grandfather gave you!" Bryan said nostalgically as he momentarily fondled it.

"Oh, my dear Bryan, how I wish he were still alive sitting right now at the center! How so different and wonderful our lives would be!" Then she looked over at Tracy and reached across Bryan to touch her arm. "Except were it so I should never have met my dearest friend."

Bennet leaned across John to Lance and out of earshot of the lord of the manor: "Why does your father seem so aloof, my lord?" asked the baron. "This is so unlike him—especially on an occasion to honor glorious victory. Why, to look upon him one would think we lost!"

"Alas, it seems victory is not enough," the young lord said forlornly.

Sir Bennet chuckled. "Oh?...Did he want us to return with his enemies' heads on stakes as proof?"

"Nay, but it seems he wants the king's."

Looking surprised, the broad knight, clacked, "In sooth?" The baron grinned. "Surely, you jest." He rubbed his coarse, cropped, slightly graying goatee and looked over at the lord of the manor, tearing away at the pheasant and drinking it down with hefty drafts of ale.

Lance cast a glance and said, "I'm not the court jester but I hope my father is. Further, he threatens to disinherit me if I do not carry *his* banner to this vile purpose."

"But I trust, if he is indeed serious, you will not go against your father's wishes," he said confidently. "After all, our loyalty of knighthood is to him foremost."

"Not when his wishes go against the Crown and our Order," the young lord retorted unhesitatingly.

Bennet glanced momentarily at the old lord, then said despondently to the young lord, "Besides which, it is to him that I owe my scutage."

"Good grief!" Lance sputtered in disbelief. "Why would a trusted, heroic knight be beholden to him?"

"The time my battle wound crippled me for two years."

"Oh, is there no end to his meanness!" Lance chafed. "And, my God, that was eight years ago! Surely, my grandfather did not levy such a thing upon you!"

"Nay, it was imposed *after* his death."

Lance shook his head, glancing over momentarily at his father. "The scoundrel!"

"Well, whatever, it is almost paid in full." Bennet. stroking his hairy chin, again glanced over at Kalab the lord of the manor. He added,

"Perhaps your father has good reason."

"Sufficient reason, aye. He wants to be king; but I wouldn't call that reasonable—rather, treachery."

Sir Bennet raised his tankard, restrained a smile, then quaffed the ale. He looked out at his banner knights' becoming more raucous and merry. "I suppose, your father—perhaps rightly—thinks Henry is not from the cut of kings."

The young lord turned to his other comrade and looked at his battle-scarred face and said seriously, "What say you to that, John?"

John gestured to the cup-bearer to refill his heavy metal goblet and replied, "In my days as squire to your grandfather, I remember him saying that kingship was inevitable because it was far better to distrust one in command than two dozen battling barons hungry for land and power."

Lance nodded. "Aye, I see the merit....And there's the possibility that Henry will grow with the awesome responsibility."

John raised the massive goblet and drank a toast. "In truth, more than your father would. Still, I like the idea that you would then be in line for king."

Bennet grimaced to the remark, then raised his drinking horn and toasted, "To the horns of dilemma, then!"

"Nay," said John, "that implies a choice—there is none. The old man is probably bewitched from what I hear at the alehouse."

Bennet looked taken-a-back for a moment, then responded rather unconvincingly, "How can that be? Witches don't really exist."

"Well, maybe in his mind they do," John said.

"Enough said, my loyal friends," Lance commanded, "let us drink and let petty power mongers fantasize all they want. As for Henry,...well, it is suffice to say here lies a start, a new era. Henry is all we have." Lance raised his drinking horn, and said loud enough above the din for his father to hear. "To the king." John raised his goblet and repeated Lance, then added, "To Henry!"

Sir Bennet, hesitated, glancing over at Kalab who was scowling and shaking the breast-bone at them. He leaned to the drinking partners and whispered, "Apparently our old warlord thinks otherwise!"

Bennet looked again with a gleam in his eye to the sulking Kalab, who was mad enough to throw the pheasant remains at them. Instead Kalab growled, "Fools, under my roof the toast is meaningless!"

Lance responded with a chortle and lightheartedly said, "Oh, father, put away your grudges for tonight and be merry....I therefore, change my toast to the most powerful and glorious lord manor in all the land!" The other two knights joined in with a hardy yea.

Kalab grinned sweepingly, wiped his greasy face in his sleeve and raised his huge drinking horn. "Now you make sense, my son; I am glad that you as well have put away your monkish fantasies." Then he looked down the table—his daughter and the new knight playfully cooing—he yelled to Tracy as he pointed to the empty chair next to him, "What's keeping Lady Erinysia?"

She was jolted momentarily but said in a nervous tone, "I'm sorry, great lord, but I have no idea where *your* great lady is."

Rhonda turned to him with an annoyed expression and rasped, "Father, please, we are enjoying ourselves. Must you dash my spirit with concern over that dreadful woman?"

"Don't wag disrespect, child!" he warned; then he sharply turned from her to signal a servant girl to dispatch the new mistress of the manor.

The girl curtsied, then hesitated and said, "Yes, my lord, but I know the lady shall be here shortly. She is preparing a surprise for you and your knights of victory."

"Oh? Well, make haste to hasten her," he snapped. The girl sprung to the arch behind the dais.

The tempo of song, melody and rhythm accelerated as the honored knights increasingly made merry with their women. Suddenly as if on cue the song and dance minstrel stopped, and hurried to a dim corner where their small table was. The flutist and drummer quickly quaffed down their wine, while the dancing girl and guitarist sat down and refreshed themselves. The drummer left behind his light drum and ran to the corner up front to the right wing below the dais where a huge kettledrum rested. The flutist hurried to the center and just below the dais and piped an eerie tune.

A door from the donjon midway up the dining hall swung in. A beautiful woman, decked in a bawdy dress likened to Spanish peasantry, thrust forward alluringly a willowy leg. The flute tweaked excitedly. She raised her dress and short-stepped into the aisle and then swirled along the first table to the center area below the dais. The knights gasped to silence and gaped at her daring as the free-flowing dress revealed her pubic hairs surrounding a tassel of green round a tiny sparkling jade. She cocked her head gracefully to the lord of the manor, tongued her lips, then abruptly turned back to the eager expectations of the men. The flutist let loose a sustained ear-piercing note, and she arched her back, extending her arms above her till her palms reached the floor, complementing the arch. She raised one leg and her gown slid up her thigh; she repeated this with her other leg. Her dress now to her hips, she spread her legs for all before her to see the tawny wonder. The flutist reached his highest pitch, then slowly wound it down as his body slowly twisted to the floor. She righted herself, half snarled at the men, leaned forward and beckoned seductively with her arms that they come to her. Two knights eagerly stumbled after her and she laughed coarsely and danced away.

The drum slowly followed the beat of her bare feet, the toes adorned in a variety of rings, as they nimbly glided along the polished flagstones. Her graceful arms and hands were constantly, seductively, in delicate, sensuous motion while her eyes sparkled at the knights under spell— to the annoyance of the ignored women at their side. She pirouetted along one table lane. Knights reached out for her, pawing her smooth dark legs or her alluringly exposed shoulders. Some could not refrain from touching her long raven, flowing hair fanning out over her shoulders and back as her eyes, though in constant orbit, seemed to burn into every man's soul. The flute again pitched to high levels as though in competition with the maddening thumping drum which vibrated the captive loins of the - enthralled men. When she reached the end of the table she reversed herself and briskly rolled closer to the men who each vied to catch her in his arms and to hold her in eternal ecstasy. But like a snake she coiled in out of their arms. Reaching the head of the table she skipped to the other side and repeated her coy, coquettish manner.

Upon reaching the end of the table she deftly jumped on to it and continued her dance, gracefully avoiding outstretched arms and the platters of carcasses and fruit. Not one knight could resist reaching out for her elusive legs or ankles. Approaching the end of the table she slid to an entrancing prone position. Slowly she reached for an apple from a platter of fruit beside her. Suggestively she bit into it and rolled the morsel in her cheek, then frowned and spat it out. Looking over her sweaty bare shoulder, she seductively rolled her lips, then turned away and hypnotically waved the apple before the eyes of a knight beside her. Breathlessly panting he managed to resist trailing his beard down her hot thigh which he had jack knifed and held tightly in his arm. He snapped at the apple several times. She let him nibble on it momentarily as her thigh slid out of the crook of his arm and elevated round his neck to press his mouth into the apple. She squirmed away from the knight with the apple stuck in his mouth. The kettle drummer pounded furiously as she leapt from the table and beat her feet against the flagstone at a maddening pace while twisting her body like a serpent. Hurriedly she returned to the man with the apple and tore it from his mouth, tossing the core to the dogs. Then she whirled round and round till she dropped to the floor and the drumming stopped.

The flute squealed into prominence and the woman uncoiled and leaped onto the dais, pirouetting round the table, she threw her arms round the surprised younger lord, edged his face toward her lips and kissed him hard. Whirling away she circled to the front of the table onto which she jumped up in front of the lord of the manor, raised her skirt to the bodice, then dropped, stretching in front of him. She reached out, gracefully her hand toyed with his beard, then her fingers lightly stroked his mouth. Suddenly she tugged furiously at his beard and his faced plunged into her breast.

Rhonda pushed back her chair, burned her eyes at the woman and scampered out of the room, crying. Bryan turned to Lance and looked at him pleadingly. Tracy scurried after her.

Lance rose up staring over at his father hungrily sucking her breasts. With fury in his eyes, the son barked, "How dare you bring dishonor and lechery to my mother's house and offend the innocence of my dear sister!"

The lord of the manor raised his head and scowled at his son. Then he grinned and said in ignorance, "Dishonor and lechery, you say? Why, my boy, this is Lady Erinysia— your new mother."

Lance flushed and reached where his hilt would be, but he was without it. He jerked round and followed after his sister. He paced across the anteroom, but before he ran up the twisting stairs, he paused a moment, wiped his brow and muttered, "My God, had I my sword I think I would have killed him!"

While passing the lower landing of his mother's room, he heard sobbing. He gently opened the door. Tracy was on the bed trying to comfort her. Rhonda lay face down sobbing into her mother's pillows. In her hand she clutched a miniature portrait of the dear departed mother. He sat down on the side of the high bed and stroked her long hair unbraided by Tracy. He said softly, "My poor baby sister, so this is what you've been exposed to in my absence. Who is this woman?"

Rhonda choked on her sobs, her body quaking. She said, muffling into the pillows, "A witch!"

"Aye," he humored, "but what other being? I'm sure I've seen her before."

She rolled on her side and looked up at her brother with misty eyes. "No other but a witch—I swear, our father is under her spell!"

"Is it true? She's not just a passing troubadour? He actually *married* her?"

"Yea," she sobbed and brought the portrait to her tiny breasts. "Our father's bitch and....Oh, I cannot grasp the word."

Tracy looked up at him. "Wife,... my lord."

" Zounds!" He enveloped Rhonda's shaking body in his arms. He looked at Tracy. "When?" he asked Tracy. Rhonda jerked a convulsive sob, and he held her firmer and let her cry. He lowered her gently to the pillows and caressed her face, parting the wet strands from her cheeks.

Tracy held back her tear-filled eyes to say, "They married nary two months after you departed from your mother's funeral."

"Oh, no! That soon?"

"Soon! Rhonda blurted, "Why at all?" Then she became calmer and looked into her mother's face. "Not two months in your tomb, dear Mother; this bed still warm from your fading presence, yet did he take rude ceremonial vows that fixed the witch in *your* bed."

"Witch, bitch, both or either, why does she seem familiar to me?" Lance re-echoed.

"And why not? She was Lady Hunter and widowed in half the time of our father's. The Earl of Huntersland was murdered while you were gone."

"Murdered! Earl Hunter gone!—incredible!...By whom?"

"No one knows—except, I'm sure, the witch knows."

"Rhonda, no, my little one, let not that lively imagination of yours dip into dark mires," he chided mildly. "Perhaps she and our father, lonely in kind and lacking normal stamina, did allow themselves to ease their sorrow," he added unconvincingly.

She rolled her head violently in the pillows. "Now whose imagination runs wild—and in face of her ribald performance tonight!" She sat up looked at her mother's picture again, then lovingly laid it by her side. With clearing eyes she looked over at Tracy and fell into her arms.

"Oh, my dearest, you were my strength in that nightmarish time!" She slowly drew from Tracy and looked up at her brother. "At first, I too thought such comforting motives in the make believe portion of my mind that he so soon should hurl our dear mother into blasphemous oblivion. But, oh, Lance, how he has changed!—no longer the sweet, kind father we once knew."

He grimaced and said bitterly, "Aye, but no longer is he tempered by our loving mother."

She burst into tears and then clung to him. He held her awhile.

"She seems calm enough, if not asleep, to take her to her room now where I can prepare her for the night," Tracy said.

"Surely, she can stay here in her own mother's room!"

"But she wouldn't want to. As she said they sometimes sleep here and the witch Erinysia has taken private occupancy here and thus defiling your dear mother's memory."

At his chest he fidgeted with his tunic and moaned, "War is not as bad as this!...And, you sweet lass, in the midst of it, too."

"I thank God for that—to be here to comfort your darling sister," she said emphatically.

"You are a king's treasure, dear Tracy."

"I'd rather be a treasure of a knight—alas, my station makes that impossible," she said looking up at him with obvious admiration.

"Oh, think not on it; the time will come when some young gentleman, will perceive the crystal clear nobility within you."

"Some...?" she murmured. She wanted to bite her lip for the utterance.

He picked up his sister and Tracy led him up the winding steps.

The intense pitch of revelry continued well into the night. Then one by one each of the carousers yielded to fatigue, nausea and heavy drink, slumping over the table or falling back off the bench. The knights more prone to love than drink and venison, stole off into the shadows of the wards or into the stables with their women, most of whom were ignorant, some innocent, serf girls. The knights fortunate enough to be in the graces of noble ladies tailed off into the sundry partitioned apartments for guests adjacent to the hall and at the foot of the donjon.

The former Lady Hunter was dozing lightly in her current husband's limp arms. Kalab's harsh snoring and heavy breath reeking with drink, stirred her in the dim light of the only candle left burning on the dais table. All the wall-torches and table candles burned out. She carefully squirmed from his arms and stole over to Sir Bennet. She shook him from his stupor and motioned that he follow her, putting her finger to her lips. One of the hounds on the dais stirred and growled; her eyes burned in the darkness as she waved her arm as though in discourse, and the receptive animal rolled over with a whimper and lay still. She tiptoed out the hall onto the twisting stairs; she paused at the first landing. She decided against entering the mother's room. And as if on air passed Rhonda's room and reached the uppermost landing to the tower. The baron followed—heavy with drink, struggling up the stairs, though alert enough to steal quietly—to grasp the opportunity awaiting him.

At the doorway to the lord of the manor's room, Bennet was pulled in by Erinysia as she closed the door behind him and slid the bolt. He wobbled and squinted while she undressed before him. He fell back in a chair agape as he marveled at her gorgeous brown body, deliciously highlighted by the flickering red of torchlight. She slinked toward him, straddled his thighs, unbuttoned his kirtle and licked his hairy teats.

3. Rhonda

Owing to Rhonda's pleas, the lord of the manor agreed to reconciliation with his son. Besides, Kalab reasoned that his forces would need rest and reinforcement before he could launch rebellion. Lance welcomed the reprieve, and his father's cordial manner. He attributed his father's ranting on his return as volatile envy germinated by Erinysia, and would soon dismiss it. Several days at home convinced him that Rhonda was right—that he was indeed the victim of an enchantress, though he had not seen Erinysia since the evening of her dance. He suspected that because she was aware he had no use for her that she was avoiding him.

He had several meetings with his father who seemed to Lance to be rather irrational, though amiable, and given to jocular fantasizing about the crown and hatching his very own enduring dynasty. Lance attributed this to his feeling of inferiority in marrying into a famous noble name.

A week passed when his father visited him in the stable where Lance was bathing Stars' leg. Kalab looked up at the animal and patted his nose. " My son, forgive me for sounding like a greedy old tanner last week. Aye, a fine, faithful steed indeed...have no fear, Stars will be well taken care of."

Lance glanced up while continuing to tend to the horse. "Oh, I have forgotten it. Besides, I know you....Stars will make a great stud, eh?" Lance chuckled. "Since I've been home you have lent yourself to wild exaggeration. Could it be to impress your new wife?" He looked obliquely as he stood up and grinned.

His father laughed robustly and rapped his son's broad shoulder. "Could well be, son. A man of my age, you know, with a young wife, has to seem what he isn't."

"Unfortunately father, I know you have had many young women before," Lance reminded him.

"Which, my son, it seems you haven't—that worries me." He laughed. "But you're right—verily, I've had my fill, but only because your mother was practically a virgin. No, this is different. By Jove, I think I'm really in love."

"*In* love and *out* of it so soon," Lance said resentfully.

Kalab sighed. "Aye, hard to believe,...'tis true; but, son, I shall never, never forget your mother. No finer woman was there in all this new kingdom."

"Kingdom? Then you accept it?"

"Aye, for a spell anyway. But I'd rather see my son as next in line, rather than that fool son of Henry's."

"Oh, Prince Henry will do fine—he's young yet," Lance said confidently.

"Nay, too bookish for me," the father growled.

"Times are changing, father; it is time to yield to law and hang up the sword."

Lance's curiosity was piqued by Bryan's mention of the mountain people far to the north. His proud steed, Stars, was not responding and he decided to uncover—together with another obsession he had been harboring— the secret of the fleeting northern horses. Rhonda, though she protested vigorously that he would leave so soon after such a long absence, had to laugh when he said why he was leaving when they were riding the manor's pastures.

"Not only do you leave me here alone with this witch, but you insult my intelligence with this fairy tale! Why, right on our manor, we have—well, the regiment's cumbersome war horses, that is—the finest in the kingdom and I know that I shall be able to restore your Stars. You, though a loving brother, are nothing but a restless, wandering warrior in search of adventure. Not nary a week are you by my side and already you want to traipse off in search of a steed!...To think my brother but a common errant knight! If that is not enough you intend to steal off with Bryan, and leave me without a source of joy, except for my caring for your horse." She snapped her riding stick and the horse carried her off to a nearby stream; she reined in to water it some hundred paces from where serf women were laundering.

Lance followed and dismounted to let his steed water. He reached up for her, and like a little girl as so often she had done when he was home more often in his early youth, fell into his arms.

They walked along the winding stream that cut through the pasture and the third field whose strips lay fallow. She paused and then strolled to a large boulder. Had she a cloak she would have climbed up to sit upon it as she was wont to do when feeling abandoned as the fallow field. But she was beginning to grow out of her pageboy tights and was content to just lean against the rock. She removed her hat and let fall her hair and it burst in the sun like a flame. She sighed and looked to the women. "Ever since Mother died, I've come here often just to watch the lusty washer-women , in spite of their hard lives, joke and make tales while scrubbing clothes and linen. How very curious is fate that extends to me this leisure and yet I feel so much busier with concerns than they."

"Oh, I'm sure, these poor serfs have no high responsibility and lack thought of implicit worry; yet they too are plagued with uncertainties of daily survival," Lance said, then bent down, picked up a flat stone, skimmed it along the plain of the stream, then returned to her and in his palms he held her cheeks, adding, "But you, sweet face, should have no woeful concerns—why, you're still my baby sister."

"To you I'll always be, but since our mother's passing and your being off to those horrid battles, I dread the loneliness. Somehow I must grow up." She threw her arms around him. "Oh, Lance, I'd die if I lost you too! Why can't our father see that he imposes too much upon you? How can he ask of his only son to fight his silly wars? And, now, this. My, God, it's madness to have designs upon the throne! No wonder you behave like a ruffian errant knight."

Chuckling, he gently urged her back onto the stone and said, "Let nature do your growing, not you—think not on such things. I know father has this affliction to become king; and further, even before Erinysia, he has always been unduly ambitious; yet I cannot believe that he will not snap out of it and see his ignoble foolishness and remain loyal to the Mari's ways."

She nodded hesitantly, and said, "He only reluctantly accepted them in honor of our mother." Then her flaming hair flickered in the sun as she shook her head. "Now with Mother...gone...and Erinysia on the broom handle: behind ambition that comes to fruit is an ambitious woman. Alas, I know that Mother too was ambitious, but always it was tempered by what she thought was good for the manor and her family."

"Aye, never would it be without love and honor," he qualified and smiled. He reached for her hands and they idled back to the horses. "But our father has honor too, you'll see."

"Oh, Lance, must you travel to that barren land, that awful Lodeston?" she voiced pleadingly when they paused before her mare.

He laughed and threw his arm round her. "And what do you know about Lodeston?"

She squeezed his waist and replied, "It is said that they are savage mountaineers who feed on creatures of the night and dig up graves to gnaw on bones to keep their fangs sharp."

"Oh, my," he gasped, "what books have you been reading since your mother is no longer with us to see that you read the right subjects?...Or worse, perhaps Erinysia has been telling you witches' tales!" He laughed again.

"No, I swear it's true. The minstrels say that is the reason our country isolated itself from the north some eight hundred years ago."

"I see, that explains it, then. The more fantastic the better they sing!" Lance chuckled. "Anyway, my little mare-spinner, I think it wise that I should leave for a spell. Without me in his grasp to carry out his methods, father might wish away his madness." he said with assurance and lifted her onto her roan. He mounted and added to lift his guilt, "Not for an instant would I leave except I've seen the way you handle father. You are still the apple of his eye—in spite of Erinysia. Besides, he knows he would need me to lead. Come, now, I'll race you back to the stable gate."

The lord of the manor rolled off Erinysia's voluptuous body. He lay exhausted, panting after intense love-making. Notwithstanding all the women he had taken in his lifetime, he had never experienced one as uninhibited and inexhaustible as Erinysia. Though truly she was masterly in the art of love by finessing aggressiveness and subtly controlling foreplay to ward off premature ejaculation and thus holding him under her spell of mystifying sexuality, he was oblivious to the aspect that his harmonious and relaxed response to her was in the main attributed to his wife's passing—her saintly presence had riddled his conscience. Curiously he had not been totally unconscionable in loving her ladies-in-waiting while she lived; he was intrigued that women for whom he had no true feelings could be warm and responsive, but disturbed that his wife, whom he loved deeply, was frigid in their relationship.

As he lay there and his heavy breathing subsided, he relaxed under the tickling strokes of her long nails running up and down his portly but still powerful torso. She tweaked his beard and said softly, seemingly idly, "How long, my lord, before you assemble your forces?"

"Till the time it takes to convince my son to lead them."

She propped up on her elbow. "Why him? Surely you are capable of leading your own troops."

"Ah, but not as gifted as he to lead men into battle!"exclaiming with a rasp, echoing a father's pride. "I swear on the sacred script that he is inspired when he takes to the sword. Much does he draw from his men, each of whom imagines to be equal to a dozen men in arms."

She raised her dark brows. "If this be true are you not fearful that he will wrench the crown for himself? Such warriors of influence are dangerous."

Irked, he sat up, growling, "For God's sake, Erinysia, he's my son!"

"Son?...Well, have it your way," she snickered; "nevertheless, he now resists you. And if you later convince him to march on the king, why not think you that he'll not resist in handing you the crown?"

"Humph," he grunted, as he lay back stroking his beard. Then he laughed and rolled her onto him, losing himself in ecstasy. With concealed vexation she rode him furiously until he became limp and spent again. He pushed her off and pulled the coverlet over him.

While he slept she brought a candle to the mirror on the wall and began to braid her hair. She murmured to herself, "You may not have the will to be king, old man; but surely I shall be queen!"

In the peeping dawn Rhonda stood at the drawbridge waving final farewell to her brother and Bryan as they rode off. She turned, and misty eyed, crossed back over the bridge. It creaked behind her while she walked through the bailey beginning to stir into the day's activity. As she ascended the donjon steps she heard muffled voices above her. She stealthily continued up the stairs until she reached the first landing. She was offended to hear Erinysia's voice from behind the door to her mother's chambers. She grimaced at the thought that her father would defile the memory of her mother by now bedding there with the witch. She wondered why he did not remain on the top floor. While turning to the next twist of steps to her own room, she heard the heavy latch clink from below. She took another step and receded into the shadows. She peered down, and though she could not identify him, she was aghast to see someone other than her father steal out of the room. He had briskly but softy descended the stairs. Rhonda jerked a heavy heave, choked back her sobs and ran lightly up the steps into her room. Throwing herself on the bed, she cried herself to sleep.

Late the same morning she rose, breakfasted and went to the stables to change Stars' bandage while a stablehand geared her roan for riding. Leading the lame horse in a careful walk along a grassy fringe between two field strips flourishing with corn she came upon the edge of the pasture along which was woodland. She observed her father in the distance engaged in falconry. Releasing her hold on Stars she left him to pasture and rode toward her father who had just let loose his falcon to prey.

She squinted up at the winging bird, then shook her head and said, "Oh, father, will you never give in to your boyhood pranks and let our dear wild birds enjoy their all too fleeting branch and sky?"

He turned from the bird in flight and laughed. "Oh, my sweet little girl, when will you give up childish dreams and accept the harshness of nature's way."

Pushing her out her lower lip, she said, "Really, my father, is it a dream that I should hope that man should realize that this harshness you speak of is more the harsh act of himself than that of nature's?" Their horses touched muzzles. "There, you see? How loving nature can be. Why you torment our happy birds is a mystery."

He laughed again. "No mystery, Rhonda, when the winter's bin are plentiful because spring's seeds have been protected from pecking birds."

For a moment she drilled her bright blue eyes into his soul. Abruptly he looked away and followed the flight of the falcon. She probed, "Yea, I presume, then, you see our king an annoying bird or rather, the seed of a nation."

He looked fleetingly askance, then said, coupled with a grin and a tone of vexation as he thrust his chin skyward, "Very metaphoric, my dear, but there comes a time in the real world when every man must decide what is good for himself—and the common good."

"Even though the common good be an uncommon route?" Her mare drew away from his horse and she patted its mane.

"All men of worth cut their own highways, my pet."

"No matter where they lead, I trust?...Such folly, father; for surely you must see that the highway is impassable. No further trails are there to blaze. Be content that others too succeed and improve upon our own lot. Yea, stay awhile, my father, to contemplate on what we have and thank dear God for it." She looked skyward and gasped when the falcon found its prey; white feathers burst against the blue then wafted earthward.

"So much wit of your mother have you!" He pointed to the sky. "Nay, my child, I as that falcon, fly toward one more prize."

She bridled her mare, then paused to look up again into the sky. "Behold, father, high above your falcon. There's a giant bird! I swear it is a white eagle!"

He squinted up and laughed. "A white eagle? Impossible!...Zounds, you're like your brother: you haunt me with the Mari name! I sometimes think you think your mother had virgin births. You never mention the Kalab name."

Her heart went out to him. "I'm sorry, father, but in truth I wasn't even thinking of the Mari coat of arms!"

He smiled gratefully, saying, while looking to the sky, "Yet, it does indeed look like a bird of prey." The falcon surely sensed it; for it quickly dived down to perch on his arm.

Rhonda watched the great bird soar even higher and northward. She chuckled while glancing at her father. "You're fortunate, father, that it had no interest in your falcon." She turned the mare round again and galloped toward Stars. Reining in she reached for his rope, then gently led him back to the stable. In returning to her room, she paused before her mother's room and pressed her ear against the door. She heard Erinysia's mumbling. She took a deep breath and braved trying the door to peep in, but she could not budge the latch. She pressed her ear tighter and now heard Erinysia's pitching her voice to a chant. Midst whimpers and rasping shrieks, Rhonda barely culled a word or phrase:

"....Power...must...urge....O deep darkness....throw off thy
shroud...."

A gust of wind tunneled through the tiny donjon window, and Rhonda was hurled from the door. She reached out for a chink at the top of the stairs, digging her nails into the crumbling stone to brace herself against the wall. As the wind funneled down the stairs, her hair blew across her face. The gust increased; she dug her nails deeper, but they gave way and she tumbled down the steps. Her head hit the concave of the wall. She lay there in a stupor. The wind subsided. Scratching came from behind the door above; it creaked ajar. She looked up to the landing: a black cat but for an orange yellow spot at its throat emerged from the doorway. All the more so because of enlarged vertical pupils—its piercing yellow eyes stared down at her. It crouched, then leaped, pouncing on her breasts, snarling and meowing menacingly. It raised its paw toward Rhonda's eyes. With a burst of fear and nervous gasp, Rhonda swept her arm across and whisked away the menace. The cat squealed and scurried down the steps. Rhonda lay there for a moment, rubbing the back of her head and breathing nervously before struggling back up the stairs. She glimpsed obliquely at the door ajar, but fearfully ignored it and continued up the stairs to her own room.

4. Lodeston

Bryan and Lance rode hard from dawn to dusk for three days before lush rolling plains of the kingdom finally gave way to a barren misty moor that stretched for another two days when the bogs yielded to rugged, desolate foothills of the northern mountain chain where they camped for the night. While Bryan searched for firewood, Lance unsaddled their horses and fed them oats. Low on water, he could barely cover the bottom of their feedbags. He corked the vessel without drinking from it himself and laid it by the saddles. Bryan returned empty handed.

"Nary a twig in this rock infested land!" he grunted.

Lance settled back against his saddle and said calmly, "We'll survive; but for the dampness of the haze still rolling in from the moor, it's rather mild tonight."

Bryan reached into his saddle bag to retrieve an apple, took a bite and while chewing said, "By tomorrow I trust we will reach some trace of civilization, though it is said these are barbaric people."

Lance replied, "Oh, I'm not so sure that's true; after all, there's the legend, you know."

"Bah, that's just a fairy tale," Bryan scoffed.

"Even so, it's a sign that they couldn't be that barbaric."

By mid morning their steeds were slowed to a walk on the rock beds and soggy clay. Not till noon did the men come upon a trail of shale, and able to kick into to a steady canter. Near evening they were surprised to come upon an inn nestled at the base of a lofty hill that loomed as first sentinel over a winding trail that led up into jutting peaks of the chain. They pulled up; tethered the halter strings to a rider post. "Seems I was wrong," commented Bryan; "this seems a warm sign of civilization." They entered the inviting but lonely inn.

A short, round, ruddy old man behind the drinking bench greeted them with a jagged toothy grin. "Well, now, this is a healthy intrusion, my lords! Hardly ever have visitors, that is, among the gentry this time of year—the days are too hot and nights too cold."

"Oh?" Bryan grinned, and since himself newly anointed, added, "And just how do you know we are of the noble class?"

"Oh, rock dust or not upon your riding cloaks, fine cloth pokes through," he said proudly, having observed inn clients all his life—seldom, however, their kind from the south. He rubbed his gray stubble and reflected. "Let's see, now,...it's been some months since your kind from the lowland have ventured this far north."

"Business must be bad, then, eh?" Bryan asked, grinning. "Though it seems you're well-fed." He winked over at Lance mischievously.

"Oh, sir laddie, I wouldn't say that," he replied, palming his protruding stomach. "The folks here keep me plenty busy."

"How so?" Lanced joined in. "For the last three days we've been traveling this desolation and haven't seen man, beast or shelter."

The old man chuckled. "Well, now, my lord, if there had been houses, there wouldn't be much need of my inn, now would there?" He winked and asked, "Ale or wine, my lords?" He glimpsed at Bryan and added, "Or perhaps goat's milk?"

"No, good man, I've been weaned this good while now," Bryan quipped, "but not enough that I wouldn't mind some warm wine. As you say the nights are very cold up here."

He poured some wine into a leather jack and held it over the torch behind the bar. "Aye, cold it gets, but nothing to compare with the harsh winters here. Old Sol barely winks at us in the winter time. Lashes me old bones, he does....Ceres has no heart."

Lance winked at Bryan and grinned. "Another sign for you, Bryan, they seem to know the myths." He then addressed the innkeeper, "I trust, then, you have warm beds for us tonight?"

He handed the warmed leather jack of wine to Bryan. "This skin jack will take the chill out, sir laddie." He nodded to Lance. "Aye, sir, my wife saw you approaching and already she's upstairs striking the hearth and warming the bedding bricks." Lance pointed to the ale cask and the old man filled a tankard.

Bryan sipped his wine, then said, "Still, old gent, how in the devil's path do you thrive? You need people to people an inn—and with a desolate trail as this it's hardly likely any could find their way."

"Well, ye gentlemen did, now didn't ye?" The innkeeper smirked and mumbled, "Pray, the ghosts of Roman pave-makers don't hear you call their road a trail!" He took a goatskin of wine and hung it over the hearth. "There, sir laddie, in case you have another it'll be as warm as your mother's milk."

Lance asked, "So only mountain people come this way, I assume?"

"Oh, no, sir, there are those from your area—but mostly merchants and traders from the shore's inlets. Nary your kind, especially knights, judging from those big steeds of yours."

"So these people do a good deal of trading then?" Lance went on.

"Yea, sir, but mostly with foreigners abroad. Those from your kingdom are interested only in our fine timber in the hills."

Bryan looked surprised. "Surely the traders must be interested in the fine horses I've heard so much about?"

"Oh, so ye heard of them, have ye? But ye lowlanders I hear are not willing to pay the market price. Seems only foreigners are."

"Why is that? Surely there are plenty of Arabian horses available." Lance wondered.

"For the profit, sir. Why, we knock the turbans off those light weight Arab and Spanish breeds when it comes to competition—our steeds are not only faster but much stronger. "

Lance raised his tankard, paused, reflected. "But you spoke of us before as though we were foreigners when you referred to the kingdom as ours and not yours."

"With all respect, sirs, it is not ours. Can't say that it will ever be."

"But surely, you must hear the knell of the feudal system?" Lance offered. "Verily, and eventually we shall all be under one banner now that king Henry sits squarely on the throne."

"Oh, maybe, sir, but not in my lifetime. And surely not up here in these parts. Besides, I only see things in my time. Before or after is no concern of mine....And surely this Henry chap is nothing to me."

Bryan choked on a guzzle of wine and sneered, "Chap!...You refer to the king as a fellow mountaineer!" His hand wrapped round his hilt.

Lance gripped Bryan's wrist. "Steady, Bryan, it's clear the man hears little news up here." The young warlord glanced at the old man. "Events do change even within one's life, you know. It's not just something that's recorded in a monk's scroll." Lance drank down his ale and slid the tankard to him.

The old man spread an impish grin. "Oh, I've heard of him; we have no use for a king up here. We have our own sweet royalty."

Bryan laughed, chucked down the dregs and headed for the hearth for the warm wine.

The old innkeeper continued, "I don't know why you would think we should be concerned with the feudal system, anyway. With the exception of a few manor lords, we Lodestonians live under a rule of grace."

Returning Bryan snickered, "I should never think of a barbaric tribal chief as royalty, let alone grace."

"My, my," the old man answered with a twinkle in his eye, "you Lowlanders believe in your old tales of us mountain people—so why do you not know of the important one?" The innkeeper poured himself an ale and chuckled. "If you continue on up in the morning and into the valley, you'll change your mind."

"Aye, good man, excuse my young friend. I'm sure you have your traditions too; we should respect them. Still, the time will come."

"Well, I'll not lose any sleep over it—nor any of us," the old man said emphatically.

"For the time, have it your way, old man," Bryan injected.

Lance felt his heart pounding and said, "Excuse my friend's youth; I have heard of this grace." He then asked, to change the subject by returning to another, "Why is it the horses aren't bartered among us?"

"Just custom, I suppose. After all, what use have ye? Why, ye combatant fellows still ride those elephants of yours. Ours would probably fold under from the weight of your mail and armor. Still, there are those among your gentry who buy a mare once in a while for their ladies and for travel when they're not off to your interminable wars."

The knights laughed; then Lance said, "Nevertheless, our fine warhorses do our calling."

"Aye, they do that I've heard—like Hannibal, eh?—speaking of which—I'll see to your mighty elephants now." He chuckled, coming out from behind the bar. At the doorway he took down a hood hanging on a hook to cover his bald head. He chuckled to himself and echoed, "Barbaric chief...what a surprise ye are in for!" He guffawed as he went out to see to the horses.

The innkeeper's wife descended the crude staircase and informed them that their room was ready. She motioned to a table and said, "Relax, my lords, and I'll have your venison in a wink of an eye." Lance removed his dusty riding cloak. "I'll take that, my lord, and spank it clean,." she said, then coaxed the cloak from Bryan. Lance sat down and drank some more from his tankard. Bryan went to the hearth to pour some more wine. "My, my, such fine weaving, not a seam anywhere! she said admiringly as she caressed one of the cloaks."Haven't seen such fine cloth in many a moon....Of course, the Arabs have fine robes, but no weave as tight as this and unsuitable for our climate."

Lance was curious."Arabs, eh?...Do many come here?"

The old woman answered drily," The smell of horses draws them, I suspect....Don't do them any good, though. The castle lords would never sell to them for fear they'll breed them. The Spanish are always here."

"Oh, yea, they are fine breeders, I hear," Lance agreed and nodded. "Horses are that good up here, eh?" Bryan chimed.

She nodded vaguely and said," Oh, the very best."

"Why do they bother to come, then?" Lance probed. "I mean, what can they barter, then?"

"Well, there are other things here, you know," she said as though taking umbrage.

"Such as?" Bryan piped.

"If you lived in a desert you wouldn't have to ask." She chuckled.

"Aye," joined Lance, "I've seen the rich soil here."

"Ah, yes, and the crops in the valleys are nature's best, some of which are cured well for shipping," she said with subdued pride while heading for a doorway under the staircase. "Before I dust off your cloaks, I'll freshly spin the deer to barbecued crisp and lard your potatoes....You men look like you could eat an elephant." She ducked behind the open door to a smelly kitchen.

Bryan muttered to himself, "Humph, elephants again," then sat down, sipped his wine and commented to Lance, "Odd they don't sell to the Arabs....I mean, what's to prevent those allowed to barter from selling the horses at a bigger gain to anxious buyers?"

"Nothing, I suppose," Lance said, staring at the horsehead tankard lid. "Then again, maybe the Arabs aren't that anxious, just curious. After all, their own breeds are superb."

"Oh?...But you said they are unsuitable..."

"At this time, Bryan,...but there will be a time soon when we will have to travel lighter....Don't forget the longbow we've been hearing so much of. We shall have to learn to outmaneuver them."

"Yea, I heard a direct aim can penetrate our armor," Bryan added.

Having risen early to saddle and water their horses, the two men returned to the inn for a hearty breakfast, after which the innkeeper's wife gave them fruit for the journey. The knights bent bridle and headed up the mountain trail. The higher up the slope they cut, the higher the flanking ridges grew. Cautiously their eyes searched the rising ridges on either side as well as the trail ahead.

"Weird country," Bryan sighed. " Why would anybody want to live among these rocks?"

"Security, I imagine," Lance said, squinting up at a ridge. "Far easier to assault a castle than these natural ramparts."

"Yea, be a might hard to get a catapult up this steep slope," Bryan agreed with a chuckle.

"Little wonder the innkeeper said this territory would never be annexed to the kingdom—if unwilling." Lance continued to side glance the ridges. "Apparently in these parts they value their independence."

"Or just a stubborn lot." Bryan rejoined. "Civilization is not for everyone, I guess. Besides, we ourselves haven't stepped very far from barbarism."

Lance laughed, thinking of his father. "Verily, my friend, yet it is better than going back— now that we have learned the glory of the ancients."

"Aye, my lord, yet those wonderful ancients still let the barbarians, from here as well as our Quandron, get the better of them, didn't they?"

"Our learnéd monks tell us we learn by history and thus try not to repeat the same mistakes," Lance lectured as he stared up at a shadowy pocket of the northern ridge.

"They'll be different mistakes, I wager." Bryan grinned, then noticed his lord fixed on the ridge."What is it, my lord?"

"I thought I saw something up there—probably a beast."

They slowed the horses to a walk as the slope steepened, then gradually dipped for some five hundred feet. They had to dismount to ease the destriers through the narrowing, twisting trail. Then the trail swooped upward again and they trudged ahead, leading their horses by the halters for a while. They sweated in the glaring sun and alternately shivered in their sweat under the shade of the jagged line of the southern ridge behind them. The trail finally began to level off. They decided to rest awhile. Bryan tossed Lance an apple and they refreshed themselves.

Bryan bit into his, chewed and said, "Maybe I should've had the innkeeper's wife stuff our bags with some meat. Our supply from the castle has run out. Doesn't seem to be any game up here. It looks like this trail will go on forever and just lead us to the next mountain instead of a valley as the innkeeper said."

"I doubt it," Lance observed; "it's leveling now and getting wider so there must be a good deal of traffic along here."

"Well, you'd never know it without tracks. With all these stones it's clear the mountain people don't use it much and must not care how the traders get here." Bryan bent over to study the trail.

Lance fed Stars' surrogate the apple core, then tugged the halter and urged his steed to follow him. Bryan loitered, stuck the apple in his mouth while he checked his steed's hoofs for embedded stones. As he rose up there was a sudden swish and the apple tore from his mouth; his head rocked to the side and his body bent round. He yelped, dropped to one knee and clung to the girth while he looked round and stared at the apple on the side of the trail skewed by an arrow. He decided against calling out to Lance who was well ahead and under a cover of tall trees. He ventured to peer over his saddle toward the southern ridge. He could see nothing but dense forest along the shady ridge. Grabbing the saddle with his left hand, he put his left foot in the right stirrup and drew up his right leg as though in a chair, keeping his head down. He slapped the steed's flank and the horse bolted ahead toward the tall trees whereupon Bryan braced the saddle, switched his feet and sat himself onto the saddle, riding hard toward Lance who was standing at the apex of the trail cutting through the next ridge and overlooking an immense valley.

Bryan looked behind him and then dismounted, grunting, "You were right we are being watched. Zounds, they've mastered the longbow—damn near killed me!"

Lance turned to him. "What? Someone feathered you?" He inspected his friend as if to see blood gushing from him.

"Either me or the apple! Either way he must be an expert bowman."

Over his friend's shoulder, Lance eyed the trail. "Just one shot? A warning, perhaps."

"If so it was effective, coming that close."

"Shot the apple right out of your hand, eh?—remarkable!"

"Were it so...right out of my mouth!"

"By Jove! I've heard of the accuracy of the longbow—dismissed them as mere tales—but this...I don't know...I'm afraid it was meant to kill...no warning would come that close."

"Well, it was effective, regardless. I'm ready to go home." Bryan said picking apple from his teeth. "Should we make a run for it back down the trail?" Bryan asked nervously.

"What you say would mean the end of us. I doubt that they intend to face us like true men of combat." He swiveled round and looked down at the valley. "We have no choice but to descend and hope for the best."

5. Escape

Days following Bryan and her brother's departure, Rhonda avoided her father and Erinysia early in the mornings by stopping off at the kitchen out-building to grab two apples, cutting one in half. On her way to the stables she would eat one and save the core for a colt of her favorite mare. She would then feed each half of the other to her horse and her brother's. Having her horse saddled she then would lead Stars to the pasture where she would watch him graze while she day-dreamed her happy childhood days when her mother used to take her riding, or when her brother would frolic with her when not teaching her two-handed swordsmanship with a small single-handed sword. On her return to the stables she would redress Stars' leg after soaking it in warm water. Each morning she expected to see progress but the horse continued to limp.

During the afternoons and evenings—after having visited her mother's tomb—she would read and sew in her room and have her meals there. One evening reading by candlelight, having supped, she heard a knock on the door, and her father entered to inquire about her long absence from the dinner table. He sat down on the feathery bed to face her. He stared over at her, waiting for an answer.

Barely stirring in her chair she flashed her eyes quizzically at him and asked sarcastically, "Why, the concern father?" She marked the heavy book, slid it off her lap and went on, "I should think your obsession with that hussy would preclude your noting my absence from the dining hall."

His brows arched and his jaw dropped as he cleared his throat. He said, puzzled, "How, my dear sweet Rhonda, could such a thought enter your lovely head?"

"And why not?..." she countered curtly: "Since it is clear that you are totally oblivious to my being alive, what with that witch around."

The father frowned. "That isn't true!...And why must you refer to her that way?"

"Because apparently you are under her spell....Why, you seem not even to have retained the memory of my dear departed mother....When was the last time you visited the sepulcher?"

"I need no artifacts to remind me of my deep loss," he said in a soft tone.

Her face gnarled. "Loss?...Surely it has been filled quickly enough by bedding with that woman in lieu of respectable mourning."

He shook his head. "Humph, what does a child know?"

Rhonda leaned forward; her eyes seemed on fire. "How dare you, father!...Child, perhaps, but a child who has freshly lost her mother and feels the sharper knife of adult pain!" She slumped back on the chair and held her hand to her face.

He lifted himself heavily, crossed over and kneeled at her feet, gently removing her hand from her face. "Forgive me, daughter,....I wasn't thinking...but don't you see, my little Rhonda?...If I did not feel the loss of your mother, I would not need Erinysia to fill the awful void."

With her other hand she touched his battle-scarred face. "Oh, father, am I so rash that I am insensitive to your own pain?" But then she glowered and said, "Still, only one bewitched could arrive at such reasoning that you could replace my saintly mother with the likes of her."

Nestling both her hands in his, he pleaded, "Oh, Rhonda, I swear I loved your mother endearingly and miss her immensely. True, our love was not impassioned by body, but I swear our souls were inspired by compassion and understanding."

"Oh, father, why, then, didn't you mourn our dear mother while respectfully searching for a lady with like repute?—instead of marrying headstrong this strumpet."

He pulled away from her and paced the room. "Crass of you to utter such rot....Erinysia is a fine woman. Yea, truly different from your mother. But she is all I want now in my later years—I care not for her gypsy past. I do not need a mother for my grown-up children."

"That is not what I mean, my father. There is no substitute for my dear mother. I ask only that for your own sake, for the honor of my grandfather's banner, that you seek out the bishop and have this foolishness annulled on the grounds not germane to her being a gypsy but of witchcraft and then find a woman of respect."

He fell back on his haunches, tapped his forehead and yelped, "Bah, the Church and its busy-bodies! Preposterous!" He rose to pace the room. "You just don't understand a man's feelings, my child; nor do I expect you to since you are so very young and sheltered rightly. Nevertheless, just as you know that no woman could measure up to what you and your mother had, why should you expect it of me?"

"This I understand, father; what I do not understand is your behavior and not only in your relationship to Erinysia but this business, this awful thing with the Crown."

He froze in his tracks and turned to her. "That, my child, is no business for a woman, let alone at your age," he remonstrated in a raucous voice while looking at her searchingly, hoping that the little girl in her would emerge.

"Normally, yes," she granted, "but it is very much the business of your witch, it seems."

"By the Rood, wash your tongue!....Surely, that is what your mother would have done to you in hearing such disrespect. She always knew her place, and it surely wasn't politics!"

"Are you so certain of this, my father? You don't think that mother would dare question why after only a fortnight of rest you have Lance's knights already in training at the lists?"

"Your brother's men! Ha! You accuse me of disrespect in the memory of your mother and already you have Lance the lord of the manor!"

"No, father, rather, I know who is *now* the lady of the manor."

He turned on his heels and walked rapidly to the door, then reeled. "No more of this pertness. Tomorrow I shall expect you at the table three times a day. And most important you are to be cordial to Erinysia."

She sat up erect and mewled, "Oh? and contrary to what you said before, she is to replace my mother, after all....By cordial I trust you mean, daughterly?"

"Well,...yes, I suppose I do."

The fire returned to her eyes as she looked across the room. "Then, Father, you are indeed a fool!" Her chin reared up and she cried, "Forgive me, Mother."

He stormed back toward her, wrenched her from the chair and struck her on the cheek and growled, "If you persist in this brazen chimera, you are no daughter of mine!" He threw her back onto the chair and left the room.

Rhonda, rubbing her cheek, uttered to herself, "Nor you a father of mine."

"You must have patience, Bennet," Erinysia said softly while lying naked in bed, fondling a necklace of tiny diamonds highlighted by a large emerald.

"But I cannot take even the thought of that fat grizzly old man touching you, much less bedding you," Baron Bennet replied as he hungrily rolled his eyes over her voluptuous bronze body.

"Well, you have me in bed now....You agreed...without him we cannot march on Henry. Even then the old man will meet some resistance in rallying the men without Lance," Erinysia cautioned, caressing her nipples with the dangling emerald.

"Aye, no question there," Bennet admitted reluctantly.

"Besides, we must move soon,...else the brooding son to contend with on his return from the north," Erinysia urged, however confident her thought that she would never see Lance again.

He tweaked her ear and whispered, "Aye, a mighty contender indeed....And, you too; for I question your trust. The crown may change your ways," he mused with a sly look.

"Nonsense!...What good is a crown if shared; I must be rid of him and son....I trust *you* to be content with the rôle of chancellor without designs on the throne."

"Ha! No gamble for you." He reached for her hand and placed it on his lips. "I am soft clay in your hands," he admitted sheepishly while drooling on her fingers.

"Good, then I command you to love me now; for I must get back to the old man's bed." She held the bodice end of the necklace between her fingers and as if a pendulum swung the heavy emerald.

"There is one gamble, however, in your plans for the girl. I fear it will boil the blood of Lance, stirring him to undying revenge—more so than in behalf of his father," Bennet said with a tremor.

She knitted her beautifully trimmed black brows. "How so? When you have sent the band of cut-throats to eliminate him."

"I've seen him escape death many times before."

"Even so, he shall be rendered powerless without an army....But surely the men you sent are competent."

He coughed and confessed, "I haven't yet."

She jumped out of bed and reached for a jagged dagger on a table. "If I hear correctly, I should run this through your yellow belly!" She paced across the flag stones, slapping the flat side of the blade on her thighs. Then she paused over him and pointed the blade directly at him. "Have I underestimated your daring?" She faked a surprised expression. "Why, you still fear Lance!"

"Aye, and well *you* should. He is formidable. And that's why I cannot convince the assassins. They want an outrageous reward—too rich for my blood."

"You trifle over cost!...I shall see to it that they are handsomely rewarded. But I expect them to leave early in the morning."

"They don't want promises; they want it now," he stressed.

"Then it shall be. Tell them you will have it, and I shall meet you before dawn on the watchtower by the donjon with more than enough."

Bennet stroked his beard and smiled. "You, too, must fear him if you are willing to go to these lengths."

"Nay, but I'm well aware of the complications if he should return. Why even now we have a problem with old Kalab and his daughter. The doting old lord, I fear, will relent under that spoiled child's badgering." She put her knee onto the bed and leaned over him and stroked his beard with the dagger.

He took the dagger away from her and said, "What's this, my marvelous magician—you don't have the old man under your spell yet?"

"That's not my worry; rather it is Rhonda I cannot range in on." She chuckled. "At least not yet." Her eyes burned into his.

She rolled over onto him, then set herself upright on her knees and swung the necklace back and forth. In the dim light her cinnamon body was even more appetizing, particularly as the low candlelight picked up the subtle glimmer of the necklace lending a sumptuous shimmer to her velvet skin. Erinysia lowered the necklace to trace it along his neck and shoulders, sending shivers down to his thighs. Suddenly she tossed the necklace behind her and her long fingers began caressing his hairy chest which heaved with every gentle stroke.

"You speak of the old man—I, too, for you leach my manhood for yourself and leave me a doting, powerless fool," he said, while she slid her wet mouth sinuously down his body.

Later as he slept deeply from her untiring love-making, Erinysia left the room and stole into the dark corridor to return to her husband's bed.

Rhonda—having risen out of restlessness from her spat with her father—had stepped out from her chambers to descend the donjon steps and check on Stars. In hearing the door below her closing, she pressed her back to the dark dank wall to see Erinysia take the first few steps up to the tower rooms. Out of the shadows of the concave wall the black cat jumped, arched its back on seeing the girl and caterwauled. Erinysia hurried up the steps and then glanced over at the frightened girl.

"Well, my little innocent, are you learning the lessons of the night?" she meowed rhetorically while approaching the petrified girl mixing her stares from Erinysia to the cat, which now was pressing its furry ribs against Rhonda's night robe. "Here is another lesson for you that you will not learn from the church sisters." She quickened her descent and grabbed one of the braids and jerked Rhonda's face into her bodice, pressing the girl's cheeks into her warm breasts while she kissed Rhonda's neck and ear. She yanked back on the long red braid and kissed Rhonda's throat and worked up to girl's lips and kissed her hard, then softly. Abruptly she released the braid and Rhonda ran back up to her chambers, crying hysterically while Erinysia laughed wildly which pierced the heavy door Rhonda slammed behind her. Distressed, she whimpered, "Oh, the disgust! And the gall to wear my mother's necklace!"

Erinysia picked up the cat, cooed it momentarily as she said to it, "A pity I cannot keep that lovely for my pet too. But then, you would be envious, wouldn't you, my fiery feline?" She opened the door to the manor lord's room quietly. "Yea," she whispered in the cat's ear, "you would kill her in her sleep the first night she slept with me." Before slipping under the covers, she returned the necklace to its jewel box, which she slid under the bed.

More restless than ever, having cried through half the night, Rhonda rose from her rumpled bed before dawn, dressed and headed for the stables. She walked out Stars and her dun mare, then mounted the latter unsaddled and gaited slowly while she looked back to see how well Stars was progressing. She heeled her mount softly to a trot and to her delight Stars was able to keep up. In the corner of her eye she caught Erinysia and Bennet on the turret. In anger she heeled her horse, forgetting Stars who nonetheless, quickened his gait. Then, remembering, she reined in the mare and waited for Stars.

In a copse in the middle of the pasture she rested her back against a tree while watching the two horses grazing. Away from the castle she felt more relaxed and watched the sun stretch from the awakening eastern sky. She wondered about the strange white bird of prey. She then dozed off until disturbed by the stocky figure crouching in front of her and caressing her cheek with a blade of grass. She was startled till she saw that it was the Baron.

"Why the frightened look, my little lady?" he asked innocently.

"Oh, dear Bennet, I am racked by the witchy winds of fear—the terror of that uncrupulous gypsy."

He took her in his arms, patted her head and assured her, "Oh, you mustn't feel that way. It is just that she is so very different from your dear departed mother."

"Oh, Bennet, do not refer to my mother in the same breath." From habit of trusting her brother's knights, she clung to him tighter while weeping into his chest. Then she pulled away, remembering his strange behavior with Erinysia. "What awful business on the tower this morning had you with the witch?"

"Eh?..." He grunted, momentarily surprised. "Why, she's been beseeching me to send out a squad to have Lance return home."

"A likely story," she said, shaking her head, "unless it is to urge him to carry out her designs to have my father on the king's throne."

He laughed. "My, you always did have a rampant imagination!...Nay, my pet, she hopes Lance could dissuade your father."

"Really?" She half quizzed, her eyes lighting up.

"Aye, this talk of witchery is pure poppycock. But I'll grant you she's a crude gypsy, but trying hard to become a lady of the manor."

"Crude, indeed!" Erinysia's attack on her the night before was still vivid in her mind.

He picked her up and took her deeper into the copse.

"Ben, where are you taking me?" she asked, startled, mixed with jest. He laid her down into a patch of soft grass.

"There, my child, relax now." He stroked her hair, then his lips caressed her hair and found her ear. Her body stiffened to raise herself up; but his strong arms gently edged her back down.

"Oh, dear Baron, you mustn't! What is happening here?—my God, she has cast a spell on the entire castle! Ben, please, cast her out!" She struggled without success as he continued to drench her ear. She freed an arm and reached for a nearby stone and rapped it over his head, stunning him momentarily for her to free herself and run out into the pasture. However, he caught up with her and threw her into the tall grass and ripped open her loose toga. She screamed and scrambled away, then rose up and began to run back toward the castle. Again he caught up, but this time Stars limped up and bit the back of his collar and shook him to the ground. Stars reared up to crush him, but Bennet rolled away, then drew his sword and plunged it into Stars's throat on the steed's downward thrust, which nonetheless took its toll as Bennet writhed in pain when a hoof thumped his thigh. He tried to get up, but was temporarily immobilized along side the mighty steed, rattling with dying snorts.

Rhonda had run for her horse. She mounted and gazed through tears over at Stars as it tumbled on its flank. She bridled her horse and galloped away from the castle. She angled southeasterly toward the shore.

6. Lucia

The two errant knights, having led their horses off the trail, had continued under growth down the sharp decline. Not until the trail stretched out moderately did they chance the open. They mounted. Bryan raised his shield to his shoulders. Stretched before them was a huge barley field, bordered by dense hedge, beyond which a pasture spanned a thousand yards to another growing field. There were many sheep grazing in the shadows of a mountain to the east. They trotted along the declining trail which leveled out along the barley field. The men's eyes constantly rolled to the mountain sides. The knights were certain they had seen movement earlier in the shadows to the east, but as the sun reached near the zenith, they saw no movement but did detect some shiny objects through the foliage half way up. Bryan favored that side with his shield; still, fearlessly the two men continued on. The big pasture yielded to another hedge and a field of summer wheat. Sweating under the baking sun, they removed their riding cloaks. The men could see thatched roofs peeping through the trees fifty feet up the base slope of the mountains. In another pasture west of the growing strip were magnificent horses gleaming in the sun at the foothills of another mountain. The men bridled their mounts through a path in the wheat and headed toward the herd of horses; the animals jerked their heads toward the intruders and eyed them suspiciously while nervously pawing the grazing field. A buckskin stallion whinnied, bared its teeth, reared up then skirted some hundred feet further away; the herd followed, then went about its grazing calmly.

"Great looking animals!" Lance burst out.

"Yea, that they are, but small compared to ours," Bryan observed.

"But powerful and swift all the same—far superior to our own generic riding horses." Lance countered. "I wonder how they got here?...obviously Arabian, but stronger."

"Ancient traders, I suppose."

"Or perhaps descendants of strays from the old Roman days," Lance speculated.

Out of the trees of the western slope thundered a white horse; upon its mount was a rider in white garb seemingly dwarfed by the powerful steed. As it drew closer, Lance grasped his hilt, then popped his eyes at a young woman riding bare back, her golden hair sailing in the wind. She held the rein in check and came to a sudden halt some twenty feet by their side. Both knights looked agape at this beauty who flashed a pearly smile that rivaled in the sunlight a bright white toga that covered one shoulder, revealing a bronze-skinned slope of the other veiled partly by glistening blonde strands. Lance's horse snorted and jerked its muzzle toward hers. Lance could not refrain from eying the slender brown legs that wrapped the steed's gleaming white girth. Her steed, was not an albino, but the traces of gray were barely visible. It snorted back and bared its teeth at the larger bay warhorse. The girl caressed the white mane to calm her steed, and said to the visitors, "Welcome, stout knights. How rare it is to see such men of worth from your land below."

"How rare to see such beauty as you from any land," Lance replied with a smile and thinking of the old inn-keeper laughing at them the night before.

"Ah, how *rare* your kindness." she said, blushing. "But then your eyes might be growing old before their time." She stretched another smile.

His gray eyes flashed and then rolled up to the grass topped ridge behind her to depict an emerging line of bowmen trained on them. "Not old enough that eyes cannot see your welcoming committee," Lance groused.

She laughed and turned to Bryan who raised his shield in front of him. "Oh, fret not, gentlemen; our bowmen are proud and love to flaunt their skill."

"Indeed, like taking an apple from one's mouth!" Bryan growled.

She laughed again; then looked sympathetically at him."Forgive me, young man; truly it was a dangerous trick that smacked of a tasteless jester. Be assured the archer has been chided."

"Chided? Why, with my sword I'd like to broadside him on the rump!"

She giggled and said, "Perhaps you'll have that chance, but I must warn you he is no stranger to the sword either."

"Takes more than an acquaintance to the blade to match the skill of knighthood," Bryan persisted. Lance reached over to Bryan as if to calm him.

"Yea, so I've heard from tales of yore—from Thor to Arthur." She drew closer and took the lead. "Come now, let us make up for our inhospitality." She cantered gracefully along a northward access through the wheat field, and the knights followed, though not as gracefully.

Lance drew abreast of her and said, "You ride extremely well, my lady—especially for a woman."

"Not unusual around here. We are tied to a horse before we learn to walk. What brings you here? Or are you lost?"

"Lost in the sense we are in strange terrain, but purpose brings us here," Lance replied, his gray eyes still casting admiration.

"How very good, for we too are people of purpose and do not admit to idle curiosity, although I must admit we are curious about ye." She glanced down at his enormous sword hanging from the saddle and with a sly smile uttered, "I trust you are not here to conquer?"

Both knights laughed, and Lance glanced over his shoulder at Bryan who now seemed relaxed since his encounter with the arrow. Lance studied her delicate profile and the confident manner in which she held the reins and rhythmically moved with the powerful muscles underneath her. "It appears, my lady, that with your presence you have conquered."

She flushed and smiled at him, then said gropingly, "What then brings ye here to our rugged parts; for I fear we are a people who do not exactly warm up to strangers, since thankfully we have so long been isolated from your contentious world."

"Your manner," Lance reacted, "belies the rumors of inhospitality, though our minstrels sing of it."

She looked askance."Oh, really?—they tell tales of us?"

"Aye, especially of your fine steeds." He omitted the other personal tale.

"Yea, it seems that those who know of them, think them unique." She glanced over at his destrier. "To me your steed is unique, though, I confess, too bulky for my taste. I'm sure it serves you well."

"Aye, *the great horses* are extremely trustworthy. Alas, my faithful gray of long service is now lame, and I do not quite feel as one with this bay."

She leaned over and patted her horse's mane. "Yea, I too would know the empty feeling were I to lose Orion here."

They continued through the wheat field's grassy path. Then she wheeled the rein to a cross path and then onto a pasture on the other side where cattle and more sheep were lazily grazing. Sheepherder in seeing the riders removed their caps and bowed. Women and children, scattered in sloping yards that rained down from farmhouses nestled into the mountain side, were busy with chores; but stopped, held their hands above their eyes and squinted at them. One by one they knelt as they passed. One little girl sporting about a flock of ducks near the trail, looked up at the blonde-haired rider of the white horse, curtsied and squealed buoyantly, "God bless, Princess Lucia!" She acknowledged the little girl with a nod and smile.

Lance again thought back with a smile on his lips to the innkeeper's reaction to Bryan's utterance of "tribal chief."

The two knights with reserved anxiety conditioned from many battles, observed that from the ridges of variant levels bracing the long, wide valley there rose up out of scalped top areas of the ridge scores of longbow men in a line that extended midway up a huge snow-capped mountain that closed the valley a half mile away from the last cluster of farmhouses. The horses with Lucia's silvery one in the lead loped along the trail that now was hardened by cobblestone and circled at the base of the closed end from where a second trail ascended and into which the blonde beauty wheeled her horse. The two knights paused at the cross section and gazed up at the overpowering sight of a castle sculpted out of a huge mountain, shorn of its top. As overwhelmed as they were by the sight of the castle, they were struck by its insignificance in relation to nature's overwhelming slabs surrounding it and hovering above. They followed her up the trail. She waited for them at the foot of a bridge. High above them a waterfall cascaded from near the snow caps into a reservoir some fifty feet above the highest chiseled point of the mountain castle. Out of each side of this reservoir gushed a stream through slab troughs to a reservoir below the entry to the castle. The drawbridge spanned the lower reservoir of active swirling, sparkling water. Lance marveled at the contrast to the murky, odorous moats of the lowland castles. With these overpowering natural defensive environs, Lance as he crossed could readily perceive why the drawbridge chains were rusted from disuse. They passed under the long cavernous arch of the portcullis—that too apparently seldom down. Curiosity-seekers had been standing and mingling with bowmen on the natural parapets carved out of the mountain and had peered through 'V' shaped crenels that left testimony to a natural ridge.

As the riders entered, the crowd merged down the many granite steps into the bailey, and bowed as their princess passed. The bailey was the sculpted mid-riff of the mountain's slope. To the sides were cave-like shoppes and smithies. The ward had not the expanse of an ordinary lowland castle bailey, for it abruptly terminated some hundred yards into the mountain side, whence hundreds of small windows pocked the horseshoe facade circling high above the ward. At the center point of the concave were huge bronze doors, over which was a densely sculptured arch that would have rivaled the great cathedrals of Europe, except that the theme of the sculpture was not religious, leastwise not Christian. Humanism seemed the theme—daintily robed women figurines and sparsely clad men, along with nude cherubic child- figures hovered the great arch.

Her sandaled foot swung over the mane and the princess in her dismount gracefully slid down the girth. She signaled her visitors to dismount and follow. Young boys in flaxy garb immediately tended to the horses, leading them to temporary livery next to a blacksmith station. The heavy doors were swung open by strapping flanking guards. They were unarmed, non-helmeted and wore light skinned jackets; their legs were bare but leather strapping twined their thick set calves down to ankle boots. As the knights passed under the long arch the eyes of the guards followed them.

When the visitors entered the high vaulted hall they were struck by its lack of dankness customary to Quandron's castles. Great arches and colonnades abounded in lieu of the traditional dining hall aura, reminding them of a temple even though there were tables and benches here and there. A great dais resembled a predella of marble with many candle stands and a large table of polished wood and rich, high back pillowed chairs, in lieu of crude benches and chairs the knights were accustomed to. In the middle was a large throne-like chair fully upholstered in white and gold, behind which on the wall was sculptured in relief a battle scene of horsemen armed with swords, spears, but predominantly bows and arrows. Hovering above were apparently gods and goddesses clad in military gear, directing the fray on wingéd mounts. In the bend of the vaulted ceiling above the sculpture was a large painting of a blonde woman with a placid look and outstretched arms, heralding in one hand a golden sword. Lance was struck by its close resemblance to the princess.

A lanky man with a long gray beard came out from one of the side colonnades. His long velvety garment trailed along the polished granite floor as he headed toward the dais. He greeted Lucia and respectfully bowed his head, then looked at the knights suspiciously. Lance looked up and was struck by the old man's height. Lance was over six feet and seldom had to look up at anyone. Lucia briefly brushed her hand on Lance's shoulder and said to the old man. "My proud patrician, have you no smile for our visitors?"

He brushed a hand over his balding head, and replied, "Lucia, my dear, whenever you are out on a hunt, I never know what your skills will return."

She cackled. "Why, surely, your grace, you can hardly think of these noble guests as prey!"

"At least permit me to think of them as unexpected guests." He unfolded his tenseness and extended his hand to the men, looking at them apologetically. "Excuse me, gentlemen, but this pesky girl so often springs surprises on me like a naughty schoolboy."

"Perhaps it's because you would rather counsel a boy than a silly girl," she said, giggling. She took the visitors by the hands and sat them at the dais. The old man sat at the end and gestured that Lucia take the high back chair in the middle. She shook her head slightly and sat instead next to him to directly face the knights. A smiling, hefty servant girl immediately came on the scene with a golden ewer and poured them wine in silver cups.

The old man sniffed the wine, then abruptly quaffed half of it down. "Judging from your dress and long heavy swords, it is clear as Sol's high day that you are knights from the ambitious south?"

"Aye." Lance nodded. "But why ambitious?"

The patrician with a grin turned to Lucia momentarily. "Perhaps 'noble' is a better word as used by Lucia; still let us venture 'nobly ambitious.'" He swallowed more wine. With no attempt to hide a childlike jest, he asked them, "Is it true, mighty warriors, when not making battle, that most of your time is taken up by hunting down dragons that burn the countryside with their hot breaths?"

"Oh, very true, your grace," Lance said without hesitation; "for dragons lurk in the avarice and ambition of men and therefore they abound the countryside."

Lucia smiled and said buoyantly, "I like that answer, sir; it shows that there is more to knighthood than the horrid romance of brutish blood-letting in itself."

Concealing his umbrage, Lance offered, "Forgive me, my lady; although it is true there is the crude romance in battle scars to remind us of the price of law, it is not looked upon by knights of worth as simply fanciful."

She held the cup to him and said coyly and with a mischievous smile, "Here's to your very noble attitude, my lord; may it always ring true and never ring to man's dangerous fancy."

"You have my word: that too rings of truth, my lady." Lance glanced over at Bryan and both raised their cups in tribute.

She turned her head to a servant girl, waiting by an arch tunneled behind the dais, and clapped her hands. The girl jumped and disappeared through the cave-like arch. Lucia turned to her visitors. "Let us as well dine, then, to this ring of truth. Besides, I'm sure ye men are starving from your long climb up the mountain trail and then the hot trek through the valley."

"Indeed, my lady," Bryan bounced, "this altitude far exceeds the lower country's highest point. Why, I'm sure even the descent into this valley is far above our highest hills."

"Oh, to be sure," the old man inserted, "right where we sit is still almost a half mile above sea-level." He tapped the table and the wine girl jumped to replenish his cup. "What say ye to our valley?"

Wiping his brow, Bryan answered, "Hot..." and stretching out his arms while grinning, he said with a chuckle, "and big as our moors but without the barrenness!"

Lance offered," Aye, your people truly must not be without. Your valley is alive with growth."

"True, we give many thanks to the spirits at harvest time," the old man said wistfully.

Bryan joined in again, "But I'm surprised the valley isn't one huge lake."

Lucia offered, "That's exactly what the valley was in ancient times. Why, even in these times, during spring the snows from the peaks find their way to the basin."

"Hah, no wonder it thrives," Lance said. "I noticed too that you have an ingenious irrigation flow from the mountain slopes."

"Oh, yea, busy as beavers are our people," she quipped. "Seriously, we cannot take credit for that. For as long as our people's history those dikes have always been there."

"The Romans, perhaps?" Bryan said, after sipping his wine.

"Even before them some say," the old man added proudly.

Lance interpolated, "Verily the Romans are responsible for the herd of steeds, I take it?"

"Yea, of that we are certain. They stem from the Roman garrison that was here."

"They are magnificent specimens," Lance said zealously; "but you must trade an awful lot to have so few in the valley."

Lucia chuckled."Oh, Sir Lance, there are many places where they roam, mainly near sea level for exportation."

"Oh, yes, I heard from the innkeeper below that there is much foreign trade," Bryan joined in.

"How is it you seldom deal with us Quandronians?" Lance added.

The old man glanced at Lucia, then to the men. "Oh, we have our reasons—such as a higher price abroad—especially Spain, the land of stores of gold."

Lance arched his brows. "I can assure you, your grace, that I myself would meet the highest bid to have one of your horses—particularly one for my sister. Small, but powerful and fleeting horses are a rarity at home."

"How very brotherly!" Lucia said, smiling genuinely. "No need to bid, good sir; your sister shall have her horse."

"How very kind of you," Lance added, amazed. "Still, I insist on paying."

The trays of meat and vegetables were served. "Let's not think of business right now. Relax and refresh yourselves with our hospitality," she said buoyantly.

The patrician carved a healthy sliver from the breast of a goose and leaned over and dropped it on Bryan's plate. "Yea, by all means, proud knights, eat hearty and have more wine. I've heard you Quandronians are no strangers to the art of making merry." A servant girl placed a golden brown pheasant before Lance. He had wanted to inquire about the bowmen, but decided it could wait as he bit into the juicy fowl.

Three lovely girls of pre-adolescence danced nimbly out from the colonnade. Their pink diaphanous gowns flowed with their long dark hair shimmering under torchlight as they swirled to the light tune of a lyre. They clustered in the middle of the hall and bent their lithe bodies to each other like a closing flower and then, like petals opening to the morning's rays, they stretched their arms delicately, extending them upward while their torsos gracefully eased backward. In unison they rose up and eurhythmically danced and sang a tale of yore:

> *Powered by a steed with flapping wings so high*
> *A golden chariot from the ominous turbulent sky*
> *Swooped down onto our grassy plain*
> *And a charioteer stepped onto the new domain*

To declare that forevermore this endowéd land
To be at one with benevolent command.
"No more," said he, "would savage war
Among disunited tribes of yore
Smoke the plain and parch the crops
From valleys to mountain tops."
He shot an arrow into the mountain cave:
"Henceforth this will be the nave
To the makings of an enlightened realm
With pliant justice at the helm."

When the girls danced off behind the colonnade, the patrician signaled the servant girl to pour some more wine from the golden ewer. Albeit the knights were inclined to ale—the inn being an exception for Bryan—they enjoyed the wine which was sweet and light, unlike the heavy wine at home. Lucia covered her silver cup and vacantly shook her head.

Bryan took an ale drinker's gulp, then asked, "Tell me, sir, if you will, the meaning of the song?"

"Oh, it goes back many centuries when our culture was fused together from thence savage nomadic tribes," the old man said proudly.

"I see," mused Lance, "this god of yours made them one people."

Hesitating, the patrician nodded. "Yea, but in reality, he was a mortal, a Roman centurion. Apparently a garrison was left behind to explore the riches of what to them at least was a strange new land while the invading legions returned to Rome. I suspect the garrison was forgotten if not totally abandoned and eventually it merged with our ancients to give it order and legislation."

"Of course, and whence came these marvelous horses," Bryan injected.

"Yea, and most of our customs," the old man added.

"But..." Lance said, looking admiringly over at Lucia, "it doesn't explain the golden hair of your daughter, though she seems to possess somewhat the rather prevalent olive skin of your people."

"Yea," the old man responded with a grin and looked askance at Lucia, "Lucia is nonetheless a direct descendant; her complexion is of her mother, who is from your country."

Lance arched his brows. "How fitting, since in reality we are really one and the same country."

"Oh?" The patrician eyed Lance suspiciously, but did not pursue the concept. "Of course, you understand she's not my daughter. The king passed away in his prime. Soon she shall be queen when Libra returns for the twentieth visit of her life."

Lance looked over at her sadly. "Forgive me, dear princess, I rashly presumed."

"A plausible presumption, so think not of it." She wrung her slender hands. "It's been a decade now since my father's burning bier journeyed the seas well beyond horizons's gate. I am comforted that my mother still lives...you will meet her later."

Bryan swirled the wine in his cup and asked, "Cut out my tongue, if I be rude, but how can there be a queen without a king?"

Lucia laughed. "Oh, you find that odd, do you?"

Bryan groused, "Again punish me, dear princess, but I really do."

"My people not unlike a colony of bees do not find it so strange."

Lance broke in, "What my friend means, my lady, is that in our parts, primogeniture applies only to males. Our land would never accept leadership from a woman—however, enchanting."

Bryan drank down his wine and raised the cup to the wine girl. "Yea, my lady, I don't question your ability to lead, but I find it incredible that the men here could accept this custom. Surely your legendary centurion would not."

Lucia covered all but a seeping tone of annoyance. "Oh, as in the lyrics he did not place gender in 'benevolent command'....I should think that in light of the history of fighting among yourselves that such a custom of authority would be difficult to accept; whereas here in our modest land we have sent to oblivion the cadaver of petty differences and conquests."

Lance detected her annoyance. "Please, my lady, we are not here to offend. On the contrary, I defend your noble ways and hope soon that our own country grows and puts an end to its internal differences. In faith, the divination of our new king may bring this to fruition."

She gratefully acknowledged his soothing tone, but pursued the subject with an air of suspicion, "I have heard of this, for which I congratulate your countrymen. But will this put an end to your need of acquisitions? Will your Henry be content with what he has?"

Lance slumped back in the chair as if jolted. "Why, what is it you mean, my lady?"

"Once united, will your country turn elsewhere for its conquests?" She looked searchingly into his eyes.

"Not on my scroll is there written such a possibility," he said with indignation, then lightened while expounding: "To me a king is an administrator of justice, a legislator, if you will, and not a warrior—such is the character of Henry."

"Well spoken, my lord," said the patrician.

"Agreed!" Said Lucia cheerily, then glanced at her chancellor, adding, "Dear Cicero, we should dub this knight legislator of our court!" She raised her empty cup to Lance. "Sir, you two must be our honored guests and stay awhile."

They had been escorted to a large room, one of many that had been scooped out of the mountain. Warm baths awaited them. As they soaked in their respective tubs, they were amazed by the abundance of hot water. A young, lovely servant girl timidly entered the room and laid out bright colored togas on the beds. She curtsied, blushing without looking at them, and dismissed herself.

"I rather hoped she would stay and bathe us," Bryan quipped, grinning from ear to ear. "Wouldn't mind a little pampering from the likes of her."

"Fie, Rhonda should hear you," Lance countered with a chuckle.

"Cut out my tongue!" Bryan whined and dunked his head.

Lance laughed. "Rather than risking its being cut out so often, I advise you wag it less."

"O how I miss her!" he said coming up for breath. "I hope we did the right thing, leaving Rhonda alone with that witch!"

"Rhonda can be as bewitching, have no fear," Lance said confidently.

"Ah, yea, indeed! Your sister has bewitched me since my page days!" He slumped back in the tub and luxuriated in the warmth of the water and in thoughts of his red-haired damsel.

Lance stepped out of the tub, dried himself and sat down on the bed. He stared at the strange dress. "I don't know about wearing this confounded thing. Seems indecent without britches."

Bryan yelled over, "Maybe that's why they accept a young queen for their leader. Men don't feel like men without pants."

Lance laughed and wormed into the toga. "Good Lord, it's like wearing a kirtle without pants!"

"Well, at least you have more hair on your legs than I to lessen the feel of nakedness," Bryan observed with dejection.

"Of course, it can get awfully hot up here...maybe that's why....Have you noticed how warm it is in this strange castle?—not dank like ours," Lance said as he was about to reach for his sword belt, then thought how ridiculous he would look.

Bryan worked up a lather in his flaxen hair. "Yes, I've thought about it, but it's no mystery when you look through that window." Bryan waved his wet arm above. "God, its sash is like a tunnel shaft...must be twenty feet in depth....Clever, though how they sharply widen and slope the sash so as to see out, right down to the valley." He dunked himself, then rose out of the tub, grabbing a towel. The two men dressed, both laughing at the soft skinned sandals, so accustomed were they to their heavy leather boots. Bryan looked to an ancient Roman shield on the concave wall, then turned to Lance. "What you said earlier...about Henry...you know, about justice and all that. Do you really think he's going to be that good?"

"No, but I think the king has a good heart."

"Ah, but is it a stout one?"

"We shall see."

7. Bennet

"**M**ock me, will you!" Erinysia, snarling, screeched with raised arms to the bleak sky, then dropped her arms and looked at the battered Bennet with disgust. "How could you have allowed that chuff of a girl to escape?"

"The gods were with her—especially, I swear, Pegasus did spur Lance's hobbling charger!" he said, dropping to one knee and reaching for her hand.

She jerked away. "Spare me your fancies!" she scoffed. "The fact is my knight was outwitted by a frightened child and defeated by an ailing horse!"

She paced the watchtower, then stopped and peered through a crenel to the south as though Rhonda would appear. She turned back to him. "You say you think she's was heading in the direction of the city?"

"Aye, though she probably will not make it—what with the thieves and ransom highwaymen on the way," he said hopefully, rising. He too peered over the crenel in apprehension that a vengeful brother would scale the wall.

"Let us hope no ransom note is sent to grizzled Kalab.... Pray, they haul her off to some distant land. But if she reaches Henry it will spell worse trouble. We must therefore convince the old warhorse now."

"Agreed, but will he listen?" he asked, adding, "He might not feel prepared to lead the men without his son distilled by the Mari vintage rather than the fruitless Kalab branch."

"You forget the wherewithal of fruitful wonder whence I stem," she prompted as she looked to the northern sky.

"Ah, yea, but folklore has it: your origin was denied the garden in which to bear the fruit."

Eyes glazed fiery red, face contorted and her long curving nails poised at his frightened eyes, she snarled, "Dare you question the legitimacy of my claim and purpose? Bow to the fates that Lilith did not hear you—else your life would be no more!"

He fell to his knees and tugged on her pleated gown; she pulled away, and he toppled against the cylindrical tower wall. Grinding his forehead into crude mortar, he begged, "Forgive my doubting. Oh, my love; have compassion for a sworn knight whose vows were hurled to oblivion, yet pop up to haunt me still!"

"Nonsense! Your vows are to Lilith. There are no others! There are no excuses for your bungling," she slashed, icily staring down at him. She then urged him to his feet, bending him forward over the battlement. Extending her arm she added, "Out there lurk the demons of your past. Thus, we must shake the old man into action!"

"Aye, forthwith we must march against Henry!" he said, reasserting his manhood.

"Any news of Lance?" she said, clearing her throat in trying to hide a nervous tone; for in spite of the immense power spiraling within her, its greater purpose was unbroken ground.

He righted himself but could not look her in the eye. "No, but hopefully he is dead," he asserted though he too was wary.

"How so? If you yourself could not handle but a dash of a girl?" She turned back to him with a trace of a smile. "Perhaps the gods interceded in his behalf too....And why so sure now?"

"I feel swallowed up by the immensity of your growing power. Besides,...a very different situation—you paid the cutthroats well and to receive the rest of the reward they will be on guard against his craft."

"Oh?...And you weren't?" she said, looking at him searchingly. "A little distraction perhaps?—the child's blossoming beauty?" Erinysia reeled, leaving gruffly to head to the master's rooms.

Bennet continued along the parapet to inspect the guard. He paused at the north side and peered over the plains and squinted hard as though looking for someone to appear out of the distant fog on the moor. He rapped his fist against the stone ledge and reflected on his fateful day some two years ago:

> For seven years Bennet had been a loyal officer to Lance's forces and willingly committed his own fairly trained contingent. Nevertheless, he was not inclined to causes as was Lance. Simply put, his constitution had precluded any alternative other than to be on the side of a winner. It seemed but a short while ago that Lance had sent him to Earl Hunter's castle to conscript more troops in order to rest some of his own gallant forces. Bennet met Erinysia, the then Lady Hunter, and was immediately swept up by her spell-binding presence.
>
> After a night-long session of bold, perverse and passionate love-making in her room adjacent to the earl's, Erinysia persuaded him that the earl would never relinquish his troops because he yearned for the throne himself. Before dawn they stole through a private passage adjoining the rooms and brutally murdered the earl in his sleep. Initially

her plan was to then accuse Bennet of the murder, but when the guard on the other side of the door had heard the earl's groans and entered, Bennet promptly ran his sword through him. Erinysia then ordered that the guard's body be placed over the earl's and then stuck her dagger in the dead guard's back. She would report that she entered just as the guard was attacking the earl and that she ran the dagger into him, though too late to save her husband. Bennet argued that it would not be believable when others saw the wound in his chest from his thrust. She grinned and took a dagger from under the earl's pillow, smeared it with the guard's blood, then placed it in her husband's hand.

Bennet looked to the sky and uttered, "Oh, God, what a wretched knight am I to abandon its noble oath for the likes of her!...Forgive me, dear Rhonda!" Suddenly a black thunderous cloud rolled overhead and lightning streaked down, pulverizing the merlon next to him; its dust fell at his feet.

8. Angus

Lucia and the visiting knights trekked over a natural igneous bridge spanning the natural reservoir that horseshoed round the castle. She led them up a twisting trail to a cavern some fifty feet below the floor of the old man's cave and far to the right. The widespread floor of the cavern was strewn with thatch and hay. The knights smelled the immediacy of horses while entering. Further in were timbered stalls and a host of horses; among which were their own towering over the others but for a powerful, buckskin stallion. Lance eyed it with interest. Lucia paused by Lance's bay, patting its brownish muzzle. Emerging from another stall was her white horse led by a stable boy. He walked it toward two other sleek horses already saddled with the knight's gear.

She turned from his destrier to the horses in readiness; she mounted her own. "I thought you'd like to try our horses and give your own leviathans a rest. I should like you to lend an eye to some others on the plain by the sea."

"There's no need." Lance announced, rising up on the stirrup. I like that buckskin you have over there," Lance said definitively.

"Oh, really, and why is that—as if I didn't know. You still like big ones, eh?" He nodded with a grin. With the flip of a hand she said, "Well, then, it's yours. Would you like the stableboy to saddle him for you?"

"No, don't bother now. It seems we're ready to go. I'll work with him another time....And, aye, in my trade, I need power; the buckskin will provide that as well as speed. It's magnificent! I'll wager my bay weighs no more than three hundred pounds and less than a hand high than this buckskin. If you have anymore of these, you could make a fortune from the knights in Quandron."

"No, he's one of a kind; however he did sire a foal. So maybe it's the beginning of another breed." Then she chuckled. "Funny, and we thought it was a freak and thought of hitching it to a dray."

"Horrors!" he squealed. "And now over my dead body!" They laughed.

"I would've bet my stipend that Lance would never give up the traditional warhorse," Bryan offered, checking his horse's girth.

When Bryan mounted, Lucia nosed forward, the knights followed her, looking at each other quizzically when instead of exiting the mouth of the cave, she led them further into it. The knights without their heavy armor felt comfortable upon the smaller horses. They were surprised by their strength. Knights of Quandron as a rule thought the riding horse but a lady's horse. The Lodeston horse seemed a far more powerful breed. Lance glanced back at his bay charger busily feeding himself at a trough filled with golden grain. The cavern narrowed into a long tunnel, torch lights along the way. After several minutes the torches yielded to a shaft of natural light. Lance eyed the gold effulgence returning to the back of her hair and his heart skipped.

The men were surprised to breathe in moist salt air. The tunnel widened and the light increased. Emerging onto a rich green plateau, they were immediately struck by a restless herd of horses that had eyed the visitors. They seemed to number in the hundreds. There were many foals among them.

Lucia waved her arm in proud presentation toward the herd. "These are our pride and joy and in the main our breeders. As you can see they are more powerful—of course, not as much as the buckskin—still as sleek as those of the valley. Though not quite as large as your mighty steeds they are nevertheless capable of carrying great weight and still much faster."

"Aye, I can see that—wondrous!" Lance exclaimed, though he was more taken in by the girl so radiant in the sea's breeze lashing her hair and light riding robe. Several spirited ones strayed off from the herd, whinnied and kicked into a graceful running gait, powerful muscles shimmering in the late afternoon sun.

"Fast indeed!" cried Bryan.

She bridled to the fringe of the plateau; the men followed. Her horse pawed the escarpment. The men pulled abreast and looked down the steep cliff in amazement that they were so high up. Bryan whistled. "How strange to see so much more ocean than there lends from our own beaches! Why, the horizon looks to be a hundred miles out!" He whistled again.

"Yea." She turned to him and smiled. Then she rolled her eyes along the horizon and said contemplatively, "Still breathtaking to me even though I have looked out on it all my life. Wondrously mysterious to see so much of the earth covered by its watery mantle. Yet the sages say that its all embracing arms is symbolic since they believe all life sprung from it as we from the womb."

Lance looked puzzled, then grinned. "What with the Roman influence about, I should think they would say that life sprung from Rome."

"Oh, true, yet even there I presume it was once under the law of Neptune."

Lance laughed. "Sounds Hebraic—what with Noah's ark."

"Well, perhaps..." She let out a chortle. "Since the people here believe that these very mountains will someday return to sea," displaying a tone of mild disbelief.

Bryan stared down at the waves lapping the rocky shore and chuckled. "That would take some doing—my God we must be hundreds of feet above it, if not a thousand!"

Lance laughed. "Noah would believe it....I assume, then, princess, that we are in the end but fish." Lance snickered, then added, "Our churchmen would not accede that Adam and Eve are but fish."

"Oh, but I didn't say that. Still, somebody had to venture forth to set up housekeeping on dry land." She laughed and bridled round, then glanced pixie-like over her shoulder. "Is not the symbol of Christendom a fish?" She trotted closer to the herd and the knights followed. "So, my lords, what say ye to my herd?"

"You have every right to be proud, my princess," Bryan said. "They seem in sundry ways to have the mark of superiority."

"Yea, though they may not have the might of the lowland's common bulky mounts, nor the endurance of your loyal Destriers, so necessary to your combatant purposes, they compensate the rider with the sheer pleasure of moving like the wind."

"Aye, I can see that," Lance agreed.

"And to boot, the traders say that once adjusted to denser air in other lands their endurance increases."

"And still as fast?" Lance asked skeptically.

"Faster."

Bryan was admiring a red stallion that had bolted from the herd and was running like the wind. It seemed a little smaller than the norm of the herd. He thought how much Rhonda would love such a horse. He could not refrain from bolting after it.

The red started zig-zagging and branching playfully. Bryan caught up with it and impulsively leaped from his horse on to the back of the red. The wild one lurched and Bryan clung to its flaming mane. The horse then rose almost perpendicularly, pawing the wind and shrieking savagely. Bryan slid down its sleek back. The red skirted a few yards away, then turned to rise up again. Lance had followed and quickly darted between the red stallion and his friend. The wild horse, snorted, arched and dashed back to the grazing herd.

Lucia rode up with a wary expression on her face until she saw Bryan stand up with a big grin on his face. She laughed, then said, "Should've warned you that they are wild and spirited."

"Oh, I could see that, all right, but I just had to get a closer look," Bryan said with excitement in his eyes.

"A closer look of the grass, you mean," Lance jabbed.

Bryan scowled in good-humor, then said to the princess, "He's spirited indeed—like the devil."

"If you can break *her*, it's yours."

Bryan jerked his head and slapped his forehead. "Oh, no, bucked by a mare!"

Lucia laughed. "A mare would be more appropriate, anyway for a girl."

"Aye, and it's very kind of you to offer it, princess. I shall be out here in the morn with a coil of hemp and stay the entire day if need be."

"That's good—your spirit matches the mare's. But please be very careful, some of these horses with savage spirit tend to kill if they shake you loose."

"You are too generous, princess; please permit us to pay." Lance pleaded.

"Now, Lance, I'll hear none of that again," she chided. "Are we not friends?"

For the evening Lucia's mother, Queen Margaret, made preparation for a feast. She was elated that they had visitors from the lowlands, whence she herself had hailed. In fact, she knew King Henry during their childhood when he was then the son of an earl. They grew very fond of each other and later it developed into young love. She was crushed when he forsook her for another young beautiful girl, who, she learned later was also forsaken when Henry's father found about the relationship and married him off for political reasons to a daughter of a powerful duke.

Margaret's father had been a successful merchant and developed extensive trade with Lodeston. Heartbroken over young Henry's rejection she traveled to the north with her father. She met the then young prince of Lodeston during this visit with her father who had offered to open a foreign trade route for their horses. Strangely Margaret was drawn to the new land

and yet knew not why; notwithstanding that the prince was attractive. Almost instantly they had fallen in love—partly motivated by her desire to forget Henry. Within a year they married. Happily in love for many years, along with an inexplicable phenomena within her, she was able to adjust to the northern culture. Not until his death was she aware that she had also harbored a yearning for her own country and hoped to return there for a spell with her daughter. However, she started having strange dreams—always about the ominous southern country alive with gnomes and wizards intent on eliminating the human race as she knew it.

A diminutive woman, she nevertheless conveyed an air of authority and determinative action. At the moment of her husband's death she made clear that his blood's dynasty would continue to flow in his daughter's veins, regardless of the council's grumbling that no woman had been on the sovereign throne for over a thousand years of legend. Nor did she feel any urgency for her daughter to marry the many suitors of the valleys' gentry that had approached Lucia. She had the utmost confidence in her daughter to rule on her own, particularly in light of Lucia's apparent indifference to marriage, in sharp contrast to her intense interest in the study of politics and law. Margaret was convinced that she had been drawn to the land to serve a greater destiny through her daughter.

The patrician and council barons of other valleys were seated at the dais. Successful merchants, tradesmen and their wives were clustered at tables under the rugged vaulted temple-hall. Lance and Bryan were struck by the moderation of the evening in contrast to the bawdy behavior of their own countrymen. Quiet conversation was the rule at the tables while the minstrels spun their tales of yore. Though the tables were laden with large quantities of food and drink, the highlanders ate mannerly with utensils and drank moderately.

There was a pervasive hush when the *Graces*, the three little girls, danced across the polished floor. All eyes turned respectfully to them and ears strained when the girls sang another myth in a soft pitch that wafted through the hall like a delicate summer's breeze. Their gay colored gowns of rich silk—purple, yellow and green—shimmered in the torch and candle light, along with their trails of scarves of white and gold. Their eurythmic bodies danced about like butterflies fluttering in and out of the pleasurable arrestment of all—including Lance who was left with no doubt about whom they sang: *a golden goddess would walk the valley of life and lay a white and gold mantle of peace and justice upon its rich loam.*

Bryan snapped out of his trance when the *Graces* departed. He chewed on a large piece of venison and resumed studying across from him a burly, black-bearded nobleman in green dyed doeskin, resembling the attire of the woodsmen of the lowlands, except for the finer cloth and tailoring complemented by a gold chain medallion out of which was etched in relief an arrowhead.

For some time now Bryan noticed that the baron, lightly salted at the temples, had been glaring at him and then occasionally mumbling when leaning over to one similarly attired but of smaller stature. Finally Bryan's curiosity drove him to ask, "Good, sir, earlier you were introduced as Baron Angus and chief defense warrior. What does that mean exactly? Since it is obvious you have no wars here as we do below, and it seems these high mountains take care of defense."

The baron lifted his barreled chest and laughed, revealing a missing tooth from an otherwise fine, white set. Resting his massive wine cup, he said raucously, "True, lad, you are a good observer. But it was once thought centuries ago that the sea too was our defense, but venturesome ships from other shores proved otherwise. And as a man-of-war yourself, you know more than I that the greater share of war is a strong defense, without which no aggressor has to think twice."

"Aye, well said," Bryan replied; "there's little respect if man or country has no will to protect itself."

The baron raised his cup to Bryan and grinned. "I suspect you felt the force of respect when the apple ripped from your mouth."

"What?" Bryan's brows rose. "You were there?"

"It was my arrow, lad," he said coolly with a grin.

Bryan dropped his venison to his plate, rose abruptly from the table, toppling over the chair. He grasped his hilt and grated, "You damn fool—you could've killed me!"

"True," he remarked calmly, "had you moved an inch,...but then you wouldn't be here to whine about it."

"Whine!" Bryan raised his sword part way from his scabbard. "A foolhardy move like that will more than offend your ears, sir." He withdrew his sword all the way.

Lance sitting at the end, several chairs away quickly leaped to his side and restrained Bryan's arm. "Calm down, Bryan," Lance pleaded. Bryan ignored him as he leered at the baron.

"Heed your friend....My, my, I thought knights were patient gentlemen who were strangers to temper," the baron said dryly.

Though held by Lance, Bryan blared, "Aye, even in the heat of battle. But that's what separates knighthood from the likes of you. We set out to do battle honorably, knowing our enemy will not dishonor himself with cowardly assault!"

"I must differ, hot spirit," Angus said coldly; "the longbow has changed that—no longer is it necessary to face the enemy in so-called noble, antiquated engagements."

Bryan jerked from Lance's grip and pointed the sword across the table. "It is necessary now; for I challenge you to mortal combat," he intoned menacingly.

"Bryan!" Lance cautioned, gripping the knight's wrist. "Think of our other code of honor—we are honored guests. You speak of honorable combat but are rude to these good people under whose care we profit. Cover your sword. Not all people think as we. They too are entitled to their strategy of survival, however different."

Bryan reluctantly lowered his sword, but still glowered at the baron. "Bah, strategy without honor is but cowardice. Only little boys hide behind trees and mountain tops to fire their slingshots."

"Enough of this, Bryan!" Lance rasped. He glanced over at Lucia and her mother apologetically.

"Aye, my lord, out of deference to you and the princess." Bryan returned the sword to the scabbard while he continued to glower at the baron.

"Of course, laddie, if you really want to challenge me, I shall accept." said the antagonist. "Matters little to me whether you meet your Maker with an arrow in your head or a crushed skull from the mace," the baron said brokenly and with malice.

Bryan leaned over the table and rasped, "Then a primitive club it shall be against my deft sword."

"No, Bryan, swallow your anger, show your true mettle. Consider that this man knew nothing of us and thought us encroaching on their land," Lance argued, however difficult to swallow it himself.

Bryan reared back from the table and glanced at Lance. "Their land? Why, it is part of the kingdom and will in time be rightly annexed to Quandron!"

"What's this I hear?" The patrician, Cicero, screeched, leaping up from his place at the opposite end. "You dare come here to tell us this?"

Lance waved his hand as though a trifle and cracked a smile. "Forgive him for his fiery youth, your grace, all of you here I trust will excuse him; the wine has inflamed his tongue. He put his hand to Bryan's mouth. "No such purpose, Cicero, I assure you in our coming here. We are but two carefree knights on a holiday from battle and wishing only to meet our *sovereign* neighbors...and to see for ourselves the wonders..." glancing at Lucia, "of your native steeds." He removed his hand from Bryan. "My spirited friend owes all of you an apology for this outburst." He glared at Bryan.

Cicero banged his fist on the table and balked, "We'll not accept! So incensed a comment has no tag of contrition!"

Bryan corrected him. "Oh, but it has, most noble patrician! As my lord has said—it was, together with the baron's rude arrow, indeed the wine! Truly, I do see you as a sovereign people who are well ruled by you and your lovely princess," Bryan said contritely, turning his head from the patrician and again in deference glancing over at Lucia.

"I, too, Cicero," the baron said, turning to the patrician, "agree that his inflammatory spit admits of no contrition. I therefore accept his challenge and forever silence his hot tongue."

"Lance placed his hand over his hilt and warned, staring at the baron, "Do not, noble warrior, overstep yourself. An apology, granted, is owed you from my friend and me, but do not stir the coals, or you shall answer to me."

Lucia stood up abruptly and shrieked, "No more of this, testy men! The apology is accepted and hot tempers are thereby doused. I believe Lord Lance that his journey here is innocent. For were his intent otherwise surely these two men would not venture alone."

"Spies, my princess," Cicero pointed out, "are a stealthy lot. Who can be sure they are not here to get the lay of our land and report back to their king?"

"Pardon me, your grace, but that is preposterous!" Lance cried indignantly: "It is not in our matrix of honor to engage thus."

Lucia went on as the patrician looked at the knights with skepticism. "And what if they were? What is there to report but an impregnable defense to rival the most fortified castle in the lowlands?"

"Oh, most true!" cried Bryan.

"Aye," Lance supplemented, "if our knights had wings, or rather steeds descending from Pegasus, there is no way. And I thank you, my lady, for your trust. I swear on my shield's crest there is no such intention. Bryan simply is victim to the haughty beliefs of our countrymen in thinking there are no bounds to its borders."

She looked at him warmly and beamed a confident smile. "Good! The matter is closed...except..." she eyed the baron, you, too, Baron Angus, must apologize to Sir Bryan."

" 'Tis impossible that I hear you right!" He looked at his princess with bafflement.

"Then cleanse your ears; for your reckless exhibit today incensed me, let alone Sir Bryan! Though I know there is no better archer than you, what you did was reckless for which I had reprimanded you. Now I insist that you apologize to this young knight."

Pawing the polished granite of the dais table like a contrite dog, Angus mumbled under his breath.

"Speak up, Baron Angus!" she persisted.

He raised himself up as though a wounded animal. He extended his hand, still mumbling to himself. Bryan took his hand. The baron said partly convincingly, "Lad, my princess rings a bell of truth. What I did this morning in reckless jest showed no respect for deadly weaponry—no more than children playing with fire. I apologize for that." They shook hands.

Bryan edged a smile, then glanced over at Lucia and smiled gratefully, realizing he would have drawn Lance into a fray and ultimately their demise by the hangman's rope. The baron bowed to the princess, then left the dais.

Later Lucia visited her mother's chambers. Lady Margaret was dressed in her bed clothes, but sitting in an elaborate padded chair reading a scroll by candlelight. Lucia sat down on the bed, fondling for a moment the lapel, on which was pinned a tiny gold horseshoe, of her rich velvet night robe, then said, "Rather warm welcome for our guests this evening, wouldn't you say, Mother?"

Lady Margaret lowered the scroll to her lap and glanced over with a smile and chuckle. "Yes,...but I should rather say it was a hot response that we received from our guests."

The princess laughed. "Yea, especially from Sir Bryan, though Baron Angus deliberately provoked him."

"That as you know is the baron's mettle. Still, Sir Bryan went too far."

The princess absently fingered her golden hair and pondered, "Wine or no wine, I wonder where such a fantastic idea came from?...Do you suppose there is some truth to it?—in that King Henry is perhaps thinking of invading?"

Lady Margaret laughed. "Heavens no, my child, why, Henry is a peace-loving man—I knew him from my childhood, as you know. Of course, that doesn't rule out other Quandronians from being covetous." She thought back to the time after her husband's death when Henry coveted her. She shuttered and shook off the memory.

Lucia fussed with her lapel and questioned nervously, "Surely, Mother, ...Lance would not..."

"Don't fret so. Of course not, I can see that he is clearly a man of honor. Still, it is not altogether untrue, you know..."

"What, Mother! Speak out."

"Goodness, child!" She looked squarely at her daughter. "Why, I believe you are attracted to him!"

She blushed and folded her hands in her lap. "Oh, Mother, really!"

Lady Margaret smiled slyly and lightly brushed her lips with the tip of a finger. "Well, after all, why not. He is a handsome gentleman, despite his scars of battle....But I was not referring to him....It seems from this ancient scroll," she said lifting it briefly from her lap, "that the Romans considered this peninsula of ours as one without borders. Some eight hundred years ago there was a great battle between Quandrons and our ancestors for territorial rights. Furthermore, there were still controversy and bickering for two centuries afterwards. Apparently it hasn't ever faded from the lowland consciousness."

"So? Let it never fade—for all I care! It will never come to pass! We are what we are and so shall it always be."

"**T**he wrong horse, lad; but no matter," said Bryan, with coil of rope over his shoulder and mounting Lance's warhorse. A small stableboy mounted a pony. They both rode through to the cave's end and out onto the plateau. The early morning mist drooped heavily over the plain and ocean. They searched the herd. The stableboy found the red one and drew it out of the grazing cluster. Bryan cautiously loped toward it as he uncoiled part of the rope, tying one end to the charger's halter. The red's eyes blazed as Bryan drew nearer. It jerked away, kicked, then trotted several paces to resume grazing. Bryan held up awhile, then moved closer, while widening the noose. Adroitly he let fly the rope and the noose dropped round the damp, glossy mane. The red reared up, shrieked and ran off. Bryan slackened the rope and paced the running-gait commensurate with the wild mare's. Only for several seconds was he able to keep pace and then the wild horse churned up the soggy turf and left the larger horse well behind. The rope became taut and the red steed slowed as it felt the powerful drag of the powerful charger. It stubbornly tugged on the rope, raising on its haunches, winnowing and pawing the air savagely, but the strength of the larger animal and the tightening of the noose were too much for the red, slowing the mare to a trot as the bay closed the gap and Bryan pulled in the rope. The stableboy rode up and tossed a second rope round her neck. He then rode the rope to a nearby trunk with a stubby broken branch hanging from it. He jumped from the pony and secured the rope round the tall stump. The beast's red body began to lather as it struggled savagely to free itself. The opposing pull of the ropes wore out the red and she snorted in temporary defeat.

Bryan moved closer while the stableboy wound some of the slack round the stump. Bryan dismounted and edged over to the frightened wild beast which bared its teeth and snapped at the intruder ferociously. The horse tried to paw the air when Bryan crept up on it and hung his body over its slick back. The horse whinnied nervously and kicked up its rear legs. Bryan hung to its mane. The wild mare strained her head back, snapping teeth in desperation and barely missing Bryan's arm. The young knight went back and mounted the bay horse to lead the red round the tall stump. Bryan gave just enough slack to run in a circle. The red mare ran at a furious pace round and round. As she felt the pressure of the rope constraining it more and more; she stopped in her tracks and tried reversing herself, but Bryan held the rope taut. She whinnied hideously, trying desperately to rid herself of the constraining ropes but could only raise the fore hoofs several inches. Then to relieve the pressure she loped docilely round the stump while Bryan released the hold from the opposing side. He

edged Lance's horse closer as he recoiled the rope. The wild beast shook
its head savagely and its eyes blazed at its determined would-be master.
Bryan spoke to it softly and dared to pat its mane; the mare jerked its jaws
and almost snapped off his hand. Bryan dismounted and returned to the
red's flank; he removed his dagger and cut one noose. He spoke to it softly
again and patted its mane; the horse pawed the turf lightly this time and
jerked back her head, her eye softening. Bryan threw his torso over the wet
smelly back. The beast snorted, jerked its muzzle upward, pawed the turf
deeply and trotted, round the stump, heaving its back along the round, but
Bryan still hung heavy.

He yelled to the stableboy, "Cut the rope, laddie." The boy ran the
knife's edge over the hemp. Before it was cut through, Bryan grabbed the
mane and threw his leg over the mare's back. The red reared up broke the
rope and bolted. Bryan pressed his knees to her girth. The two, for a
moment as one, braced the ocean's winds until the mare jerked up violently
several times before it reared up almost perpendicularly. Bryan gripped and
tightened the noose. Suddenly as he began to slide off its back, he yelped,
then let go the noose and fell to the turf. He let out a scream. The horse
twisted round and reared up again, his fore hoofs churning the air above
Bryan who rolled his body over and over, howling with pain with every
turn. The well-trained bay galloped over and maneuvered broadside the
wild mare, veering it away from its fated rider. The wild horse bolted away
across the plain. The charger lowered its head, snorting over the gushing
blood from its prone rider. The stableboy galloped over to the knight who
was desperately reaching for the reins. The stableboy stared in fright, then
jumped down, pulled up his kirtle and pressed it into the knight's chest
wound while with the other hand he fidgeted over an arrow broken several
inches above its entry.

Bryan groaned, "Don't boy!...Don't try to remove it! The head has
punctured my back....Roll me over carefully." The boy's eyes blazed
frantically at the black arrowhead protruding from the knight's right
shoulder blade. Bryan reached up with his left hand to his steed's stirrup.
"Help me, lad; put my hand in the stirrup and lead my horse back to the
cave. I can't move my right arm—no way I can mount."

"Forgive, me, sir, but I mustn't. I am strong. I can put you onto my
pony." With nervous grunts and motions, the boy managed to raise him to
his feet and then snaked under his left armpit to rest him against the pony's
girth. Then he lifted Bryan's left leg over the pony's back."Grip the rein,
sir, while I lift your right leg." The boy pulled on the ankle and got his hand
under the boot and mounted him securely. As he started to lead the pony
back to the cave mouth, the red steed thundered toward them. He reared up,
neighing hideously, then galloped closer. The charger swung round,
neighed back, reared up its immense hulk, and the red steed quickly

swerved away and galloped off.

Lucia was certain that among the herd on the plateau there was just the right colt for Rhonda. It was a blue roan, known for its high, but gentle spirit. Lance, nevertheless, was free to choose any that he deemed more suitable, if Bryan were unsuccessful in breaking the wild red. They had gone through the cavern passage sometime after Bryan and the boy. When they reached the plateau they were shocked in seeing the riderless bay and behind Bryan slumped over on the boy's pony.

Lance quickly dismounted and ran to them. He was horrified to see the blood flowing from his semi-conscious friend. His first instinct was to wrench the arrow out of him. Lucia cautioned him. She urged, "We must get him back to the castle where my mother can care for him. She is knowledgeable in medicinal arts. But first get him down from the pony, so I may strap a bandage on him to slow the bleeding." Lance carefully set him down while Lucia tore off the hem of her riding bliut. She crisscrossed it tightly round Bryan's chest and over the shoulder, twisting it round the arrowhead and back in front. Lance carefully lifted him onto the powerful bay and headed toward the cave.

The boy told them he had noticed a figure on the ridge when Bryan was breaking the red mare. "I thought nothing of it, my princess, until too late and the dirty deed was done. Only a second before, when I was cutting the rope for Sir Bryan, I saw the figure fix an arrow to his bow. I yelled but the wild beast was neighing so madly that the poor sir couldn't hear me."

"Did you recognize the cowardly culprit?" Lance asked anxiously.

"No, sir, all adults look alike to me. But I do know he was very stocky and wore the forest green of our archers."

"Yea, obviously an archer he was....And I suspect," Lance said gritting his teeth, "which one. What say you to that, Lady Lucia?"

"Oh, Lance, I well up in shame that one of my people could do this!" Then she nodded grimly. "Apparently, there can be no other but him—the very least of nobility and integrity."

Lance turned from her pleading look and to hide the anger in his eyes. She looked to the sea and said, "I promise the baron will face our justice."

He peered up at the jutting ridge above the cave. "Not if I get my hands on him first."

"Oh, Lance, you must not! You will never leave this valley alive!...Angus commands too many of our fighting bowmen."

"Commands! But you are their princess!"

"Yea,...but as Bryan implied last night, there are those who resent me; for they cannot accept a woman on the throne."

"My God! Then you too are in danger!" he exclaimed fearsomely.

"Not true—our customs are too established for them to rebel. Even if they did, they would not harm me."

"I would not chance that, my lady."

"I have no choice."

Lucia had the queen mother-to-be summoned to the guests' rooms while she had the servant girls strip Bryan of his bloody tunic, wash the wound and carefully sat him on the bed. The mother gently eased him back and rolled him on his side to cleanse his wound. She ordered Lance to coax into the wounded knight a good amount of wine to relieve his shivering from shock and to help ease the pain of what she had to do. She waited for him to slip into fairly relaxing sleep. Carefully she snipped away the vane end of the arrow from his chest. She saturated with a strong smelling ointment a wad of cotton and gently dabbed the dry wound, then pressed into it. Bryan let out a whimper but fell back into unconsciousness. She had Lance hold the cotton bandage while she cautiously rolled him further on his side. With a small dagger she deftly cut away the exploded tissue round the arrowhead in his back. Resting the dagger on his back she nimbly worked the index fingers under the arrowhead, then lifted the arrow slightly. Bryan stirred. She backed off momentarily, then picked up the dagger and slid it under the arrow fin and with her other hand gripped the head and deftly in one even motion extracted the arrow; quickly she pressed a bandage over the wound. Bryan groaned, exhaled heavily and fell into a deep sleep. Satisfied there was little bleeding, she lifted the bandage. She then took a leafy plant, crumpled it in her hands and then squeezed its juices into the wound. She took a second wad of cotton, left it dry and applied it to his back. With the help of Lance and Lucia she dressed the wound.

"Your young knight will live, my lord," she said confidently. Turning to an old woman servant, she gave instructions and left the room. "Obviously his lung was spared or he'd be dead by now."

Lance and Lucia eyed each other across the bed. Both were much relieved. She brushed back her tresses and said, "Please, Lance, do not interpret this heinous act as a reflection of our people."

"Have no such fears, my lady; I know they are a respectable lot. There are, alas, those individuals in all races that seek to dishonor the noble character of their people. That is why we Quandrons have knighthood—to redress dishonorable action."

She expressed concern. "But you will leave the redress of this ignoble action to me?"

He hesitated, his lips quivered, then stretched a smile. "Under the circumstance, my lady, I have no choice but to yield to the grace of your sense of justice. Ordinarily I would search him out and kill him on the spot. But since your situation here is tenuous, I shall not place you in jeopardy."

"Thank you, my lord; I see now why chivalry is ascribed to knighthood."

Together they met with the patrician in his chambers. Cicero was circling his desk of granite slab. He paused in front of it and rested against it. Cicero rubbed his gray beard and said, "This is most unfortunate as well as painful to the young knight. I fear there is more than a personal motive here. You know as well as I, dear Lucia, that the baron has expressed undue concern over the coronation. At first I thought he would adjust to this. Apparently my explanation to him that although a queen has never ruled in centuries past, it is perfectly acceptable and the rule of law in our land. Alas, the baron has other ambitions and this dastardly act proves he is capable of anything."

"Yea, your grace," the princess agreed, "I feel I must now make this known, even though I swept it away as harmless lunacy....You see, not two moons ago, Angus proposed marriage. I laughed it off, since neither of us ever had such leanings, as a foolish fantasy of his widowed state, having lost his wife to the nether world. But then I learned from my mother that he had made the very same proposal to her!"

"Good Jove!" Yelped Cicero as he circled behind his desk. "Why was I not apprised of this? Why, this is heresy! Obviously he meant to undercut you by marrying your mother and positioning himself as king!"

"Yea, in retrospect, I should have informed you. Still, he seemed loyal in spite of being twice rejected. It is clear now, however, that he was ill-affected and his ambition lies beyond serving my mother, me and our subjects."

The patrician had wrung his hands while she spoke and now he pulled his beard and said impatiently, "We must act on this immediately before he assembles a rebellious force to cast you to his hounds!" As an afterthought he turned to Lance. "I know how this must seem to you, proud knight, but I trust you understand that the stability of our little country exceeds revenge for your fellow countryman."

"I understand but I fail to perceive how you can overcome this pressing political problem by bringing him to justice," Lance said, mildly shaking his head. "Will not the people think the punishment of Angus was in behalf of a Quandronian, rather than for the security of the state?"

"Eh? I do not follow," the patrician said, rubbing his thinning hair.

Lance raised himself out of a folding chair and paced awhile, then turned back to the old man and offered, "The masses seldom perceive the value of justice when one of their own countrymen is sacrificed for the justice due a foreigner. Particularly in this case. Have you forgotten Bryan's outburst in the temple hall in front of scores of your countrymen?"

Lucia blurted "Oh, my, I had forgotten that! In his pool of blood and sorry state my sentiment glossed over that he had expressed himself like some common spy."

"Aye!..." said the patrician, "which also angered me to say the least."

Having circled the room in random fashion, wringing her hands, Lucia said nervously in reminding them, "Gentlemen, you also forget how nobly Sir Bryan voluntarily apologized for his statements with sincere contrition; and that it was the baron who required my reprimand before he came forth with an apology. Moreover, it was the baron who twice endangered Sir Bryan's life."

The old Cicero rubbed his head, then struck his fist into his palm with finality. "By Thor, that's right!"

Lance smiled at the old man's fickle decisiveness, then turned to the princess. "In sooth, my princess, but your perception is high-minded; I rather doubt the people would see it in that light."

"Noble knight, it seems, contrary to your prior headstrong resolution, that you now propose we take no action at all." She brushed back her hair and shrugged.

"Aye," he nodded. "I do propose that you do nothing, else stir up rebellion. But I do not suggest that *I* do nothing."

"I am with your drift." She put her finger to her chin. "Still, if I let you challenge him, what's to prevent him from calling on his followers?"

"Nothing but honor. For if his ultimate ambition is to overthrow you, he must prove his mettle and meet me in single combat."

Her dark brown eyes sparkled with admiration and drew closer and touched his shoulder. Then suddenly she shook her head violently and withdrew. "Oh, proud champion, I cannot, will not let you do this!" She paced in a tight circle near him. "Angus is very dangerous;...and though no swordsmen, he is deadly with the mace....More so, I fear his marksmanship with the bow and arrow—I doubt that he would ever chance close combat."

"That is my concern, good princess, not yours."

She looked up at him with petulance. "Have you somehow retrieved a wizard's crystal ball that you now presume my concerns? Besides, should you lose—and for that matter should you win—there is no guarantee that his men are not bent as he and attack us, anyway."

"By the ghost of the Centurion, princess, you ring true!" Cicero blurted, ramming his fist in his palm. "We must assemble the loyalists quickly to our side and smash this omen hanging heavily over our valley."

"I don't know, my old stout heart," she said with a long sigh as she went behind the desk and slumped in the chair. "Oh, I do not doubt that we can muster superior numbers, but I dread the spilling of innocent blood."

Lance leaned over the desk. "Then, let me, my lady, seek out this demon! I beg you. It is truly my battle, not yours. Had I not arrived all would be well."

She buried her face in her hands for a moment, then looked up, brushing back her hair. "I thought I explained that—regardless, Baron Angus is an enduring problem." She looked at both of them squarely but could not muster a tone of conviction. "I shall summon him. Perhaps he shall understand the sprawling consequence of his deed and submit to exile."

The old man shook his head. "No, my soon to-be-queen, thou must be firm and hang him!"

"I assure you, grand patrician, I shall be firm; but I'd rather not be ascribed to as the hangman's queen." She clapped her hands and two castle guards entered immediately. "Take this knight to the fiery cavern high and behind the castle. Handle him with the utmost respect. I shall let you know when I am ready to release him."

Lance glared at her. He swiveled on his heel to the guards, instinctively reaching for his hilt, but he was unarmed. In desperation he asked, "My lady, I do not understand!"

"You will, my lord, and hopefully forgive. For I cannot chance your taste for vengeance to swallow our state."

The guards took him to the stables and through the familiar shaft leading to the ocean and the plateau. Half way they urged him into an opening along the gnarled igneous walls. One of the guards took down a lighted lantern from the wall and maneuvered in front of him and led them up twisting, roughly chiseled steps to an elevation of about a hundred feet to a wide shelf that apparently connected to the peak. They crossed over another hundred feet or so into another passage with an ascending ramp. At the fifty foot apex of the ramp, they began to descend abruptly but the declining ramp was chiseled into steps. The lead guard hung up the lantern, even though there were no torches along this bending wall, for the steps were discernible in a dark red cast which graduated toward scarlet, coupled with intense heat. The discomfort worsened as they further descended. Beads of sweat rolled from them. A muffled noise Lance first heard when they had turned to the imbedded stairs, now became a roar in conjunction with flashing light spreading an effulgence of blazing embers. The noise became as pervasive as the din of battle as the steps blended into a bending path of faint decline. The path widened and rolled out a huge semi-circular rim revealing a cavern dazzling in scarlet that vaulted thousands of feet into the deep, interminable shadows above. The source of the roar below was deafening; Lance edged out on the craggy apron. Raging was bubbling lava, which sporadically lashed out tonguing flames and rocketing white hot scintilla. Across from it was a tree stump; an axe next to it. He blinked in disbelief as he heeled his boot into the solid rock bed. He backed off and glanced at the guards quizzically. One shrugged and waved him back. The other pointed toward a narrow shaft fifty paces back. Lance needed no coaxing as he felt the immense heat virtually singeing his beard. Still, he turned and looked again at the violent action churning sparks and balls of flame high into the stalactitic vault. They walked along the shaft for a while as the red glow from the raging pit diminished and torches spaced on the walls began to illuminate the way. They came to an iron-gate. A sentry was sitting on a stool.

The sentry eyed Lance's confused expression. With a toothy grin the sentry yelled above the din of the pit, "And what do you think of the devil's work, stranger?"

Lance managed a smile but answered rather solemnly, "Aye, hell it is. And though this settling place of yours is about as inviting as limbo, it's at least much cooler than the raging demon at the end of the shaft."

Guffawing and nodding all too knowingly, the sentry opened the gate. Lance noticed that it was not locked. One of the guards put a hand on his shoulder and urged him behind the gate, saying considerately, "Further down you'll find it cooler and a cot to rest on. Of course you'll have to work the broom—not much business down here."

"My, but aren't you soft-hearted," the gate sentry said to the guard. "But I can see we have a gentleman here."

"Yea, and treat him well; the princess does not think of him as a prisoner. Put the lock on the gate all the same."

"Oh? Just a guest in hell, eh?" the sentry snickered.

The other guard piped in. "Nay, from what is brewing in the air, it seems that hell will be above." The two guards left the gatekeeper.

Lance moved deeper into the tunnel and began to cool. On each side there were unoccupied cubicles, each with a cot, wash basin and bucket. A little further down and somewhat cooler, though still moist and warm, an old man in a clean but ancient tunic and himation sat on a cot, staring at Lance blankly through straggles of hair over his eyes. In a crackly voice he greeted the knight, "At last someone to talk to other than that prattling gatekeeper. He never listens, but I think the roar of the fire pit has made him deaf."

"Indeed it would, old man," Lance concurred.

The old man lifted his left arm and beckoned to the departing gate-keeper. "A little crazy too—he's always bemoaning his stay in hell as a curse."

Lance noticed several phylacteries fastened to his veiny arm. "Better a life-span of hell than eternity in hell like the rest of us."

The old man chuckled. "I could see you were alien—from Christendom, I gather?"

"Aye, as all of you should be."

"Nay, too much fuss over religion—much too serious."

"I should think religion was serious with you—judging from those relics round your wrist."

"Our business is restricted to what we understand, young man," he countered firmly. "I leave mystery to God's hierarchy."

"I'll yield to that, but tell me....What I don't understand is why a sentry at the gate—for just you and me?"

"Oh, he's not here to guard me or you. He's here to guard the pit—round the clock they guard it."

"Then, in sooth, they guard the gates of hell," Lance said with a smile.

"Not exactly—that's my duty—they are here to alert me."

Lance leaned into him to ask, "And what have you got to do with it?"

"Oh, it's been so long, yet oddly sometimes like only a Sabbath or two, I sometimes forget my purpose." He parted some twisted strands from his forehead, rubbed his thumb across his heavy brow. "But purpose I do have, I trust."

"How can you possibly have any purpose in this God forsaken hole?—much less forget if you had." Lance eyed the strange old man curiously.

"On the contrary, it is far from forsaken. That's what gives it purpose; nor is it so strange that one should forget why he is doing something....After all, are we not in a world where fallacy endures daily? How often have you risen with the dawn and as though in a daze, wondered what the aim was for the day?"

Lance grinned and said, "Aye, that oft does happen. But overall there is a driving force to give me direction."

"Then you're fortunate and obviously a nobleman." He chuckled.

"Being a nobleman has nothing to do with it—at least not anymore where I come from....Well, perhaps I should say our intent is to give purpose to everyone."

"My how democratic." The old man chirped.

"Oh, I wouldn't go that far. Perhaps I mean some dignity in lieu of purpose."

"A wild horse has dignity but no purpose; on the other hand, a trained horse has no dignity but surely purpose," the ancient reasoned.

Lance paused a moment tufting his beard round his scar, then said, in a puzzled tone, "Maybe one under yoke; though even there it depends on the owner's care....Kindness goes a long way....I feel our destriers have great dignity because we care about, and for them; and surely, no one can argue that they don't serve our purpose."

"I gathered you are or were a knight."

"How so?—without tabard or sword?'

The ancient pointed. "By your hands—they are ruddy, powerful and scarred. Court nobleman have lady's hands." Lance laughed; the cellmate went on with a sudden light in his eyes, "Of course, now I remember the point of my being here!"

Lance scratched his beard and grinned. "Surely not based on anything I said."

"Oh, precisely,...You see, all the great myths begin with a benevolent god who nonetheless has deep-seated anger. He is like a father who resents the ingratitude of a spoiled child. As long as the child needs his guidance and care, he remains under his roof. Once, however, the child rebels to a degree that he is capable of exercising his own mind, whether responsibly or recklessly, he is no longer bestowed the right to his father's care or to dwell under the protective shade of the tree of life."

Lance interjected, "Vaguely, I understand your drift, but how can it possibly connect to what I just said?"

"Your knighthood for one thing. You took an oath—I assume a generous one—to defend the rights of others who are violated. You, in a sense, restore their dignity in order to carry out the aims under society's governance—in a sense you toss them a twig from the tree. But you don't—nor are you expected to—rise to question that aim no more than you would your destrier. We tend to look at individuals as a set of values within a system, not individuals within themselves."

Lance shook his head in annoyance. "What's wrong with that? It seems to me there is no more noble purpose than to serve in behalf of the state just as my destrier serves me to benefit that state."

"Nothing whatsoever, and indeed noble. But what if your great horse begins to resist your commands? Would you still be a caring loving rider? Would you set him free on the range? Or would you butcher him or hitch him to a dray?"

"Nay, I would first try to retrain him."

"And if unsuccessful?"

"Hmm, I really don't know."

"But if you really had the dumb brute's welfare in mind you would not have to think about returning him to his original state of dignity, which may be all the purpose the animal needs."

"Aye, I see your point, but how does that apply to complex humans?"

"The same individual you rushed to defend may be the next you defend against. Not that he has changed as a person but only that his direction in society might have changed that does not suit its aims. So it is not the individual that you care about but the protection of society's laws."

"Why, of course, if the same individual has now violated another, he must be under my blade!"

The old man nodded pensively. "In truth—thieves, murderers, molesters— transgressors of all kinds deserve a thrashing. "Still, I'm sure it has crossed your mind many times that the world would be better off without these wilful individuals."

"Absolutely, I have: *Why were they born to begin with, I would ask my tormented soul."*

"And I would agree that they never should have been put on the face of the earth just as I question the need for the cruel, vicious carnivores that roam the earth or that there be un-god-like catastrophes as earthquakes and plagues. But that is not realistic. The world is designed in itself and we can only help that it, within itself, somehow alters its design; and the same for individuals that wreak havoc on us—that somehow miraculously they change for the better. And your work in this world is precisely that. Your chivalric ways and unselfish duties will no doubt inspire many inclined otherwise to do good in the world. Yet that is all we can do is hope."

Lance nodded, then suddenly added, "Or change it by the sword."

"Yea, but only if the sword were in your hands and not in the hands of a tyrant. Thus, my young cell mate, is my purpose."

Lance shook his head and grimaced. "Well, I'll leave that to you and trust that you know what it is you mean." He chuckled.

"Oh, verily, you will know."

"You are a strange mystery, my elder."

"Oh, not so,...simplistic in a way"

Lance chuckled. "Aye, but in a strange way."

"But to me, stranger, still, is that you are here. Why, 'tis plain you are a nobleman from the lower land."

"Ah, strange is your princess; for she has a unique sense of humor sentencing me here." Lance chuckled.

"Strange, you say? For that darling girl has not a strange streak in her. You must have done something dreadful for her to send you here—rarely, as you can see, is this place occupied." The old man parted his thatch bristle shock from his dark gray eyes looking quizzically. "Perhaps she had a wider reason."

"Why so?" Lance perked.

"Who but she would know the tailoring of her reasoning?" the old man said. "She threads a special style."

"Aye special, but hardly mysterious....And darling, you say? Aye, my impression too," Lance intoned rhapsodically, then snapped, "Yet why are *you* here?...Seems cruel for one of your age to be doomed to this pit."

"Has my talk fallen on deaf ears as the gatekeeper's?" He laughed and said, "Let us just say that this is my home for just a spell."

"I find it hard to believe that anyone would volunteer to stay in this hell hole," Lance said, raising his brows.

He chuckled. "You would change your mind were you to reach my age. I come here to bake the creaks from my bones and the cold from my fingers and legs. Better the sweat of this place than the sweat of labor at my age."

Lance put his hand on the old man's shoulder and sat down beside him. "By the way, my good man, why *are* all the cells but this empty? Is there no crime?"

"Oh, the usual crimes of passion—drunken brawls, family hatred. Drunks and husbands are hitched to ploughs to work the fields till the pugnacious spirits leave them. And justice is swift—noose or arrow is the choice if murder. In the old days it was the fiery pit."

"But is there no theft, no lesser crimes than murder?"

"Oh, the people here have abundance—no need to rob. Of course, among the gentry there is always theft but with them it's legal." He chuckled. Lance laughed. The old man's tired eyes glanced at him, then glittered. "Of course, their grain bins are not as full now that our darling princess reigns."

Lance perked, "Oh? How's that?"

"The share of the manor strips have been diminished by her rule. Therefore the people have a generous take now."

"I gather that wasn't the case when her father ruled, eh?—much harsher?"

"Aye, although a good ruler; still, the princess is fairer. Of course, she claims that the new rule was in her father's will, but I know it came from her pure heart—because she's a child of Ceres."

"Oh?...I thought it was the Lady Margaret." He chuckled. "You highlanders do take things seriously, then?" He smiled at the old man and winked. "Perhaps though with tongue in cheek?—Why Ceres? Surely you must mean Eve?"

"Oh, yea, either way, but as I said on what can be understood; for there is ambiguity in the biblical name. There is no mystery about Ceres, no stipulations, she just yields up the fruit of the land naturally, without question, without apology."

"Well, then, why not Christ? Surely he gives bread for the soul!"

He laughed. "Oh, come now. Even if we did believe in him, it has nothing to do with this world. He's in the past and mostly in the future."

Lance shook his head in puzzlement, rose up and went to the bars and eyed the passage way. He could see the gate silhouetted against the flickering fiery background. He turned back to the elder. "You said that the gateman watches over the boiling pit and in your behalf? Why?"

"Ah, there lies the ambiguity!...Sages thousands of years ago predicted that its flames and boiling rock would leap up and tear off the rest of the peak's top, flooding the valleys with fiery water and lay the base of nourishment for the tree of another millennium."

Lance laughed. "My, that's a long, tedious watch! I should think if nothing has happened in all that time it is never going to happen."

"I suppose, in a way, it is like your monks who rise each morning expecting the Judgment Day. We, on the other hand, dread the coming of

Lilith."

"Lilith? Surely, you don't believe in that fantastic notion!"

"You believed in the legendary princess," the ancient said with a wink in his eye.

Lance's jaw dropped. "My God, how did you know that?"

"The human species is made up of, as you put it, *fantastic notions;* our heart pumps figments into our brain."

"Hmm, like the tree?" Lance uttered confusedly. "That's twice you mentioned it....The one growing out of this impregnable rock?"

The elder nodded slightly. "Yea,...thus the ambiguity."

9. Rhonda

By noon she and her dun were exhausted; for the last mile she had dismounted and led the mare by checkrein to rest it and relax herself. Moreover, she was sore from riding hard and long without a saddle. Continually she sheltered her eyes from the hazy sun as she squinted down and along the twisting trail hoping to see a home or inn—she knew she was still two day's ride from Castle City. Spacious rolling plains opened up beside the trail which became wider.

Finally she discovered a camp where two men were sitting round a smoky fire. A donkey and an old draft horse were tied to nearby trees. A battered cauldron was set on stones in the middle of flames. The suggestion of victuals aroused her appetite, though the aroma was not much more appealing than the wash she had seen the women boil by the river of her castle. The men were dressed in little more than rags and their mien disheveled and dirty. Instinctively she mounted; stopping was out of the question, even though she would have welcomed the respite and perhaps some nourishment. She mounted and gently heeled her tired mount to a canter.

Nevertheless, one of them, a sandy-haired rogue in his twenties, obviated her having the luxury of her volition. He had been watching her attentively as she was coming down the trail. When he saw that she was going to pass them by, he jumped up from the campfire, and rushed to the road, stepping in front of her and grabbing the rein.

"Now, missy, that's not very neighborly of you to pass us by—and without a word of greeting."

"This is not my neighborhood; now let go, peasant," she demanded.

"Now, missy, peasants are hard working people, and I have never worked a day in my life. So you have no cause. It seems, though, I have strong cause to call you a horse thief, since you have no saddle, and this fine filly must've had one strapped to it," he observed with a grin of yellow-green teeth barely perceptible midst his hemp-like beard. "Clever of you to sell the saddle already!" He went to reach into her coat pocket.

She slapped his hand. "You have a sick imagination, rogue!"

"I know wily wenches,...and sick indeed is imagination 'cause it doesn't lead to loot." He grabbed her wrist and with his other hand, still clinging to the rein, stretched it to its limit into her bodice.

"You filthy swine! How dare you!" she shrieked; she backed away; his hand was constricted by the rein.

He shook his head, let go her wrist and tugged her belt. "No dare, untamed missy, just plain sight. Why, I reckon you stole the fancy coat and breeches and the dyed doeskin boots. Oh, if only you had big feet!—I'm in dire need of a pair."

"Your sight is far from plain with the fancies you add to it," she countered. "Can you not see how perfectly my clothes fit? I cannot say the same for you. Why, that sword you have, though poorly crafted and unworthy of combat, surely can't belong to one so misbegotten—obviously you're no Achilles. Vulcan himself must be thundering a bellicose laugh throughout the clouds of Olympus! Now off with you before I report you to the king's knights, one of whom is my brother who has a sword two times the length and thrice the weight."

Proudly he tapped the hilt above his sash and smirked "Now, who has a running imagination?" He laughed. "If of noble blood, then what are you doing here on this lonely road of thieves? Surely, you would not leave your brave brother's side! And what are you doing in a torn, though costly coat? Have you no ladies-in-waiting?" He laughed again, but in hearing her talk he surmised she was from the gentry. "But I'll believe your tall tale, my lady, and therefore you must accept our hospitality for quite a spell." He reached up to pull her from the horse. Rhonda raised her leg to shove a foot in his face, but he grabbed her boot and toppled her from the mount. He picked her up by the collar and led her and the horse to the camp while she squirmed and screamed.

The middle aged companion, short and very fat, wobbled closer while her antagonist set her by the fire. He took her braids in his pudgy hand, then pressed them to his quivering jowls, after which he ran them under his bulbous veiny nose. Though she pulled her hand away several times, he insisted on smelling a hand so white, clean and smooth, that he had in all his life never seen so close up. "My," rubbing his gray stubble, the fat one said, "she smells so good I should prepare her for the cauldron. What a wonderful stew she would make."

The younger rogue grated, "Bah, that's all you think of is filling that belly of yours—too many years as a miller, stuffing yourself with the grain you stole. How many times do I have to tell you that belly is so cavernous that you will never be satisfied. That's why you belch and eternally unleash smelly winds from your fat ass only to stuff the barrel more." Then he looked into Rhonda's watering eyes. She lowered her head into her drawn up knees. "Never fear, my lovely, we won't eat you....Never get our ransom money that way." He chuckled.

Rhonda looked up and burst out laughing. "Ha, ransom, you say? Why, my father has disinherited me!"

"Wonderful!" cried the fat miller. "Then we shall have a fine meal after all," he added, glancing over at his sandy-haired companion who frowned back. "What say you, Sandy? In truth, I tell you, I've heard from a mariner that there's a treat in store. He says a tribe at the lower end of the world indulges in such sweet cakes which he claims to have tasted and approved, saying it is far better than the juiciest fowl and tenderized venison. And, he says, this is all from colored skin. Think, then, Sandy, what this pearly thing would yield—why, I'll wager, on the level of royal taste!"

Rhonda laughed nervously and cried, "Why, this is inane—and utterly grotesque!"

The fat miller grabbed her hand and licked it. "Ah, in truth, so sweet!" She wrenched her hand from his grip.

"Oh, turn off your blubbery, blathering mouth!" yelled the sandy-haired one while half drawing his short sword, coupled with a threatening look at the miller. He slid the blade down again and turned to the girl, who had lost her haughty humor and now sat shaking in fear and adjusting herself closer to the fire. "Don't play the fox with us, my haughty missy," Sandy cautioned. "If this is in truth, and no one wants you, then there are other ways a pretty lass like you can bring us instant booty, you know."

She cupped her ears and squeezed shut her eyes as she drew closer to the fire as overcast and frightening circumstance chilled the air. Sandy pushed the miller away and rolled himself closer to Rhonda who was rubbing her hands over the fire, hoping to alleviate the cold, fearful shivers winnowing her body. He put his hand under her waistcoat; she recoiled and slapped the busy hand and scowled. "That filthy hand be assured will no longer reside with the wrist when the Lord-Protector meets up with you!" she shrieked caution.

"Ha, my pretty, you forget your family has abandoned you. Why, then, should a brother care—and surely not the lofty commander of the famous Mari!"

"Hah!" she exulted, "One and the same!"

"Oh, no!...The mighty Lord Lance! Heaven have mercy!" The miller begged clutching at his fellow rogue's collar, "Jesus, let her go!"

Sandy pushed him back onto his broad billowy rump. "Bah, she's a liar! First she says she's been disinherited; now she threatens us with the

Lord-Protector being her brother, no less!"

"Sandy! For the sake of my precious life! We cannot chance having the warring Mari swooping down on us!"

"Precious! That's worth a horselaugh!" Sandy sputtered, then glanced at her and added, "Besides, your so-called Lord-Protector brother would have to know of your pretty predicament, wouldn't he? Why in his lofty position, I'm sure his thoughts are not on you. And surely, no noble would immerse himself in the nether world of us commons."

"Humph, subcommoners! For surely neither of you strike me as having the common decency of those working our fertile strips for the good of the commonwealth," she boasted.

The miller clapped his hands. "My, what a spirit—oh, truly straight from the gentry! Show mercy, Sandy, lest the mighty knights of the land hack us to bits!"

"Bah," Sandy grunted, frowning at him, then over at Rhonda, "the common poor, you mean, for the good of the uncommon wealth of the nobles."

Jowls drooping, the fat miller said disappointedly, "Oh, no, your wisest, now turned fool. We must therefore make the evidence disappear. Why not then prepare her for the cauldron? Ah, it would outdo the Lord's supper!"

"Zounds, fool of fools!" Sandy scowled.

An elderly, scrawny man approached bearing firewood. His low forehead wrinkled even more in seeing the damsel. "Jumping Jove, what have we here?...Surely she descended from the heavens!" He dropped the sticks and rotted logs; the old man clasped and shook his own veiny hands and exhaled, glancing at the miller, "By Jove, your lowest, there is no doubt she's drawn from nobility's womb. Meaning...in store for us is a mighty ransom as fat as you, eh?"

"True, but very dangerous," the still wary miller inserted.

Sandy looked at them with disappointment, coupled with belated worry, and growled, "I fear the blubbery fool might be right, after all."

The miller bounced to his knees and his eyes popped glee. "Ah, good sense has returned. Good! Let us tie her to a tree and begone from here!"

The elder looked at them in puzzlement. "What are you balmy to pass up this opportunity?"

"Yea," as you say," the miller nodded, for we'd be balmy to court this slip round the country side being the sister of the immortal Lord-Protector!"

The elder fell to his knees. "Is this in truth, Sandy?...You have gone mad?"

"Nay, old man," the young rogue groaned, then gesturing to the miller, "but the swine has: to believe the bewitching tale of this little whore. Just the same we cannot chance the dangerous implications of a ransom." He looked over at her and touched her cheek which immediately recoiled. Then he stared at each of the men. "Think, my foolish band; just look at her!" He wrenched her braids and forced her face to the fire which blazoned her delicate beauty. "In our permanent possession is this not a lifetime of king's ransoms if we put her to work in God's oldest profession?"

"Youth!" cried the eldest in disgust. "What you propose—slavery!—is far more dangerous! Why, to charge handsome funds we'd have to pander to the gentry! Clearly this lovely thing would cry her heart out and spill the beans to them. And then God help us if the pig here is right!"

The fat one fell back on his haunches and looked to the sky. "God forbid I'm right—nay, I cannot think on the awesome Mari anymore!"

"That's the spirit!" Sandy cheered the miller and turned to the old man. "And damn the nobles! Not a hair of her will they get! They would want her for the entire night—no money in that! No, you unthinking old man, the foreign mariners and the king's sailors at the seaport I am thinking of. With their speedy, anxious loins, she will make us a fortune in a single day!"

"That's a long journey for my delicate feet!" cried the fat miller.

"For your fat body, you mean," countered the old man.

Rhonda buried her face in her hands at the sordid speculation.

10. Kalab

With a glistening polished horn of potion in her hand, Erinysia entered the old warlord's chambers. He was sitting up in bed sucking and licking his lips in hot anticipation. Sashaying in rather modest sexual undertones, she approached the bed and said tenderly, "Drink, my lord, but slowly, tastily, letting its warm unctuousness settle on the tongue, slip it gently off to dwell under a while to caress the sublingual gums."

Kalab chuckled. "Ah, the mouthful falling from your lips is more than a match for what's in the cup." He eagerly took the horn, ready to guzzle.

She placed her hand on the vessel. "Nay, my loving lord, chug not, but rather suspend the swallow for it to pamper your throat and only then ever so gently let it ooze down to fire the blood to set you into action."

He shrugged his battle scarred shoulders and replied, "My dear kitten, when you enter my room, I am ready. Your beauty is incomparable. Why, I'd have to be dead if I were not sexually attracted to you this hot, blistering moment!"

She giggled and pecked him on the nose while handing back the drink. "Nevertheless, my aging tiger, you must drink—you'll perform better and longer."

"My dear, what I lack in performance you will more than compensate by your fiery nature. However,...drink I shall." Yet he hesitated and added, "Unless, of course, it is a trick to make me sleep." He roared with confident jest and then ignoring her sensuous, lingering instructions, gulped it down, wiped his mouth and beard on the coverlet. "Now as you say I am in total readiness, he piped and held out his arms."

Erinysia looked to the high ceiling. "Oh, damn you, Eve, for the gross reconstitution of man to spineless swine!" She paced the foot of the bed, then swiveled and stared at him. "Must I bed again with fired loins designed for no other aim than rapid limpness?...I'd prefer the latter first and challenge it to rise by dancing round it while suggestively disrobing."

He roared again and yelped, "I know every inch of your body—no need to exhibit it. I need only that its softness press up against my damnably agéd flesh....Come now," he commanded, holding out his arms again, "no more of this. Clear the game board and cope with the reality of my hardness."

She dropped her heavy robe to the floor, then removed her flimsy gown, lifted the coverlet, and trailed the gown caressingly along his hairy chest, stomach and legs. She put one knee on the bed, leaned over and kissed him fully on the mouth. The old man pulled her down onto him and ran his hands crazily down her sinuous back.

Because she too had taken the aphrodisiac she responded wildly to the extent that she would not let him roll over on top of her. Indeed, as the old man had suggested, his potion was unnecessary, for it was Erinysia who dominated through the night.

Long after the tumble glass had depleted, they both rolled over exhausted. However, she continued to fondle him while he was on the border of sleep. She said, "My lord, I'm beginning to think you do not wish to be king."

"He could barely roll his head in the pillow. "Huh,...Oh, I'm worried about Rhonda....The search party has not found her yet....I wonder what she's up to? You don't suppose Henry had anything to do with her disappearance?...No, of course not," he added, answering his own question, "he wouldn't dare....No, it is her own doing—her mother was strong-willed."

Erinysia suggested innocently, "Perhaps she went to find her brother."

The old man's head jerked up from the pillow. "Alone? On that dangerous northern trail!"

Nonchalantly she said, "You just said she's strong-willed," then added ominously, "however, I think you underestimate the king. What better way to head you off than through your daughter?"

He propped up on his elbow. "Why would that stop me? It would serve as juice to attack now. There is no negotiating with kidnappers. I would have to take the chance."

"Then, you must rally your men," she emphasized, tapping his chest.

He fell back and rolled away from her and muttered, "Oh, I know I'm right—she's off somewhere with her damnable horse because she's mad at me....Why, at this very moment, she's probably with your other stepdaughter!"

Erinysia's dark eyes lighted up at the prospect. She then began to run her long fingers down his spine and then curled a finger under his hairy rump. "My Lord, you cannot go to sleep yet. It is your turn now."

He mumbled into the pillow. She went on tickling his testes until he rolled back over and smothered her breasts with busy rubbery lips. He looked up at her fiery eyes, "Oh, my bawdy widow, witch, and wife, you kindle this tired old body with the raging fire of youth!" He kissed her wet on her mouth and then went back to her breast to wallow in their warmth and softness made all the more sensuous by his hot saliva. His mouth traveled to her thighs, which suddenly locked. He tried to force them open, but she pushed him off, sat up and jumped out of the bed. "Why now tease me?" he quizzed. "I was satisfied—aye, totally spent and prepared to sleep, until you aroused me but now you do this to me." She laughed and danced round the bed as he bounced round on knuckles and knees in the bed, panting like a dog.

"Do you blame me?" she asked while picking up her light gown and caressing herself, careful that the candlelight played on her bronzed body. "*You* may be satisfied...."

"Good! Then I'm here to satisfy you! Come to bed again and I shall!...Verily, like never before!" He reached out and grabbed her gown to pull her onto him, but she let go and danced round the bed again. "Bah! Women! Annoying, delicious mystery!" He jumped out of bed. "Hah, now I know!...It is said all women fantasize about rape!" He grinned. That's it, eh, my little cat?...You purr in anticipation of being taken forcibly!"

He caught her by her flowing hair and forced her down to the cold flagged floor almost hitting her head on a nearby table. She giggled as he salivated her body and held fast her arms. Still her thighs locked; he let loose one arm to try to force her open. Just then she reached for the leg of the table and toppled it. The candle-holder fell; she gripped it and with a short stroke rapped it onto his head with just enough force to hurt him but not make him senseless. He rubbed his head and rolled off her. "Zounds, bitch!"

"I don't fancy to rape as some wild fancy brought on by some cheap mix of aphrodisiac, my lord," she said coyly while rising and prancing round him. "I must be relaxed but in full control."

"Then what is your problem?" he asked still rubbing his head.

"You, my lord."

"What by the Holy Rood is that supposed to mean?" he growled as he pulled up his naked body and threw himself onto the bed face down.

While stroking his back she said, "Your body alone cannot satisfy me. I need your power. Yet you persist in this cowardice."

He rolled face up and jerked up his torso. "How dare you accuse me of cowardice! I can stand up against the best of them."

"Then, why do you procrastinate? Is it because you are too old for war? And you need your son to fight your battles for you?"

"If a man—hell, any other woman—said that to me I'd run him or her through to the bowels. My son gave up fighting for me. That traitor fights his battles for that damned Henry!"

"Aye, and why not? Did not my jeweled dome show you the reason?" she rasped crudely. Pointing to the corner of the room where on a shelf the crystal cabochon dimly pulsated through a silk covering chrysoberyl or cat's eye, she added, "Perhaps again you would like to see the enactment of siring what you believed to be your son." She ran to the dormant cabochon, slipped off the covering and waved her hand. Suddenly from its idling state it burst a glow of green and yellow flashes with dashes of red illuminating the spacious room.

"Oh, you are so damnably cruel, witch! Enough of that bastardly act!"

She shook her head defiantly. "Alas, I fear the fire in your eyes are not enough to head off Henry's dynasty before it is inscribed in marble by the deeds of Lance for the benefit of Henry and young Henry?"

"Aye, be damned sure I'll not let that happen!"

"Then firm up the loins, throw off the skirts of Mari and assert the name of Kalab!"

"Aye King Bal it is!" He reached out his arms for her and added with bravado, "There's enough fire in my heart to burn out the king's castle if I have to!"

She placed the red and gold silk cover back over the dome, which subsided. She moved close to the bed and ordered. "Then you must not loiter but muster your men in the morning to march on Henry before it is too late and Lance's loyalists defect to Henry."

"*Damn!* ...Woman, why do you insist that my men, the ones I originally trained and kept in provisions would desert me?"

"Ah, but then you trained them for your father-in-law. Then as now the banner of Mari hauntingly waves! That is why Lance is in control of the army and thinks its force is under his rule and Henry's. Why, the tag of Kalab means nothing to him!...You must reclaim your manhood before it is too late."

"By God, I'll rip that damn flag down from the tower myself!...And burn every last one of the purple tabards in the army!...Still, I wish to see my son again—I need to hear his reaction before I make a move. And, oh, where is my Rhonda?"

She frowned, pouted and abruptly jerked back from the bed. "You want my body but do not trust my mind....Moreover, what good would that do? Lance can't tell you what loins he springs from!...And did I hear you say 'my son'?"

"Oh, the torture!" He pressed his palms against his face.

"Then put and end to the torture of your old wife's adultery by terminating Henry I and the potential II and claiming the crown for yourself," she snarled.

"What is an old man to do with a crown if without a son? If what that cursed catty crystal of yours shows be true, I have no son to carry on the reign."

"You have a daughter; see to it she marries wisely. Besides, what do you care? It is the land you want and your revenge." Her lip curled up.

"Aye, so sorely I lust for both....And as you say...why not Rhonda? Why, I shall make a man of her to carry on!...But, oh, where is she?"

Erinysia edged back toward the bed, ignoring his question. "And as you say; if you love me...why not for me?" she reminded him, trailing her gown over his shoulders.

He reached out for her but she stepped back. "Aye, for you, you beguiling wench....Then I yield, but only if you come back to bed. Who knows but there may be enough juice to make a new son!"

She dropped the diaphanous gown to the floor and pressed her breasts to his sweaty, bearded face. "You shall move to action, then?"

He hungrily sucked her breasts, then murmured. "Yea, yea, I shall yield to your ambitious wiles." He pulled her down on the bed.

Her thighs crossed and ankles locked, she said, "In the morning you will call the troops to arms?"

He smothered her face in kisses, then murmured, "Aye, at dawn I shall be dripping with power and meeting with my officers."

She sighed and opened her legs.

Though extremely tired from his power-driven escapade all night and into the morning, Kalab summoned his two commanders—Baron Bennet and Sir John, the latter warrior also had fought under Kalab's command as well as the grandfather's. Similar to Bennet he had a thick powerful figure but aging flaccidly. His gray beard and graying bushy eyebrows helped draw from the white shining scars of battle across his forehead and both cheekbones.

The old warlord poured them wine into two immense horns and motioned that they partake. Leaning over and pressing his knuckles onto the table, the master of the manor began, "My trusted knights," but he looked squarely at the elder, "the time is ripe—with or without Lance. The king is rolling in unilateral strength. We will have no autonomy left if we continue to let him rise in power. Thanks to Lance and you fools Henry is a bloody schemer, who has already surpassed those damning Clergy-robbers in money and influence, leaving us to his mercy. There is no end to his levying inordinate shares on our tithes. Verily, we are under his thumb....Aye, I concede my own stupidity for permitting this self-anointed king."

Bennet put down the horn tumbler into its cradle and inserted crafted innocence. "I can't argue with you on that score, my lord....Still, is it not too late? For what is there to do?"

The old warlord raised a fist then crashed it to the table. "Why an assault on his castle, what else!"

"Good grief, my Lord Bal, you dare speak treason before knights sworn to the loyalty of the king!" said the old thick-set warrior."

Kalab looked with surprise at his old comrade. "Treason? Was it not treason on Henry's part to appropriate for himself those lands?"

"But it was through marriage!" John reminded him.

"Through theft, you mean. He had no right to the old Duke's lands that were left to his son!"

"Need I remind you, my lord, that the Duke's son died?"

"Yea, very timely and mysteriously," snarled the warlord.

John added, "Granted, but...no proof of treachery."

"Oh, Henry is too shrewd to leave a trail! Nevertheless, I know." He said gazing out past them. "Besides, what divine right has Henry to declare himself king?"

"The Church has given him Her blessing!" the old warrior prompted. "And then there's the Document."

"Aye, like an apple in a hog's mouth!" Again he slammed his fist on the heavy table. "Damn those paper tigers—roars, nothing but groundless claims. Testament or Document—just fanatical ranting of mere mortals."

"You forget, old war-charger, that your own son believes in Henry," John persisted. "It might well be a scheme for power; still, it is primarily unification. We cannot go on forever fighting among ourselves."

"You, John, of all fighting men should say that!" The old man's brows raised as he looked at his old friend with legitimate surprise. "The feudal system has worked for hundreds of years!"

"But at a very dear price—merely anarchy pitted against anarchy," the old warrior said in a low, deliberate voice.

"I fear, my friend, you and your horse are ready for pasture. It seems you are losing your steel nerves; or worse, Lance has so bent your ear with the feminine sop of the Mari Order you can no longer think straight."

John, with sadness in his eyes, shook his head and reminded him, "You forget we both did fight under its flag and still do."

"And you, John, did once believe in the tried and true of the feudal system. Henry's way is disruptive."

The two old warriors stared in silence at each other. Bennet eyed askance his fellow officer, then turned to the old warlord and said, "My lord, I couldn't agree with you more..."

Sir John broke silence, "What's this?" He stared at Bennet quizzically. "Our first loyalty is to the King and Lance!"

Kalab shook his head, seemingly shocked. "Sir John! You dare say that in my presence! There is one loyalty and that is to me! I grouped your armies decades ago into an unsurpassed fighting force. Without it there would be no Henry. Now, with it back under my command there will no longer be a Henry!"

John was struck dumb. He blinked his eyes and then roared, "I can't believe my ears!...This is John you're speaking to! For three generations—before this castle was built—the Mari Legion has always been the finest fighting force in the land. You were planted here to sustain the tradition simply by marriage; otherwise, the command would have gone to me to carry on after Lord Mari died."

Kalab clenched his teeth and fists. "So that's it, is it? The demon Envy resists me! Is it my fault you lacked the skill even to squire me!...Why, else would Lord Mari, a man of great perception, choose me as his son-in-law?"

John cleared his throat and murmured, "Oh, I think we both know why!... But put that to rest...." Kalab fidgeted and receded. John went on, "Think now of your son,...and the great path to peace he carved out of the wilds of anarchy.... My lord, this is madness! There is no turning back; the turn of events now has solid footing. The old ways are gone." Sir John pleaded.

Kalab rebounded. "Bah!" Kalab looked coldly at his old friend in-arms. "Mere fancies are always volatile."

"But Lance is fully committed—he would never consent—it is no fancy to him! He believes in the Great Document."

"Damn the Document! It is nothing since I never agreed to it. As far as I am concerned nothing has changed. I am my own destiny. I don't need a king to direct me anymore than I need the Church to haunt my soul."

"Yea, Yea," inserted Bennet, "there is no doubt about it; the king complicates our lives!"

"Good! At least you, Bennet, are loyal to me and spare me the trouble of hanging you." He turned and stared guardedly at Sir John. "What say you, John? Are you with me?"

The old warrior grasped his drinking horn tightly, then asked, "What option do I have, Bal?"

"The dungeon or noose."

He tilted the horn and drank dry the wine; he released a feigned bellicose sigh. "Well, then, I am with you, my lord; yet there's Lance..."

"Bah, forget Lance!" he snarled. "He has forgotten us—what with his being on some schoolboy fantasy."

"Of course, Lance no longer is a factor," rejoined Bennet with alacrity. John glanced over in disgust, then bowed his head.

Kalab smiled in triumph. "Now that we agree. See to it the men do not carouse tonight. Before dawn on the morrow assemble them to march. We shall camp on the first knoll at Henry's castle by sundown three days hence. In the meantime, order the carters to see that provisions are plentiful and the wagons well-greased."

11. Second Arrow

The princess on the dais sat in an enormous high-back chair, which doubled as a throne. (Through the castle grapevine it was said that a top craftsman was planning a beautiful new throne proportionate to her size to be presented to her on coronation day.) The big dais table and its many chairs had been moved back against the wall. Her eyes followed the strapping baron as he paced in front of a bench table on the lower level. He stopped at one end, turned and leaned over the table and said in an annoyed tone, "What you propose, my princess, is lunacy."

"What you so cruelly did to that young knight was beyond description—amoral," she countered.

"But to expect me to accede to exile for the mishap of a lowlander..."

"Mishap!" She raised herself out of the chair momentarily, then settled back.

"Yea, though I'll not deny it was my arrow, they had no business coming here to check on our security and study our horses." Angus strutted back up along the table and faced her. "Oh, how can I convince you that they are fraudulent interlopers?"

"Whatever they are and their motive, they are our guests. Not only have you injured and insulted them, but you have perpetrated the same dishonor to our proud country for your ignoble act," she snarled, and rapped her tiny fist on the chair's arm to emphasize all the more her indignation.

Angus snarled back, gritting his teeth. "Nay, rather I am protecting our country!..." Then he collected himself and nonchalantly asked, "And have you forgotten that I proposed to you?"

She was inclined to laugh at his straight face manner. "No, nor have I forgotten your proposal to my mother! Yet you have the gall to question *their* motives! In truth, you are not thinking of our country but of your own welfare."

"I do not deny that either of you beautiful women would enhance my well-being."

"Humph, never mind ours!" She rose from her chair, circled it and grasped its wings. "However you might have once been loyal to my father, it is clear that you have no intention of being loyal to me, nor to my mother—and most assuredly you do not have our country fastened to your heart for all to share. The effrontery of your dastardly act as hunter of humans today and the conniving manner in which you have insulted my mother and me for the sake of your lust for power leaves me with no alternative but to exile you."

"Then, why not sterner justice? Summon the guards and spear me down," he said, folding his powerful arms.

"You know why."

"Then I refuse your wish and repeat my proposal of marriage. It is madness that you should think that the people of the valley would accept a virgin queen as leader of the land. They merely tolerate you because they hope eventually you will marry one of their warriors of nobility. But they also feel that you are like your mother and could possibly marry outside the race. And with these young knights traipsing about your hem it is perceived that is your intent."

"How dare you!" She clapped her hands to summon the guards. "And to suggest that my people expect me to rush into marriage—any marriage—because I'm insecure as a leader is deceitful whining from a frustrated bowman and suitor. And even if there were the remotest possibility that they thought that, I would not give my hand to one I despise!"

He seethed, bending his arm and tightening his fist. He moved forward and shook his fist; but stepped back, quickly placed his arm to his side, when the guards entered. He said venomously, "You leave me with no other course of action, princess." He turned on his heels.

The princess, knitting her brows, stared at him. "On the contrary, there is no choice."

She said to the guards, "See that he is put in chains for the night. In the morn he is to be carted beyond the moors and our boundary and there abandoned. And tell the men on the bridge tower to lower the gate tonight, lest he have restive comrades in arms." They nodded, bowed and escorted him out of the temple hall.

Lady Margaret, having overheard his concluding remarks, when she had entered the hall through the colonnade, ran to her daughter and put her arms around her. "I know you can be stubborn, my child, but I must advise you to release Lance. You must know the baron has backing; Angus would never have taken action such as this on his own."

She looked at her mother with kindness and said, "I may be stubborn,

Mother, but not stupid."

"Good, the mark of a queen. Then, you know that you will need him."

In their rooms, Lance stood by the window overlooking the valley, thinking of the strangeness of the ancient man some inestimable feet beyond and above him. Bryan, recuperating rapidly from the arrow wound, was sitting up in bed, while a young girl had just changed the dressing. The girl smiled and picked up the basin to leave. Bryan said to her, "Ah, my angel, if anyone deserves a gem from our country's treasure, you do, kind child." She giggled. He watched her leave and thinking that she could not be much younger than Rhonda. Then he looked over at Lance who had returned to a chair. "Lance, I'm getting restless and a bit worried. I'm surprised that you don't feel the same after being locked up. I want to return. I don't trust that Erinysia," Bryan reaffirmed, "That's the main reason I want to leave here as soon as possible to see that Rhonda is safe."

"Zounds, Bryan, you're yelping like a gossiping old hag! Why, my father is the victim of his own foolish dreams. Besides, my father promised he would wait for me to return."

"Well, maybe the lord master is just a ranting old man, but with that Erinysia snuggling up to him, I'm not so sure that the state of affairs isn't serious by now."

Lance rose and went back to the window. He squeezed his chin. "Hmm, you could be right about Erinysia; still, she would have to reckon with me....Are you sure you're well enough to travel?"

"Aye, I'm fit as a custom visor. Just thinking about seeing the little redhead again makes me stronger." The maiden returned with a train of strong young servants bearing jugs of warm water for Bryan's therapeutic bath. When the young servants receded, and another maiden entered to help with the bathing, Lance left his fellow-knight with a wink and a smile to the bliss of maidens bathing him.

Lucia had just dismissed her court from the great hall and was ready to leave herself when Lance walked in. She motioned to a guard. "A chair for our visitor, please." She stepped down from the dais and greeted Lance and then led him to the chair set next to hers. He remained standing until she sat back down in the throne.

"Young Bryan is healing well, my mother informs me."

He bowed before sitting and concurred, "Aye, and he's quite anxious to be up and around in order to break the red mare for my sister."

She smiled. "That's a good sign!—but an alarming amount of horse flesh for a little girl."

"I still wish I could pay you."

She shook her lovely head and frowned. "Absolutely not!—consider it good will between our nations."

"Ah, that indeed shall be affirmed in any case."

"Yea, I believe you."

"Of course, and Bryan shall begin a good-will mission on his return. In any event, I'm sure my sister will be thrilled with your gift—she loves horses so." He grinned and winked. "Of course, both Rhonda and Bryan will be thrilled to be together again."

"Oh?...It is that way with them?" She seemed embarrassed.

His eyes twinkled. "Yea, in a way. Rhonda has adored him since she was a child and he a page. It's no surprise, therefore, that Bryan's rapid recovery thanks to your mother's marvelous ministering induces anxiousness in seeing my sister again."

She bowed her head momentarily, sighed and said softly, "I suppose, then, you plan to stay on?"

He looked askance for a moment; then back to her and dropped his eyes. "Actually,...well,...I know I shouldn't...duties to the Order, you know....But I've grown...attached...sort of..."

"Attached?...to the valley?"

"Yea,...to the valley...it is beautiful."

"Oh, I'm so glad you like our home."

"I do, yea,...but something else..." he looked over at the guard; he was relieved to see him engaged in conversation with the kitchen maids who were waiting for the princess to leave so they could set up the hall for dinner.

She giggled. "Of course, you mean the buckskin, but he's yours, Lance! You don't have to remain on account of him."

He cleared his throat and lowered his voice barely audibly, "Don't play with me, Lucia; you know what I mean: I'm attached..."

"Oh, that word again!" She mocked disappointment. "Are you saying you're attached to another maiden, is that it?" She smiled confidence.

"Of course not!...attached...attached to *you*."

"My, how nice! Like a pair of oxen under yoke."

He frowned dumbly. "It's you I mean, far more beautiful than the valley."

She cupped her hand over her mouth to hide the stretched lip ready to let go more giggles. "How very sweet, Lance!" She let down her hand. "I've never been compared with a valley before." Her lips puffed out a controlled giggle.

He raised his brows in exasperation and inhaled; then yelled out, "No damn it, I mean I love you!" The kitchen maidens burst into laughter while the guard was trying to quiet them down, till he too was drawn into the laughter. Lance turned round and on impulse put his hand on the hilt till he realized how ridiculous it was. He turned back to the princess who was cuffing her giggles. He took her hands down, and she convulsed into laughter to rival the kitchen maidens; then he joined in with a hearty laugh.

Having doubled over and holding her sides, the princess finally got hold of herself and looked over at the maidens and put her finger to her lips. She said to Lance, "My sweet, clumsy darling, let us go to my rooms and finish this jumbled conversation. The girls must prepare for the supper hour."

Sitting together on the settle, he said, "I'm sorry I was so awkward downstairs. I'm new at this, you know."

"Yea, so I gathered——and flattered that you are!"

"Alas, I suppose, though, in spite of my feelings I had better head for Quandron."

She bowed her head, sighed and said softly, "Perhaps...for the best since I do not wish to confine you again. I am very sorry I did that to you, Lance."

"Think not on it. You did what you felt you had to," he said chivalrously. Then he chortled, "It was interesting meeting the ancient vigil."

She laughed. "Yea, one of my mother's favorite myths. She claims he's been here almost before time." She laughed again. "Must be a northern weakness to weave tall tales." He laughed and nodded emphatically.

Just then a guard rushed in. "Forgive me, your highness, for breaking in unannounced. A messenger has just reported that the exile escort was attacked just short of the moor."

"Oh, no, were they hurt?" she asked with sincere concern.

"Only two have returned to tell of it; and they are wounded so seriously that the innkeeper's wife is tending to them. The poor fellows were lucky to get that far. The innkeeper sent the messenger."

"Oh, my," she brought her hands to her mouth aghast, "you must dispatch a medical team immediately; the men must be under my mother's care."

Lance grew impatient and prodded, "And Angus? What of him?"

The guard answered, "A fugitive, Lord Lance."

"Did the wounded say how many were involved in the attack?"

"Only that there were many more than their team of eight, sir."

"Hmm, not very accurate reporting." Lance frowned.

Lucia finally composed herself to ask Lance, "What do you think? Do you suppose he is back here?"

"Obviously, why else would they rescue him?...The extent of it hinges on how many were involved and how organized they are."

"Then you're saying this is only the beginning?"

He nodded. "Well, it is clear now that I am not going with Bryan."

"But why?...You mustn't remain. Bryan must have good reason to be concerned over your sister."

He chuckled. "Or love sick—either way, she'll be in good hands once Bryan arrives. That's why I want no mention of this to him because if he smells trouble here his first loyalty would be to me."

Lucia and Lance accompanied Bryan, who was leading the red horse, along valley's trail edging up to the mountain pass. Lucia was giving some pointers on the care of the spirited animal. "But I'm sure," she said, turning her head to Lance, "your sister, apparently a lover of horses, will see to it that Red becomes well adjusted."

"Aye, princess, you can be sure of that," Bryan interceded confidently but wondered if Rhonda had been able to adjust to her new stepmother.

She flexed her body toward the young knight and said with a glint in her eye, "Still, I should've chosen a less spirited one."

"Ah, but this beauty will blend with her hair as they romp off into the wind!" Bryan rhapsodized.

She laughed. "Which is it?—poetry, admiration or love?"

Lance smiled over at them. "A mixture of all, but mostly the latter, verily." His words rang in his ears as he watched villagers gathering round the princess whom all seemed to adore.

The princess drew up her horse to acknowledge them. Lance signaled that he would continue on with Bryan, who bade farewell to the princess, and the two men rode up the trail that cut through the joining slopes of the two mountains that seemed to serve as eternal sentinels of the valley kingdom.

Half way through the exit, Bryan asked as he veered his horse and Red from a low hanging branch over the trail, "My lord, you won't dally here too long?"

"Dally?" Lance repeated with a grimace. "Why, no, I shall join you within a fortnight."

"Good, sir, but I trust you will make it sooner; for I am really concerned. I don't like the smell of the politics brewing in our lands."

Lance chuckled it off. "Oh, it just Chimera stirring in my father's fanciful head. I'm sure when you arrive there the smell will have gone." Having met the old man in the cave, Lance was experiencing an ominous consciousness. Had Bryan not been wounded, he would have been back home already. Under the circumstance here, he could not abandon Lucia. He glanced back at her. She seemed to be dancing her horse to the delight of children that had circled her.

Bryan flicked the feather in his cap with mild disgust and moaned, "I don't know, Lance. I hope it isn't in *your* head!...It seems the princess has clouded your thinking....Could it be love?"

Lance laughed. "Not true—not entirely, anyway." He winked. "If I'm wrong about the situation at our castle—or in Henry's court for that matter—remember, there can be a formidable force here, you know."

Bryan's eyes flashed. "Ah, so that's it! You think Lucia might take advantage of the situation?"

"No, I'm not saying that—on the contrary. In Henry's struggle—and I still believe he is bent on forging an enlightened nation—politics can go awry when petty men are reluctant to yield to law, in which case I prefer she be on our side."

Bryan winked and jerked his head. "Well, you couldn't pick a better bedfellow, eh?....Still, I'm not sure which side is which—as I don't trust the king as you do....In one respect your father may be right. The king takes advantage of the proud Marian Order as though he were commanding it instead of you."

Lance smiled and shook his head, and said, "Aye, that is precisely the perception from a decentralized view. I admit, I don't always agree; still, as long as Henry respects the autonomy of the flag regiment and legion, I have no argument."

"Ah, but does he?" Bryan inquired, arching his brows.

"Time will let us know. The legion must remain independent to check tyranny. That is why even my father must not gain control of it. And that is my grandfather's bequest."

"Aye, truly a wise man," Bryan joined solemnly.

They spurred their steeds up the trail to the crest where they bridled to a halt. Taking in the lad's eyes, the warlord said, "Be careful going back—no dragon slaying on the way. I'll soon join you."

"Yea, my lord, sooner than soon; for I do not share your optimism....Though I should have lingered awhile to see Angus thrown into hell's pit that you described." Then he laughed. "Not very Christian of me, is it?" Bryan withdrew his sword, held it in salute for a moment, returned it to his scabbard, then bridled round and cantered down the winding slope.

Lance watched his friend in arms awhile. He did not have the heart to tell him that the princess did not serve up capital punishment on his behalf. Nor would he reveal Angus's escape since he knew from a recent report that Angus was in propitious custody of another fractious manor lord at a castle in the foothills further to the west. Had this not become known, Lance was going to accompany Bryan till he reached the border. He was glad he did not have to, sensing that Angus would inevitably lead an assault on the princess.

12. Sir John

Sir John waited till dusk before he sent his squire to enter selected tents circling the moat for the purpose of summoning to his tent Lance's lord captains and lieutenants of the Mari flag regiment. The officers—all staunch loyalists to Lance—were puzzled when informed earlier of the orders to march on Henry. Disgruntled, they demanded clarification when they arrived at Sir John's tent. Charles who had come by horse since he was at the back end of the moat dismounted and rushed into the tent with his sword in hand. "What is this treachery I'm hearing?" he snarled, his heavy red moustache rising up one side of his cheek as he looked suspiciously at the men.

"Don't jump the blade, Charles," Sir John said calmly; "hopefully we are here to foil this mad attempt by an old man gone berserk."

"And how do you propose that?" the fiery redhead asked, sheathing his sword. "Why, with Bennet's obvious betrayal, and the old man's stratagems behind our back we do not command enough foot soldiers to side with us."

"I know that," the old warrior said to the younger soldier, "but we can at least pull out with the Mari nexus to camp north in the foothills and send for Lance."

Charles slid his blade in its hilt, stroked his red whiskers to ponder a moment, then shook his head. "No, there's no point to that. We must join Henry's forces now. If we slip out of camp within a few hours we shall be there by the morrow." Some of the others nodded or expressed agreement.

Old Sir John pleaded, "Men, listen to reason. You all do know that without Lance present, the king will never let our regiment through the gate. He'll perceive us as a Trojan horse."

Charles blurted, "He's hardly in a position to reject us with the weak force he has on hand!"

"Poorly trained, yea, but sizable nonetheless," John countered.

One of the officers, his arm still in a sling from the latest battle, addressed the others, "Sir John rings true; the king is not a trusting soul. I doubt he even trusts himself. In fact, he might try to place us under his sole command. I go along with John: Wait for Lord Lance and then decide on what action to take. Lance might perceive this as an opportunity."

"An opportunity for what?" quizzed the redhead.

Sir John broke in, "What Robert is saying is that Lance has reason to doubt Henry's public purpose."

"Pshaw, that's no news—we all know that!" Charles, snarled, turning to Robert. "But, captain, are you saying that the old man could be right? And that we bring down Henry now?" Charles absently gripped the hilt.

Robert shrugged and yielded to John who shook his head vigorously, emphasizing, "No, definitely not!... Kalab," John continued in a lower, very serious tone, "has meaner ends....Particularly now that he is in cahoots with that bitch."

Charles blurted, "Witch, you mean."

"The same...at this moment we are crossed with the lesser of two evils."

The wounded knight, Robert, added, "At least with Henry, whatever his purpose, there will be unity."

The redhead snickered, "Aye, united under his fist, eh?" He turned to John. "Why does Lance put up with this uncertainty anyway?" John darted a squinting glance at him as though to tell him to drop the subject; but Charles went on anyway, "We all know the people love Lord Lance. To hell with divine right; it is the people's right that counts—he should be king!"

Ayes and nods bandied about the tent but Arnold, third in command under Charles, objected, "You know yourself that Lance does not want the crown. He swore at his mother's death bed that he would give Henry time and that of young Henry as well in order to sustain the Mari defenders as objective overseer."

"Bah, there's more to it than that!" Charles grumbled.

"Hold your tongue, Charles!" John warned. His eyes walled to the officers to change the subject. "This is not the time, men, to be discussing such matters. Paramount at this moment is to get out from under this treachery with as much force as we can muster. I've communicated with the Captain of young Earl Hunters' command...."

"By the bloody Rood, what are they doing here? I thought they split off from us after our final battle for rest!" Charles squawked.

"Aye, but apparently Kalab has been scheming for sometime, trying to get the young earl under thumb."

"Under that damned witch, you mean!" Charles inserted.

"Aye," Arnold agreed. "Don't forget as Lady Hunter she had a strong influence and I can't believe she relented so easily to the children when the old earl died."

"Humph, you make it sound like he died of natural causes!" Charles growled.

Arnold added, "We can't prove she had a hand in the gruesome murder. We have to yield to the court's findings."

John pounded his fist on the table. "Enough of this, men, come to order and the matter at hand. Chiefly, is to point out that the captain of Hunter's legion is disgruntled in being here. I trust him even though he was not free to divulge his reasons for being on the scene. However, his Mari detachment is up in arms and wants to rejoin us; he said he's willing to look the other way. So my plan is that Arnold, who is the only one that the King will trust to a degree, since they are cousins, will abscond with the Hunter-Mari company to the castle city tonight while the rest of us head north."

"Then we slip out with the regiment tonight and join with Lance?"

"Aye, and Gregory has already been dispatched ahead to find him," Arnold added.

All the men joined hands.

Later, as John was gathering up some personals for his saddle bags, Charles entered the tent with a young woman in a hooded robe. "This lass wishes to speak to you." Charles chortled. "The chit brazenly made it clear that she would speak to you *only*."

"My, my, must be important, then, eh, lass?" Sir John said with a kind smile.

"Oh, very much so. You see, I am Tracy, the handmaiden to the great Lord Lance's sister."

"Yes, of course, lass, I remember you from the banquet...Has Lady Rhonda a message for me?"

Shaking her head, and placing her hands to her cheeks as though ready to cry, she took a deep breath and sobbed. "If only it were so. No, the Lady Rhonda, has been missing for too many days now."

"Missing?...Disappeared out of thin air?" Sir John reacted.

"The witch's doing!—I'll bet my finest chess pieces on it," Charles chimed in.

"Oh, yes, good sir," she agreed casting a glance at Charles, then she turned back to John. "But not directly that I know of. You see, the last time I saw my lady she was caring for Stars, you know, Lord Lance's faithful destrier. Later when I went to look for her I found the poor animal in a pool of blood in the pasture, without a sign of Lady Rhonda."

"Oh, no, I do not like the sound of this." Sighed John. "I feel you're right, Sir Charles—it seems we shall all become victims of bewitchment before this ends."

"Could the witch be holding her hostage without the old man knowing it?" Charles asked.

"Not in the castle, sir," Tracy said. "I've looked everywhere. And the Lady Rhonda's horse is missing, too. I think she was terrified of something and ran away."

"Why do you think that?" John asked.

"Because I told the black witch, and she told me back that she would take care of it and that I was not to utter it to a soul. I was so frightened of her that I kept silent, but I went about looking for the Lady Rhonda myself. But it's been almost a week now. I fear for her."

"Brave, lass," Charles sympathized, patting her hooded pate.

"Indeed." said John. "Now, my dear, have no more fear, we shall take up the search immediately—we'll find her."

Tracy bowed and John brought his calloused hand to her cheek. "Oh, thank you, sir, I do so much miss my lady and friend. I can't bear the thought of her being out all alone with so many churls lurking everywhere."

Sir John felt embarrassed and then swallowed hard when he felt her warm tears on his hand. "You seem sure that she's run away, then." He said to Charles, "Have my squire escort her to the castle safely."

John and Charles met with the regiment, but the two knights—so strongly bonded to Lance, felt an urgency to find his sister—circled the castle and headed eastward as the rest went north under Robert's competent command.

13. Vanished

Confirmed by trusty Elm, the castellan, later the next morning that indeed the Mari regiment of crack knights had fled into the night, the old manor lord paced quickly to the watchtower to observe the assembly of fighting men in the outer ward. Clearly the number of horsemen had diminished noticeably. He turned back to his vassal and said, "I suppose Sir John is nowhere to be found?"

"True, my lord, all of Master Lance's loyalists have vanished," said the old castellan, nervously twisting his long gray beard and tugging on the sleeve of his bliut, trying desperately to conceal his satisfaction.

The warlord went to his table-desk and poured wine into two horned vessels. "Come, my old friend, drink with me."

The old servant sharply bowed his head. "I should be honored, kind lord."

"Kind, is it?" the old warlord queried with a fleeting smirk. "Even though I know you do not approve of what I am about to do?"

The old confidant's hand shook as he slowly raised the horn to thin, crackly lips and stared warily at his lord while he took a long drink. Putting the horn back on its cradle he said, "You know, good master, that I am very fond of Lance."

"Aye, since he was born, old friend. Why, you and your dear wife were closer to him than I was—that I admit."

The agéd castellan brushed the thin hairs on his wobbling head. "Forgive me, your grace, then why?"

"My quarrel is not with Lance, you know that."

"Yea, but I also know that young Lance is loyal to the Crown," the steward said somberly while twisting his beard again before taking another drink—a sip this time.

"Bah, the crown!—More so to his mother!" The warlord said before guzzling down the wine and slamming the horn into its resting place. "Who needs a king? The country has managed from the dawn of time without the ilk of squeamish Henry." Kalab looked to the door. "Why, if I had my way...I would not want the throne. The old way is better."

"Still, Lord Lance says we need law not the unbending gauntlet, and Henry is a legislator, but I care not of that. Who am I but a lowly castellan."

"Lowly?" Kalab raised a brow. "Why, you make it sound as though I've reduced you to a porter!"

Taking another light sip, Elm clarified, "I simply meant my authority is with servants, not nobility. Though you say your quarrel is not with Master Lance, I am worried that it shall come to that."

The warlord laughed. "No, my friend, not without his men behind him. Oh, he can whine and bellow but it will be harmless chatter in the wind."

"But do you not fear what Sir John is up to?"

"I'd be fool not to; he is a fierce knight and the defectors with him. Still, they are but a handful against the might that remains under me."

"Aye, but will your mighty force fight well without the wondrous Mari to inspire them?"

"Damn the regiment! And the ghostly Mari! I am in charge and shall inspire my troops even more!" The old warlord turned to the window again, adding, "But I cannot fool you, old fox; verily I am sorely disappointed."

"Verily,...and there is still Henry's army—and he seems to have the support of the people."

"Bah, his generals are blockheads—he can do little without Lance." Kalab picked up the horn of wine, held it to his lips, smirking as he stared at the old castle steward. "Oh?...The people, too, you say, and does he have your support as well, old Elm?"

"That is beyond my wit, my lord; I have loyalty to the only home I've ever had—the castle of Mari."

He laughed again. "I see, but not its master, eh?"

"Oh, he, too. I care what happens to you, your grace."

The warlord choked on his drink. "In a hog's eye you do!" He laughed and added, "Rhonda and Lance are the extent of it—you, too, see them not as belonging to the name Kalab but rather Mari."

His face reddened, but replied, "Nay, they are simply fixed to this castle as you." He took a sip, lowered the horn shakily. "I cannot say the same for the new mistress, who means to do you..."

"Enough of this, Elm." He took the horn from his servant. "Go now and fetch the lady whom I know you despise."

The old servant bowed and back-stepped to the door and left.

The warlord went to the window and observed Bennet on horseback crossing the bridge to review the foot-soldiers for readiness. He turned abruptly when he heard the door open. He was startled to see Erinysia in a coat of mail whose links emitted a dark red lambency. "What's this, my pet? You intend to join us in the fray?"

She drifted across the room and gave him a peck on the cheek. "No, but I intend to accompany you to the encampment to see that you don't falter and scurry from kingly purpose."

He chuckled. "Am I so helpless without your bewitching influence?"

"There's no need of dark magic if your vengeance does in truth run deep." She eyed him inquiringly.

"Well, it seems there was a need of your talents to keep Sir John at bay. Apparently his hide is too tough for you."

"Oh?" She arched a brow.

"Aye, he has fled—apparently to dispatch Lance."

She lightly touched her lips and conjectured, "Or, worse, to join Henry more likely."

"Doubtless, but in the main he will get word to Lance."

She heaved a sigh. "No matter...what with our strong alliance."

"What, with the devil?" He laughed.

She smirked. "Perhaps."

He eyed her skeptically. "Be clear with me, witch. If I'm to lead this foray I must know what else you've brewed up."

"Will this do—my ex-husband's army of eight hundred strong?" She smiled beguilingly, stroking his balding head with the tassel end of her dark braid.

"Aye, I've learned of it just this morning." He grinned and said almost with glee, "But is minus three hundred now."

"Impossible!" she shouted and strutted round the table.

"No, my dear,...apparently there are indeed limitations to your powers as extraordinary as they are. It appears the Mari legacy is not bewitched."

She shrugged. "Is that all? No matter, they are more trouble than they're worth. Five hundred or eight the Hunter force will serve us well."

"Even without their magnificent chargers, the Mari detachment, eh?" The old man curiously seemed to be enjoying himself.

"I shall be their charger." she said coolly.

"Oh, the explanation for your armor, then." He grinned, then he moved closer to her. He ran his stubby fingers down her long, high cheek and said with awe, "Regardless, my pet, your powers are remarkable! How now did you manage the Hunter force to come over?—why, his children hate you to the core."

"The simple turn of a key—the contemptuous children are captive in their own castle."

He shook his head in wonder. "It appears you really do want to be queen as much as I want revenge on Henry!"

"Oh, my tired lover, speak not *only* of revenge; for to be a queen I must have you at my side as *king*—do not lose sight of that," she said convincingly.

"Oh, you'll see to that....But tell me, how could you be so sure the Earl's army would not simply free the children, especially by action of the Mari detachment—more magic?"

"Certainly magic, but trickery too, forged orders from Lance before the detachment ever arrived at the earldom. As far as the Earl's forces are concerned, it was widely known that the commander of his forces has been under my spell for some time now." She winked.

"Ah, yea, when making love with you I prefer to forget your torrid history." He pouted as helplessly as a child.

"Well, in this case, it was his wife. She was and still is my lover....Nevertheless, that history, as you call it, is what will make you king."

He shook his head in disappointment. "And I thought *I* was your lover!"

"Ah, but you are, my grand lord!...But you know my intriguing appetites," she said smugly.

"Aye, like a giant black widow spider's."

She drew her dagger and playfully dubbed his head. "Pout not, my love; there isn't a woman lover in the world that can match your love."

"No, but I'm sure there are a hundred men!" he grumbled.

She laughed; then moved her dagger to his shoulder and dubbed him again. "Now, Grand Knight of the New Kalab Order, rise and let us move toward your destiny."

"Not so fast, my dear," he muffled into her dagger-buckle. "I may be under your spell, but I am not mindless. We cannot march on Henry with Sir John on the loose."

She withdrew abruptly. "But your bravado..."

"Mere lines spouted by a nervous, frustrated old fool!" He got to his feet and went to the table to fill his drinking horn, which he raised to her. "Aye, old fool, but an old soldier as well who knows enough not to enter battle without knowing where the enemy is."

She knotted her face, waved her dagger downward to castrate him, as it were. "Why, you're not just a fool and shadow of a soldier but a woeful coward!"

"Whether fool or coward, I'll not set foot toward Castle City without first dealing with those haughty knights." He gulped down half the contents.

"And you call yourself a soldier!" she snarled, then rebuking him with a short, sharp laugh. "To battle John's forces now would inflict heavy casualties and substantially weaken us."

He wrinkled his brow. "Oh? And what of your powers. You speak of my bravado, what about your boast and standing here in a coat of mail?"

She waved her dagger like a wand. "Oh, the sorcery will be there!"

"Will, you say? Then you are not fully equipped yet, I gather? But you want to send our troops against an impregnable castle!"

She plopped down in a chair, and then got right back up and ordered, "Help me off with this cumbersome thing, since obviously we are not going to march today."

He grinned and went over to assist her in removing the mail. "You know, my dear, you should not remove it. This is a great opportunity to test yourself and your sorcery under combat. Why not join Bennet and me in our forthcoming engagement with the renegades?"

She gave a startled look. "Then you intend to follow through on this—even though you don't even know where they are? I tell you it is madness. Without Lance, they will not be as formidable. Why for all we know they could've fled in cowardly fright."

He shook his head. "Oh, but I know they couldn't. As much as I despise them now, rest assure they will fight fiercely."

"See, then, my point is correct. Why chance meeting them when we don't have to?...I tell you they will sit on their hands in the saddle waiting for their leader who will never arrive."

"Just what do you mean by that?"

"Oh, never mind, my intuition pricks me that Lance is no longer a force to worry about."

"Bah, you have no powers! Why, you're a charlatan! A spinner of tales!"

She stared coldly. "We shall see who the spinner is!...Within a tumble, rest assure I shall be mounted at the lead with Bennet to track the regiment. It remains to be seen if you will be at my other side."

Destiny was taken off hold, though deferred to another aim. For the triad indeed led the force to the north with the confident hope they would track down the famous Mari flag unit. After a day and a half search, the old warlord's massive unit came upon the Mari camp a mile short of the Quandron northern border. Kalab immediately deployed his units into a three hundred-yard arc despite Bennet's advice to set up camp and to attack in the morning.

"Surely, our men are not tired after a mere three hour morning trek," Kalab, countered. "Why give them time to prepare?—or worse, skip out on us."

"I was thinking of the horses, Lord Kalab," Bennet reminded him. "Their's are rested. Even on equal terms we could not measure up to their jousting skill."

"Granted but our foot soldiers outnumber theirs five to one. Besides, we have Erinysia on our side claiming to conjure powers of legendary proportions. So return to your battalion and ready them for the bugle call."

Just then Erinysia pulled up her all-black gelding but for a small red star round each eye. "My lord, the attendants refuse to set up a tent for me."

"There's no time for such luxury. This will be a battlefield in moments," he grumbled. "I thought you came to fight alongside?"

She pursed a lip and raised a brow. "But, my lord, I am after all just a woman!—surely you jest."

"And surely you are different from most, are you not?...Thus, stay by my side and conjure your vaunted necromancy to protect our forces. Though far outnumbered, the enemy will wreak great damage."

"Then you admit now what I warned you against!" she scorned. "There is no need for this wasteful encounter!"

"Not if you do what you're supposed to do!" he reminded her.

"Not without my tent!" she said, pouting.

"Bah, "You women...make demands to be on equal footing until it becomes clear it is truly a man's world!...If I have this tent set up for you to take a nap while we risk our lives, it could be overrun and burned to the stakes and I shall be forever without my protectress!" He laughed mockingly.

"You underestimate me, good lord. I need the tent for the sorcerer's cabochon, I can not summon powers in broad daylight without cover. Why there isn't a tree round here for miles."

"Why, there are two big shady ones not a two hundred yards ahead!"

"I'm not stupid, my lord, to attempt necromancy midst the din of battle!"

"Now order the tent set up behind the lines, or I shall leave you to this foolishness and return to my castle."

"The castle of Mari—*your* castle, eh?" He shook his head and then added, "You shall have your tent, damn you!" He bridled round and shouted to an attendant, "See that Lady Erinysia has her tent. But draw it up a good distance back from here." He turned to her and said, "We shall see, if you measure up to your boasts, my lady." He heeled his destrier ahead. "Sound the bugle!"

Bennet was so sure of the opponent's skill that he himself would not dare lead the charging jousters. He left it to his commandant while he remained behind to lead the foot brigade. His prediction held true.

Though their leaders John and Charles were not with them, the magnificently trained and equipped warriors waged heroic battle.

In the first pass a hundred of Kalab and Bennet's jousters were unhorsed while every Mari knight returned with not so much as a dent in their armor. Sir Robert cut short the return in order to gain ground and have his foot troops move in closer. On the second pass he himself would lead them with sword in his good hand. His squire begged him, "Sir Robert, you mustn't, you're our only leader! It is too dangerous to face the pole with just a sword! Let me ride for you!"

"Just a sword, Richard?" Robert laughed. "A sword forged in the Mari smithy is worth a dozen enemy lances! Nay, I need you here to lead the infantry as soon as we have gained more footing. We'll not return this time. We intend to break through and continue on and raise havoc in close ranks."

"Oh, my gallant knight, 'tis suicide! Lo! There must be thousands of them!"

He laughed. "Suicidal I'm not! We know when to strategically withdraw." He raised his gauntlet and the courageous knights lined up with their lances poised. He turned round to the hundred foot soldiers under the Mari flag. "Brave lads, admit no light of day between us when we pole the louts and my loyal squire gives the call to arms. Have your weapons ready for the unhorsed enemy and those now scrambling for their horses from the first pass. Squire Richard, sound the bugle." He snapped down his visor. The bugle pierced the day, and the two hundred horseman thundered toward the warlord's line.

Midst the rumble of hooves, the thump and clatter of lances, the roar and bluster of brave men, Robert and his men broke through the dense lines of horsemen onto the surprised foot soldiers. Their mighty swords swooped down on frightened, though well-trained men, but who never before had to face the skill and fearlessness of the Mari elite whom they once fought on the side of. And indeed the Mari infantry, worthy of knighthood itself within the borders of any other manor, followed closely behind, though far outnumbered. With spears, swords and chains the infantry did untold damage to the unhorsed knights before they continued through the huge swath paved by the fearless knights.

Bennet quickly ordered the bugle blast of retreat and his battalion axiomatically responded on the run, away from the fearless regiment. The old warlord seeing this cowardly act, and though feeling vulnerable, inspired his men to fight all the more fiercely. But when he saw that Robert and his cavalry were ferociously hacking away but fifty feet from his line of reserve, Kalab too ordered the bugle blast of retreat.

Satisfied, Robert held up the advancing lines. For he knew his men would tire into the afternoon and eventually be surrounded by the enormous army. He ordered the withdrawal and on the way back to camp razed everyone of the enemy still standing.

At dusk the Mari regiment had buried its dead and made room for the wounded on the wagons, rather than place them in tents. Sir Robert before a select assemblage—since strategy obviated assembling every one—ceremoniously read the *Hail Mary* in homage to the dead. Deep sorrow was compensated by the consolation that on the other side hundreds would have to be interred in contrast to the forty Maris.

Captain Robert called his lieutenants to his tent to lay out plans of escape. Although they regretted having to withdraw after inflicting an estimated three hundred casualties in all, the lieutenants yielded to the cunning of Sir Robert—rather than to risk another open skirmish—that they should scuttle the camp and head for Castle City, and have Sir Arnold capitulate with the king who would surely trust them after this glorious skirmish. Sir Robert was certain that Sir John would approve in knowing that when Lance got word he would instinctively know where to find them.

Lying on a cot in her tent, the warlord, exhausted and disappointed, rolled his head to Erinysia mumbling incantations over her cabochon, "Humph, a lot good that mumble jumble did us today!"

"At least I predicted what would happen, you old fool! Still, have heart, it is near nightfall now when I am most effective."

He rolled over and sat up at the edge. "If you think for one moment that I would order an attack at night, I should think some demon has *you* under a spell! Especially against those crazy Mari fighters!"

"Ah, have no qualms; you will not be needed."

Robert's men—tents folded, carts packed—were ready to abscond when suddenly appeared a monstrous apparition of swirling green dust enveloping their ranks. The file scattered, some hurled their spears. Three swordsman circled the phenomenon and tried cutting through it, only to be caught in its vortex and with a hideous, continuous sucking pop, were swallowed up. One mounted knight aimed his lance and charged it—horse and all disappeared into the howling mass. Robert quickly warned, "No more, action against this monstrous witchery! Disperse the column and try to out-run it!" Robert, in spite of their objections, ordered the cavalry to head for Castle City on the run but that each was to take a foot soldier with them. As the knights scooped up men to ride with them, Robert urged an infantry man to leap up behind and then hold another by the purple tabard as he scooped another in his good arm and then carried them a safe distance from the demoniac swirling mass whose powerful sucking force within seconds digested dozens in rapid tandem. Robert continued to bear many to safety in this fashion. He noticed the demon was losing speed and more men were escaping its deadliness. After a quarter of an hour—and scores fated to its decimating jaws—the whirling mass turned red and was able only to tear limbs from howling men but could not suck them in. Just as suddenly as it appeared, it disappeared in a puff of red smoke.

After tending to the wounded and securing them to litters, Sir Robert reorganized the column spacing them as much as was feasible and headed into the night, confident the witch had expended her energy.

14. Northern Battle

Lingering distrust of her visitor and fearful of leaving the valley unguarded, Lucia at first resisted Lance's advice to launch an assault upon Angus's marauders. However, when reports flowed in that the rebellious force was burning defenseless villages and capturing women and children who she feared would be sold into slavery, she was devastated to think that one of her own countrymen could stoop to such atrocities. After consulting with her officers of her force of eight hundred men, she acceded when they convinced her that the reputation of the Quandron Lord-Protector was all the evidence they needed to do as he suggested: three hundred crack archers would remain to protect the valley while the main body would attack the marauder's camp fifteen miles beyond this first mountain chain to the common meadow of the country's sheepherders.

Lance immediately set up strategy. His inkling was that Angus whose pride and ambition—akin to Kalab's—driving him to confrontation would welcome battle on any terms to prove to Lucia that a woman should not be sovereign. Furthermore, Lance was certain that Angus relied on the military inexperience of the princess and her lieutenants, along with the exile's presumption that the princess would never trust a lowlander to lead her troops into battle. A few days before the main thrust, Lance had sent a hundred horsed archers on a hit and run mission to ambush the marauders on their return from raiding a village. The archers inflicted substantial casualties to insure that the marauders would be in camp to reorganize and reclaim their momentum.

The castle horsemen lined the breadth of the valley at the foot of the castle to await their princess. The men were saddled, silently searching the empty plain; the horses snorted and restively pawed the grass. In his purple tabard over mail, Lance—not yet confident to enter battle on the buckskin—mounted the tried and true warhorse and descended from the cavern stable. The bay clapped its giant hoofs on the rocky trail. All eyes turned to this man of war, fixed to his confident air and the purple hood and mantle draped over the powerful steed, displaying the colors of the Mari. As Lance passed in review he held up for a moment the crested shield—eagle and scroll. He then lashed it to his saddle and raised another. The men cheered when they saw on the second shield, the white on gold crest of a branch and golden apple from the tree of knowledge. He steered his mount several paces in front of the skirmish line, then turned in his saddle, awaiting the princess whose white horse was balking somewhat in bearing her across the drawbridge.

Commoners swarmed round her, wishing her well, touching her boots in the stirrups, crying out to her that they loved her and that Ceres was with her. The beautiful white horse reared up a few times, then loped to the warhorse's side. The princess flashed up a smile at Lance. "This mantle of light mail you insisted Orion wear does not agree with him—nor for that matter, do I care for it on me."

"As sovereign, ironically you must adapt to compromise—since you insisted on accompanying this expedition," he reminded her.

"I don't feel like sovereignty! Why, you treat me like a little girl with all your preconditions!"

He laughed. "Aye, but you pouted like one, don't forget."

She pushed out her lips. "Such a price to pay for love."

"Aye, and a lasting love," he responded, "I want you to survive a volley of arrows!"

Recasting her lips from pout to purse, she said, "Yea, and you too, my love." She bridled round and faced her men.

With calm, sweet, but firm voice, she said, "Staunch men of our blesséd valleys, this day shall be the mark on history's calendar commemorating this moment of glory when Ceres weeded treason from her garden of flourishing justice. Let us hope that though we toil to this end that only sweet sweat and not blood is spilled so that ye may live to herald with your own lips to your dear children the glory of the day that sustained our heritage. Therefore we march against the infamous camp of our own countrymen gone awry by the notorious Baron Angus."

The men hailed her, "Long live our princess and queen."

She motioned for them to advance. She steered her horse onto the trail edging the rich, green plain. Her force began to file into a column. The defense in the hills cheered them on as did the people alongside the trail. Lance spurred abreast of her. She glanced over and said, with a mock snarl, "Here it is but early morning and already I'm roasting in this drapery of iron chains."

He laughed. "You think this is bad; wait till you don the full armor the tinsmith made for you."

"Oh, horrors!"

Three tumbles of the hourglass before dusk the plucky band deployed to the top of the mound leading to the meadow. A dozen men rode ahead at a fast gait to chase the sheep from the line of advance. The marauder camp sounded the bugle and men could be seen running from their tents and mounting their steeds. Lance observed that they were only a handful and advanced on each fringe of the plain. He surmised that the main group had already planted themselves under cover squarely in a large patch of grazing wheat. He cantered over to a cart that bore his armor. An attendant helped him on with it. He returned to her.

"Oh, no, full armor!" she cried. "I hate to think what you plan to do."

"No different from a marshlander putting on his boots—simply accouterments of the trade, my love," he replied, turning to the attendants who brought up a lance, which he thought he might need in the event more hordes of horsemen came out of the shadows. He looked at it admiringly as he buckled it to his arm. "'Tis a shame you do not have knighthood here; your fine craftsmen are wasted."

"There are other things to forge than weapons, my lord."

"Aye, agreed, my lady, thus the purpose of our Mari regiment to persuade others to aim for those other things."

"Ah, yes, the famous Mari! My mother told me that your grandfather founded the selfless force of good....I can well understand your pride, which at this moment I fear you are going to do something reckless with that awesome pole."

"Nay, no such word in knighthood, rather, duty."

"Noble knight, is there nothing I can do? Lucia looked at him helplessly. "I'm new at this. What do you propose I do?"

"For the moment nothing till we send a team of the cavalry to join those who have dispersed to head off the horsemen before we advance full force into the meadow." He quickly turned to a royal officer, "Take twenty men to the east fringe, try not to engage them in close combat until the arrow has had its chance from horseback. I'll send more archers in support to dismount and plant themselves strategically."

"Aye, my lord, and the west flank?"

"I'll take care of it. Wave the men rounding up the sheep to join me to the west."

"But, my lord, there are only a half dozen!"

"Aye, but there are roughly only thirty on that side, you have some fifty to contend with. We don't want the enemy to think we are afraid to face them undermanned. Besides, I'm armored and have my trusty thruster." He bridled back to the princess, hailed her with his lance and galloped off.

She cried out after him, "My God, Lance, you aren't going to face them alone!"

He never looked back and angled westward as the horsemen who had dispersed the sheep to the east turned back to join him. By the time he reached him, Lance had already met the marauders' column head on. With merciless precision he leveled his lance at them; one by one the first half dozen howled in pain as they were jousted from their mounts. The others, never before having witnessed the skill of knighthood, came to a halt, bridled round in fear but too late to escape the arrows of Lucia's horsemen that had finally reached them within range of marksmanship. Lance pulled up his destrier and glanced toward the tall wheat. Deliberately, he bridled through it to flesh out some to be certain his conjecture held true. The fear of being thumped by the probing lance or trampled by the gargantuan hoofs propelled several of Angus's men to leap up and run back to camp, some dropping their bows. He noticed the other fringe was now engaged in close combat. Lance fired an order to his horsemen: "Sweep over there and tell them to disengage so that the archers now in position can pick off the rest." He returned to the main body to prepare for the advance.

She pouted again. "Oh, Lance, how little or greatly could you love me to take such a risk? I'd rather you renounced your love and live than to die just to escape my heart!"

He laughed. "No time for talk on the battle plain, dearest."

"Oh, what bold, mad thing is next on your mind? Please, my lord, what can I do?—I feel so helpless."

"Again nothing, princess, until we see the bulk of the enemy," he offered calmly. "I suggest you hold the garrison here. It doesn't seem that Baron Angus is set out to do conventional battle; otherwise he would have made an attempt to storm the castle. I give him that much credit; for he well knew the castle is impregnable. In battling noble opponents, the Mari doesn't have the problem of marauders. In this case, we have no choice but to deal with him on his terms or else he will continue to sack the countryside."

"Alas, I know, and I hope you forgive me for my cowardice in hoping he would end his looting and leave our borders," she said meekly.

"Think not on it." He looked to the plain. "I wager their bows are already pulled back waiting for us to approach the tall wheat."

"But why didn't they shoot at you when you were so close?"

"Nay, they'll wait for the rest of us."

"Poor strategy, methinks, to let escape the leviathan of battle!" she chortled.

"Oh, I doubt Angus knows what strategy is."

Suddenly she cheered. "Look Lance, the archers have felled the marauders!"

"Aye, and look where those who escaped the arrow are running to," he observed.

"Ah, yea, into the wheat field! To confer with their leader, I suspect," she said excitedly. She stood up in her stirrups. "I trust, his men would not dare advance without Angus first advancing to the front to show that he is a true leader."

"We soon shall see," he said.

She kicked the white's flanks and jolted forward.

Lance broke to her left side; cautiously he scanned the wheat field. He could discern widespread restless movement in the wheat other than the soft sway from the breeze. He dropped his visor, unbuckled the lance and let it fall. He bolted forward at fast-gait, raising the shield level.

The princess shrieked, "Brave knight, don't be a fool! It is our battle now!" Despite her protest, wisely she held up her men to see if Lance could flesh the enemy.

He quickened his steed to a furious gait as arrows began to bounce off his shield and his steed's blanket of mail. Just as suddenly as they volleyed, the arrows stopped. Lance reined to a trot and lifted his visor, lowered his shield and looked down into the wheat field and the many heads that popped up barely above the rusty grain. In a calm, commanding tone, he said as he unsheathed his long heavy sword and lowered it effortlessly with one hand, "Stay your arrows, men; for I do not see a leader among you. Obviously, then this cannot be war, if you have no leader. Why, look ye yonder and there you see your princess boldly in the lead of men ready to do battle for their country, while you seem not to have cause other than to protect a miserable field mouse." He swiveled his head in search and yelled, "Where is that field mouse Baron Angus? If you are here show me your yellow flaccid spine and gray tail that I with sword shall lop off." He could hear whispers and choked chuckles in the wheat. "Yet little would it lend to my honor to vanquish a paltry mouse; therefore, I order you to stand up and reveal yourself like a man and face me in noble single combat. Then would I feel the honor in redressing the wrong heaped upon a loyal, gallant friend. Just as I know these men here in the golden tresses of your beloved Ceres, are gallant and loyal and are much confused that they find themselves perpetrators of a cowardly ambush upon a knight and their royal princess. And now what's worse that they now find themselves hiding in a wheat field while their lovely princess sits proud and in the open on her glorious mount. Rise up then and give these men cause to fight, if so bent they shall avenge your death. For I vow you die today!"

"Don't listen to this vile Quandron tongue that wags with serpent's venom!" the baron cried out a hundred feet away, crouched in protective wheat. "He rings with the voices of the ancient Quandronians who mean to strip our defense and enslave us no less than the Romans had."

"Fie, Angus," Lance's voice jumped, "it is you who rudely intend to usurp their generous princess of sweet justice to wear the crown for yourself. And if you hold your princess in such contempt then what can these fine marksmen expect other than tyranny?"

Quickly the Baron, also bedecked in armor, rose out of the wheat, ready with tensed bow and with lightning speed let fly the arrow. Lance deftly veered his steed and raised his shield as the arrow deflected off the edge with a singing flutter and a clang. Lance dug into the flanks and the horse swept across the swishing wheat. Bowmen in his path scurried, others cowered from this undaunted flair of courage that had come upon them with daring speed, power and terrifying whoops of battle, the likes of which they had never seen nor heard before. The baron stood firm and let fly another arrow. It glanced off the knight's helmet, stunning Lance but only momentarily tilting him in the saddle. Quickly shaking it off, releasing the rein momentarily and ripping off his helm to throw it down, Lance resumed his charge, swinging his sword from flank to flank as though it were a single hand blade. The baron momentarily froze in terror at the oncoming howling knight and the thundering steed. His boots vibrated from the onslaught; the baron broke out of his trance and threw himself out of the path as heavy hooves brushed by. Over and over he rolled in the wheat as Lance pulled up and headed for him again. The baron scrambled for a mace and ran for his horse on the fringe of the wheat field. Just as he mounted and raised the heavy barreled mace over his head, Lance swung his sword, cracking the mace like a tree struck by lightning. The baron toppled off his horse from the power of the blow. Lance dismounted and jumped on the bulky, cowering body. The fearless knight was about to run him through when hordes of bowmen now armed with maces and battle axes circled round the knight. One shirking his fear advanced and swooped down on the knight with a mighty swing of his battle axe, knocking the sword from Lance's hand. Rolling under swinging axe, Lance scrambled for his sword and jumped to his feet and deftly parried two-handedly breaking the arc of the attacker's axe and plunging the sword under the assailant's breast plate and into his hip. Lance withdrew the sword and quickly parried off several deadly clubs of others who had joined the fray. With incredible speed and skill, one by one he felled the attackers. More mustered courage to approach him; some hesitated what with the marvel of his savage courage. Raised brows and pleading eyes of the baron, however, caused them, however fearful, to edge like inch worms toward this untiring knight of battle.

Suddenly the wheat field was alive with swishing hooves as the princess led the horsemen through the field. The bowmen on the flanks trained in. The horsemen scattered the rebellious resistance. The men assaulting Lance turned in terror at the advancing horses and ran for the ridge. The baron in one last effort grabbed a fallen follower's club and charged Lance madly. Lance stepped aside but thrust his sword in the rebellious leader's swinging arm. The baron screeched in pain. With pleading eyes he turned to his men fleeing the wheat field and pathetically waved them back to battle. Alone but for a heart full of fear, he switched the mace to his other hand whirled it over his head. In final desperation he charged Lance who deftly with his sword tripped the baron who fell into the trodden wheat. Then the knight thrust his sword into the back and through the heart of the baron whose death swooped in without a sound.

Lucia's horsemen everywhere were herding the fleeing rebels. Hordes of Lucia's bowmen closed in to flesh out any others cowering in the wheat. Rebel bowmen who with anxious alacrity rose up with bows on their shoulders and hands skyward. Lance turned round and saw the princess ride up to a group of defeated men and say, "I shall consider this, however grave, a lapse of discretion. There was never a question of sovereignty. I am your sovereign; no need for another. Your baron was clearly a traitor, not only to me and your country but he betrayed you with his vile ambition. Return now to your fields and valleys. For you, the noose of treason does not swing. But mark, you shall be for the rest of your lives taxed heavily in restitution for the families' you have ignominiously looted and the for the shame cast upon our heritage." The defeated men bowed their heads with nary a word but sighs of relief abounded. Slowly they dispersed as the horsemen led them out of the field.

Then she turned to a small group of leaders and said ominously, "As for you manor lords who have abused the leadership endowed by our laws, it remains to be seen as to whether you will be dropped in the lava pit." She leered at a partially bald, thickset warrior with hemp-like beard and her voice grated, "You, Dane, above all who were so loyal to my father, might well be the first to burn in the Christian hell of which we hear so much—until now thought little of." She bounced a smile off Lance.

The cowardly warrior dropped to his knees and pleaded, "Oh, sweet princess, I swear, I did fear the madman Angus who threatened the lives of our families if we informed on him!"

The princess scowled. "Ah, the usual rationale of traitors who are never themselves responsible for their treachery. Are we not a race of free wills and decisions? Why then would you take up with the likes of thieves and murderers if you are not thusly bent yourselves?" She turned with instructions to her field overlord: "See that these cowards that mock their own noble blood, are incarcerated in the cavern cells nearest to the pit so that they may with nervous sweat think hard on their dastardly deeds."

The princess bridled over to Lance who had just mounted his battle-proven steed. She looked up at him with admiration and said gratefully, "I am ever indebted to you, my foolhardy champion."

He shrugged it off, and removed his mail headpiece. He stared down at her for a moment. "I hope you are not being foolhardy in pardoning these cutthroats."

"No fear. Still, the poor souls were but pawns," she said confidently.

The victorious defenders of the tree of knowledge rode off toward the castle in the mountain. Well into nightfall they reached the mountain trail to the valley. A team of horsemen rode ahead to lead them by torchlight through the rocky trail. In the valley scores rose from their beds to hail the conquering brave.

"Imagine," the princess said as they approached the drawbridge, "all my fighting men seemed captivated by your action in battle. Already they are weaving tales about you to the people at the roadside."

"Aye, as was I filled with tales since a boy about the legendary princess of the north." He laughed. "And you, my princess, are you also captivated?"

"I was enchanted by a fool—a magnificent fool." She laughed.

Lance smiled again. "I too was taken in by a brave young princess—aye, a legendary princess indeed!...Verily, the drawbridge will be down tonight,...thanks to your fleeting steeds with yours in the lead."

She chuckled. "I had thought it was your powerful steed's haunches I was behind."

"Aye, but soon abreast to save my hide!" He laughed.

Bound in chains in the hot mountain cells throughout the night, key supporters of Angus had been brought by guards in the morning before Princess Lucia and Cicero. Lance and the princess' mother Margaret were also present on the dais of the great dining hall and court. A guard singled out Dane and by the collar chain forced him down on his knees before Lucia. Dane bowed his head in contrition, but slowly raised it as Lucia inquired, "Have you and your commanders had sufficient time to sweat out the evil implanted in ye by the devil Angus?"

"Verily, your highness, the evil in spirit is no longer with us, nor does the evil of still others linger."

She leaned forward with a surprised look. "Still others?"

"Aye, your highness, the main accomplices."

"Accomplices? Why, surely you men are the accomplices," she corrected him.

"Granted, sweet princess, but I meant the three men from the Lowlands."

The princess quickly glanced over at Lance, then at Cicero who was leering at Lance with suspicion. Lance nonchalantly shrugged innocence. She turned back to Dane, asking, "What were their plans and by whom were they sent?"

"Believe me, your highness, I speak the truth in that I do not know from whom. They did not say—or possibly Angus did not disclose it to us.

But we did know that the knights under your hospitality were to be assassinated and that we would be rewarded handsomely. I did not see any harm in that since we all looked upon your two visitors with suspicion, anyway. Further, the men who met up with Angus seemed from the southern gentry, one I'm sure was a knight. They seemed intent to carry out their plan."

"How could you, Old Dane, be a part of this? We have laws; in addition, I take umbrage that any would dare ascertain for me the integrity of my guests." She glanced again at Lance, then continued, "Nor does this in any way explain rebellion. Was that too the idea of these Quandronian conspirators, and if so, to what purpose?"

"Oh, I'm sure they were not, my princess. Rather, it seems Baron Angus was enraged by your sentence. When the three men rescued him, and he returned to the castle of Baal, it is said that over and over he mumbled 'Exiled be damned' while carrying around his mace and thumping furniture to pieces."

"Then, it seems, he intended to kill his princess as well," she inferred with a heavy frown.

"Oh, no, your highness!" He corrected her with an emphatic swivel of his head.

"How sweet of him!" The princess chuckled nervously. "I suppose, he intended exile for me."

"Nay, my lady,...marriage." He grinned. "He wanted you for his queen."

"*His!*...Humph, the nerve!" She turned to Lance and scowled. "And, proud knight, you had to kill him robbing me the pleasure of killing him myself!" She looked down again at the rebel. "And where, treacherous Dane, are these Quandronian criminals now—still at the notorious Baal's?"

His eyes walled to her and he said, "Cowards they are, your highness; they murdered the crippled Baal, who was furious that Angus would bring foreigners into his home. Then Angus in turn murdered them!...Not to avenge Baal, but for their treasure."

Lance rose and addressed the princess, "Your highness, may I speak?" She acquiesced with a nod. The tall knight walked from behind the dais table and approached the bearded man who cowered closer to the slated floor with Lance's steps. "How can we be sure," he turned and asked the princess, "that this traitor is telling the truth?" He turned from her and glared intensely at Dane. "There are ways, you know, to see that you tell only the truth." Lance gripped the man by the beard. "You are sure these men were of my country?"

With pained expression old Dane sputtered fawningly, "Oh, yes, great warlord. I am not that foolish to lie in your indomitable presence."

"And just how did you know they were from Quandron? Did they announce it?"

Dane shook his head and said with a grin, "No, sir, but they certainly had the accent—the same as yours—haughty they were."

Lance grinned back and went on, "Did they bear a crest? And...you say they were knights?"

"No crest—black robes they wore—but, nay, only one I'm sure of was knight," Dane said.

"Oh?" Lance arched his brows.

"Aye, by his long sword and a much larger steed—like yours."

Lance paced, rubbing his chin, then addressed Dane again, "This reward you speak of—what was it, this so-called treasure, Angus murdered for?"

"Ah, yea, splendid!—jewels they were, my lord."

Cicero joined in from the table, saying, "Yea, Sir Lance, I vouch for that: we recovered them and they are magnificent jewels."

Glancing at Cicero, Lance said, "I should like to see them later, good patrician." The venerable old man nodded solicitously.

Dane was beginning to look much too relaxed; Lance squinted and grabbed him by his collar-chain and wrenched it. "You had better not be telling tall tales to save your neck."

Through strained voice Dane uttered, "I am but a warrior, sir, not a weaver."

Lance smirked. "And not a very good warrior at that; for your sake pray that as a weaver of tales you are just as bad."

"Oh, indeed, your supreme, poor in both. In all fairness, and for what pride I have left, I could war quite well until facing a mighty foe as you!"

"Nor would you be alive to tell of it..." While releasing his hold on the hapless warrior, Lance looked briefly over at Lucia, then reminded Dane, "but for the kindness and mercy of your princess,".

"Oh, you're so right, so very right!" Dane peered round the knight and gazed gratefully at the princess.

Lance pursued, "Did you notice anything else that might have led you to believe that these men were noblemen?"

"The boots, sir,...fine boots like yours. Only the nobility from the south wear such leather." Dane touched the knight's boot, then added, "And, yea,...the jewels."

"Distinguished jewels were they?" The knight piqued.

"Aye, crown jewels—that's what they said."

"Crown jewels," Lance repeated.

"Aye, so delicate were these gems that I would have to believe they came from Henry himself."

"Watch your tongue, old man," Lance warned, pushing Dane who toppled back over his haunches. Lance reeled, appealing to the princess. "This cannot be!"

Lucia stared back with a painful expression.

Later that evening Lance requested an audience with the princess. He felt that she was still not sure of him in spite of his enormous victory in her behalf. She was delighted with the request and quickly changed her gown to a stunning white silk toga more in the fashion of ancient Greece. A braided belt in gold complemented the dress and accentuated her narrow waist. Her dainty crown was studded with tiny diamonds and pearls. When he arrived he was in awe over her graceful beauty. She greeted him warmly. He wanted to kiss more than her slender hand. He was disappointed by the interruption.

Cicero entered with a guard carrying a small jewel chest, which was placed on a foot-locker. The guard, however, did not leave; rather he stayed by the door. "These are the jewels Dane spoke of," said the patrician.

Eyeing the chest, Lance said, "My God, my mother had one just like this!" He glanced at the princess who had a confounded look.

Cicero politely dismissed it, though he still cast a suspicious look. "Perhaps they're common in Quandron." He unlatched the lid.

Lance's eyes bulged when his mother's familiar brooch sparkled up at him. "Now, I wish they *were* the crown jewels." He chuckled nervously. "Well, that clears up the suspicion of the king unless—and highly improbable—he is in cahoots with Erinysia. It is said, however, there were no limits to her relations with men."

Cicero added, shaking his head in a mix of disbelief and suspicion, "Or she—this witch you speak of—is in collusion with your father. It certainly rings of treachery from one of them."

Lucia gasped, "Your father! Hmm, rather close to home." Her eyes shifted to the guard at the door.

"Oh, we're engaged in wild conjecture—believe me, my father is harmless and not well," Lance assured him, having seen worry and suspicion in their faces. "Besides, even if we took him seriously, it is Henry's throne not yours he wants."

Chancellor Cicero momentarily glanced at the princess, then back to Lance. "But what of the assassins that old Dane claimed were here to send both of you and Bryan to your Maker? And how can we be sure that was the purpose? They could be knights lurking in your support. Why they could've been from your very own castle!" the chancellor speculated warily.

"Impossible—not with the flag regiment and its detachments left in charge," Lance jumped, stabbing in the dark, "For all we know Angus himself could have hired them to do the dastardly deed in exchange for asylum up here...or perhaps this Baal fellow."

The patrician shook his head. "Nay, he was just a grumpy old man that would threaten the tax collectors every year, but nevertheless, pay them. I am saddened that he was murdered."

Lucia joined in. "The poor soul died without a friend in the world. I'm surprised he even would let Angus hide out in his castle." Then she nodded reassurance, not from the muddy knowledge at hand, but from a somewhat shaken but growing faith in this knight. "Still, you might be right about Angus's motives."

Lance glanced at her in gratitude, then turned to sit down on a heavy chair by the bed and stretched his legs. Cicero pursued, "While the conjecture flows, then why couldn't the king be involved?"

"I doubt it very much: I couldn't believe that of Henry, particularly....He could never take seriously something as preposterous as my father and Erinysia, much less, send murderers after us. And how could he have gotten hold of my mother's jewelry?"

"They could've been stolen while you were away fighting, and with your dear mother gone, who would notice?" Lucia offered; then she smiled and added, "If so Henry didn't get much out of it, did he?....After all, he wouldn't give up a treasure just to have Bryan out of the way. Not much of a bargain with you still alive to wrest away his throne, is it?"

Lance laughingly said, "Especially since Bryan was treated like a king by your mother to nurse him back to health and then to leave us so soon...of course, I'm glad he did go to see to Rhonda's safety. Still, I'll wager, he'd be raging mad right now if he knew what followed."

Lucia laughed too, then became serious. "He would've given up his limbs to be with you on the battlefield today."

"He missed little, nonetheless: they were unworthy soldiers," Lance said haughtily.

The patrician coughed and broke in, turning back to the gnawing subject. "Maybe the king was informed of your father's ambitious plans."

"Even so, it would be preposterous for him to search out *me*, his ally," Lance jumped.

Cicero went on. "Just the same, if the king thought there were some sort of conspiracy, it would be logical to track you down. I mean, what could your father possibly do without you at the lead? Furthermore, in light of all your victories on behalf of the kingdom wouldn't Henry be in a grasping mood for more?" Cicero studied Lance's eyes.

Lance laughed. "If that were the case, why would Henry want me dead?...In truth, I do not intend to do anymore battle except in defense; but he doesn't know that yet. As I mentioned before, this is but wild conjecture. This seems more the doing of common thieves—and Angus was probably responsible and told this story to save his hide—of course, he didn't know he would die in battle."

Lucia had been pacing the floor nervously with these questions that seemed like an inquiry. Suddenly she said angrily, "My dear Cicero, we do dishonor to this hero who led our nation today by these questions." She approached the patrician and took his hands in hers, bouncing a smile off his confounded expression; she dismissed him with: "These questions are upsetting to me as well, my dear chancellor. Lord Lance may be right—we are just stabbing blindly in a bat cave; besides, I wish to be alone with him to honor his great achievement today. I owe him that." Cicero was stunned but simply bowed and left with the guards. Lucia also signaled the maid-in-waiting to leave.

Both alone, she sighed and sat down in a cushioned settle. On the table next to it was the jewel chest—she wished she had had it removed. She beckoned that he sit on a chair opposite her as she said, "I suppose, now you will be leaving us?"

"Aye, but I confess, I'm not as anxious...though I should be for other reasons."

"Indeed, for it seems there is business at home," she said harshly. "Of course, if Cicero had his way you would be detained. But to my way of thinking totally unwarranted."

He smiled, in face of taking note of her tone but continued, "That makes me very happy that you have faith in me....In truth, your highness, I shall miss you. You have been a great hostess and ally."

"Ally? How very strange." the princess reacted with disappointment. "It sounds as though you have some use of me."

"No, my lady, I simply meant that in the context of our having joined in battle against Angus."

"There may be a time in the near future that we may again meet on the battlefield." She leaned toward him and stared into his eyes. "I trust not as adversaries."

Lance gaped. "Good grief, what are you implying? Surely, you don't think..."

She sighed again, then said, "Oh, I don't know what to think right now. Ever since you arrived, events have been swimming in my head."

"In faith, not all bad?"

She smiled. "No, of course not. Still, there is some question." She looked over at the jewel chest.

"Aye, a puzzle to me too." Lance reached over to examine the brooch, then held it up to her. I remember this brooch; my mother wore it often. She also had a magnificent necklace of small diamonds and a large distinctive emerald. I wonder why it is missing? I know Rhonda always admired it—hopefully she has it."

"Oh, yes, I hope so too: A daughter needs something precious to hold in remembrance....Again, though,...I have no guarantee that Angus took it upon himself to overthrow my rule."

Absently he nostalgically fondled some jewels, then said sullenly, "Alas, guaranties are hard to come by. All I can say is that to my knowledge no one in Quandron has designs on your state and if in fact they do I shall hunt them down."

The princess glowered skepticism momentarily then focused onto his eyes. "These men from the south Dane spoke of could have been behind Angus's plan to overturn my throne—why, how do I know you and Bryan were not the vanguard...here on pretext?" She brought her palms to her face whose cheeks were damp in rolling tears of ambivalence. Then she sat erect and wiped away her tears, squinting puzzlement at him. She squealed, "I'm a wretch for having such phantoms in my head."

He dropped a ring back into the chest, rose from the chair, paced, then paused before her, searching her beautifully soft-toned face for a moment. He sat down next to her and took her hand. "Dear Lucia, I cannot deny any possibility in this insane world. But this I can deny: no such conspiracy subsists in my being or Bryan's. We are knights and take our Order seriously."

"But they too were knights!"

"We don't really know that; yet, if so, no single group is without its cankers." He squeezed her hand. "Please, Lucia, you must trust me."

"Why? How? In light of this box!" she rasped, gesturing to the jewels. "From your very own castle!"

"Ah, and how would you know that but for my own admission?"

She studied his eyes, then said, "Yes, I grant you that; still, you cannot deny that someone within your castle..."

"Not necessarily," he interdicted, though he himself looked incredulous, "chances are they were stolen. On the other hand, I might have grossly underestimated my father and his witch in particular."

"Oh, nothing makes sense!" she clucked. "Perhaps stolen by your own hand."

Smiling and lightly shaking his head, he countered, "You really don't believe that, Lucia."

Instinctively she pecked him on the cheek. "No,...I know, you know, I couldn't believe that." She chuckled through her tears.

He took her hands and brought them to his lips. "No, Lucia, you are not just an ally, but a dear friend. I have dreamt of you all my life, that is, of the legendary princess. And now that you are so real and more than my wildest dreams, I would never betray you." He circled his arms round her and held her tight.

She relaxed in his arms and muttered, "Perhaps, we are allies in the single purpose of love?" He kissed her on the lips; she swooned and settled back on the couch.

He whispered in her ear, "There is no perhaps in our lives. It is absolute love."

The patrician tapped his staff on the slate floor as he walked back and forth along the long table, glancing repeatedly at the princess. Finally he paused before Lady Margaret and appealed to her, "Is there no way you can drum sense back into your daughter, your ladyship?"

Margaret smiled. "Not when dealing with the illogic of love."

"Bah! Hero-worship if you ask me—why, this knight could've staged all the heroics and killed Angus to keep him from revealing the truth."

"Even to the extent of having his own trusted knight on the brink of death? Hardly." Lady Margaret reminded him.

"Men of ambition have no loyalties." He stomped the staff hard.

"O ardent advisor," the princess said in a kind voice, "I know you have only the defense of our country and my safety in mind. Yet look into this more: in truth, he is ambitious but in the correct way—why, he has in the heralded capacity of Lord-Protector restored law to Quandron."

"Restored! Bah, conquered you mean!"

"No, my chancellor, you do not understand the ways of feudal lords. They are unjust tyrants who enslave their serfs for their gain. They are not enlightened as you and our tradition exemplify—Angus excepted. Many are but nobles in name and wolves in fact."

"Then your knight whom you have taken a fancy to should have remained there to keep the peace and not cajole himself into our ways of living."

"Do you overlook already" she jogged him, "that he in fact kept the peace here in our own valley?"

He glanced at the mother then askant at the princess. "I've already explained his sinister purpose for that."

She raised both arms and pleaded softly, "Oh, my clearheaded adviser, in your anxiety to protect me you are under a cloud. Do you realize that Lance is in command of a supreme fighting force? He at anytime could have invaded us full-scale. Why, all this? Nay, I am convinced he is an honorable man that lives by the highest code of knighthood."

"If he has such a fighting force, then why would he solicit help from us?" he grasped.

"He didn't. It was my idea to commit our forces if he should need us — despite his proud objection....I firmly believe we are beholden to him; for had Lance not been here, our people would have been at the mercy of Angus and I a very unhappy bridesmaid." She looked over at her mother.

Lady Margaret laughed. "Or bride and I the matron of honor."

The sun was setting as he straddled his new horse whose mane glistened from the soft rays. In looking over the valley he thought with the exception of Lucia and his darling sister there was not a more beautiful sight in the world. It seemed even more beautiful and permanent now that the battle was won. After last evening's engagement with Lucia, Lance was more reluctant to leave than ever. He chuckled to himself that perhaps Bryan was right: that he was indeed enchanted by the legendary princess. He laughed at the thought of the old warlord under Erinysia's spell and that he was after all his father's son. However, deep down he knew that he had at long last surrendered to love—and ever so willingly and delightfully. It was now clear why so many women in his life meant little to him. At thirty-five he was proud of himself for waiting for that single star sparkling on a clear night for him and him alone.

Nevertheless, belonging to the highest order of knights he must fulfill his oath by returning and restoring order to the kingdom. He was convinced now that his father was foolish enough to grant to Erinysia the privilege of his mother's jewelry and consequently something stronger than an old man's fantasy was in the wind.

She touched his shoulder as she came along side on her white horse, almost pink in the low rays. "I'm sorry to have kept you waiting Lance."

"Don't be, my love, for there is no finer waiting station in the land than here," he said jubilantly.

"Oh? My dear Lance, do you really mean it?" She beamed.

"Aye, and to prove it, I shall return as soon as I can—to stay."

She radiated and leaned over and lifted his hand to her cheek. "Oh, my darling, would it were true that you would return soon. But something inside me tells me otherwise."

"Why, what do you mean, Lucia?" He studied her face. "There is indeed something strange in your look. Even though you have my hand, it is though you were in a distant place."

She caressed his scarred hand and voiced tremulously, "No, dear love, I am here. I told you it is within me...a strange feeling as though there is some other me....Did you ever have the feeling that you were truly held speechless?"

"Aye, when I first laid eyes upon you."

She giggled. "No, seriously,...I feel as though there were another voice pent up inside, not yet ready to echo in my brain."

Perhaps it is Cupid, trying to get you to write verse for me; I know since meeting you I should rather be a poet than a knight."

"Why, Lance that thought in itself is all the poetry I want." She leaned over and kissed him on the cheek. "But again, be serious....However much I love this valley, my head is filled with Quandron. I see real places in thought and dream even though I have never been there. Somehow I have this feeling that our destinies are intertwined there and not here."

Gently he pressed her hand. "Well, I'll have none of it. I just committed myself to spending the rest of my life *here* with you!"

"Oh, you're so precious!" She released his hand and heeled her horse. "Come let us ride through our valley of love." He bridled close to her, and the steeds in harmony cantered gracefully along the trail. Soon crowds filed along the trail to greet them and the horses slowed down.

An elder in the crowd stepped out and touched her horse. Lance held back the checkrein of the buckskin for fear of trampling the old man. The elder asked the princess, "Your highness, is it true that Old Dane and his treasonable cutthroats are to be hurled into the hot pit?"

"Aye, aye, boil their yellow blood!" chanted a young farmer. Others joined in agreement with sundry cheers and yeas.

"Nay, my good people" she answered with a smile. "Gratifying it is that you are outraged. It shows your loyalty. But till now those men were stalwarts of trust. They are contrite now. And I firmly believe they had been duped by the madness of Angus."

"But surely they are to be punished," the elder pursued.

"Oh, yes, be assured of that. They will remain captive and under guard to do labor in the fields."

The elder tugged on his gray beard and shook his head. "Your highness, forgive me, but that is no punishment to work our beautiful valleys."

The princess laughed. "How very true, to a masterly farmer such as you; but to a nobleman and his soldiers, trust me, it is no labor of love." The young farmer laughed. "Aside from that," she continued, "it is tradition of our modest nation not to do harm among ourselves."

The persistent elder shook his head again and flapped his beard. "But your highness, those callous thugs meant to do harm to you!"

"Yea," agreed the young farmer while several women next to him nodded to each other. "Those devils need a hot bath in the red lava."

"Oh, good, loyal citizens, liken not to their ways! Besides, they were deceived into thinking I would do harm to the valley."

"Never!" chanted the women. An elderly one added, "Why, you are the sunshine of our beloved valley!"

"Thank you, thank you, my darlings," she said spreading a warm smile. "But, good people, give thought to this: justice is our way. Our justice requires understanding of even those who wish to do harm—yea, even these men, who now acknowledge their wrong-doing and understand my intent now, are seeing through the clear window of our justice. And someday they shall be given the privilege to once again serve our land with honor." She pointed to a lad leaning on a hoe some fifty paces away. "You all know that young man yonder who just last year stole an only cow from the young widow Rebecca. What could be more offensive and devastating to a mother trying to rear four young children? In truth, such a dastardly crime deserves punishment, but more important is restitution, which our justice achieved. This lad is now productively working the field strip for the family he offended and in so doing is also developing into a true, selfless citizen, which is the ultimate end of punishment born of justice unique in that it expresses a constructive nature dear to us and salvaged from under the Roman rubble of centuries ago."

Though not fully comprehending, the crowd, in tandem nodded and uttered variant agreement. They then began to disperse as Lance edged back alongside. The princess glanced at him and whispered with an endearing smile, "I thought we'd be alone." She smiled at the sea of faces and bade farewell, then wheeled her horse back to the castle as Lance followed and when the crowd was distant he pulled abreast of her steed. He looked over at her. "My, your highness, you certainly do have a good manner with your people."

"Is there any other manner?" she laughed.

"Apparently not for you. I noticed that your dungeon cells were empty but for the old man," Lance commented.

The princess laughed. "Yea, there for medicinal purposes—says my mother when she's not on one of her mythological tirades."

He grinned. "He mentioned it. But he can weave a tale or two himself. He told me he has golden apples sent to him by a mysterious lady."

"I shouldn't put it past him to have visions of Ceres. The apple is the key to the sustenance of knowledge," she said nonchalantly.

"So?...That's the thrust of your coat of arms, eh?...Not like the one in the cave, I take it."

"Heavens no!" She glanced up and smiled. "Ironic, isn't it?"

"Aye, and the ancient's axe that leans in readiness." he chuckled.

"Oh, it depends on one's perspective....well, he has help now with old Dane and his group down there to keep him company."

He rubbed his chin. "And you really mean not to sentence them to death?" She nodded. He absently gripped a silver horseshoe on a chain Lucia had given him before battle and said, "But, my God, there is no worse offense than treason."

Her eyes danced on his. "To them it wasn't treason. They were defending me against you, remember?"

He shook his head, then lifted his brows as he sighed. "Still, I suppose, were I in their boots..."

"See?...The key to justice....What is it your Jesus said?"

"Oh, that...Do 'unto others as...'"

"Precisely."

15. Bryan Returns

Bryan had met Sir John's messenger midway through the vast heath separating the lowlands from the mountains of the north. Gregory, barely Bryan's elder, the young knight with a cheerful unbearded face, greeted, "You're a happy sight in this barren land."

Bryan laughed. "Aye, my mirrored thoughts as well. But, my speedy Gregory, what news have you that makes you thump the sedge?"

"Aye, and with only four hoofs." He looked at the beautiful red mare. "Are you into horse-theft now?" He laughed.

"A gift for a very special person," said Bryan with a smile.

"Beautiful!" Gregory said as he looked at Red again, then looked seriously at the fellow knight. "But to the matter—crisis is stirring in the winds, I fear, and why I'm here to fetch you and Lance." With raised brow he asked, "But, Bryan, where is the Lord Protector?"

"Love it seems is stirring in the northern wind," Bryan quipped and laughed. "Our, mighty leader has been smitten by a princess."

"What! The legendary princess really exists?" Gregory chuckled. "My, the confirmed bachelor stepped right into a story book, eh?...Well, we have to tear out the pages and fetch him."

"The situation grows worse, eh?" Bryan groaned. "The Lord Kalab is set to do wrong, I suspect."

"Indeed, and why I must dispatch Lance to join the regiment camped on the border and then from there onto the king's castle."

"Good grief! That serious! Then old Kalab wasn't just ranting out of fantasy!"

"Aye, that is why Sir John decided the regiment should slip out from under Kalab's clutches."

"Then let us make haste back through the mountains. But tell me how is fair Rhonda in this sour situation?" Bryan asked.

"Bad news, I'm afraid. I met a lass just as I was leaving camp. It seems Rhonda has disappeared mysteriously."

"Oh, no!" Bryan pulled back on the reins."Oh, my friend, overlook my slight, but I cannot get myself to escort you to the north, knowing Rhonda is in need."

Gregory reached over and tapped Bryan's shoulder. "Aye, I know how you feel about her. And Lance would want you to make haste. No matter to me, I know fairly well the territory—up to the mountains, that is. Just tell me how I can locate him."

"He's at the main castle in the valley to which you take the main trail. When you come upon an inn, you're almost there. The nice old couple will direct you from there. But be sure when riding the trail that you bellow out your purpose, lest sharpshooting woodsmen nail you to a tree."

Gregory guffawed. "I've heard their longbows are always on the hunting mark. But have no fear; caution is my middle name. You know me....Why, I'd talk Christian charity to a dragon before I'd engage one in combat."

Bryan laughed and spurred southward. The messenger continued on to the north.

By noon three days later Bryan approached the watery border. He got down from his horse and let it drink from the stream, although he was anxious to meet up with the regiment, hoping there would be recent news on Rhonda. Then he unhooked Red's checkrein from the saddle and let him join the destrier. He took a venison chip from the saddle bag to eat while he filled up the water sacks. Hitching the replenished bags to Red's traveling pack, he squinted across the stream for signs of the regiment. To his horror he saw buzzards low in the sky across the glistening stream. His anxiety cut short resting the horses and he began crossing, worrying about the regiment. After a two mile canter, his eyes blinked and smarted from the glitter on the plain. Squinting and shading his eyes was no help. He dismounted and went to the red mare and retrieved a helm and put it on. He mounted and lowered the visor to see what caused the intense reflections. He was aghast to see that the sun was glancing off shields and breastplates. Countless bodies of warriors stippled the meadow, and hundreds of buzzards already on the ground feasting. When he reached the scene, he dismounted and had to lift the visor to hold his nose from the putrefaction under the hot sun; he returned the helm to Red's pack. Red snorted and whinnied at the presence of the scavengers and the smell of death since all this was new to the mare. Bryan walked through the grisly scene of battered armor and shield, broken spears and swords at phantasmagoric angles protruding from untold hundreds of cadavers. He waved off the voracious birds with his sword. He was surprised to see so many of Bennet's coat of arms on the bodies' bloody tabards. The purple ones made him gasp until he examined one of them closely and saw that threads were removed and hastily sewed over was a large K. He could see the outline of the eagle so he knew they had originally been the purple tabards of the Mari and inferred what Kalab had done; yet he wondered why such madness could evolve after their glorious victories to defend the realm. He surmised, of course, that the regiment had clashed with these ill-fated warriors but a day or so ago, but he was mystified by the colors. He knew, of course, if indeed this was the result of a battle with the Mari, which was obviously victorious, that the regiment never would have left its dead exposed as this. When he swung his head to the east and then slowly to the northeast border he saw crosses a half mile away from the border sticking up from the freshly spaded earth. He led the horses toward the sacred ground. Tears came to his eyes in seeing the names of so many he knew and fought with carved into the crosses. He bowed in prayer for a good spell. He finished his praying with: "Despite the horror, O Lord, I thank Thee that there are but forty of our wondrous warriors compared to the countless toll of the enemy." He rose up, crossed himself with sword in hand and added, "Be at peace, honored men, for your sacrifice shall be avenged. The gallant Lance will see to it."

Bryan arrived at the old warlord's castle in the evening, following two more days of hasty travel. By the lack of tents beyond the moat, he surmised the rebellious army was gone. He hoped it had returned to its senses and abandoned Lord Kalab. When he crossed the bridge and into the outer ward, the old bridge-tender called down, "Well, young Bryan, I see you're back from the mountains. Your foolish trip might have saved your neck. The master's men are all gone to unseat the king."

"I was afraid of that." Bryan gulped. "But surely you don't mean all of the Mari detachments!"

"Aye, I do—of course, the flag regiment went off somewhere in search of the Lord-Protector. How is it Lord Lance is not with you? Or did old loyal Sir John find him?"

"Nay, I wish he had."

"Yea, in truth, things would be different....Just like Sir John, you could rest assure the young master, I swear, would never dare look into the witch's eyes!" he bellowed over the squeaking winch as he drew the bridge back up. "That woman could crack the crosspiece on the chapel's cross. Once her icy orbs did catch my old tired eyes and the hair on my brows turned from gray to white!"

Bryan snapped a chuckle. "Verily, old man," but then quickly asked solicitously, "The young lady Rhonda—have you news of her?"

The old man descended the bridge tower steps half way, sat down and ran his hand over his bald tawny head. "Nay, and sad, such a lovely lass..."

"Speak up, man—hang me not."

"Hang her not—'tis better that we heard nothing. Let us pray she's safe from eely Erinysia," the old man moaned, cradling his stubbly chin in his hand. "But if there is news of her, the loyal Elmer will surely know."

Bryan hitched up the horses and headed for the keep's steps leading to the lower level of the servant quarters. The chatelain answered the knock on the door by crackling for him to enter. Elm blessed himself and his eyes lit up. "Glory to God you have returned—and where is the young master?" he said anxiously.

"Still north of here shamelessly, since I can see in your eyes that he is sorely needed here." Bryan did not attempt to hide his resentment. "Elm, have you any news of Rhonda? It grieves me we were not here to protect her from the witch."

"Yea, it saddens me too that the young master had too much faith in his father. Lance was away too long for the good of the king while his witch-doting father cut them both to the quick. And now, I fear his daughter...might...nay, nay to such thoughts!" he added shaking his head and tugging his beard. "If she's in trouble, verily, though unwittingly, the manor master is to blame." He shook his head again and looked with sad eyes to the young knight. "Nay, I haven't uncovered anything—the poor dear. Still, I know she lives."

"Of course, but that you might have thought otherwise rings ominously," Bryan said warily. "Good man, what sort of dark place is this that she should turn to running away?"

Elm grinned. "Ah, the fleet faith of the young! Yea, surely, that's what she has done—so strong-headed she is. I suppose, the insult to her mother's memory was too much for her."

Bryan heaved consolingly. "Verily and sadly...still, there is more here surely....And where could she have gone?"

"At first I thought perhaps to the king," Elm offered, scratching his beard. "But then, I reasoned that since she did not know him, and young Henry very little, she probably went to see her friend at the earldom."

"Maureen? Why, of course, how logical—a friend in need," again the young man consoled himself.

Elm solemnly and slowly shook his head and said in retrospect, "But now I hope I'm wrong; for the old earl's knights and troops have allied themselves with my master—I should say, with the feisty witch."

"Surely the young earl would not be a part of this!" Bryan attested but with a tone of skepticism.

"Does it matter to her Lady Wiliness? Verily, my own good master is not in his own mind. Why, he barely showed concern for his own daughter's whereabouts." There was a light tap on the door. "Ah, my warm ale!" He called to the door. "Come in, Tracy." He looked up at the worried knight. "The ale will warm your heart, good Bryan. Worry not; I shouldn't spew my concern. Rhonda will be fine."

"I pray to Christ you're right," Bryan said, mixing despondence with optimism.

The pretty lass entered, and in seeing Bryan her eyes glowed bright. She almost dropped the ale but quickly put it down on a table near the door. "Oh, thank God, the saints in heaven have finally awakened! Sweet Bryan, sir, have you news of Rhonda?" And the young lord...is he here? Oh, do tell me, sir, where is the master Lance — in his quarters? Surely, he's here and has come to rescue her."

"Nay thrice," he said sadly. She sniffled into her smock. She picked up the ale and put it down at a table near the bunk and smoothed the pillow. As a little girl she would never enter Elm's room without admiring the finer bed linen that he had earned over the years of loyal service to the Mari crest. When she later became more friend than handmaiden to Rhonda, she too earned the same and a private room, unlike most of the servants who had to sleep on coarse bedding of flaxen and straw. "Thank you, Tracy, you've been a good girl." She smiled and then turned a concerned look to Bryan.

"I hadn't realized that you remembered Tracy," Elm said, lapsing into one of his periods of forgetfulness. The young ones laughed more to break the tension of concern.

Bryan said smiling and taking her hand. "Old loyal Elm, you can remember what Lord Mari wore at his wedding, yet can't remember that I was the first to greet Tracy since her parents handed her over some years ago for their tallage much in arrears."

"Ah, yes, indeed I do now! Oh, what piercing arguments Lord Kalab had with the young master's mother over that!...Alas, she was already so ill, she yielded to his iron ways....Never before in the century old tradition of the Mari was such cruelty administered!"

"There you see? Now, I never knew that." Bryan chuckled. "Yet, I should have; for never did I meet a kinder person than Rhonda's mother."

"Oh, so true," Tracy chimed with a far away look, "and because of Lord Kalab's action, she took me into her heart, even though she was dreadfully weak from the slow, nagging illness....Oh, dear Sir Bryan, what are we to do?..." Her face scowled impatience. "Oh, why isn't the young lord here? Is he not the Lord-Protector and yet he is off meandering somewhere as an errant knight when his dearest sister needs deliverance!"

"Don't be harsh on him, Tracy. He really had no idea that Erinysia had turned his world upside down. But be comforted, for very soon he will be here to set things right side up again."

"Oh, yea, yea, I know he shall. But in the meantime my dear Rhonda,

I feel, is in danger."

His eyes flickered hope. "Then you do know of her whereabouts?"

"Nay, if only I did." Her eyes angled to the earthen floor.

"But at least your intuition spells danger only and therefore at least alive."

She looked up, flashing umbrage. "How else would I think of her—good heavens, dear knight!—even if I hadn't seen her leave the castle very early in the morning of her disappearance a fortnight ago."

"Oh, dear child," old Elm said as he beckoned to a chair, "come, sit down awhile and tell the young knight what you know."

"By all means, Tracy," Bryan added, while taking her hand, "please recount that day."

"Well, as you probably already know, she was dedicated to taking care of Stars, master Lance's mighty animal who so bravely carried master Lance through many battles."

"Yea, verily, but go on, my child," Elm said impatiently.

"Lady Rhonda was wont to bathe his wounds, then would mount her own horse and gently lead him to the pasture to graze. When she did not return I went looking for her." She wrung her hands momentarily, then raised her apron to her eyes. "All I could find was poor Stars at the edge of the pasture near death. I ran back for the stablehand. He later told me that Stars was dead when he got there. In the meantime, I had run to tell Master Kalab, but that mean old witch intercepted me on the stairs—with that awful cat in her arms—and forbade me to see him. She said she would relate my story to the lord master. She then told me, because I was hysterical, not to tell a soul, lest all in the castle worry needlessly."

"And did she tell the Master?" Bryan jumped.

"I doubt it; for it was another three days before Baron Bennet was informed by Master Kalab that the poor dear was missing and to conduct a search party."

"Oh, the castle truly is plagued by a witch!" cried the old man.

"All that time and you said nothing?" Bryan asked irritably.

She glanced up beseechingly. "Oh, sir Bryan, I feared for my life—she has searching black eyes that flare like coal! When the witch Erinysia told me to say nothing, I could feel that it was a warning as her frightful cat eerily caterwauled."

"I know, Tracy," Elm said sympathetically, putting a hand lightly on her pate; "she truly is foreboding and that cat from another world."

"Yea, verily it seems." Bryan nodded and asked, "And Baron Bennet—did he return with any news? Did he go to the old earl's castle?" Bryan pursued.

"He never went, my knight," she said. "At least that is what the stable-hands told me."

"He would stoop that low? Oh, far worse to lose the oath of chivalry to kin than the oath to a king!" Bryan's face gnarled and twisted toward the old man. "It seems, Elm, black magic indeed has hold of this place."

"But there is some light, Sir Bryan," Tracy offered. "You see, I overcame my fear and stole out of the castle to Sir John's tent. He promised he would immediately search for her."

"Ah, the loyal John!" He sighed. "Oh, Tracy, forgive me for my scolding you before. You are an angel—a very brave one."

"Thank you, kind sir, but I still wish I had gone to Sir John sooner."

"Don't be hard on yourself, my dear," Elm said, patting her on the cheek. "You did your best for which we are grateful. Now take young Bryan to Lord Lance's rooms to rest his travel-weary body."

"Aye, unfortunately I am exhausted, else I'd be off right now, but no, any old bunk right here in the servants' quarters will do. I must leave well before the crack of dawn."

Tracy escorted Bryan to a small room with a cot in the servant's quarters. At first she was going to offer him her room, but thought it might seem inappropriate. She seemed embarrassed when placing the candle near the straw bed with a heavy jute coverlet. "Are you sure, Sir Bryan, that you wish to sleep in this grimy bed?"

"You forget, dear Tracy, that most of the time we travel widely and sleep anywhere we can drop our saddle—preferably under a tree."

"Then, I imagine you are used to hideous animal calls in the wild—we have her damnable cat that wails all night. I think the witch left it behind to annoy us, but it terrifies me."

He laughed. "Well, at least it's not a mountain lion."

"Still it's awfully big and mean." She went to the door, then turned round. "I have a bowl of water in my room I didn't use. I'll be back with it so you can freshen up."

"Oh, you're so kind, Tracy, but really don't bother."

"No bother, it's natural with me. Been a domestic for many a year now," she said with a smile as she left, leaving the door open.

Bryan sat down on the bunk and wrestled off his boots. He clinked them to remove the peat and road dust, set them down and rubbed his stocking feet awhile. Then he took off his tunic, shook it vigorously and laid it on the back of a chair. He lay back on the bunk. In spite of its crudeness, it felt good to stretch. He had been spoiled by the royal hospitality of Lucia, and the kind nursing of Margaret. The long trip took its toll. He hoped Tracy would not return. He closed his eyes and within seconds was asleep only to be wakened by a scream and a bang. He ran to the doorway to find Tracy pressed against the wall in the passage way.

Spilled water and the wash bowl were on the floor. "What's wrong, girl?" he asked, now fully awake.

"That evil cat attacked me!" she wailed.

"You mean frightened you."

She shuddered and shook her head. "Oh, no, sir, it actually pounced on my back and clawed me!" She turned round to show the tear in the blouse.

He examined her back. "My, that is a mean scratch—more like a gash. It's broken the skin badly. Do you have any more water in your room?"

"Yea, I have a bowl set aside for Old Elm in the morning." He picked up the bowl on the floor and followed her into her relatively richly furnished room. Tracy sat down by a table where the bowl of water was, loosened her blouse to slide it down over her shoulders. "This is embarrassing, Sir Bryan."

He proceeded to bathe the scratches. He was astonished at the depth of the clawing. "Good grief, that cat must be from another world. You're actually bleeding."

"Verily? No wonder it hurts."

" Zounds, if I see that damnable cat, I'll lop its head off!" Bryan howled.

"It won't do any good," she said definitively . "You know what superstition says about felines—well, with this one it's doubly so that it must have eighteen lives, maybe more! Why, Old Elm has tried poison, but it just gets more ferocious. Even the cook swiped at it with his chopper—took its tail clean off—within an hour glass it grew back even longer!"

Bryan chortled. "Methinks you've added to the myth; or perhaps the superstition pertains only to the tail."

She glanced up over her shoulder briefly and said seriously, "Oh, no laughing matter, sir—mark, *this* is Erinysia's cat."

"Aye, from the same egg." He continued to bathe between her shoulder blades. He was taken in by the delicacy of her v-shaped back; she did not carry the usual healthy heftiness of a peasant girl. Shoulders, too, were sensuously sloped, though slightly bony. He flecked some silky strands covering the wound and placed them over her shoulder to join the abundant hair falling over the breast. He became unnerved. His legs wanted to drive him out of the room as he thought of Rhonda. Suddenly before his eyes the claw cuts vanished. He patted dry her back with a towel and looked again. He gently ran his fingertip over where the wound had been—silky smooth flesh with not a trace of disturbance. His finger continued its journey up to the shoulder and across to the other. Other fingers joined when the vanguard reached the nape and vacillated. Her shoulders momentarily tensed, then relaxed, and she wobbled her head which stopped and bowed when she felt his hot lips on her nape. His hands gently stroked her shoulders, then traveled down to her young breasts and twirling some silky shocks to assist in his fondling of their delightful fullness and smoothness.

Her face turned up and back hoping to find his eager lips as shivers took hold of her body. She sighed. "Funny, there's no more pain."

"That's because there's no more wound. An angel took pity and deemed no back as lovely as yours should be marred," he whispered nervously. "Loveliness conjures miracles."

She twittered, "It seems, Sir Bryan, you ought not to be a knight, rather a surgeon."

"Right now I wish to be only a lover." He caressed her cheek and his mouth found hers.

Her lips slid off his to squeal, "Oh, Sir Bryan, we mustn't—consider our dear Rhonda."

He pressed his lips to hers again, then relinquished for a moment to whisper, "Aye, we mustn't—'tis true—to think of Rhonda."

"Oh, dearest Bryan, though I am but a chambermaid, I see her as my dear friend. It would be wrong!"

"Perhaps but more wrong to pass up this wondrous moment—why, your loveliness is like an awakening—not unlike the excitement before battle!"

"Oh, dear, you mean to do battle with me?" she said with rising brows.

He guffawed and pulled her up from the chair to kiss her passionately, then whispered huskily, "Forgive me if I sound surprised, but you are indeed so lovely."

She put her cheek to his muscular chest and whimpered, "Ah, but not as lovely as the Lady Rhonda...were she here you would not know I exist."

He picked her up in his arms and said, "Well, now, she isn't here—think no more of it." He kissed her again and took her to the femininely modified crude bunk and gently laid her down.

While he was disrobing she protested softly, "Oh, we mustn't, dear Bryan! This,...this betrayal of our dearest friend."

He dropped his riding tights and pressed his groin onto her soft, limp, accepting body. She cried, "Oh, be gentle, my sweet."

He swallowed her words with his hungry mouth. She tightened her lips, jerked away, then whispered, "Please, kind knight, I've never done this before."

Bryan opened his eyes when the castle tolled the dawn. His head jerked to see Tracy next to him. He looked around and realized it was not the same room: the last thing he remembered was dozing off in the room Tracy assigned to him the night before. He shook Tracy. Her eyes fell on the proximity of his bare chest. She squealed, "Oh, my God, what has happened? What are you doing here?" She looked down at her bare breasts and spontaneously reached for the coverlet. She gasped, "Oh, my honor! Oh, Sir Bryan, how could you!"

"And what of my honor—my knight's honor?" He jumped out of bed and saw his pants in a heap on the floor. He bent down to retrieve them and was startled when the cat, growing twice its size, arched its back, from under the heap, leaped, grazing Bryan's shoulder with his claw, then vanished. Bryan dabbed his shoulder with the cloth from the night before. While squeezing into his pants and looking at the sobbing girl, he rued, "Oh, dear Tracy, this is as much a mystery to me as to you. That damn cat in truth is not of this world. It seems we've been bewitched. It is not as it seems." Tracy glowered at him and turned down the coverlet. Bryan mewled, "Oh, no, my dearest child!" as he stared at the blood stained sheet. "Oh, darling child, forgive me!" He fled from the room.

As a knight of combat Bryan was eager to try to locate the Mari forces, but as a knight of chivalry his concern was with Rhonda. The latter code took preference. When mounting his horse in the heavy morning mist he decided to head for the earl's manor, hoping she was under the protection of her friend Maureen. He signaled to the bridge-tender who raised the portcullis and lowered the bridge. The youthful knight mounted and cantered out of the castle gate as thunder rolled and rain thickened the early mist. His face turned to the watery sky diffused with lightning streaks as the thunder was displaced by the piercing caterwaul of the demoniac cat. He jerked his head at the shameful vision of waking with Tracy curled in his arms, ironically feeling secure, unaware at that moment her virginity had been ripped away by her protector.

Tracy rolled over, and wept into the pillow, then riled, "Oh, my sweet dear Lord Lance, I so much wanted to save this for you!" Her eyes opened by the flickering of lightning on the wall upon which loomed a large silhouette of the cat arching its back. She sat up and turned to the tiny window through which the enlarged cat illuminated its piercing eyes. In a trance she slipped on a robe and left the room and out into the ward, unaware of the teeming rain drenching her—aware only of the cat's hideous wails as though in rutting. Before the gatekeeper could lower the bridge in the blinding rain she crossed it; and wandered off, swallowed up by the thick atmosphere.

16. Captivity

All through the first night of her captivity, Rhonda had struggled with her binding trying to free herself from the churls of the highway. By dawn she was asleep; her cheek in the dewy sod. Sandy wrapped her in a foul robe and picked her up. He fastened her to her dun by wrapping rope round her boots and cinching it against the ankles, then girthed the mare. She offered no resistance as she was half asleep. "That's the good whore; accept your ways and we'll all be rich, once we get to Dawnport." He grinned over at his comrades, busy packing the donkey and the dray horse. He put the rein of her horse in his teeth and strode along.

The fat miller offered, "If you're not going to ride that fine animal, I'd like to—Dawnport is a long way."

Sandy pushed back his tattered feathered hat and grimaced. "You're dumber than I thought if you think I would let your weighted flab upon this expensive animal. Nay, at the marketplace it will heap three months supper for all of us."

"Yea, that noble animal," agreed the old man as he picked up his robe to straddle the donkey, "is worth a good twenty sides of venison—the trouble, Sandy, is we'll never get to sup on them."

"For want of your wonders, old man!—pray?" Sandy scowled.

"As sure as you're not a Jesuit, there's the sheriff who'll hang us the morning after!" the old man guaranteed him.

The miller laughed while successfully—in his third attempt—mounting the resistant, winnowing, ancient dray horse. Triumphantly straddled he said, " Zounds! and to add to the gloom, we'll hang twice for that prize tied to it!"

Sandy spit out the checkrein, ripped off his hat and threw it down on the road. He raised a fist. "Doomsayers!—*cholera morbus!* Why, you two are chapfallen flunkies to warlocks!"

"Chirrup on," cried the old man; "just remember, we ought not to be traveling the road under the sun."

"Bah, who's going to notice her in that raggedly cover," Sandy spouted.

"See here, Sandy, that's my church cloak!" yawped the miller.

Sandy glanced up at the groggy girl momentarily, then shot back at the fat man. "Yea, relic in truth!—since you haven't been to Mass since your First Communion!"

"Not so! I was married in the church!" the miller fretted with a scowling look.

Sandy laughed and reminded him, "By sword at your back!...Then abandoned the little mother, anyway!"

The old miller grunted, "Bah, she uncleanly bewitched me!" then heeled his dray horse.

Rhonda began to whimper and slump over further. Sandy leaped up on the mare's haunches, steadied her and said, "A chirp out of you and I'll put a muzzle on you, linguistic lass."

As they traveled the morning hours, Rhonda was becoming unmanageable, squirming and trying desperately to slide her feet out from the boots, despite Sandy's threats. In seeing some carters ahead moving in the opposite direction, she chanced screaming until she felt the tip of his blade at the small of her back. "Just one more peep and I stick this between your ribs!" he warned.

"Even though I'm valuable to you? I rather doubt it," she said bravely, though she did not dare yell out again. The carters, used to strange sights on the road between Castle City and Dawnport were indifferent and went right by them with only side glances at Sandy's tense grip on the hilt. and a dagger in his other hand. They were content that they got by without being robbed by the motley group.

"Verily, " he said when they passed, "you are a diamond in the rough; but remember, we have survived without you."

"Well you might have to, after all; since it is obvious you intend to starve me to death. I haven't eaten in over twenty-four tilts of the glass!"

"Ah, so you *are* of noble birth! Why, peasant girls have gone days without eating when their menfolk have a mind too." He reached into his goatskin bag and drew out a small piece of mutton, broke it off and handed her the smaller piece.

An hour after noon, they pulled into a grove to relieve themselves. Rhonda was totally mortified and refused to get down from the horse. "My, ye nobles are disciplined. You didn't even ask to 'uri' this morning," he snorted. "Afraid to remove the chaste-belt, I'll hazard."

Rhonda scowled. "How dare you pry! You incorrigible lout!"

But as they were ready to continue, she demanded to be untied and let down and to find privacy in the trees. He laughed, but agreed. With immodest alacrity, the miller wanted to escort her, but the old man checked him: "Come, now, find some decency under that flab of yours."

"Ah, that I have! Would you believe it? I was mistakenly circumcised by an infidel midwife!—clean as a maiden out of a hot tub I am!"

"Now I know why you always disgust me!" The old man chuckled and led him back to the dray horse. "There's your pleasure—what with your sensitive tool, I imagine the old dray's motion gives you plenty of thrills."

"Now who's disgusting?" the miller grunted.

Rhonda threatened to wet her undergarments if Sandy continued to follow her into the trees. He bellowed, "You win! I couldn't get a tuppence for you in a soiled, smelly chemette." He turned away and walked back some twenty paces while she headed another thirty paces before she found a tree distant enough. He cautioned, "You go any further and I swear, I'll not leave your cherry to the first customer!"

Behind the trees Rhonda, more mortified than frightened at this moment, cried and tears commingled with the puddly urine. She looked up through the trees and whimpered, "Dear Mother,...surely your immortal soul will help me!...Dispatch good Bryan to my rescue....Oh, my brother, you too hear my prayers!"

17. Lance and Lucia

"**O**h, I know you must go," Lucia pined. "It's selfish of me to detain you this long. I too have grown accustomed to the so natural feeling of being with you."

Lance nodded with a smile. "It seems love works that way. Strange, I go through life thinking I'm satisfied to a great extent being rather content within myself. And then when it strikes, I can't understand how I ever lived without you!" Lucia, misty-eyed, turned to pat the mane of his bay muzzling in the stable trough while Lance cinched the saddle of the buckskin. "Of course," he added, "I did carry with me for many a year the wonderful legend of a princess." He smiled at her as she gazed at him "Apparently," he said, it was fate that Stars was badly damaged in battle. "I had thoughts for sometime about an altogether different kind of war charger, but I never would have followed through until old Stars was ready for the pasture."

"How flattering!" she said petulantly. "I owe our love to a horse!" She drifted over to him and lovingly punched his arm.

He chuckled. "Not entirely true,...don't forget the haunting princess in my head....So, you see, I really did come up here because I sensed you would indeed be here to tantalize my heart."

"No matter, I'm just happy you did." She tenderly rubbed his arm as if to soothe a bruise from her mock punch. "Lance, you really meant what you said the other night? That you would actually give up your high position after the rumbling down there is over and return here?"

He glanced down at her wonderfully dark but warm eyes, and said softly, "Aye, and not only what I said in the valley but just now: I can't imagine life any longer without your presence."

"But what of knighthood and your duty to the Mari? I wouldn't want to be the cause of your abandoning your ideals," she said, showing legitimate concern.

"Once a knight always one, I suppose. After all, I'd still be your champion."

"Why, Lance, how sweet!" She hooked her arm in his.

"As far as the Mari is concerned, I should leave it in good hands. And if they need me I shall be on call—provided, of course, all's well here and safe to leave you for a spell."

A brief smirk crossed her lips, then she smiled. "Hmm,...yea, I should have to live with that and promise to be understanding."

He grinned and chortled. "Understanding, eh?—like last night when you so abruptly cut short my advances."

"Understanding cuts two ways, my love," she said. "But, Lance, I'm surprised; you never let on that it bothered you."

He chuckled. "My training in the arts of chivalry, I should imagine, but more my infinite respect in itself for you." He stroked the golden strands cascading one side of her face. "I'm ashamed that I brought it up like some frustrated farm boy trying to lure a kitchen maiden into the barn."

She giggled. "Oh, Lance, you're being crude. And don't be so hard on yourself....Why, as faithfully as the lava bubbles behind and below the castle, I thought you were a perfect gentleman."

"Then, by God's oath, we should marry," he announced curtly—surprising himself.

Her eyes popped and she smiled sheepishly. "Why, dear Lance, you've never broached this before." And then she laughed at a comical image in her mind: or is Cicero correct that in the folds of your mind lurks in kind the political plots of an Angus?" He looked dumbfounded, and she laughed again more intensely and added to the quip: "If not me, my mother then?"

He half smiled, and replied, "When you become queen, you can also be your own court jester, eh? Besides, your wild joust does not take into account the high ethics of chivalry....Please, Lucia, do not mock me! You know by now intrigue is not my bent."

"But to do battle and love of knighthood are your natures. Perhaps I would not be understanding. How could I lead my country while my husband is off to war in behalf of his country and not mine?"

"Surely, you don't expect me to renounce my country, nor my Order altogether!"

"Of course not," she said indignantly, then grinned. "However, now that you mentioned it...." They both laughed. "You know, Lance, were I a commoner, you'd expect me to become a Quandronian."

"Aye, without question, on the other hand, were I not a landholder and of noble blood, I should unhesitatingly remain forever by your side as your husband and champion." Then he smiled and added, "Of course, were I a peasant, you'd have nothing to do with me."

"Why, Lance, that's unkind of you!" She sulked and reached for some hay to feed the buckskin. Then she turned to him and looked over his shoulder as though someone were coming, but in fact, she saw something in her mind and said strangely, "It is all academic anyway."

"What's this? Have you been misleading me?"

"Nay, a thousand times nay!...I truly love you; I was referring to the two countries. I mentioned before I sense a proximity to Quandron now...as if strangely linked and not just geographically. I cannot explain it further, but mark me, something like that will come to pass."

"Perhaps, not so strange, after all," he answered, "because of our being at one."

"Yea." She nodded while with her thumb she tufted his beard over his scar. "I'm sure of it," she added; "in truth, it conjured up this feeling, yet I think it goes beyond even that."

"Sounds ominous. I hope it doesn't mean you become united by marrying Young Henry! I couldn't bear it!"

"Lance! Shame on you for such a thought!...No,..." touching her lips with her finger, "my intuition envisions no such thing. It is a blur of commoners of north and south joining hands in the valley and children of both lands dancing merrily in the rolling plains of Quandron."

He kissed her on the cheek, then drew back and laughed kindly. "It seems, my love, this intuition comes with scenery; why then may it not ladle up a crown of Henry's."

"Oh, Lance, you are usurping my position as court jester that you just now granted me!" She waved a little hand in front of him, then smiled coquettishly and asked, "Why must intuition be doomed to dark shadows while thought itself struts freely into the sunshine of the mind?"

"Oh, my sweet darling, feel free to strut whenever you wish!—I love it!" he said, squeezing her hand.

She swept away all other matters and raised her heels and hung her arms round his nape, then softly addressed her anxiety, "My dear, brave knight, I shall miss you deeply."

"And I you, my love." They kissed long and soft.

She whisked her tears with her fingertips and nervously chuckled. "As much as your old horse?" She chuckled.

He laughed. "That'll depend on how well I do with this new beauty you gave me." He patted the nose of the buckskin.

"Oh, his speed will more than make up for the minor loss of strength," she assured him. He then embraced her again, craving for an instant—that she indeed were but a peasant beauty permitting him to sweep her onto the buckskin and ride north.

"Then, you really must go?"

"Aye, I must—if for no other reason than to see to Rhonda's welfare."

"Of course, apparently no one is safe in your homeland, 'tis unthinkable how your country thrives on political intrigue as though all down there were soiled as our Angus."

"My country hasn't the luxury of your nation's long tradition and stability."

"Henry, then, is not of divine right?" She squinted surprise, though she already intuited he was not.

He laughed. "Oh, I suppose a case could be made, like the longest family tree."

"What, no mighty deeds, no magic sword imbedded in a rock?" She tittered.

He grinned and replied seriously, "We are a realistic lot."

"Yea, and I suspect, why your father, too, thinks he is entitled to the throne as well."

"How so?" he asked, spreading surprise across his face.

"Well, why not he out of the blue like Henry? Was not Henry but another warlord?"

"Nay, but his father was."

"So why shouldn't your father have the right to contest the throne?"

Lance laughed and squeezed her in his arms. "Be careful, my love; you shall be giving ladies-in-waiting designs on your throne. Nay, you forget one important aspect: the Document."

"Ah, but it is not a mysterious tablet inscribed in ancient times as my ladies are well aware of ours."

"Granted not as dramatic, still, an agreement by honorable men is just as enduring."

"Oh? No women, eh?" She chortled. "But I take it your witch intends to change all that."

"Aye, and why I must no longer trifle here."

"So, that's what you call it!" She jerked away and tended to the bay warhorse.

He reached for her arm and pulled her close to him. She mildly resisted. He kissed her on the ear. "My love, forgive me. I meant it only within the rigors of knighthood."

"In the end,...knighthood is all that really matters," she said petulantly.

He pulled her gently to him. "Nay, you have stormed my heart! My remark came from the bowels of my country, which, I swear, if I stay another day I shall renounce in favor of my locking you in my arms forever."

Just then a castle guard ran through the stable passage. He cleared embarrassment from his throat and said, "Excuse me, your highness, but there is a messenger awaiting your goodly knight at the conference hall."

Gregory, stared into his tankard in seeing across the table the stunned, yet incredulous look of Lance after having heard the news. "My father *and* Bennet, you say?"

"Aye, my lord, both." He fondled the tankard as if indecisive about taking another quaff. "Our code of knighthood has gone to hell, it seems." He took a hefty draft, then crashed the tankard on the table.

"And fatherhood!" Lance added angrily. He looked askant at Lucia who was some distance away, pacing nervously. "I'm sick, Gregory, to think that I left the scene like the errant king who went abroad to fight a distant religious war while his country boiled in treachery." Lance decided to join Gregory in drink.

"Then I hesitate to tell you more." Gregory gulped down some more wine.

"Oh, better, I trust, for never could there be worse."

"Your sister has not been heard from."

"What cryptic gist is this? Speak!" Lance's brows arched and his knuckles bleached round his tankard handle. "God, so help me, if a hair on her innocent head..."

"We just don't know, my lord. She has disappeared from the castle of Mari."

"Oh, no! A hundred tentacles to Erinysia's witchcraft!" He jumped up from the table and tossed the tankard into the hearth. "Three hours rest for you, Gregory, no more and away we must."

Lucia moved toward him. "No, Lance, though you are rightfully upset. The late hour and now the rain forbids haste. Let this good man sleep the night; by the morn you shall both be fresh."

He cast controlled resentment at her, then turned to Gregory. "Aye, the princess is right. And selfish of me after your long journey. Indeed, refresh yourself and rest the night."

"Thank you, my lord." Gregory emptied his tankard.

Lucia signaled one of the guards. "Escort this loyal knight to Lord Lance's rooms while I speak to Lord Lance alone."

Lance paced the floor, then turned when the guard and Gregory left. "Oh, good queen, words will have no meaning now. Foremost is my darling sister. Henry, the nation and its intrigues be damned!"

She touched his arm and said, "My sentiments are with you—still, you are not yourself right now."

"Oh, more than ever now—a wretched, irresponsible brother!"

She laid her hands upon his face. "Nay, my dear, twist the finger of blame to the south. You cannot be headstrong and jeopardize all the more your dear Rhonda and unthinkingly embark on revenge. Rather, think this out; for I see it as a larger scene and for the time your sister is safe." She caressed his beard and looked up lovingly. "Trust me, even though you take my intuition lightly."

"The sweet word *safe* makes a believer of me," he said brokenly. He cleared his voice and pronounced, "But duty and honor call. Damn my country! It's clear to me now that I *will* return to your arms—all else but the immediate unfinished business at hand is dwarfed."

"Oh, Lance, would that you consent I send my longbowmen along in search of your dear sister!"

"Nay, that would but slow down the trip back."

"Nevertheless, Lance, how do you know that even your own men by now have not been infected with witchcraft?" she inquired with alarm.

"You heard faithful Gregory. Sir John will not succumb."

"Perhaps, but what can you do with a handful, however courageous they doubtless are?...Lance, I'm frightened." She clung to him.

"Have no fear. I shall get to Henry, and together we shall succeed." He said confidently.

"Oh, that woman—sorceress!" she cried. "Why, methinks she even affected Dane and the others."

"Very possible—granted my father is ambitious, but always checked by the Mari honor. This parasite has spread a plague. I'm now not sure how far she will go."

"What do you mean?"

"I know your people are rather skeptical of us lowlanders, thinking we have designs on your borders. As long as Henry's kingdom is retained that shall never come to pass. Why, even my father, under my grandfather's tutelage, respected your borders. And Henry, with his ties to your mother, surely. But now I'm not so sure, my love, that even you and your country are safe with this wild woman. It is imperative that we stop her."

"You think she's that powerful?"

"Aye, unless Gregory is a tall-tale teller or bewitched himself. So, my dear, think not on my abandoning you, rather, that I too champion you." He again embraced her. "I must reluctantly bid you good night. I shall leave before the cock crows. Wish me God speed."

"Yea, good night, verily—goodbye, nay—for I shall join you in the morning with the full force of my army."

He broke his embrace. "Nay, I cannot allow that!...I fear with my babbling I alarmed you! What you propose is madder still!"

"You seem to forget that I do not take orders. Is it madness to put an end to madness?—for I see it all clearly now...yea, intuition does indeed strut from out of its shadows."

18. Maureen & David

A dowdy nurse of the earl's daughter escorted Bryan to a locked room in the keep tower of the earldom. "You'll be able to talk to the dears through the serving peep, sir."

"What!" Bryan blurted angrily, "This is an outrage! No one here has seen fit to free them?"

She shook her head and looked up with confusion in her eyes. "Oh, no, sir, no one dares defy the orders of the fierce Baron Bennet!"

"Bennet!" he cried as though it still had not sunk in. When Gregory had told him that he suspected Bennet's treachery, Bryan was skeptical until he crossed the border and saw the Baron's coat of arms on many of the dead. "Zounds, what sort of sorceress is this that can turn the finest into monsters!" he wailed.

"Ah, then, you too can taste the foul witch's deadly brew!" The nurse said, then called through the peep of the heavy oak door, "My dearies, are you there?"

"Obviously!" answered an angry youthful voice. The young Earl came to the aperture. "You will pay dearly for this betrayal, nurse!"

"Oh, my kind young master, find it in your heart to forgive a fearful old woman," she sputtered remorsefully. "Still, I'd rather your gentler justice than the ferocious stroke of the baron's blade."

The young earl frowned at Bryan. "And who are you?—one of Bennet's treacherous dogs?"

"Nay, from the honorable legion of Lord Lance."

The young man gripped the serving sill, smiled and yelped, "Glory be to God!"

"Yea!" high pitched another voice. A young girl about the same age as Rhonda ran to her brother's side. "Why, of course, I know you. You are Bryan! Rhonda so often speaks of you!"

"Aye, and she of you....Your fears, Maureen, are at an end. I shall have you out of here at once." He turned to the nurse. "Fetch me the chatelain immediately."

"But, Sir Bryan, the key-keeper keeps no more. They are in possession of one of the Baron's knights left behind to oversee our every move."

Bryan looked at her skeptically. "Then why was I admitted without resistance?"

She shrugged but ventured, "I suppose the bridge-tender thought you were sent from the Baron."

"And where can I find this unknightly knight who now keeps the keys?"

The nurse wrinkled her round face. "Oh, as is his custom, with one of the kitchen wenches. I think he's slept with every one of them thrice over already. I'll take you to the old earl's apartments. I'll wager that's where he is between the sheets and soft flesh—oft he has pairs with him." She turned to the peep. "We'll be back, dearies, for now my hope swells with the strong hand of one of the Lord-Protector's loyalists!"

Bryan followed the nurse back down the winding steps and through an arch leading to the passage way to the deceased earl's rooms. She pressed her ear to the door, then nodded to Bryan. She stepped away, then light-footed back to the arch, leaning her back to it. Bryan unlatched the door and flung it open, his hand upon the hilt as he entered. A blubbery bare, hairy chested rogue abruptly sat up in the huge bed, his mouth agape. A young girl, barely of pubic age howled and jumped from the bed nude. She reached for her calico dress and held it up to her delicate, undeveloped body. When Bryan drew his massive sword, she fell to her knees. The startled man jumped up, wrapped the coverlet round his stocky body and knitted his heavy brows, inquiring, "What is this intrusion?—how dare you!"

"Nay, how dare you dishonor knighthood by your treachery and, as I see now, bedding with a mere child!" Bryan riled. "On with your pants, dog, so I can kill you honorably." He leveled his sword at the shaking man who dropped his wrapping and wiggled into his britches. Bryan spotted the keys on a table and motioned to the girl. "Take the keys to the nurse outside; then, young lass, get you to the chapel to cleanse your soul." The girl repeatedly and submissively nodded as she crossed in front of him to retrieve the keys. "And for God's sake put on your dress," he ordered. The girl complied hurriedly and ran out of the room, sniffling. Bryan stepped over to a chair where a sword and girth hung. He drew out the sword.

His pants up, still several inches under his bulging belly, the knight observed nervously, "I see from the crest that you are one of Lord Lance's men."

"And so were you, I gather, as was Bennet till this betrayal of the king, and to me, worse that he defiled the detachment flag of the Mari!" Bryan excoriated him, holding up the renegade's sword.

Tensely the self-appointed key-keeper, abruptly corrected the menacing sight in front of him, "Not true, swordsman, I was one of the old earl's castle knights."

"Then you are doubly treacherous! Especially in smearing the memory of the good earl by abandoning his children!" answered the righteous knight.

"Now, let's be reasonable, my good man. What say you espouse the new cause and join Bennet's ranks? And I shall overlook this violation," the renegade offered dumbly.

Brian laughed. "You, dog, are the violator! Bennet's ranks, you say?

Surely you mean the witch Erinysia's who now seems to be in command....And are we forgetting the old warlord Kalab altogether? You are indeed a dishonest man. Had I more time I'd have you hanged in the ward, so unworthy of my knighted blade." He tossed the frightened man the sword.

"But sir, unworthy verily, for I am no match for you. That's why I've been left behind."

"Your foreboding is true. I shall make short work of you. But treacherously skilled you are enough to scare the wits out of the staff, molest children and lock up the earl's dear brood." Bryan aimed his blade inches from the protruding belly. "My sense of honor to redress your infractions diminishes all your lowly fears."

"Kind, sir, yea, your honor is too high for the likes of me. I am guilty, true, but I possess none of your skillful morality. I, like the underlings, shrink before the menacing baron." He fell to his knees. "And now I shrink before you and beg mercy."

"Stand like a man; up with your blade, coward."

"Aye, coward I am!" The fat man dropped his sword and fell supinely, moaning into the floor.

"Then die a coward!" Bryan raised his sword to thrust, but hesitated. His honor prohibited him. He sheathed his sword and pulled the groveling man to his feet. "Then you shall exchange the children's cell for the rest of your miserable life."

The fat man, gratified that he was unworthy to be called a knight, blessed himself and said, "Oh, gladly! Aye, under lock and key forever—ah, to go on breathing..."

At the cavernous dining hall, the siblings were feasting on a heaping platter of assortments they had not seen since their three week long incarceration. Bryan watched them with satisfaction as he drank from his tankard. Young Lady Maureen heaved a sigh, dipped her dainty fingers in a bowl of water, dried them with a towel and sat back in the chair that seemed to swallow her. "My dear Bryan, I thank you again for my freedom, but I shall hold you accountable if I turn into a pig." She twittered. "So much have I stuffed myself, I must seem to you to have an apple imbedded in my mouth."

He grinned. "Trust me, little Lady Maureen, no such grotesque vision has caught my eyes." His expression turned grim as he leaned forward. "I fear, however, the speculation concerning Rhonda's fate. Having been captive, you, of course, know nothing, I gather?"

She gripped the arms of the huge chair and arched thin brows. "What's this—my darling Rhonda is missing?"

"Aye, and thankfully—having stumbled on your grim situation—why I came here, thinking that she had sought refuge here."

Pushing his plate away, the young earl joined in. "Thankful, indeed, good Bryan, but how now this sad news of Rhonda? What would bring about her wanting refuge?"

"The wicked Erinysia," Bryan said curtly.

The young earl frowned. "Ah, yea, how familiar we are of our so-called stepmother and her evil ways!"

"Yea, verily the dear would have come here if in trouble," Maureen cried out.

"Yea, and from cauldron to raging fire," the brother said, snarling.

"Still, she could've come here and seen Bennet's siege and decided against it." Maureen suggested.

Bryan looked surprised. "But she trusted Bennet." Then he wondered if Bennet could possibly be so deeply under a spell to do harm to the sister of the Lord-Protector.

"And so did I." Maureen said.

"Aye, I see," Bryan said, while his thumb absently flapped the tankard lid repeatedly.

Maureen broke the silence. "Pray, she is safely with the king."

Her brother snickered. "Little consolation what with old Kalab probably storming the castle this very moment."

"Surely her own father would see that no harm comes to her," she said.

"Aye," Bryan agreed, "provided the old man is in his own mind."

"Slim chance with Erinysia in control," the young earl said grimly while stroking the new phenomenon of stubble on his chin from his captivity.

She wailed, "Oh, that woman! Once my stepmother! Ugh!"

Bryan drank down the ale and added, "Furthermore, I don't trust the king. If Rhonda's there he might decide to hide behind her skirt by holding her for a ransom or a deal to save his own neck."

Maureen squealed, then laughed. "Oh, good Bryan,...why, that's treason, yet it strikes me funny!"

His brother chided her, "It doesn't strike me that way." He turned to Bryan. "And you too...I shall forget you said that, Sir Bryan—after all, you're upset over Rhonda."

Maureen shot back, "Oh, my brother, you are too serious." Then she giggled. "Maybe I would be too if young Henry were king—he's so handsome!" She had a good laugh, then burned a serious stare onto her brother, adding, "You know very well that our father always felt the elder Henry didn't have the qualities to be king and simply tolerated him. You heard him say that above all the first king of a new nation must be extraordinary."

"Aye, I concede; he did in truth. But as implied he accepted him in spite of it for the sake of peace."

The cup-bearer poured more wine for Bryan, as the knight looked over at the brother, "Tell me, your grace, what is it you plan to do now?"

The young earl looked back with searching eyes. "With the earldom in disarray, I simply don't know."

"Surely, you must retrieve your army," Bryan offered matter-of-factly, "before they perpetrate treason—if they haven't already."

"But will they listen?"

"Good grief, David, they must respect the memory of our father!" Maureen shrieked.

"Aye, verily, it is our birthright."

"And our pressing duty either way is to press onto Henry's castle," Bryan said urgently. He glanced over at Maureen. "You, Lady Maureen, should remain here and reassert castle authority. I have already had the skeletal force here to swear before me their renewed loyalty to the earldom."

"Nay, sweet Bryan, I go where my brother goes—nor could I rest here thinking of dear Rhonda's fate."

19. The Prince

Some ten days before Bryan's return, outside the port city, the ruffians camped at dusk for the night. To the relief of her olfactory nerve, Rhonda, because the evening was warm, immediately removed the smelly robe when Sandy positioned her close to where they were starting a fire for cooking. She drew up her knees and buried her face in her hands, unable to take in the phantasmagoric situation she was in. She choked back the cries deep within and prayed. As Sandy was leaning over to strike the fire, she, grimacing painfully, peeked between her fingers at the sword tucked in Sandy's frayed sash. Suddenly she lunged and in one sweeping motion she grabbed the hilt with her two hands and jumped to her feet to hold them at bay. Brandishing the blade threateningly before them, she back-pedaled toward the mare. The fat miller laughed and reached for his dagger hanging from his rope belt until she deftly parried and slashed the back of his hand from which he yelped in sharp pain. Rhonda dexterously maneuvered the sword before their surprised eyes and warned, "Indeed, you subcommoners, I know how to use this—how could you think otherwise, knowing I am the sister of the greatest swordsman in the kingdom?" The young one, nevertheless, stalked toward her. She backed up faster, turned her head to reach for the reins of the mare.

Instantly Sandy leaped toward her but she quickly reeled and sunk the swift blade in his arm. He shrilled, "My arm! You bitch!...Why, you've been baptized in witches' brew!" He started toward her but felt the tip of the blade in his chest as she extended her arms. He backed off, dropping to his knees to nurse his arm.

She, still gripping the sword, released one hand and mounted her mare. The fat one, having tried to suck the pain from his wounded hand, again reached for the dagger. Balancing the point he took aim. Comically it fell like a wounded duck far short of its target. Rhonda heeled her horse and headed in the opposite direction, favoring the dark highway to the fearsome city of cutthroats she had heard about. Sandy rose up in disgust, scowling at the miller while picking up the dagger. He ran after the mare; as it gained ground he poised, and with his good arm he was about to fling the weapon till he heard pounding hoofs behind him. The horseman had been riding out of the city and immediately had spurred his horse to fast gait when he noticed the distressing scene ahead. He easily overtook Sandy who reeled and had to jump out of the way lest he be run down; he ran back to camp.

Rhonda turned in her saddle; then sighed and slowed to a trot when she saw the dark horse turn abruptly toward the grove encampment to but a few paces from their fire. A young handsome nobleman, very finely dressed, drew his sword and arced it down slowly toward the men. Rhonda quickly returned and pulled up her mare. She chose to remain mounted and slid the sword out from under her belt. The stranger addressed her, "I trust, good lady, that you do not wish to remain in the company of these rogues."

"I certainly do not, kind sir, " she responded and bridled round her horse.

He smiled broadly, showing clean white, noble teeth "I suggest you ride with me." Rhonda, nodded, sliding the sword back under her belt, and gladly complied while clinging to her horse's bridle. He bridled round to face her captors and warned, "If I see you thieving kidnappers along this trail again, be assured I shall run the three of you through with a busy blade."

The old man bowed. "But, my lord, you are taking this the wrong way. We never intended, your very highness, to do harm to this poor girl in distress."

The fat man wobbled closer and then bowed again, saying, "True, true, our prince, we meant only to feed her for her journey."

"Enough of this," the young nobleman interjected, "I know the ways of you highwaymen and your lame excuses. You are to break up this camp and leave the kingdom at once or spend the rest of your days in my father's dungeon unless I decide to kill you personally."

The fat one untied the donkey as the old man scurried about in preparation for breaking camp while the young one bemoaned his lost treasure and mounted the dray horse.

When the prince sidled alongside her. He arched his brows and sputtered, "Good grief! If it isn't little Rhonda!—how is this possible?"

For the first time in quite a spell, she laughed. "I'll tell you, good prince, while we ride. The quicker I'm away from those louts the safer I shall feel.... I thought I recognized you."

"Then, with your being without a saddle, would you care to ride with me?" he asked.

"No, thank you, your highness, I've ridden this way many times—though granted, not for any distance. But, I'm fine—just happy to be free of these grimy clutches."

Rhonda and her rescuer rode hard for an hour. She slowed to a trot and said, "Good sir, my mare is not used to the hard riding I've put her through these past two days." They dismounted and walked the horses for a while. He observed that her mare was very tired.

"Well, my lady, we shan't make the castle tonight, nor an inn for that matter. Around the bend in the road there are sheltering trees under which we can spend the night," Prince Henry suggested.

"Oh, my," she murmured in jest, "that doesn't sound very proper coming from a prince, especially." She had remembered the prince from when he paid his respects to her mother's passing and knew him as a perfect gentlemen.

"No fear, I shall find a tree a good distance away." He laughed. "We have no other choice. There is not a farm house for miles yet. And it is too dangerous for us to continue along the road at night—especially with a tired horse."

She agreed, "Yes, dangerous in the daytime as well—besides, my horse needs the rest more than we."

The prince nodded in agreement. "Yes, I gathered your steed is most important. I wouldn't dare suggest a while back that we abandon your filly."

"In the Mari tradition, we Kalabs are as loyal to our steeds as they to us," she prompted the prince with a dazzling smile. Rhonda was famished and devoured an apple the prince had in his saddle bag. In seeing this he gave her his apple too, which she politely rejected. He unsaddled his horse and placed the saddle under the tree, spread out his cloak for Rhonda to lie on and cover herself while he picked out a distant tree to prop up against.

She cried out after him, "Oh, my lord, there is no need for you to be that far away. I would feel safer if you were somewhat closer—not too close, you understand," adding a giggle. "Besides, I am not sleepy, even though I have had horribly eventful days."

He stepped toward her and sat down next to her and propped himself on his elbow, "There, I can see your eyes now. I don't like talking to a shadow. I don't think I should make a fire; it would draw attention."

"Tell me, prince, what have you been doing so far from the castle?—and coming from the notorious Dawnport, no less! I trust you didn't lose your way in a hunt."

"No, I'm no huntsman. I don't like killing. I know that sounds cowardly since I enjoy a good meal of pheasant or venison. I suspect, if we didn't have plenty of huntsmen to fill the castle storerooms, I should have to settle for barley and roots."

She laughed. "Sounds sensible to me, rather than cowardly—and, of course, hypocritical. I am guilty of the same. I dare not look in the eyes of our livestock....And, I hear that the poor at Dawnport wait at the pier—oh, I shiver from its grotesqueness—for foreign rats to disembark so they can sup on them." He laughed. She squinted at his shadow. "You know, I don't like talking to blank faces either. Please turn round so the moon falls on you." He raised up and adjusted himself. "There I can see your eyes now....You still haven't told me you've been doing in that horrible city."

"Oh, nothing really,...the king sent me along with the castle guards to insure against the theft of an arrow shipment from Lodeston. It's fortunate that I got bored, leaving the men to tend to the carters. I hate to think what might have happened to you had I not decided to chance the highway when I did, rather than wait till morning. Not that I'm anxious to return to the tedious court scene. My mouth and ears are not prone to the verbal nonsense that goes on at the castle."

"Strange coming from a prince, I should think you would relish that—after all, what else is there to politics but tongue wagging," she said with a chuckle. "I certainly got enough of it from listening to my father and brother."

"Oh, really? I thought your famous brother was too busy fighting battles to be bothered with the political side of power."

"Well, yes, that part is true. But this last time he came home he was in constant argument with my father."

"Yes, of course, your father, I heard he's in disagreement with mine."

Her lovely teeth shone in the moonlight as she shook her head and laughed. "Yes, I hear too. But nothing serious, you understand,...I mean, he is, of course, loyal to the Crown."

"Yea, I'm sure he is, " he said unconvincingly.

She yawned. "I think I'm ready to close my eyes now....Oh, by the way, how coincidental—Lance is in Lodeston. I hope he's home by now."

"Really, and what is he doing there?"

"Oh, he's looking for a Pegasus, I suppose, to replace his faithful mount that was wounded severely."

"Yea, they do have fine steeds, but inappropriate for knights."

"I'm surprised to hear that the king would have dealings with those barbarians."

He laughed. "Well, actually they refuse to engage in diplomatic relations with us—a very ancient grudge."

"Then why the shipment?" she asked.

"Oh, it was arranged by an exporter from Spain. Lodeston doesn't know it was for us; otherwise, it would've been carted overland."

"Oh, my, do you think my brother could be in danger up there?"

He laughed again. "The world renowned Protector in danger? Hardly!" He raised himself up and covered her as she rested her head on the saddle. He stepped away to the nearest tree and leaned up against it. She felt secure with him—in spite of one noble's betrayal already—and had little trouble falling asleep, though she kept the highwayman's sword by her side.

An hour glass or so after the rescue, the daring highwaymen, who, having lost their treasure, decided to return to the outskirts of the castle city. Along the way, they discovered the escapee's camp. The churls kept watch some hundred yards from Rhonda and her rescuer.

20. Lance's Call to Duty

Lance's protests again the next morning fell on Lucia's deaf ears. She had alerted her band of men the night before to prepare for the journey to Quandron. The two knights cantered out of the cave to the assemblage of five hundred horsemen strong, mostly longbowmen. "Are you not glad that I insisted you wait till morning?" asked Lucia smiling, her eyes sparkling across Gregory and Lance, whose heart beat over her long blonde hair burnt pink streaks from dawn's light diffusing the peaceful valley. Her great white horse sidled the larger buckskin stallion worthy to be Lance's new charger. She motioned for the band to follow, then looked up at Lance. "With such beautiful weather as this we should make short work of your destination."

"Aye, there's no arguing with a woman's intuition. But I hate to disillusion you, dear Lucia, for weather is far different—often inclement—once we leave the valley and your protective mountains."

"Yea, I know from my mother. Well, we shall enjoy it while it lasts." As the long column of daring men laced through the valley trail, a sprawling black cloud rolled swiftly over the formation. Lucia laughed. "Serves me right for boasting!" She brought forward her hood as heavy drops increased in speed. Suddenly it was a fierce driving rain as gusts swept through the valley. At first the horsemen quickened the gait as though there were cover to take. The foot soldiers too ran but not for long as the rain became so torrential and blinding, men and horses were crisscrossing and bumping into each other.

Over the howling winds, Lance bellowed, "Stay, men, hold the steeds. We can only hope it ends in a moment." He felt over for Lucia and he locked her to him.

"How very strange, Lance," she shrieked to the rainy winds, not being able to see his face. "I swear, this is no native storm. Never has there been anything like this."

"Aye, I agree." he wailed. "There wasn't a cloud in the sky but a minute ago."

"I wonder,...nay, foolish tales...still, Indra..."[1]

"Who?"

"Oh, no, impossible." She satisfied her own questioning.

A prodigious squall moved in. Clattering shields and spears were in the air. Lance shrieked, "Hold onto your gear, men!" to no avail, so deafening was the wind. He lost touch with Gregory and heard Lucia scream. He reached out for her. She was not in her saddle. He slid off his steed and carefully let himself down, not knowing where she was and careful not to let go the reins, lest she be stomped. "Lucia, Lucia, why aren't you answering?" He stretched his arm in the vicinity and felt nothing but debris. He had to chance letting go the reins. He heaved relief when he felt a young tree and gratefully wrapped the reins round it. Untethered and on hands and knees he felt round and muttered his blessings when he felt her drenched hair and hood. "Oh, my Lucia, are you all right? Speak to me. He touched her face and traced his finger to her lips. which quivered; he softly pressed his lips to hers, then uttered, "Lucia, Lucia."

He felt her squirm in his arms and then moan. He held her tight and kept his body over her to protect her from the stinging, driving gusts. For thirty minutes the legion was immobilized and then as suddenly as it began the fury spent itself. Another half hour was spent for the band to reorganize—archers gathering their caps, bows and arrows, the royal guards hunting down their spears. Next they dried off their steeds and saddle gear, all dried their shirts and tunics while some helped the carters edge the wheels out of muddy ruts. Lance bathed Lucia's bruise from something that grazed her cheek during the driving rain.

She would not listen to him when he begged her to return. He and Gregory moved about the ranks to tend to dozens, who fortunately were not badly hurt. One, however, was seriously kicked by a horse. Villagers carried him to a nearby house. Finally the contingent continued on and proceeded up the trail exiting the valley into the mountain pass.

---

[1]Hindu god of rain and thunder

21. Another Attempt

The highway rogues very early broke watch and stole upon the opening of the woods. While the sandy-haired one crept toward Rhonda to retrieve his sword, the others jumped the sleeping prince who quickly woke and fought them off but not before the fat one had wrested away the prince's sword. The miller held the prince at sword's length while the old man started to tie his hands behind his back.

To the chagrin of the sandy-haired highwayman, shaking his head that they had attacked the prince too soon, he looked up at Rhonda whose sword point was but inches from his beard, follicles of which tingled near his throat. Still braced against the tree trunk, Rhonda slid back up onto her feet, keeping the sword with both hands steady at his throat. She looked over at the prince. "It appears our recent acquaintances have come for early breakfast," she said, then chuckled. "'Tis a pity we cannot accommodate them."

The fat man looked over perplexedly. The prince kicked the sword from the pudgy, inept hand. The old man flinched and Prince Henry slipped his hands from the loose rope and retrieved his sword. "I'd kill you both on the spot if you weren't such pathetic fools." He picked up the rope intended for him, then threateningly brandished the sword, warning, "Stay fixed in prayer to Assisi that I too at the moment have his forgiving saintliness."

But Sandy abruptly scampered from the blade point when Rhonda was distracted by the prince's action. The young outlaw daringly leaped at the prince and knocked him down. The other two men quickly pounced on young Henry and tied him to a tree while Sandy held Rhonda at bay.

Determined not to become imprisoned again, she chanced engaging in a duel. She knew he did not know how, yet she was not sure she could deal with the others if they too charged her. She held the sword high and stalked him, circling round him ever closer while keeping her eye on the other two. The miller rose up from tying the prince. He gripped the dagger in his bandaged hand and began to move in on her.

The prince yelled out, "Rhonda, please! Don't do this! I can make a deal—a handsome ransom when they come to their senses!"

"A deal?" repeated the miller as he turned back to him. Just then Rhonda wielded the sword and gashed the miller's shoulder blade. He let out a howl and fell to the ground, groaning in pain. Quickly she turned and parried Sandy's inept thrust. But the prince's sword of superior quality broke her blade. Sandy swung round and grinned, then stalked her.

"Don't, Sandy! The prince said he would give us a fortune," the old man shouted as he kneeled down to tend to the wounded miller.

"To hell with a deal! He'd have the king's guards on us at the blink of an eye!...This she-demon has humiliated me enough!" He thrust the sword;

she dodged it.

"For God's sake, Rhonda, get on my horse!" yelped the prince.

"Swallow your tongue, nobleman, or I'll cut it out!" He said, not taking his eyes off Rhonda. "It's good you escaped the thrust, my witch, because I have another sword that never misses young pretty lasses." He grinned and tugged on his crotch.

Though reluctant to leave the prince, she ran for her dun, but had trouble mounting because of no stirrups. Sandy grabbed her leg half straddled and pulled her down, tearing her riding tunic. Slamming her to the ground he tore open her chemise to below her breasts. He smothered them in hungry kisses despite her screams and her fists pounding on his back. The heavy sound of thundering hooves displaced her screams. The attacker looked up at two mighty destriers charging toward him, each mounted by husky knights.

Sir Charles jumped down from his mount and pulled him up from the crying Rhonda and by the throat his immense hand held the terrified outlaw above him. His eyes blazed at the helpless, cringing malefactor. Charles said to him, "Behold the rising sun, sinner, for the last time!" Charles grip tightened until Sandy was limp from strangulation, exhaling into hell. Charles swung round to toss the body to the other transgressors only to find they had already scampered off deeply into the woods.

Rhonda while adjusting her torn riding tunic, said to Sir John who had knelt beside her to help her up, "Oh, faithful Sir John, thank God you arrived!"

"Aye, my dear, and none too soon. I regret this delay, but we didn't know you were missing until your loyal handmaiden informed us," he said sadly.

"Oh, darling Tracy!...Yea, yea, thank God for her too!" she mewled. He helped her to her feet and dusted her off, then went over to the prince while Charles galloped into the woods to retrieve the runaway rogues.

Bending down to unleash his bonds, John said in a surprised tone, "Your highness, how is it you came upon this sordid scene so distant from the castle?"

Getting to his feet, he replied, "By the same route as yours—Lady Fortune. Though I bungled my unwitting mission, I at least delayed Rhonda's fate for you to set it right."

John nodded agreement. "The good lady in sooth; for, after scouring the city, we chanced upon your guards at Dawnport. We thought we could at least see to your welfare along this dangerous road while still continuing the search for our leader's sister."

The powerful Charles returned with the two rogues draped over his giant destrier. By the collars he threw them to the ground.

The miller climbed to his knees and cried to the prince as he was chary in even looking at the merciless knight, "My prince, why this treatment? Why we had nothing to do with this. It was the young...late... Sandy who forced us to return so he could get back his foolish sword."

"*His* sword! You mean *stolen*! Commoners don't have swords!- —which further proves your roguish ways." Sir Charles said

Rhonda, partially relieved, slashed out, "Indeed, except having one didn't mean he knew how to use it—thank goodness!"

"Oh, so right, my lady," cried the elder, "never had he used it except to open pumpkin."

The prince laughed. "Aye, bumpkin, that I believe." Then he knitted his brow. "But a weapon in the hands of the likes of rogues is still lethal to the defenseless."

The old man, still face down, rolled over and struggled to his knees, "Lethal! Oh, no, sirs! Why we are Christian souls who merely beg for alms. As you can surely see I am but frail and thus included with the poor defenseless you speak of. No longer am I strong enough to work for a living."

Charles bellowed, "And strong enough reason to rid the kingdom of your useless life!"

The old man clapped his hands, "Yea, useless it is; but still a precious life in the eyes of God, I hope you find." He looked over at Rhonda for a trace of mercy.

"Oh, Sir John, I am so grateful for my life," Rhonda pleaded. "Let us be gone from here. Leave these pathetic fools to their own misery. I believe they were but ignorant dupes of the younger one who got his just deserts. And they too someday when they meet their Maker."

Charles protested, "But, my lady, they deserve to meet Him now!"

"I know, dear Charles, but one is enough for now. Please, let us just leave."

Sir John grabbed their collars, dragging them, and lashed them to a tree. "Pray wolves will do the job."

22. Margaret & Ethan

Back at the mountain castle in the north at the time of the valley storm, Lady Margaret was suspicious of nature's ravage, but it subsided, and she was assured her daughter was unharmed and continued on. Lady Margaret subsequently set out for the fiery pit and directly went to the cell of the old man.

Margaret placed a basket of fruit on a small table by his bunk where he was sitting. She sat down on a rugged little chair across from him and asked, "Did you feel the force of the storm above from here, Ethan?"

He shook his head and then stared at her momentarily. "But I knew its sound and fury from the roaring pit spewing out its hot venom."

"Ah, as I suspected," said Margaret, "then the force was not from nature's normal course."

"Verily," he nodded, moaning, "not since the passing of your king has the pit belched thus."

Her eyes went to the igneous floor while she said, "I thought then his death was mystifying. Still, the physician diagnosed it as a natural heart attack, however robust he was."

"Nothing is natural when Lilith fires up her anger to supernatural force." He answered sullenly, waving his arm in the direction of the pit.

"Then you still maintain her raging soul is at the bottom of the pit?" she asked warily.

He chuckled. "Oh, my dear Margaret, still skeptical. No surprise, though since I have to explain it to every generation....Why else am I here? Why, her burial plot north of Eden, it is said, could not refrain from vomiting up her corpse."

"A corpse?" Margaret squinted skepticism. "An immortal!"

He laughed and popped a grape into his mouth. "Oh, even they need their relics, you know. A bone here, a shield there, memorabilia everywhere....Why, didn't your Jesus have one?" He chuckled, adding, "I understand it didn't stay too long....Still, I suspect even spirits grow an attachment of sorts to their shells."

Lady Margaret took in his ancient wrinkles then squinted into his eyes so blanched their irises could barely be distinguished from the white. "But why here, Ethan?—so far north, I mean."

"Why, it is the legacy of the Quandronians. Of course, they paid a very high toll to rid their land of her. You see, although she was dead they verily believed her soul was still encased for three days," he said, plucking another grape.

"They came by sea and in the middle of the night hoisted her coffin up the deep cliff . At dawn they fought our bonny coastal men to reach the cavern so they could send her to the legendary black, inactive abyss. As they hurled the coffin to its bottomless descent, they were horrified to see the abyss erupt into a belching fire. Few escaped the singeing heat to tell of it."

Lady Margaret squinted and lightly ran a finger up and down the straight bridge of her nose and asked, "How did these aboriginals of our people conceive of the fantastic notion that Eden was in Quandron?"

He grinned and wriggled a finger. "Oh, not Eden, my dear, but north of Eden."

She reflected a moment. "I see, like east of Eden, eh?—then again, who knows what that means?"

"Oh, it has meaning in that once geography entered into it Eden ceased to exist—after all, it was a state of mind."

"Well,...nevertheless, I never heard of such a tale, though I come from there." Margaret said, perplexed.

"The ancient Quandron legend-tellers were forbidden to pass it on. The consensus was to forget the terrible she-demon that had harassed their land."

"Yea, and ever since you have been here to guard its activity." She stared at him and added, "Some four, five thousand years, eh?" And he jiggled his head inconsequentially. "Then why the storm?" she pursued. "Did you doze off?"

"Strange, you should say that. I may nod off but my eyes are open to jar my sentinelduty." He flipped up his very long beard, taking it between his palms and vacantly rubbed his hands. "I must confess, though; lately...oh, perhaps some several years..."

"Lately!" Her jaw dropped.

Grinning, he said, "My time is not measured like yours, you know."

"Oh, yea, I should've realized; but when you say several years, do you include the time of my husband's death?"

"Verily, exactly then," he admitted as though his memory had been wakened.

Her brows arched. "Ten years....Strange."

He looked over at her with a serious expression. "There's a powerful witch in the lowlands, you know."

"I've heard the visitors speak of her."

"Ah, yea, I met one of them—seems a fine young man, in spite of his war credentials. Of course, we might need him."

She knitted her brows and asked, "Because of this witch?"

"Aye, an evil one that overshadows all others. She is a direct descendant of Lilith."

"Oh, no!" Lady Margaret's jaw dropped. "And my daughter is heading that way!"

"Fret not, my mere mortal, biblical proportions will be her fate." Ethan said.

"Good grief! Are you saying Lucia is in danger?" she creaked, clasping and unclasping her hands.

"Perhaps, if this witch senses her presence she will feel threatened and conjure up obstacles in Lucia's path."

"Oh, my,...biblical, you say...but why?" Margaret got up, wringing her hands, and paced the floor.

"Because it is written:
> *And the beautiful descendant of Eve with her golden bow*
> *and silver arrows will challenge the reign of terror forged*
> *by the dark daughter of Lilith*."

"What!" she shrieked. Are you saying I have brought a beautiful daughter into the world practically by proxy to satisfy the whims of jealous women?... Asinine!"

"Nay, she is yours truly, Margaret. A bewitching damsel in her own right with a sense of justice just as you have, my lady. You should feel proud that she is the chosen one hopefully to end this curse upon the land. Feel secure, my Lady, for if this horrid witch is defeated—only Lucia can do that—and Lodeston is saved. For it is also written:
> *Beware the terrible daughter of Lilith who will prevail*
> *upon the high country and raise her mother from the*
> *eternal fire of hell. Pray, thus, for the fair daughter of*
> *Eve!*"

"You say secure,...proud...how can I be when my daughter is so cruelly fated? Why, she isn't even prepared for such an assertive, imperative task. Her decision to march southward has no biblical bearing."

He grinned and nodded his head slightly, slowly. "We cannot be certain of that. Forces wind sinuously through mysterious paths. I trust Lucia now intuits her calling."

She sat down again on the edge and leaned toward him. "I cannot take that chance. She must be warned...to turn back. My God, Ethan, she could've been killed in the storm!"

He closed his eyes and pressed his fingertips to his temples. "Fear not; already she has thwarted Lilith at the first turn."

"She has?" She gaped at the old man.

"Aye, trust me."

"But how can my daughter possibly be able to face up to Erinysia's powers?—why Lucia's barely an adult."

He grinned. "Because you as a mother think of her as still a child....Nay, Lucia will tap her resources lying spiritually dormant when she needs to."

Margaret wrung her hands and looked to the red glowing walls symbolizing the pervasive power raging but a hundred feet away. "But this demoniac daughter of Lilith is far more experienced. And it seems to me to be easier to do evil than to defend against it."

The old man chuckled. "Do not underestimate your daughter. Besides, she now has a champion. Don't forget her power is not for its own sake but rather for the common good of man."

"Nevertheless, I fear for my little girl up against this awesome power."

Looking at the walls again and crooked her head, she added, "Listen how it roars so restively....I fear it is breathing fire and sorcery into its agent's evil aims." She rose up and stretched her legs around the cell, then turned to look at him inquisitively and said, "You know, ancient one, I never could understand Lilith's fate at Eden—such a tragic figure. Her story, till now, has always drawn my sympathy."

"Aye, as I suspect," he said with a grin and twinkle in his eyes, "a woman should. After all, it was Adam who turned creation of the human race upside down. Granted he was the stronger of the two physically, but Lilith's mental capacity was superior and clearly dominant, though not dominating. He depended so much on her thinking that he tolerated her until he matured."

Margaret paused, tapped her forefinger on her chin, asking, "But why just tolerate? Heavens, I should think he would have had the highest respect for her."

"Respect is extremely difficult without love," he said reflexively; "besides, there was no precedence, don't forget."

"But why didn't Adam love her? Verily, she was loving and caring."

Fondling the phylactery on his forehead, he said with a faint grin, "Yea, but only as a queen to her subject. His resentment grew over time driven by the thought they had been created as equals—and of course, they were not."

She chuckled. "Perhaps God is a woman, eh?"

He laughed. "Many cultures do believe that....Nay, God is clearly male and a father. Actually he created Lilith to be more a mother than a wife for Adam. Thus in the father's frequent absentia, she was truly godlike....Adam resented this distance between them. He wanted a wife, not a mother. When Adam tore Eve from his rib they both—and as is often the case in carnal love—alienated themselves from the mother. As a result, the couple lost touch with divine knowledge, deteriorating into an animal existence."

Margaret's eyes sparkled. "Until..."

"Yea," the ancient sage extrapolated, "until Eve ingested *human* knowledge."

She sat back down on the chair. "Thus, the reason for our worship for Eve who led us out of the darkness and in the process diminishing the importance of Lilith."

"Exactly," snapped the old man, "and the supremacy of Adam."

She wiggled her head. "Still, I do not understand why God punished Lilith for Adam's ingratitude."

"Is not a mother always held responsible?" he asked rhetorically.

She nodded vacantly and sighed. "Yes, as I this moment weigh heavily in responsibility for the fate of my child." She sighed again. "Well, as tragic as the story is I am stuck with the humanity of myself. And at this moment Lilith is the enemy for interfering with this humanity, however imperfect....Yes, we must protect our paltry being."

"Yea, ironically the price of free will and freedom," he said wistfully. The old man rose and gently lifted her from the chair. "Come, we must intervene with careful incantation of deception to quell the fiery pit." They walked along the tunnel and out into the open pit. Ethan went to the edge and looked down, then turned back. Etham cautioned, "At all costs we must keep Lilith here in this formless state. If permitted to take shape, she will be too much for Lucia."

Margaret shook her head. "Oh, God, why?...After all these thousands of years!...Why now?"

"I suppose she had to wait for the coming of Erinysia," the old man offered.

"Yea, and, I suppose, the challenge of my daughter," she mused sadly. Suddenly a great surge of flame shot up from the center and vaulted the shadowy heights. Hundreds of bats were disturbed and flew high and out of the mouth of the volcano.

Ethan strained his eyes to the black hole above. "Hmm, what do you suppose she wants with ugly bats?" He looked over at the tree stump—out of its roots a leafy shoot was thriving, hovering over the pit. He reached for his axe.

Forty leagues from Lodeston castle, deep in the center of the moor separating the two lands, were the two highway men who had escaped before the prince's guards could locate them shackled in the grove off the road. For weeks they had traveled by night through Quandron to avoid being arrested. On the way, they looted manor strips for food, which by now was spent, by their having been on the desolate heath for several days. Each would take turns at walking while the other would mount the fatiguing draft horse.

It was the elderly rogues's turn to walk and he was staggering from the ordeal of intensive travel. He protested, calling after the fat miller, as he continued to lose ground, "What a lout, you are to expect one of my age to walk this devilish ground! Nor was it coincidence that you rode while I trudged through that stinking graveyard of battle back over the border. Fiend, though you are, have you no respect for the agéd?"

The miller swiveled round resting one hand on the haunches of the animal and laughed. "Stop the whining, old man, I could have left you tied up for the king's men."

The old thin man nodded. "Yea, and better off I'd be, verily. I'd bet my dying wish that Sandy is in heaven by now."

The miller almost fell off the horse from laughter, then finally sputtered, "I'd have more of a chance to make heaven than Sandy—and I have no chance at all!"

"Jesus forgave those rogues on the cross, remember," the elder reminded him.

"Yea, but they were Jews! We are doomed Catholics!" the miller countered emphatically...."And you forget that it was your own stupidity that let your donkey get away," the miller added.

The old man shook his bony face. "Aye, put too much trust in him—no gratitude in that animal."

The fat miller yelled out. "I see smoke ahead. Maybe a camp where we can get some food! I'm starving."

"Who'd be camping in this God forsaken peat ditch!" groaned the old man. He stopped in his tracks and squinted into the fog. "Thank thee, Lord!" he yelped as his spirit quickened his pace. The miller heeled the horse and as they drew closer three women could be seen preparing a fire. One of them went toward a horseless cart and helped a younger woman take down a large black pot.

The miller jumped off the horse and approached them. "Ah, sweet, lovely ladies, what godsend sight you are for hungry gentlemen! I trust you have a meal for that wonderful looking pot—and plenty, too, I wager from the size of it."

An old gray hag looked up at him with a wide toothless grin and rubbing her bony hands, said joyously. "Indeed, now we do and plenty plump!"

23. King Henry

Henry the king, though still handsome, was not an imposing figure and from years of inactivity his lean body became flaccid. With the help of the Lord-Protector's loyalty, he maintained an authoritative air as he grew with his position. In his own right, he was adept at law and constitutional governance. The pocket of insecurity he possessed was attributed to the times; for he was fully aware that his sovereignty was continually threatened by his ambitious and vain barons unable to accept a unified system.

As a very handsome, lean young earl he was considered a courtier and ladies' man and never entertained knighthood, in part, because of his size, to his father's disappointment. Had it not been for his father's arrangement of a power-related marriage, setting the stage for royalty, he would not have become king.

The Sovereign Document was conceived and developed by the Mari lineage. It was reluctantly accepted by the disunited barons of the lands in face of the huge army, Henry's father had mustered by the merging of two powerful families, along with the shadow of the powerful knights under the Mari crest. Upon Henry's father's death, the barons seized the opportunity to rebel but were still too stubborn to actually unite their forces. Fortunately for Henry, the Mari regiment under the leadership of Lance's grandfather–despite Kalab's objections–remained united in the defense of the Document as the only true course for peace and prosperity.

Henry was thankful that his son, though no match for a knight, at least was a swordsman and not unlike his grandfather was somewhat adept at power politics. When his son apprised the king of Rhonda's plight and the probability of treachery at her castle, the castle guards and Henry's army were alerted and in Lance's absence, placed jointly under Sir John and the cousin to the king, Arnold. Prince Henry was liaison officer to the king. The bulk of the army, however, had been relieved after its tour of battles under Lance and had to be summarily dispatched. As a result of not being at full strength, John deployed the Mari to the battlements to direct the archers in the likelihood of attack.

The king had been impressed by Rhonda's fiery spirit and of her loyalty to the crown as related by his son. He perceived, of course, that she was of the same cut as Lance and not of her devious father of whose ambition the king was well aware. The great heavy doors swung open to the throne room and Rhonda, eclipsed by the flanking guards, entered in stunning attire supplied by Lady Rita who had been the first lady-in-waiting to the queen, whose last bequest was that she remain to officiate the castellan's affairs of the castle. The king with alacrity rose up and stepped down from the throne platform to greet her and quickly motioned that she sit with him at the large table to the right of the throne. He offered her wine.

Tactfully she lowered her eyes for a moment, then flashed them up at him and said, "If you do not mind, my king, I should much prefer milk."

He laughed. "Why, of course, my dear,...after all, in spite of your ordeal, you are but a child." He snapped his fingers at a servant girl who quickly left to fetch the milk.

Rhonda chuckled. "Oh, please, your majesty, you put too much into my request. I have on many occasions had a sip or two of the stronger liquid. It is simply that milk might favor a rather jittery stomach. Actually I should rather just cool water except that I have not eaten anything, but for an apple, for nearly three days."

"What's this? My son, and knights for two days didn't see to your needs! And you've been here in the castle for the past six hours and Lady Rita has not seen to it that you be fed?"

"Oh, no, my king, all have been very kind to me, and Lady Rita very hospitable. It is simply that I have been unable to eat...in light of..."

"Dreadful episode, indeed." He reached across the table, took one of her tiny hands in his white puffy ones and said gently, "Of course, my dear, you've been through a sinful time with those felons." The servant girl returned with a mug of milk. "Bring this dear girl some fruit before she wastes away."

"Oh, really, your majesty, this is fine," Rhonda pleaded lightly. The servant girl hesitated, but the king knitted his brows and the girl went off.

"Once the milk soothes your stomach you will be ready for some much needed nourishment," he said authoritatively. "Now, tell me, little one, of this terrible woman at your father's castle." He added uneasily, "I met her once when she was the wife of the Earl. She seemed a rather pleasant woman; but with her great beauty, one, especially a man, could easily be deceived."

Rhonda absently fidgeting with the mug responded, "Oh, truly, she is beautiful and until recently rather amiable to me. But a great change has come over her—perhaps I should say that her true possessive character has come to the surface. She too has instilled in my father a change for the worse in my brother's absence."

He frowned. "In truth, had he not run off, Lance surely would have interceded." He tensed his fingers round the tankard and chafed at the thought. "You know, Rhonda, he was supposed to report to me when he returned from his great victory—so very unlike him to simply send a written message."

"Oh, sire, verily, were he on the scene it never could have happened. And, alas, it's true, he has gone off to satisfy his curiosity about the northern lands."

"Yea, so I heard. A rather childish quest, it seems to me." The king looked away from her for a moment, then continued, "I wonder what could have drawn him there?"

"Yea, I've wondered that too. Surely, he would not journey just for a horse."

"Hmm," he stroked his trim still blondish beard and mumbled to himself while Rhonda sipped her milk, "could he be thinking of another conquest?" He shook his head and cleared his throat. "Nay,...why, those people are too barbaric....Still, I had no idea he felt so strongly to the point that he would abandon his little sister and bewitched father." He chugged the wine, then slammed down the mug. "It is unlike Sir Lance to be irresponsible," the King declaimed vehemently, obviously irked as though for the consumption of others, though they were alone at the table.

Rhonda hesitated, then agreed softly, "I said as much...terribly disappointed that he would not stay the while, even for my own selfish reasons. On the other hand, he took lightly my wariness that father was under Erinysia's spell. Besides, he was so distraught over his loyal steed's wounds that he left Stars in my care and wanted really to see for himself the truth of the great herds of the north."

"Aye, aye,...I've heard of them. They...say...they have a long line to the ancient Roman centurions who conquered the northern chains—nothing, however, can come up to our great drafters....But, no, my child, it could not be that. I shall just have to consider it an irresponsible act that, nevertheless, I must condone because of his great service to me." He squinted at her momentarily, then uttering worrisomely, "But verily, I trust, by now he is on his way back to set things right at your father's castle."

"Of this I have no assurance—I truly hope he has had enough of his boyish foolishness," she pouted. "He's been gone much too long already."

The king pondered as the servant girl returned with a bowl of fruit. Rhonda eyed the gleaming red apples and thought of loyal Stars lying in his own blood. She could not take one; rather she plucked several white grapes. The king fondled an apple for a moment then set it down. "Of course, from what Sir John has reported, it is clear that your father will not come to his senses on his own volition. It seems unbelievable that he could think that his son's recent conquests were in his behalf and not of the kingdom's."

"My father is not himself of late, your majesty—I rather doubt he has his own will any longer." She sighed, staring at the grape between her fingertips. "I truly believe the woman has bewitched him all too deeply, sire."

"Yea," he uttered with resistance, "I've heard the same upon the death of the Earl. Still, there is consolation that she cannot hold an entire army under her spell—surely not those who fought under Lord Lance."

Plucking another grape, she said, "In my father's current mental state, I fear he looks upon those troops as his own. I heard him say as much to Lance."

"What? And in face of such treason, your brother did nothing?" The king grabbed an apple and flung it along the great hall. A sleeping hound awoke and chased after it.

Rhonda quaked and said nervously, "Oh, my king, surely you don't think my brother...why, Lance was so shocked and in disbelief that he could not take him seriously."

"Now that I hear this I am even more disappointed that your brother would traipse off on a wild fancy. Why, he swore to the Document! And so did your father!"

"You may think me a child, good king, but it is thoroughly a grown woman's intuition that my father would be as loyal as truly Lance shall always be had the foolish old man not been put under a spell."

"I rather doubt, young lady, that one unwilling can lend himself to bewitchment. Let us hope that the son is not also thus inclined."

Rhonda's eyes widened. "Surely, you don't believe that Lance was lured away!"

"Who knows the ways of witchcraft," he said. He pictured in his mind the lure of the valley.

Rhonda thought of Bryan: she was sure he would not let that happen to her brother.

24. Rita

After her session with the king and another restful hour, Rhonda, near sunset and before the dinner bell, went out onto a balcony adjoining her accommodations high in the donjon. Lady Rita joined her and sat Rhonda on a stool to brush the long red hair, emitting faint auburn in the setting sun. With an admiring look, Rita said, "You have lovely hair, my child—soft and silky like a toddler's. Your mother had such hair—very same shade too."

Rhonda, on a high stool, craned her neck, looking up momentarily, "You were such great friends, especially in your early years. Mother spoke favorably of you many times. I remember how she looked forward to your visits."

"Alas, when you lose a dear friend, you regret the visits weren't often enough....Yes, long before she was betrothed to your father, we were as close as sisters....Oh, the good times we had!...And so many suitors at our feet."

Rhonda giggled. "I can imagine. You were both so beautiful....I mean, you still are."

Rita kissed her pate. "Oh, my darling Rhonda, you are so sweet, but I accept without regretful ado the wrinkles now."

"They become you—and so few, despite the many times you smiled so lovingly on others. You're still such a handsome woman."

Rita laughed. "Yes, handsome is the term for those my age."

Rhonda jerked up an apologetic smile. "Forgive me, Lady Rita, I did not mean...."

Rita squeezed the girl's narrow shoulders. "I know, my dear....Did you know the king himself had a twinkle in his eye for your mother in his bachelor days?" She put the brush down on the balcony ledge.

"Oh, my, no....Were they lovers?"

With wrinkled fingers Rita arranged a few strands of Rhonda's hair about her face. "In a sense they were, that is, secretly....Mind you now, nothing obscene between them." She seemed to gulp down the words. "Your mother, needless to say, would not be part to a scandal. No, the king, a young earl then, was a respectable suitor. It's just that he knew his father who had once before interceded would not approve: he had other plans for his son."

"Of course," Rhonda interspersed, while leaning over the ledge and looking down at the rather busy vigil on the parapets, "marriage of political expediency, no doubt."

"My, perceptive for just a dash of a girl! You see, the king's wife and queen-to-be was the daughter of a very powerful duke who had harnessed a third of the current kingdom. Through matrimony the young earl would eventually lay claim to half of what is now the kingdom, out of which was born the Sovereign Document authored by your grandfather."

"Yes, and thanks to my brother, the king now has virtually all of the kingdom under his control," she said proudly.

"Why, my child, you say that innocently without a trace of bitterness or sarcasm." Rita uttered wide-eyed. "After all, in these barbaric times the strong bestow the honor of royalty to themselves."

"Lance is not barbaric—too steeped in the Mari tradition—firmly believing the only road to lasting peace is through loyalty and unity." She stretched her neck to observe the prince below heading toward the parapets to inspect the guards. She continued, "Patriotism overrides personal feelings....I, however, unlike my mother, would probably be vengeful."

Rita burst in, "Such sweet irony—the son of the woman the king truly loved became his powerful defender of the crown," Rita rhapsodized, leaning over the ledge. She noticed the prince too. "Young Henry is a good boy. He should make a good king....But truly he's no Lance....Your brother even as a tot took to the martial arts but he never would resist his lessons from the monks. He was destined to become a warrior with kindness—so very rare."

"Kind indeed, Lance was more like a father to me and fortunately yet sadly more a son to my grandfather than to...." Her voiced trailed, then added, "I was so disappointed, though, that he left for the north. It was so unlike him."

"Men of war—even in Lance's case—always on the edge of death become restless," Rita said, slipping the brush handle into her sash, and then looked out to the northern horizon, chuckling. "Why, now that Lance is over thirty, I shouldn't be surprised that he's thinking more of serious romance than this political dream of a truly united land."

"Oh, my, why would you think that of Lance?" Rhonda asked pertly. A thought she would never entertain.

Rita faced her and winked. "Oh, I'm sure he has had many lasses enthralled by his looks and power on many tours of battle. "But...why?...Why, precisely because, as you said, to avoid the expediency element. Your brother is a very independent force."

Rhonda flushed briefly with embarrassment, then chuckled. "I suppose you're right. When home he never mentioned to me that he was serious about any damsel—perhaps it is high time for him to consider a lasting relationship....Yet, heavens, surely there is no attraction in the rugged north other than a curiosity over its horses."

Rita beamed a smile and chuckled out, "I trust, then, you are unaware of a legendary princess in those mountains?"

Rhonda arched light red brows, stood up and rested a hand on the rail. Momentarily staring at her and then breaking into laughter. "Oh, Lady Rita! 'tis you who are the romantic! My brother is too practical to run off to a strange land for romance, much less after a fairy tale, when he could have virtually any charming woman in his own country." Rhonda crossed her arms to cover her bare shoulders. "There is a chill in the air."

"How thoughtless of me. Come inside and warm yourself by the fire. The dinner hour is approaching." Rita said, draping her shawl over Rhonda's shoulders.

Rhonda curled up in a chair by the immense hearth glowing with subdued summer embers. Rita proceeded to brush her own graying hair before the warmth and pursued the subject. "It's no fairy tale, little one."

"You yourself just said she was but a legend," Rhonda reminded her.

"That I did. And the legend goes centuries back. But now there really is one of flesh and blood. In fact, however little known, she is the daughter of one who was once years ago in this court."

"Oh, my," Rhonda yelped, "how intriguing! But how would Lance know that?"

"Oh, I don't think he does; yet—and in spite of the practical label you've pinned on him—he could very well be searching for the legend. After all, he is a knight, and not unlike most, endowed with romantic notions." Rita drew a chair by the fire.

Rhonda giggled. "My brother?—hardly! In search of a dragon or the Holy Grail I should believe,...but a *princess*?"

"Your brother is also very much a man. And since I knew the mother, the daughter is sure to be very beautiful indeed."

"This woman...who is she?"

Rita flustered and dropped her brush in her lap. "I am not at liberty to say."

"Oh, my, then, even the mother is a mysterious legend!" Rhonda chuckled. She looked to the fire for a moment. "My mother," Rhonda began, "you know, must have been broken-hearted by Henry's rejection."

"Oh, I shouldn't go that far—disappointed, as I said," Rita assured her. "Such a raving beauty would never know the emptiness of being alone. But why do you say that?"

Rhonda lifted her chin from her knees and momentarily glanced over. "I swear, she never loved my father. My grandfather arranged the marriage—rather on impulse, I've heard."

Rita abruptly turned away her face, rose and went back to the hearth, warmed her hands and looked over at the girl staring into the embers. "One as lovely as you had to be conceived out of love. You must not think otherwise."

Rhonda chuckled. "Oh, dear Lady Rita, that is only in fairy tales and perhaps in exceptional and very fortunate lives. Why, I think the peasantry has more privilege in the affairs of love than we of the gentry."

Rita poised the brush and thought, "But limited in selection nevertheless because their environment is so small. We at least are exposed to the gentry across manors and borders." Then she chuckled. "Still, you're right; we are still but objects of choice, no better than items of the marketplace."

"Yes, sons of the nobility with less demanding fathers are more or less free to choose....That cannot be said of us women."

"My, my," Rita said laughingly, "a woman already, are you?"

Rhonda stared into the fire. "I guess I cannot lay full claim to that as yet....but when I think of the young knight Bryan, I can't imagine my feelings changing much from what I feel toward him now."

"I don't believe I've heard of him," Rita said, picking up her brush left by the chair and sat down.

"No, you haven't but saw him many times when he was a mere lad. Until recently he was my brother's squire, but proved himself in battle....Alas, he is an orphan and of common blood."

"Oh, you poor child," Rita moaned. "Still, if he is as you say a man of achievement, he will eventually be awarded land."

"Verily, if my brother has a say....But in the meantime, I am at the mercy of my father's will."

Rita absently picked a long red strand from the brush and compared it with her gray, then said. "In my day I was fortunate that my father's will respected my own. Fortunate, that is, until my betroth was slain in battle over curséd land."

"You must have loved him very much, not to consider marriage again," Rhonda said sadly. "Was there never anyone else?"

"No, never,...I suppose my heart died with him. And of course, my father was considerate by not trying to impose a relationship on me....So, you see, Rhonda, not all fathers are demanding. Besides he fared well when I took this position after the late queen insisted I be at her side....Yes, he got his share of land."

"Well, it's good to hear we are not all chattel, then," Rhonda retracted.

"Or cattle, eh?" Rita laughed. She crossed over and cupped Rhonda's cheeks in her hands. "But in your case, my sweet, it is not inevitable. I've noticed young Henry is taken in by your loveliness. You surely must be flattered."

Rhonda blushed. "If true, it still does not change my feelings toward Bryan," she said longingly. "I'm sure it is but a passing fancy on Prince Henry's part."

Rita pondered. "From this current situation I'd rather doubt your father would superimpose his will anyway...what with his having such hatred for the royal family."

"Why, of course!" Rhonda's eyes flashed with a new awakening. "Oh, could it be because of my mother's early relationship with the king? Could he still harbor a grudge?...But did my father know of it?"

"No doubt in my mind," Rita said; "everyone knew—unlike before that."

"Before? — still another affair?" Rhonda jerked. "My, then young Henry, too, must be addicted, or is it inherent and thus father like son?—young Henry, too, but a philanderer?"

"Oh, never mind; let's not pursue wild speculation." Rita squirmed.

Rhonda dismissed it and returned her thoughts: "Hm, perhaps, then, my father's not so bewitched, after all,...at least not all Erinysia's doing."

Rita smiled. "I shouldn't go that far; verily, as Lady Hunter she bewitched the earl and I'm convinced she murdered him."

"A week ago, I should've been shocked; now, I've seen her true spectrum of chilling darkness." Rhonda crossed her arms and shivered. "Oh, I do hope my brother returns soon!"

"The king, you know, has already dispatched for his return," Rita comforted.

"Oh, thank, God," she said smilingly, then reflected with a pout; "What am I saying?...Mercy on us, that may take weeks! Longer if your fantasizing about the legend turning true. I trust my brother is on his way back already even though I truly do wish—but hardly the time for it—he would meet up with love." She stood up, drew up the shawl to her throat and strolled out to the balcony.

She leaned over the wall and from her donjon vantage point could see young Henry inspecting the guards on the battlement. She certainly was impressed by his royal demean and good looks, yet she suspected her feeling for him was out of gratitude. Her thoughts turned to Bryan. Since early childhood they were smote by each other. She could not imagine her life without him. Still, she feared that her ambitious father had other plans for her. She shivered at the thought that her father apparently on the path of self-destruction might not ever have a say in her future. But worse, if he succeeded in this reputed mad venture, the she-devil would truly want to be rid of her if not by murder, then surely to send her off to some distant kingdom.

Rita came out and put a hand on her shoulder, saying, "Forgive me, dear, if I have added oil to the embers of concern. After all, it could be but hearsay that Erinysia is a demon. After all, it was ruled that the earl was killed by his own guard."

"Yea, but suspicion is sometimes stronger than apparent truth. And if your suspicion is thus, then...my father too must be in danger."

Rita stroked the beautiful red hair. "There is no need for alarm—for now anyway. In the meantime, let us put some flesh on this frail frame of yours."

At the massive table in the cavernous dining hall, Rhonda—had she not the proper upbringing—would have behaved like a hungry peasant. Still, in her stylish manner, she negotiated two healthy servings and a full chalice of wine. So busy eating was she, that there was little time for conversation with young Henry or Rita flanking her at the table. She managed, however, to divide her attention between listening and eating.

Rita looked at the prince and asked out of idle curiosity, "Is it really true, your highness, that Rhonda's father was the only nobleman not at the signing of the Sovereign Document? I find it hard to believe inasmuch as Rhonda's grandfather was the author."

The prince turned and looked apologetically at Rhonda "Yea,...that is what the king told me—not that the others were eager to be there, but most swallowed their pride for the good of the union."

Rhonda chuckled, dipped her fingertips in the finger bowl and wiped her slender hands on a napkin. "I do not think pride had anything to do with it with respect to my father—rather resistance to my grandfather's persistence—so accustomed was he to his own levying, it seems he resented having to be levied on himself."

Rita laughed. "Yes, the two plagues on all of us—death and taxes."

"Ah, but it is taxes that keep us alive to pay them,...dog chasing the tail, so to speak," the prince reminded her. "The feudal system is too barbaric. Erinysia and the old warlord are proving that. The world cannot be run on man's ambition alone; it must have law. Rhonda's brother is the champion of law for all."

"Oh, yes," Rhonda overcame her resistance to devour her pheasant leg and pointed it at the prince, "and he takes it literally because he includes the peasantry as being protected under law and not just as chattel, but as human beings."

The prince scowled. "That's carrying it a bit too far, don't you think?

I mean, it is enough just to protect property."

"Ah, but property is the wherewithal for the gentry, but what protection is there for the peasantry inasmuch as they have no property?"

"It is precisely because they *are* property that they are protected from harm," he countered.

Lady Rita said, "Oh, but my prince, there is more to the human soul than protection from harm. That is much too negative—even the peasantry has feelings, you know, and, yes, aspirations."

"Lady Rita, forgive me," young Henry said, "dear friend and chain to my mother's memory, but that is as difficult to digest as this meal. What aspirations could an ignoramus have beyond what is comfort and work that he already enjoys?"

Rhonda inserted, "Could it be, your highness, that the alleged ignoramus's aspirations are for his children? That they may have a better life than the simple soul can only dream about? Just as I am sure our own forefathers finally realized that there is more to life than the animal existence of their barbaric days."

The prince laughed heartily. "Oh, my, I heard your mother had hired a Greek tutor for you to balance your monkish learning!"

"And why not? There is, after all, a life here on earth as well," she said, slightly peeved.

"Oh, very definitely, my sweet Rhonda, but not for everybody; there simply is not enough to go around," he said haughtily.

She was growing sleepy from the food and wine. This was just fine with her as she did not wish to continue the conversation with the young prince who was beginning to annoy her. The prince noticed her sudden silence and that she was no longer supping. He suggested that she accompany him to the parapet. She agreed, thinking the night air would do her good; in addition, she was beginning to feel that she was a captive audience in the great dining hall now alive with entertainment, for which she was in no mood.

While they walked the ramp, she said, "Explain to me, prince, this concern for the castle guards—I saw you earlier today officiating the parapets—are you really expecting trouble so soon? Surely, you don't think my father mad enough..."

"No, don't fret; it is simply a precaution. Besides, it is not your father we are worried about. It is that crude gypsy we are troubled by. She is capable of anything—you above all know that," he said confidently and squeezed her hand.

"Yes, yes, verily. Still, I keep thinking,...hoping, really,...my brother will be back and have everything under control." She withdrew her hand from his, still thinking of his insensitivity at the supper table.

"Well, that truly would be a big lift off our shoulders, but as you say a mere wish....Who's to say Lord Lance will ever be back."

Rhonda raised her brows as she snapped, "What on earth do you mean by that?"

He hesitated and looked at her apologetically. "It's just that it is said that those Northerners are fiercely savage."

"My brother can be fierce too, you know. He is too experienced in battles not to take precautions," she said without a shred of diffidence.

"Forgive me—it was insensitive of me. Of course, he could never be thwarted by uncouth warriors."

Since a little girl Rhonda never thought of Lance's being in danger. She was so accustomed to his returning in triumph and barely scathed. Nevertheless, she quickly changed the subject. "Lady Rita tells me that Erinysia actually murdered her previous husband. Is there veracity to that?"

He held up his hand and turned to one of the crossbowmen to inspect the new supply of crossbow arrows—Lodeston never exported its longbow arrows. He turned back to her. "No one knows for sure. Still, why would a trusted guard suddenly turn on his sovereign like a dog gone mad? There does seem to be foul play."

She raised a skeptic brow. "But surely, the human species is not exempt from sudden fits of anger."

"Granted, but did you know that your assailant Baron Bennet was at the earl's castle the night of the murder?"

"Oh, no,...I had no idea!" Still perplexed, she pursued, "But Erinysia did not inherit the estate. It all went to his children, Maureen and David, from a previous marriage."

He rested his hand on a crudely mortared merlon and peered through the crenel out onto the dark plains, then said, "That part is true, but she nevertheless walked away with a ton of jewels and silver. Apparently the son's payoff just to get rid of her. And with the current situation, I wouldn't be surprised that she intends to get it all back."

"Alas," Rhonda sighed, "she seems to be a woman of many sinister motives."

The prince inserted, "Aye, but mainly vengeance. She has reason to hate my father, you know?"

"No, I didn't." Rhonda squinted as she thought of her father's hatred for the king.

The prince continued. "I don't really know for sure, but I have an inkling that my father kept her as a mistress for sometime and then abruptly ended it."

Rhonda perked, "How very odd. Your father spoke of her as though he barely knew her."

He laughed. "Odd if he *admitted* to it....Speaking of motives, I suppose, I have my share. I don't respect my father for his keeping a mistress under my mother's nose—not to mention I hate the witch even more."

She looked up at him with disappointment and said, "But you don't even know for sure, so why not just put it aside? You are better off not knowing." She dwelled for a moment on her mother and the king.

"Oh, I have reliable sources. Although, I suspect, I still don't want to believe it. That's why I play with self induced vagary...but to be honest, there really is no doubt....And aside from that, he always treated my mother shabbily."

She squinted with skepticism. "Oh, and I suppose when you marry it will be different."

"Why not? When I marry it shall be out of love," he said confidently.

"How grand, but can you be sure of that? I mean, what if your father has other plans?" she asked.

He touched his hilt and said with determination. "I'd be exiled. Rest assure that would be my option." He grabbed hold of her tiny shoulders and pulled her into his chest. "Besides, dear girl, the king likes you. He would approve of my choice." He took her face in his hands and tried to kiss her.

"Please, my prince, you mustn't," she shrilled as she broke loose his hold. "You just said your relationship must be of love. And what of me? This is merely a boy's impulsiveness taken in by our recent circumstance. A silly romance over a damsel in distress." She drew herself away. "I must take my leave, your highness, I am very, very tired—apparently you are too. You've also had little rest, and it's evident you are having a semi-waking dream." She swung on her heels to run down the ramp, but he reached out and held her fast.

"You must hear me out. A schoolboy's fancy it is not. And now that I've witnessed your spirit, I love you even more! It is obvious you are not one who is easily impressed. I like that. But I warn you I shall kill the first man who pursues you."

"She wrenched away from him. "Time, sour Prince, will not lend you any favors, if you truly think that." Then surprisingly she laughed to add, "And knowing the quality of your swordsmanship, I should think that vow to be risky to your health....In the meantime, I shall consider this the talk of one who's weary and concerned for the safety of his castle. Good night, Prince Henry." She turned and headed back down the ramp.

25. A Contested Regiment

The hand of fortune turned to the earl's legions encamped in reserve behind the main force front. As the three horses bearing the young people approached, the Earl's commander hurriedly mounted and galloped out to intercept them. In a disquieted voice, he warned David, "Oh, my young grace, it is folly that you come here."

Bryan slapped the hilt. "It is folly, commander, that *you* be here."

"Aye,…still, I fear for his grace and his sister."

"Why so late?" Bryan glowering, grunted sarcastically.

"How now, captain?" David asked the commander. "It does not appear my men have joined the renegades." David noticed the small numbers.

"A company is strategically deployed for a possible siege, the rest of us in reserve—oh, your grace, I'm sad to report that your dear departed father's ranks are steeped in rancorous treason!"

Maureen edged her strawberry roan forward and inquired, "How so if the captain himself is not thus steeped?"

"My lady, in name only am I captain—more like captive. My own men look upon me with distrust in their cowardly eyes."

Bryan intervened, "Then, proselyte, who is in actual command of the young earl's troops?"

"One of Bennet's captains."

"Fie, Bennet again!…Equipped with the vigorous wings of a vulture!" Bryan wailed.

"I care not who has usurped command. I shall have it back!" David said sternly. "The men will listen to me, else my father's ghost will wage havoc among them!"

"Please, young master, reconsider!" the commander pleaded.

"Nay, why should I doubt that which is sewn into my family's crest!"

Bryan softened his tone to the commander. "His grace is right, you know. Are you now with us, captain?"

He flashed yellow teeth midst his graying beard and said, "Aye, especially now that I see the youngster is indeed of his father's stamp and seal." The four of them continued on, notwithstanding Bryan's protest that Maureen stay put.

The four were greeted not by the young earl's men but that of six of Bennet's renegade knights. "Part the way, traitors, I've come to speak to my men," the young earl commanded, scowling.

The men leveled their swords menacingly to which Bryan spontaneously spurred his horse toward them. Swiftly he felled two of the clumsy swordsmen with his two handed blade. He yawped with a scowl, "That should teach you to dare assault a knight with the proud banner of the Mari to which you once owed allegiance!" Another proselyte, while holding onto the reins tried to pull Bryan from the steed. The earl's captain quickly heeled his steed to a charge. The renegade was forced to let go of the reins, at which point the captain slew him. Subsequently, a horseman galloped out from behind a tent, jumped from his saddle and knocked Bryan to the ground and battered Bryan's armor with a ball and chain. Bryan's horse whinnied and reared up on its haunches, then came crashing down on the assailant who howled and rolled off the dazed knight. The young earl then rode up and slew the assailant summarily. The three hedging knights of the original six ganged up on the captain who was pulled from his steed. Two more from camp joined in the fray. The young earl was quickly subdued and his shoulder battered from the swing of the flat side of a heavy blade. Bryan, having steadied himself to his feet fought off four men while Maureen ran to her brother and dragged him several feet away from the fracas and the danger of unnerved horses. The valiant visitors were helplessly surrounded as another ten men from camp joined in. Maureen looked up to see many familiar faces from her father's legion pointing swords at her.

"Must *I* fight all your battles?" intoned Erinysia rhetorically and with vexation while observing Castle City from an opposite slope. She looked to the massive castle fortification of King Henry's sprawling atop the entire extent of a wide plateau. She glanced back at Bennet. "I'm amazed you can make love—but then, after all, it is mostly my doing."

Bennet flushed with embarrassment as he looked back, lest his men had overheard. Then he turned to her and scowled, but said, evading the latter reference, "Why that's unfair! We underestimated Henry's stamina and his numbers."

"Rubbish! What are numbers if he doesn't come out of his granite shell to meet us in engagement?"

"Precisely why I'm sure Sir John advised him to concede to a siege. What with ample provisions of the city their numbers could be dangerous while we ourselves would be under siege by the erosion of a winter encampment."

"Encampment! Son of Balaam! You disgust me!" she scorned. "Snow flakes in hell before we grow old and settle here in winter. The only course is attack!"

"My lady, the risk is too great! Their archers are all top marksmen."

"Risk? Yea....Too great?...Nay. War by definition is risky but if too great there would be no wars. It is hard to believe that you fought under the greatest risk taker of all."

"Your cuts run deep today, Erinysia. There is no one in the fighting ranks the world over who can compare with Lord Lance."

"Well, then, count your blessings that he is no longer a threat," she reminded him with a snarl.

Again he looked to a gathering of his troops before responding in low voice, "Keep saying that and you will believe it yourself. That we have not heard from the assassins should be sufficient evidence that they fell to inevitable failure. And you can stake all your magic and tricks up your sleeves that Sir John has gotten word to Lance."

Pointing toward the mountain, she said, "Bennet, you see the river?—were Henry not now faced with our powerful front, women would be at its beds laundering, I should order you to join them—you belong there."

He glanced back from the river and lowered his eyes. "My lady, you are most unkind. I have been your most faithful servant."

"It is not a servant I want but a man of war."

"Then you shall have him," he said solemnly and slapped his quillon.

"Good, then, attack in the morn. Use the earl's men in the first line of advance, since you are so concerned with the archers. By then their supply of arrows will have dwindled and your men can launch the attack."

"Agreed....Still, we must secure a siege round the many exits of the city."

"Won't that weaken our frontal forces?"

"Would you rather cunning John to outflank us?" he wisely asked. "Besides, we already have a company of the earl's forces guarding some of the other bridges. We can spread them out to cover more and add another company to seal them all."

"Yes, to that I agree; the Hunter force is useless in assault," she said, cooling off her impetuousness.

But there's one other item. What of old Kalab? He is wavering."

With disgust she asked, "What? He too?"

He grimaced at the reference. "Too?...He mentioned to me about a proposal to the king," he said, searching her unfathomable eyes.

"How dare he!"

"It seems your powers over him are wearing off." He could not refrain from grinning.

She tapped his black tabard with a long fingernail. "You'd like that, wouldn't you? Well, we shall see about this." She stormed off in the direction of the old warlord's tent.

Barging in on Kalab, she assailed, "What is this about capitulation with the dastardly king?"

The old warlord looked up from a table where he had been writing. "Bennet goes running to you with every vowel and consonant uttered, eh? Just how does he fit into your grim picture, my witch? Can it be I don't have exclusive petting rights?"

"Nonsense, he is nothing but a sacrificial lamb. Why, he is a poor warrior to boot!"

"True, though skilled, he hasn't heart. Still his contingent of fighting men is large."

"Whatever, he is not the point. I see the point before you is in the busy quill. Taking to love ballads to the king?"

He snickered. "Aye, grossly put but on the mark; for love is filled with lies."

"Not *our* love, my lord!"

He guffawed and choked out, "Oh, Erinysia, you are the epitome of falsehoods! If I weren't such an old fool I'd put an end to you this instant."

"Yea, a foolish court jester you've become. It appears we need to bed down more often." She stooped over to fondle his beard; he luxuriated in her toying with him for a moment, then pressed his lips to her waist. She patted his head and said, "Pray tell, my love, what is it you're planning behind my back?"

He looked up. "Aye, that would bother you that I move on my own will; for in your eyes I am but a pawn."

She ran her long fingers over his bald head. "Silly, pet."

"Ah, forgive me my choice of word—not a pawn but a pet, eh?"

She bent down and wiggled her tongue across his head, then bent back up and squeezed his bearded cheeks and said, "Stop with this game; my love, for you require finer play."

"Play or ploy for that is what my proposal is: to get into the castle and meet with Henry. Surely, he would never consent to meet us here."

"And you rant about my deceit!" She jerked out of his arms. "Poppycock! You wish only to see if your daughter is captive."

"Nay, if so, he would have gloated over it already and tried to turn us away. Still, there is the chance that she is in his stealth custody and could still be used as a bargaining chip if we successfully attack."

"There shall be no deals!" she said forcefully.

"That's where you're wrong when it comes to the safety of my daughter."

She stared at him coyly. "You're sure she's your daughter?"

He smirked at her. "Now, don't go starting that again. Your chatoyant tiger's eye cannot cast otherwise."

"Do not smear my window of truth," she cautioned, then chuckled derisively. "Are you willing to let ambition for a throne be dashed by a slip of a girl?"

"Oh, Erinysia, you are an incorrigible witch to refer to my daughter so minimally and callously," he scowled her while fingering the quill. "Nay, I still seek my vengeance, but I must see to her safety."

"The king is not a total idiot. He will see right through you. He would demand guarantees."

He laughed satanically. "Aye, that he will have." He grinned. "But guarantees never last."

She moved over and cuddled him in her arms. "My lord, we cannot afford delay. But we'll speak of this again. Come, rest in my tent where there is more comfort and more conducive to *my* incomparable comforting." She coaxed him from the table.

He uttered weakly, "But what of my message to the king?"

She snapped the quill. "Later, my lord,...why, I'll write it for you."

Having soothe the warlord in her tent till he dozed, Erinysia unveiled her tiger-eye crystal, but quickly recovered it when a messenger entered to apprise her of the prisoners just taken. She immediately left for Bennet's tent.

Erinysia glanced for a moment at the frightened girl near the entrance before staring with menace in her heart at the captain of the earl's contingent. "You, captain, most of all, turn my stomach by your bald betrayal while under my command."

"Your command, my lady? You jest, of course. I could never submit to *your* command."

"Silence!" she ordered.

"No, I have been silent too long and my soul suffers. You lied to me and told me that the young earl was held captive under a king gone mad. Only to discover that it is you who are the mad captor. I am loyal to the young earl and the poor dear here," the captain said as he gestured to Lady Maureen, "out of deference to their father's dying wish that I watch over them. Nothing else takes priority, not you, nor the king."

"King! You dare provoke me with the word! Why, Henry has pressured all the barons of the land—including your earl, my late husband—to affix their seals to his worthless paper."

"That worthless paper is *the* Document to insure peace and to eliminate just what you are planning by your witchcraft," the loyal captain protested boldly.

She motioned to Bennet's guards to take him away and commanded, "Do not wait till dawn. Hang him now."

"What! Am I not to see my wife for the last time?" The captain gaped.

She laughed derisively. "Nay, I shall spare the dear of such a repulsive moment; besides, she is my lover now."

The captain seethed, then yielded calmly, bravely and was escorted out.

The young Lady Maureen squirmed between two other guards and bowed before her. "Oh, Erinysia, and one time stepmother, spare the noble captain, I beseech you. The dear man, all my life I've known him and know that he but spoke from the heart and not the head. Spare him!" The girl sobbed and groveled at Erinysia's feet.

She patted the girl's pate and said softly, "Oh, my sentimental child and one time daughter, grieve not for those who are paid to die. Think how well the captain was cared for by your father all those years. Now payment is due." She looked over at a guard. "Take the dear child to my maidens' tent and have them see to her comfort."

The girl shrunk from the guard when he touched her arm, and then clutched at Erinysia's robe. "Oh, Erinysia, why, why are you so eager to destroy? Was not my father kind enough? Did he not take you from the gypsy wandering roads and give you a straight path to a nation you could finally call your own?"

She laughed coarsely. "Ah, dear Maureen, indeed a country of my own—all mine!" Erinysia gently stroked the girl's cheek. "Think not on worrisome Roman roads; rather at your age, enjoy the pleasures Pan's uncluttered path has in store for you. You'll see, my child." She lifted her to her feet. "Be gentle with her," she said to the guard who urged the girl toward the tent's opening.

"What now lurks in the blackness of your mind?" Bennet asked, looking at Erinysia with curiosity. "For sure, I thought she too would be hanged with the captain."

"It is my mind and black it shall remain when I choose to have it so," she snapped.

"That hardly makes for a trusting relationship." He frowned and chanced a glaring look.

"Did you not but a turn of time's glass ago agree to do my bidding?"

"Aye." He bowed his head in submission.

"Then prepare the lambs of the old Earl's ranks and march them toward their slaughter under arrows—begin the assault." She glowered at him and pointed to the exit. "But first where are the other prisoners?"

"In the stockade to cool their hot youthful tempers."

"Send the earl's son to his sister's tent. The maidens will soften him." Bennet bowed and wondered silently this time what stuff of spirit constituted her mysterious, blackened soul. "And summon here that fool of a knight that makes up the left hand of Lance."

Bennet scowled. "Foolhardy, my love, he is in a violent mood and vows to do us in. You will never break him. He thinks Rhonda's fate is your doing."

She snarled and said, "Yea, and he would have been entirely right if you hadn't failed!"

Indeed, Bennet was right: she had been unable to summon sufficient prowess and charm to affix Bryan under her command. Repeatedly she slapped the face of the steadfast knight in chains. Barely could she refrain from running a dagger through him. Frustrated, she sliced his cheek, then had the guards force a potion down his throat and drag him back to the stockade. She returned to her tent, knowing she would have the loyal knight under her spell in due time. Her tent was specially decorated to suit her beguiling femininity in her accustomed perverse moments. She stood over the satin bunk in which Kalab slept. She looked up for a moment with closed eyes as if conjuring a spirit, then looked down at him and began the pendulum action of her amulet over his head while she whispered an invocation:

> MY LOVING MOTHER OF OUR TRUE KIND, LET THERE APPEAR
> WHAT IS WHAT WILL BE AND THUS LOCK IN THE OLD
> KALAB'S MIND DETERMINATION TO OBTAIN OUR PURPOSE.

She bent over him and nudged him. He stirred. "Awake, old man to charmed appearances," she mandated.

The old warlord sat up, stretched a moment, then wrapped his arms round her rump and pressed his hirsute cheek into her soft stomach. "Oh, you wicked wench, is there no way I can be rid of you? Night and day—awake or asleep—you taunt me with your sinful beauty. I just did dream of our love-making and now awake I must submit to your delicious enchantment again."

She giggled and rubbed his head caressingly. "My, lord, have you forgotten we have a war on our hands. I need you on the battlefield. Already Bennet's lieutenants lead the earl's brigade toward Henry's battlement."

He pushed her away. "This cannot be! It is I who am in charge! I told you I wish assurance of my daughter's safety."

"Yea, that she is. A girl that sweet and innocent is in heaven, verily."

"Aye, but as an old lady; now she will remain innocent and sweet and then much agéd to heaven she will go. Meantime, I wish to warrant that she has secured this distant fate of a comfortable old age."

"As I have already said secure she is." She urged him to his feet and pressed him to the table and uncovered her bulging cat's eye.

"Oh, no, what now in your vision do I *not* wish to see?" He turned his eyes away and looked to the tent top as the crystal spread its hue of ghastly ashen green.

"Look now upon sweet truth," she said, touching his shoulder. Slowly he turned and shielded his eyes from the eerie glow.

She grabbed his wrists to remove his hands from his eyes. "Come now, my lord, you wanted to see to Rhonda's fate. See how content she is in her adoring mother's arms."

He gaped at the glowing image, rubbed his eyes but still the diminutive figures, once the objects of his love, burned in his retinae. "Oh, no!" he cried.

"Oh, yes!" she cried. "But why no? Look closely. See how happy in the fleecy heavens they romp! Would that I had that fate!"

"Oh, witch, is there no abyss into which I can toss your devilry and rid the world of such ghastly pain?" He crooked his arm to shield his eyes and stepped back.

"Pain, my lord—is it painful to see mother and daughter in loving reunion for all eternity? And why do you persist in ascribing witchcraft?—the thanks I get for trying to smooth the anxious flutter in your heart."

He pounded his chest and cried, "Smooth?—when at this moment I swear my heart is pushing its way out to thump the floor with its gravity!"

"In my kindness, I wished to spare you the harshness of its cause. But if gravity you feel then give its heaviness purpose." She took his hand and urged him toward the light which momentarily darkened then flared up a bloody red. "Contrary to your suspicion of me, look you into the reality of her fate."

"Oh, God, spare me! Pinch me that I may wake from this evil mare!" he wept and cowered from the hideous light. With gentle hand she stroked his beard, and with the other she pressed against the back of his neck and bowed his head toward the fiery ball.

"Look you into the truth and vile ways of this world, and thus take comfort that Rhonda now lives in unburdened spirit." The concentration of light dimmed and diffused the tent while under glass it cleared to a faint, misty red. The old warlord blinked to see his Rhonda grimacing with pain as Bryan repeatedly plunged a dagger into her heart.

The warlord recoiled, then grinned, chortled and finally blustered a manly laugh. "Truth, you show me?—never! No more than a common witch's tale! For never in a million moons could the faithful Bryan harm a hair upon my daughter's head!"

"Deceiving yourself by perceiving truth deceiving will not deceive the sisters of fate to splice the cut that's snapped the thread of dear Rhonda's life." She smirked at his confidence while stroking her throat where Bryan's marks still lingered from his attempt to choke her but an hour before.

He buried his face in his hands and sobbed. She touched his shoulder; he pulled away. "The touch of death is what your caresses mean," he yelped. "But in this you're wrong. Why, Bryan loved my Rhonda ever since she was a toddler! He could not commit such an atrocity."

"Ah, love is what brought the end," she said, again touching his shoulder, but again he backed away.

"Duped, deceived, stripped of my manhood, bewitched—whatever be the agent—of this I'm sure; and if you persist with this doomsaying I swear I shall strangle the black magic out of you!"

"The black magic of Bryan's envy is what did her in, my lord—not I," she said softly, soberly, though she jerked her hand again to her throat from the vision of Bryan's having tried just that.

"How can you expect me to believe you? Even aside from the obvious of not wanting to, you forget that Bryan is with Lance."

She shook her head vigorously. "Nay, he only left with Lance as a pretense. In reality, he doubled back because he was sick at heart when he learned from Tracy, Rhonda's ostensibly loyal servant and friend, that young Henry was Rhonda's secret suitor while Bryan was off doing her brother's battles."

He guffawed and slapped his barrel chest. "Well, then, perhaps cause to kill Henry's son, surely not Rhonda!"

She snickered, "'Tis surprising that a young man would know the workings of a woman's mind where you a man of great experience would not. For surely, Rhonda would never forgive him; and with his having made her lover a martyr, she would never forget his rival."

He laid his eyes upon the tiger's eye, which was now but a weak candle flicker, but he could not see it, so trapped was his inner vision from the turmoil of his heart. "Oh, Erinysia, why this cruel tale?...Why, oh, why do you impose such woe upon my already woefully human soul?"

She held his beard, damp from tears, between gentle hands. "Oh, my darling, it is not I but life's cloudy perceptions that impress gray misery onto the world." She stepped over to his armor stacked in a corner. "Come now, my lord, firm up your loins and avenge the misery heavy in your heart by at least making an appearance on the line in moral support of the initial attack. Then I promise I shall caress the hurt within and flesh it out with the many goose bumps with which your body will be blanketed."

Early in the morning Erinysia slipped from under Kalab's heavy arm, slipped on a robe and left the tent to ascend the knoll. Lifting her chin to the grim northern sky, she pressed her amulet to her forehead and muttered softly, "Why, Mother, did a mere squire—to the notorious Lance or not—not only dare resist me, but attack me as well?...Oh, shake the brute Plateos from its slumber!...And pray it cannot be that the dreadfully human Eve stirs and has conjured countermanding powers?" Just then the sky lit up with violent lightning and cracked through rolling thunder to which she hysterically laughed. She returned to her tent, determined she would again test Bryan even though she was disappointed in her self that she had to resort to a potion to sedate him. That evening she had her guard retrieve the prisoner Bryan whom she would titillate throughout the night by her wiles of sexuality.

26. *The Tiger's Eye*

From her vantage point atop the knoll opposite and safely distant from the castle, Erinysia had spent a good part of the day observing the mêlée. Her late and previous husband's soldiers under her spell had fought competently by at least establishing a siege round the city. Over her shoulder she looked skeptically to the northern sky, even though she felt moderately successful. However, Bennet's prediction held fast: Henry's archers, in spite of her spell, indeed were relatively skillful in spite of her spellbinding intercessions wreaking havoc upon them. Her own troops suffered immeasurably. Notwithstanding the heavy toll, she was pleased in that Henry's defense did not come without high cost. She had seen dozens topple from the battlements and scores of his foot soldiers that had fallen forward from the bailey wall down behind the thick rocky bulwark, whence those still alive were carried back into the castle bailey wards. Indifferently she laid eyes upon the handful of Hunter's bedraggled survivors returning to the new reserve camp in the ravine below the castle, she retired to the camp. She decided that this was the time to muster Bryan into her service.

The guard pushed him hard into the tent. Bryan, his wrists cuffed together, lost footing and landed, sprawling before the hem of her robe.

"No need of this rough-handling," she said sternly. "Remove his chains."

"But, Lady Erinysia, he is dangerous! Did you forget the last time you summoned him, and he almost strangled you," the guard protested.

"That was *then* . Do as I say!" The guard immediately jumped to her command, pulling Bryan onto his feet. "At one time, yea, he was a dangerous enemy. Now he is to become a docile, loyal servant. My most thorough guard, you may leave." The guard's jaw dropped. She chuckled. "Fear not; he is harmless now and ready to accept orders as easily as you do, loyal one."

"Even so, my lady, I shall remain in calling distance." The guard swiveled on his heels and left.

Erinysia stared up and into Bryan's lifeless eyes. She strolled round the strong body, touching him here and there as though at a bondsman auction. "Yea, I see clearly why you were picked to be at the side of Lord Lance. 'Tis a pity I've had to distil your strong spirit." She reached up and caressed his stubble and lightly ran her finger over the cut. "Such a pity I lost my temper and disfigured such an Adonis. Bryan stood rigid. "Oh, my dear handsome knight, why could you not yield and be my champion? Not only is Bennet not in the same league as warrior, he falls far short of your beauty." She slid her hand under his tunic and caressed his chest. "Pity, indeed, too thorough a job I have done to control you," she snarled, in self-reproof as she observed no response from him. Then she went to his lower parts. He gasped. She smiled. "Ah, perhaps not so completely spiritless, after all, eh?" She continued fondling him as she lifted his shirt and wet-kissed his lean chest. Suddenly he gently nudged her apart and took her face between his hands, kissing her hair, forehead eyes and cheeks before kissing her softly on her eager lips. He then loosened the collar string of her robe and slipped it down her arms letting the garment fall to the floor. He caressed the frills of her satin robe-linge, then drew her close, kissing her passionately, and with jerking whispers, "Tracy, Tracy."

She pulled away laughing. "Ah, then you remember, do you? Well, why not? After all, am I not memorable—even by that name?" She led him to the bed dressed in fine satin and quickly she satisfied her hunger for a young man as she had through Tracy's young responsive body five nights before.

As though he were a little boy, she dressed him in fine clothes and girded his own sword. "Now, sweet thing, you have your instructions and a chance at gratitude for my passion for you." She tapped his shoulder, then turned and snapped her fingers. The black cat slipped into the tent. "Merge now with my darling pet. And before you know it you will be inside Henry's castle. Do the deed and do not get yourself killed—now, that I have seen twice that there is still a delicious side of you so very much alive. Now begone!"

The cat arched its spine and its eyes glowed the same eerie green of the tiger eye crystal, and Bryan was sucked into its body and both vanished.

The young earl, garbed in a light woman's robe, entered with a supper tray and placed it in on a table covered in red satin. He bowed before her. She tapped the scarf wrapped round his head and toyed playfully with his large round ear-rings dangling. "My how beautiful you are! Did you enjoy my maidens? I must speak to them. I think you need a bit more color in the lips and cheeks. Pitiful that you did not bronze yourself in this summer's sun instead of wastefully mourning for your father." She pecked him on the cheek and said, "Now off with you—I'm sure the maidens miss you already, so bored are they with each other and common eunuchs." He kissed her hand and darted for the door and turned round to bow. She gave him final orders, "And send me your sister, the darling Maureen. Too short a time earlier today. Tell her to hasten; for I long for the gentle presence of my stepdaughter."

Several hours before dawn, Erinysia woke up in a sweat. Gently she removed her arm from under the sleeping Maureen and carefully got out of the bed. She went directly over to the tiger's eye and uncovered it. It was pulsating a dark blue light dimly illuminating the image of Bennet frowning and in a cold, low voice, warning: *Beware of Lance!* "Humph!" she grunted and threw the cloth back over and headed back to bed. But so powerful did the ball emit a new intensity that the tent glowed in scarlet. She returned and removed the cover. There in the crystal were Lance and Lucia leading an army through the warm valley aglow in the brilliance of dawn. She snapped her fist in the palm of the other hand, then tossed on her outer robe, and slipped the chain of her amulet over her head, blustering out of the tent.

The guard, having nodded off, was startled. "My lady, what brings you out into the cold of early morning?"

" 'Tis the best time to think," she said abruptly and continued on toward the other side of the knoll where she observed clear features of the castle aglow, more than usual, from excessive torchlight. "Ah, it seems, now loyal Bryan, you have agitated royal smugness!" She caressed her amulet and closed her eyes, then heard purring and felt her cat sidling her leg. She stooped down. "The deed is done, Bryan?...Be not modest, show yourself. Though Maureen is delicious I hunger for your sterner touch....Come now, do not toy with me...." She shook the cat violently. "Appear, I say!" The cat escaped her hold and ran off. "Well, no matter, if he did the deed. They'll be a propitious moment to draw him to me." She oscillated the amulet, then raised it to her lips. She stretched up her other arm to the sky and canted:

> "Great powers of the firmament, turn thy turbulence to the
> north and unhorse intrusive Lance bent on undermining my
> destiny!"

She dropped to the cold hard earth and turned her ear to it. She raised her head momentarily to giggle. "Ah, yea, Mother, I hear you stirring—ah, capital that you should at last invoke the thunderous reptile!" Erinysia kissed the earth and rose up. "Now, my dear Bryan, let us see in the cat's eye what you've been up to." She headed down toward her tent.

27. Witches' Brew

In their descent after the mysterious storm through the flanking mountains, high above on the southern face a roar was heard. Suddenly a snake crossed Lucia's steed. The white stallion reared up, then bolted down the trail. Lance spurred his new charger and followed at fast gait to assist Lucia with the reins. Lucia, however, controlled the steed after some hundred paces. Lance came abreast and they reeled round and waited for the men. They were both in shock to witness a huge dragon emerging from the tall trees on the mountain side. "My God! I can't believe my eyes!" Lucia shrieked. "The beast Plateos really does exist!"

"Aye!" cried Lance, "It must be thirty feet in length!"

Pandemonium broke out with horses rearing up, whinnying, and stomping. Riders unhorsed ran for shelter. Some of the mounted scurried away. The dark green monster lapped out its white hot fiery breath upon the ill-fated in its path. Of the brave, several horses and riders went flying from its active powerful claws. Only Gregory could control his old, experienced warhorse so he could maneuver combat readiness—contrary to what he had told Bryan—against the fifteen-foot tall assailant out of the scrolls of antiquity. Gregory jabbed its rustic underbelly, then backed off from the enraged reptile to avoid its deadly strokes and held his shield against the hot gaseous vent. Thrice he repeated this maneuver and thrice the monster countered, but lastly the monster scorched the steed which bucked and Gregory was hurled to the ground whereupon the monster trampled him with its heavy, massive hind legs, then let out a stream of flames, setting the brave knight afire.

Lance had tried desperately to come to his aid; but unnerved horses and fleeing men across the path slowed down the fearless buckskin. When Lance finally faced off with the monster, Gregory was already dead, his body smoldering. Lance—sword raised and shield high—slashed at the monster's green scaly forelegs to avoid the steel-like claws, a foot in length and sharp as an arrowhead, while he maneuvered round to get at its ten foot tail. With a mighty swoop of the sword he cut half way into the huge extremity. The monster hissing and spitting fire twisted round and with a powerful swipe of its claws smashing into Lance's shield, the immense force unhorsed the mighty warrior, leaving him at the mercy of the dangerous flames. But the already loyal stallion held its ground, and rose on its haunches to paw at the strange underbelly until the hot gases forced it to back away. Some brave men, having witnessed in their skirmish against Angus the steadfastness and loyalty of the powerful warhorse left behind were amazed by the adaptability of the new home-grown steed. They moved forward with spears to distract the monster from their new leader, still prone and stunned. The monster swung round and unleashed its fiery breath. The men backed away from the scorching heat. One soldier screamed when set afire and rolled in the path while a comrade desperately scooped up dirt, tossing it on the soldier's flaming clothes. The monster was about to swing back to the dazed Lance, when Lucia pulled up her horse, swiftly strung an arrow to her golden bow and barely time to take aim, unleashed the silver-tipped arrow. It found its mark deep between the monster's hideous red, vertical eyes. The monster howled chillingly, reverberating from mountain to mountain; blindly it clawed the air and slowly, painfully toppled and fell back, narrowly missing Lance. The monstrous thing felled three trees in its weighted, thundering fall.

The brave men gathered round their princess and cheered. Those emerging from their hiding places hailed the princess too. She dismounted and ran to Lance, who had removed his helmet and was rubbing his head.

"Oh, my dear," she cried, "Saint George is but a figment of the mind. Promise me, the next time we encounter a dragon in our path, you will keep your distance and not try to emulate the legendary saint."

"Believe me Lucia there will be no next time. I'll maneuver to the farthest corner of the earth to avoid it! I wish Gregory had."

"Yes, truly brave are knights of Mari," she said reflectively. She then ordered a carter to return the bodies to the valley for proper burial. Others threw kindling on the fallen monster and torched it; however a puff of green smoke enveloped the men. When it cleared, the fire was out and the carcass of the monster had disappeared.

The hardy band of over five hundred strong—all on horseback but for the carters—moved down from the high country without further incident. When they reached the vast stretch of sparsely heathered moor, bleak weather set in and they had to maneuver carefully through dense fog—especially the carters whose oxen and draft horses resisted moving on. At one point horsemen dismounted and carters jumped from their driver seats to guide the animals through the thick soup. Toward evening the fog lifted somewhat and they were able to organize a campsite. Lance broke off branches of a dead tree and made a fire. Lucia removed her breastplate, which Lance had insisted she put on after the Plateos episode, and then ordered the carter of provisions to sort out the food for the cooks to prepare the meals for the evening. Fires soon flared as hungry men gathered round for supper.

Lucia heard wailing and whimpering in the distance toward the south. She and Lance decided to investigate. As the wailing grew louder, they were able to descry its source of four shadowy figures circling a large cauldron hanging over a fire. Lucia halted and touched Lance's shoulder and said, "Oh, no, Lance, they aren't what I think they are."

"I'm afraid so. Verily, I haven't seen such witches since my childhood, except that I never saw one with a draft horse, however undernourished it looks." He grabbed her hand and they continued cautiously while listening to their incantation:

> "Feast, dear Lilith,
> Feast on our offering from the fool intruders
> Who failed thee in purging a helpless child of Eve.
> Chew sensually these animal innards
> Topped with the ambrosial lizards
> Out of the dying gut of Plateos
> Whom the invading knights of Roman culture
> Felled to violate the sanctity
> Of thy daughter Erinysia's plan
> To rule over cutthroat man

Who has cursed our kind
For all too many millennia."

Lance was mentally jolted in hearing the weird chant, suddenly dawning on him that he had indeed seen such witches as a boy when he had chanced upon a gypsy camp:

Outside a circle of gypsy carts, a young beautiful woman was dancing round such witches who were feasting from their cauldron. The image of the young dancing woman he realized now strongly resembled Erinysia! Of course, it could not have been her since it was over twenty years ago. He began to perspire when his memory brought forth the utterance of the witches as they clapped to the gypsy's movements and a younger—near Lance's age at the time—dark-haired girl mimicking the dancer while singing:

"The legend tells of a glimmer of gold
surrounding a princess of the north.
What then am I when coated in black
And brooding in dark shadows?"

And the witches turned to the little girl:

"Aye, a fairy tale
ripped from the womb of Eve
Fret not! Thou wilt be queen.
Look up at night's sky;
In spite of countless stars
Black space dominates.
Your destiny is therefore
To wrest her golden bow
And shoot down all heaven's stars."

Suddenly in his boy's imagination he saw a tiny blonde girl on top of a mountain, looking down the volcanic aperture, and holding out a wooden charm in the shape of a tree.

"Lance!" cried Lucia as she poked him. "You seem entranced! Wake up, do not look upon them!"

Lance snapped out of the haunting recollection. "Nay, I'm fine." He bravely and with measured steps—still thinking of the childhood scene that had vaguely beset him all these years—approached the witches, pointed his menacing sword at them, and growled, "What are you wicked ladies up to? It appears you are but serving hags to the omnipresent Erinysia; so, then, take your stew and poison her with it. Away from here you serve us no purpose."

One bent over the cauldron to dip a large wooden spoon into the brew. Her scrawny hand shook as she offered a spoonful to him. The flickering fire revealed her wizened face with toothless grin. "Purpose we do have, my lord;...why, we know how men ready for battle long for home-cooked tasties." She flipped back her hood, revealing through her thin gray hair a frightful countenance of rippling veins and ghastly crow's-feet.

"And a for a weary princess, too," said another, her face recessed in the shadows of her black hood, while advancing toward Lucia with a dipper dripping thick, ugly grayish green mucous-like substance. The princess jerked away in seeing bugs and bones wriggling in globs of slime, then became intrigued that the hand round the handle was smooth and slender. She squeezed her nose from the heavy, nauseous smell that seemed to stick in her throat. Lucia blinked her brown eyes, virtually reddish gold from the fire's reflection, when the witch threw back her hood, revealing an aged but handsome dark-complexioned woman with a streak of gray in her still raven flow of hair.

"Oh, come now, deary, my sisters and I spent hours preparing this for such a grand occasion. Surely, if it is fit for the goddess Lilith it is fit for a *mere* princess."

Lance stepped between the second witch and Lucia and fended off the offering with a short swing of the flat of his blade. The witch howled, stooped over to retrieve her dipper, then rose up to face him, flashing her wide, wild, dark but piercing eyes. He was momentarily stunned as he saw that she resembled the dancing lady of yore. He turned away and spoke to the old hag. "Enough of this nonsense," he scolded, "you mischievous, unworldly women mean to poison us with your sick ingredients, I'll warrant....And how is it you seem to know the princess?"

"No identity is a mystery to us, *Lord-Protector* of the realm," the old gray one said with a mystifying grin.

The raven haired one added, still sniveling from the sting in her hand. "Yea, Lord Lance, you should know." Her eyes burning into his.

Again he looked away, and turned to the cauldron but jerked away in seeing two human skulls bubbling up.

Brushing the peat off the emptied dipper, the younger witch tugged forward her hood and said, looking up at him with a mixture of venom and fear, said, "My lord, potions we so carefully mixed are of the killed, never designed to kill—and surely not that which is intended for our living, loving Lilith."

One of the other witches stoked the fire. Lance was surprised to see that she was young, though drawn and deathlike. He turned to the shadows. The fourth one protruded from the shadows and went to the caldron to dip a cup in to the bubbly mix. Her scaly hand brought it to a large curving mouth. In the blazing fire he could discern under the hood a grotesque apparition of a serpent. "So, I see...now why there are four of you who as a rule conjure in threes! The devil himself has appeared to pay tribute to our fighting men, I gather. What now, you fish head interloper, more dragons to block our path of righteousness?"

She hissed, flapping her split tongue. "Nay, no need...ye dolts won't see the dawn as penalty for killing my son Plateos."

Lance grinned. "My, an egg so large came out of a sickly sinuous thing like you? Witchcraft, indeed, is a deplorable art! If you're not concocting stinking brew, monstrosities give birth to monsters." Deftly and without the slightest indication, Lance swung his blade and beheaded the teetering thing. Hood along with it landed in a copse of briar, whence it hissed and howled, then commanded to its body, "Avenge, O body!" The black clad bloody body snaked out at Lance, twisting its length round his neck, to strangle him.

Midst the wails and supporting cheers from the other two sisters—the other frail one, continued absently to stoke the fire—Lucia quickly ran to Lance, and with her golden sword started cutting into the headless serpent which nonetheless kept its strangle-hold on the gasping knight, who could barely negotiate a groan: "Not here, Lucia, get the commanding head!" Lucia leaped to the briar, reacting swiftly by stabbing the hissing head repeatedly, then into its bulging eyes whose squirting blood vaporized into a pervasive red luminosity. The snake-body relinquished and slid off the nearly asphyxiated warrior who staggered and slumped into the soggy peat. Lucia ran to Lance's aid. The twisting body crawled into the fire under the cauldron and great sparks flew wildly as the frail witch cowered, then jumped away to cling to the raven haired witch.

The gray, toothless one swung round to the other two and scowled, "You wouldn't shrink from this if you discarded your mortal coun-tenance—fools you are to cling to foolish cosmetics!" She quickly dashed to scoop up the eyeless head. She ran to the fire and cauterized the head to the hot flaming, writhing body. Suddenly the head transformed into two—the skeletal awe-struck faces of the highwaymen. The witch dipped her spoon into the cauldron and spooned the potion into their mouths, revealing forked tongues. The rogues slithered out of the cauldron

Lucia assisted Lance to his feet, then lunged and deftly thrust the sword into the old witch's back. The witch groaned and dissolved. A scorpion crawled out from under the frock. Lucia poked it with the blade and swooped it into the sparking fire. The two-headed serpent rushed her from behind, but with a skillful swoop of his heavy sword, Lance severed both heads that then plopped into the boiling cauldron, howling human cries. Lucia ran down the other witches clinging to each other and was amazed to see vaporizing before her eyes two human-like, frightened women who then vanished into the prevailing red glare.

She returned to Lance who was regaining his breath. He said, "Dear

Lucia, again I owe you my life."

"And I you—my life, it seems, is your life, my knight."

He chortled. "Some knight I'm becoming—can't even defend myself against old hags!"

"They weren't exactly defenseless, you know—except perhaps the two younger ones."

"Aye, weird, eh? I saw one—the shell of my dreams."

She laughed. "Perhaps a jealous lover of yours? In any case, they didn't seem to belong."

"Nor do I think you belong here, Lucia. It is much too dangerous. Erinysia apparently is more than I expected. You must turn back."

"Nonsense—even if I wanted to, I couldn't. My detachment would return also, despite my wishes. I could never leave you all alone."

He chuckled, rubbing his throat, then said humbly, "Aye, it's clear to me now how much I need you....Still,..."

"Hush, my sweet."

As they approached the border Lance led them to the eastern trail. He turned to Lucia to explain. "There's not much point, other than brief rest, in going to the castle of Mari—and surely Rhonda will not be there. With Gregory's report it is obvious the attack on Henry's castle, where hopefully will be my sister, is under way."

The long horse column traveled through the lower kingdom's wide manorial expanse. Peasants from fields marveled at the power and swiftness of the steeds. Lance was struck by the peaceful industry that prevailed among the serfs and the past war barons now devoted to the manor itself. He felt proud that his sundry victories were not in vain, yet saddened that it could eventuate into futility with the nation plagued by sorcery. When they approached a castle high upon a hill, Lucia, cried out, "Lance, this is the first castle in the lowlands I've seen on a natural hilltop."

Turning his horse partially round to reply, "I gather you noticed, not many mottes are. Yea, there aren't many hills down here."

She nodded. " 'Tis clear as to why it is called the lowlands—sunken would be more like it....Pray, where are we now?"

"This is the Godwin manorial lands. He is a good friend—that is, if he hasn't been bewitched." He added a chuckle. "Fortunately my great grandfather laid claim to a rare prominence to build the Mari. The king, too, has the luxury—surely not one near as high as your mountain—of a high plateau to protect the city. Some of the barons have man-made elevated battlements but at the cost of cruel, back-breaking labor. Wasteful sweat, I might add, if only we could learn to live in harmony."

She looked over with admiration and said, "Lance, for a man of war you amaze me with your thoughtfulness."

"I'd prefer you thought of me as a man of peace, in spite of my trappings."

"Oh, I do!"

As the column drew nearer to the castle, to everyone's surprise the drawbridge was lowered and the portcullis raised. Baron Godwin rode out personally to greet them. He pulled up a beautiful black horse. "Lance, a godsend to see you back! I heard from the vine you were in the high country. What a stroke of luck you chanced by this manor."

"Greetings, Godwin, but not at all by chance. I trusted that you would welcome us. This cavalry has traveled a long way and in need of some rest and provisions."

"Then you've chosen wisely."

"Thank you, Baron, I knew I could count on your hospitality."

The Baron looked to the officers and the column. "In sooth, all of you are welcome guests within our walls." He turned to look squarely at the princess.

Lance gestured toward Lucia. "Permit me, Baron, to intro..."

"No need," the baron chortled, "I can see for myself she needs no introduction. Truly, you can be no other than the legendary princess of the north — a firm believer Iam. We of Quandron have heard much of you."

"Oh, my," she said with a mildly embarrassed smile, "I trust all good tales."

"Indeed, especially of your beauty. But no report could compare with the actual appearance. You are exquisite!"

She giggled. "And I have heard tales that Quandron's men are superb flatterers." She laughed. "If I may indulge that is a beautiful horse and looks very familiar."

"Thank you, princess, and well it should since it cost so much and familiar indeed, since it came from your country by way of greedy traders."

"Yea, I hear they are tough traders," said the princess, then smiled up at her champion, "but Lance has put an end to that. You are free now, Baron, to trade directly with us."

"Oh, that is good news! he said with excitement, then turned to Lance. "Of course, these metal heads like our sturdy workhorses."

Lance, eying the bucksin, vented proudly, "You don't see me mounted on one now, do you? I'm converted. I'll gladly give up strength for the agility of these grand beasts." He patted the scorched mane of his steed.

The Baron viewed the steed. "Beautiful animal, but, pray, what happened to its mane?"

He chuckled and looked over at Lucia for a moment. "A long story, Baron, but first your hospitality."

"Aye, forgive me. Onward to my home."

Later in the evening after Lucia's force was settled in the immense outer bailey, and they and the horses were fed, Lance and Lucia went up to the second landing of the square keep to the private rooms of the baroness who had invited them to join her and her husband for supper. Lucia's eyes widened over the rich display of fine foods which she had not seen since leaving her home. Lance filled his plate and in no time scraped it clean. He reached for another ale, winked at Lucia, then glanced at their hostess and said, "A very fine meal, Baroness; I must say it was clear that it contained no lizards, toads and rodents either."

The baroness arched her brows, but before she could protest, Lucia broke in. "Don't listen to his dreadful and disgusting humor, my lady. It is our private joke, and if you will pardon the obvious pun, in very poor taste." Lance broke into convulsions.

The baroness asked, mildly perturbed, "What still another joke?" Lance laughed again and almost fell back on his chair.

"Oh, my," uttered the princess, "please, Lance, behave yourself and let me relate the story." She eyed the hostess warmly, then with a serious look said, "You see, my lady, we met on the moor these four witches several days ago."

"How odd," said the baron, "four you say?"

Lance chuckled. "Well, one wasn't really a witch—that is, I don't think so."

Lucia turned to him, annoyed. "Well, if you must be that precise, there was in fact only two."

"I suppose, you're right if you're counting the one with black hair. To be more precise one was the devil's serpent!" Lance laughed freely. Of course, there was still another?"

"Lucia frowned, but asked, "There was?"

"Aye, the serpent became two-headed!"

"Oh, just eat some more and do not interfere," she commanded.

"Oh, goodness," cried the baroness, "how utterly confusing."

"Then I shall explain," said Lucia. These four witches..."

"But you said two, just now," the baroness broke in.

"Yes, I did..." she reached next to her and lightly punched her laughing companion. "Lance, you're like an unruly child. Now, let me explain this." She smiled at the baroness and continued, "When we came across them on the moor, they were clumsily dancing and chanting round a large cauldron of the most horrid blend you would ever want to lay your eyes on and even worse put your nose to."

The baroness looked over at Lance and said, "Well, thank God, then, your remark was in jest. I was afraid for a moment you were leading up to an accusation of witchcraft on my part. We are all so edgy these days from the rumors flying concerning that wilful, wily woman Erinysia."

"Oh were they but rumors!" Lance replied. "I fear she is in sooth and by no means an ordinary witch."

"Why I had no idea there were ordinary witches," the baroness said perplexedly.

"True, but this one is extraordinary," Lucia joined in. "Allow me to explain." Lucia went on to relate their experience on the moor and with the dragon Plateos.

When she had finished, the baron said, "This story coming from anyone but you, princess, I should have laughed off."

"And I too, at such a tale," the princess agreed, "had I not first hand experience." Then she turned to Lance. "You know, Lance, I realize now that Erinysia must have been responsible for that freak storm in the valley as well."

He raised his brows. "God's Blood, I forgot about that. Why, for sooth, you're right."

"What storm?" the baroness asked rather nervously. "There has been no storm."

Lucia explained, "No, your baroness, this was in my valley some five days ago." She then related the experience of the storm.

"Oh, my, my, is there nothing this woman cannot conjure up?" the baroness moaned while twitching, almost spilling her drink.

"Nothing good apparently," her husband said sardonically.

She looked at her husband with wariness. "My God, Winnie, are we safe here? I mean she has these powers at such great distances. She probably knows Lance is here. What if she raises havoc in the castle?" She glanced at the visitors.

The baron laughed it off. "Oh, she would've unleashed herself long ago. Don't forget, we're in this too when I refused to join Bennet in his treachery."

Lance perked. "What's this? Bennet solicited you in a conspiracy?"

"Aye, and the rascal went so far as to try convince me that you were the leader of the conspirators, imagine?" The baron tossed down a long draft of ale.

Lance nodded to the air. "Loyal Bennet...so hard to believe he too could be duped."

The baron set down his drink with a bang and said, "Of course, I knew he was lying about you and told him so. Surely, it made no sense that with all your victories in behalf of the crown you would turn around and betray the king." He poured more ale into his silver tankard, then added, "I'm truly ashamed that I even tolerated listening to his story, I should have killed him on the spot. And sorry for you Lance, that your father was responsible for the conspiracy,… though now so clear the poor old man is bewitched."

"In truth, but still, I hold him responsible for getting tied up with that monstrous woman to begin with. And God help me if my sister is harmed out of all this—I shall kill him." He turned to the baroness and said seriously, "Your fears, good baroness, are not ungrounded. To ease you I promise we shall be gone by dawn." He glanced back at the baron. "I am in truth very honored that you, Godwin, have offered your contingency to assist us in our goal. But in light of your wife's fears I cannot accept. They might well be needed here."

In the gray just before dawn, the baron was wakened by the tossing and turning of his wife next to him. He reached over to calm her. He was startled to feel soft fur where her face should be. He wailed in fear as he sat up, squinting in the dim light to see a big black cat smothering the baroness. The baron grabbed it by the tail, dragging it away from his wife. The cat arched its back, then caterwauled into a crouch and leaped at the baron's throat. The baroness sat up and shrilled. Fortunately Lance had risen early and was on his way down the passage to Lucia's room to wake her. When he heard the baroness, he bolted to the room and flung open the door. With one knee in bed, Lance with both hands gripped the cat's neck, pulling it away from the baron, then swung it round to the foot of the bed while increasing the strangle hold round its neck. The more he squeezed the larger the animal grew. Lance could no longer press the throat from behind. He let up for an instant to turn it toward him. The cat clawed his cheek. It grew to the size of a panther, the yellow spot increased to cover its breast, and Lance nearly let go from the increasing circumference of the neck. Suddenly he saw the face of Erinysia snarling at him, but determined, he choked it harder. Its face then transformed into the serpent's that he had beheaded. Its fangs lapped out at him. As the neck grew thicker Lance was losing his grip, he struggled to lift it and ran to the window. Just as he tossed it out, in horrible disbelief he saw the face of Tracy. He lunged in futility as though to catch it in flight. He heard a hissing sound and then a woman's scream. He looked down in horror. The great black leopard leaped across the moat and disappeared; but there on the embankment of the moat clad in the black cloak of the moor lay the lifeless body of Tracy.

28. Henry: a King's Past

In the royal conference room, Henry the king sat rigid and tense at the head of the huge table of thick oak while listening intently to his knights discuss their being under siege. A tall thin man near the opposite end stood, leaning forward, his hands spread on the table and his eyes on the king: "Why should we listen to Sir John and your cousin Arnold who have but a handful of men?"

A stocky man with a round red face released his tankard from his heavy lips and rejoined, "Why should we *not* is a better question, Lord Gideon. For one thing the handful of whom you derisively speak consists of the greatest knights in the world....Surely you've heard of the shining heroics led by Sir Robert on the moor. Frankly I see no other action than to do as Sir John bids."

The king looked at the stocky man and asked, "Why, Sir James, do you feel there is no other course?"

"My king, I do not say there is no other, but I perceive the rightness of John's caution." The king glanced at Arnold who nodded agreement.

Sir John, sitting at the opposite end, tugged on his reddish gray beard and offered, "I do not advocate caution, rather that we simply await Lord Lance."

"Bah," groaned Gideon as he rapped the table and turned to John. "What good can one man possibly do?"

James rapped his tankard and said, "We are not speaking of just *any* man."

"In sooth, you have my support on that score," Arnold bellowed.

"Verily," said the king. "Granted, what you say is widely given. Lord Lance is a powerful ally to the services of the crown; nevertheless, he is without his army. Gideon searches well; for I fear, what with Kalab camped below, that Lance in returning will be held captive by the treacherous Bennet and the infamous witch."

John rocked his head. "Pardon, your majesty, but you discredit my commander. Lance is too versed in strategy to fall into such a trap. Foremost in his mind, I know, will be to regain his troops directly."

"Why that's preposterous!" Gideon wailed. "Why would those traitors follow him?"

"I must correct you, Lord Gideon; these men, remember, are under the command of his father in his absence and failed to see any betrayal, rather, as good soldiers they follow and in all probability under a wicked spell."

"Bah, Lance's absence, indeed!...and because of his irresponsible abandonment, we are in this fix now," Gideon reminded him, then hesitated a moment before adding, "But how could those soldiers ever be loyal again after being ordered at the border into battle against Sir Robert and their Mari comrades?"

Arnold shook his head grimly, offering, "Sadly, by now I fear the spell is irretrievable."

"Aye," reinforced Sir John, "and...is not a leader who tamed the entire nation entitled to a spell of relaxation? How was he to know his father was to go mad?"

"A leader of his renown should have known!" Gideon complained.

James gave Gideon a scornful look and countered, "You expect too much even from him." He then looked over at John. "One thing bothers me, Sir John,...How do we know your messenger will make contact with Lance."

Sir John replied, "No fear of that. Gregory is resourceful. And for all we know he might have met Lance on the north trail, already on his way back."

The king shook his head and moaned, "I simply don't understand why he wanted to head for Lodeston, anyway. Why, there is nothing there but savages!" But he quickly amended, "Of course there are exceptions."

"Indeed there are," Sir John said with a smile. Lance was always fascinated by their reputation in horse-breeding. And when his trusty steed was disabled, he decided to explore the country. Of course, that was not the only reason."

"Oh?" The king perked.

"James intervened, "Why, of course, his thinking no more battles to be won, he decided to see for himself if it were ripe for the picking, eh?"

"Nay," John replied, "to think of so great a man as a spy is insulting." He frowned at the stocky knight who lowered his eyes to his tankard and became red faced.

"Tactless of me, Sir John," James said contritely, then chuckled. "Bryan would do the dirty work."

Ignoring James, the king leaned forward to inquire. "Then, John, just what was his other reason for touring such a mountainous terrain?"

"Once in the aftermath of a battle, under the stars he expressed the importance of our mission to unite the nation and to end once and for all the endless alienation. And then out of character—for he is not known to show emotion—he said that it was time for him to search out love, in lieu of war. Curiously, he said that he knew where to find that love."

Gideon yelped, "A lovely sentiment for a love-sick minstrel, unbefitting a man of war in whom you expect us to have faith!"

"Surely, John, you do not mean that he would find love there?" James broke in. "You heard the king: they are savages!"

"According to us, they are; but not so with legend."

The king rose abruptly, trembling from memories and conscience. "Excuse me, gentlemen; this is a trying time. I suggest all of you retire for the night as I intend to do. We shall continue this discussion in the morning on whether we should hold or counterattack."

In bed that evening under Nod's shadow Henry tossed and turned driven by the beautiful faces of Lady Margaret, together with Lance's mother. He was often haunted by his indiscretion of secretly journeying to the highlands to resume a relationship with Margaret after hearing of her husband's death. Although his wife was still alive at the time, he yearned for his childhood love to compensate for the love he could not have—Lance's mother. Lady Margaret was vulnerable and they made love. Lucia was no more than ten then and told simply that the visitor was an old friend. Henry had discreetly traveled incognito. The fading ember in her heart was rekindled only to be doused once more. He never returned, though he thought of it many times after his wife's death and later—most particularly, after Lance's mother passed on. But between the young nation's political struggle and his shame of his having taken advantage of Margaret in mourning, kept him from following his heart. Often he thought of his childhood and early teens with Lady Margaret when they were so happy and carefree—until he became infatuated with one who was to become Lance's mother. When Henry's father the earl had interfered with this relationship, he would have regained his feelings for Margaret had his father not arranged the marriage with the old duke's daughter.

29. Bryan at the Castle

What Erinysia had seen through her tiger's eye the evening of Bryan's exploits shocked her into a rage:

The cat had stolen past the sentries at the old palisade—so rotted away it was of little use—and reached the moat. It crouched and leaped high in the night air and landed on the castle side of the moat. It then crawled through a crack in the bailey wall and pranced across the court toward the inner ward's bailey, which the cat scaled. It glided past castle guards of the keep, some alert, others dozing. As it approached the keep steps, it hesitated, then shook itself, slumped prematurely, giving way its image and rolled on its back concurrent with Erinysia back at her tent losing concentration by making love to young Maureen.

Bryan emerged, looking puzzled as he sat up and gazed at the surroundings. He pressed the heels of his hands to his throbbing temples. He then got up to climb the winding steps. Two guards were poised on the landing with swords in readiness. Bryan drew out his blade, ready to cut them down. They were no match for the swordsman trained by Lance. He stepped over the corpses and under the doorway and onto the passage way. Quickly he retreated into the shadows of a niche when he heard footsteps. Rita passed by him. He stealthily followed her to a door she opened. He pushed her into the room.

"My God! Is it really you, my dear Bryan?" Rhonda, seated, queried with joy and ran to him, despite being startled . "But why this crass handling of Lady Rita?...Heavens, you don't think I'm held captive!" His strange, vacant expression checked her impulse to embrace him.

Lady Rita recovering from the rough-shod treatment, questioned, "You know this ill-mannered knight?" She glanced over at him, his sword still unsheathed, and scowled. "Young man, what is your purpose that you should barge in this way contrary to even the lowest code of behavior?"

He ignored her and took a step toward Rhonda who held up her hand and said, "Yea, Bryan, why this strange greeting. Just look at dear Lady Rita—you frightened her!...Come, now, Bryan, this has gone too far. Speak....And where is my brother?" Her large round eyes popped puzzlement as he stood there without emotion as though he did not know her. She repeated pleadingly, "Where is Lance?" He continued to stare at her as though a stranger. She clasped her hands and whimpered, "No!...Bryan, you bear ill-tidings! Oh, my darling Lance! Bryan, dear, hold me in your arms before you speak of my brother's death!" Her arms opened.

He advanced, glowering and slapped down her hand, and said sternly, "Speak not of traitors! Would that he *were* dead!"

"Heavenly Mother! My ears play tricks!" she shrilled and held her hands to her face momentarily, then she looked up at him. "Oh, friend from as long as I can remember, why this cruel manner? A time of siege, alienated from my father, an attempt on my life, and now you unspeakably jest of my brother's disloyalty! Oh, Bryan, please be yourself and show your love." She reached up and clung to him.

He jerked away and pushed her forcibly. Her tiny body toppled to the flag floor. Rita picked up a candelabra and advanced to strike a blow. He saw her in the corner of his eye and deflected it with his sword, then mercilessly flung her against the door. She slid down and sat frozen in semi-consciousness. He swung round and leveled his sword to the weeping girl. "You dare speak to me of loyalty when your brother dishonors his father, and then of false love when you, my Jezebel, betray our love by bedding down with that whimpering pup Henry?"

Bewildered, she barely half raised her torso with her elbow and froze with fear gasping, "I swear I see Bryan before my eyes, but he cannot be here!" When he threateningly edged the sword closer, she, grasping her crucifix dangling on her breast, slid her body back and cried, "What awful tale of fancy picks your brain that you should roll from your tongue and behavior this frightful mood?"

"Nay, fancy does not incite my anger!" He mocked a thrust of his blade. Rhonda cowered, closing her eyes.

Bryan moved closer and bent over to Rhonda who further inched away. "Oh, dear Bryan, can't you see? This is your Rhonda! It seems you do not see who I am—rather, you look past me and see another!"

"It is Rhonda whom I see for what she really *is*," he growled and then glared and cruelly grinned. "I had seen through eyes deceived an innocent virgin, but now I see a whore!"

Rita, emerging from her stupor and picking herself up, screamed, "Erinysia the harlot is what you see, curséd knight under the witch's spell! Before you is darling, innocent Rhonda!"

"Damn up your babbling, old woman!" Bryan lunged at her and with his sword grazed her hand. She howled and ran through the door ajar. Laughing, he watched her speeding down the passage way; then he slammed the door shut. Lady Rita reached the stairway where descending she shrilled, "Help, guards, somebody, dear God!"

Bryan returned to Rhonda and held the sword's tip a hair's breadth from her heart. Her elbow collapsed her shoulder to the floor; she rolled further on her side, pressing her forehead to the cold floor, sobbing, "Oh, the devil has inflicted us with woe and wile upon our souls!"

"Aye, the devil that is within you has racked my soul!" he said as he sheathed his sword.

She sighed in relief and for the first time she detected remorse, overriding the anger in his voice. Raising herself, scrambling to her feet, she stretched out her hand to him. "Bryan, I beseech you to take my hand and touch the truth. There is no slab on which to sustain your tormented tale. You heard Rita—Erinysia is the only source of your misguided perceptions and outrageous presumptions." He grunted and slapped away her hand. Aghast but for a moment she held up her crucifix and begged, "Then touch this, and the Lord will clear away the lies beclouding your foul vision."

He held it, released it, shrunk from it, and squinted at her. Then he grasped the chain round her neck and lifted it over her head, flinging it violently against the wall, crying, "Lies, all lies!"

She gasped and cried, "Is there no way to return you to your loving nature?"

"Aye, loving hotly I shall be!" He ripped her robe at the breast line. She backed away. He gripped her shoulders and pressed her into him while smothering her neck and shoulder with hard, angry kisses. Her head shook in a frenzy. He swept her up in his arms and threw her on the bed. Her first impulse was to roll over and cry, but instead she sat up quickly and tried to push him away as he ripped the last remnants from her helpless little body. He ungirded his sword with one hand while holding her down with the other, then got on top of her while she sobbed convulsively and jerked her head side to side in the pillow.

She screamed when he forced her legs apart. When he pushed against her sanctity, she cried hysterically, "Oh, dear God, let me die!"

Suddenly the door was kicked in and young Henry rushed to the bed yanking the spellbound Bryan by the hair. Bryan rolled off the bed and tackled the intruder. While Rhonda gathered her torn remnants to cover her nakedness, they wrestled on the floor but Henry squirmed from the bigger man's hold and darted back to draw his sword. Bryan laughed, scrambling to his feet to retrieve his sword, saying sarcastically, "A lesson in swordsmanship you want—well, then, first and last it will be." The two men dueled but for a moment; Henry from the start defending himself helplessly. With a mighty swoop Bryan knocked the sword from Henry's hand and readied the fatal thrust. He paused to say, "Aye, 'tis fitting that I kill you too, since you've stolen my love." Just as he was about to lunge, Rhonda tearfully plunged a dagger into his back. He gasped, staggered and slumped to the floor, blood gushing from his mouth onto the floor as he painfully coughed. Rhonda sobbed uncontrollably into her hands.

Henry bent over him and rolled him on his side. Rhonda dropped her hands from her face and fell to her knees and threw herself upon Bryan. "Oh, my love, forgive me! 'Tis not Bryan that I dirked! Nay, some other from the nether world. So, dear Bryan, you are free to return to your sweet self. I beseech you! Return as my true knight!" She gently raised his head into her lap.

A flash of multi-colors glowed about his head. He blinked his eyes, coughed, then in a weak voice intoned, "Rhonda! My dearest love!" His eyes widened as he felt the frightening flutter in his lung. "How did I get here? What is happening?" He gasped for breath and coughed up more blood. "How kind our God that in my moment of death he grants me the sight of you, sweet Rhonda."

His soft, warm eyes she had not seen since he left with her brother surged through the bewitchment only to glaze over at his final breath. She wept profusely over his body, all the while stroking his hair and kissing his bloody lips and cheek. Henry finally gently urged her to her feet. "Small comfort, I know, Rhonda, but at least to heaven he went as truly Bryan and not to some other place as his false self."

"Yea, yea, it is a comfort in no small way to know for sure it was not Bryan that acted thus....But, oh, my prince, why did my dagger have to run so deep?"

"You had no choice in your fright. Think not on it."

"Yea, I felt only for our lives—not thinking of poor Bryan's."

30. Kalab's Reversal

Urged by Young Henry, Sir John sent Sir Robert under a white flag to the old warlord. On the edge of camp Bennet intercepted the brave rider and demanded to know what the message was. Robert scowled, reminding Bennet of the code of knighthood in war or peace.

"Ha, and where was your code when you so ruthlessly routed your fellow comrades on the moor?" Bennet reminded him.

"My ears must be upside down! How dare you flip the lip of truth!" Robert slashed back defiantly drawing his sword, despite a half dozen riders round their leader. "It was you who attacked the Mari flag! Your men carried no such heraldry, for which in time you will answer to me."

Bennet wanted no part of confronting Robert's deadly sword. "Go then to the old fool's tent," Bennet lashed out and yielded the path to the tents. "He's helpless anyway."

The old man, studying Robert, rubbed his chin. "This is not a trick? My daughter is really alive?"

Robert grimaced. "Would I be bearing the crests of the King, and the Mari, yet deliver false tidings?—and surely not one of so grave a nature."

"Yea, Robert, yea, of course not. An attempt on her life,...you say? And none other than by the once loyal Sir Bryan?"

"Aye, to the first, but, according to the prince, nay, to the second question," Robert snapped. "Though it was the strong body of Sir Bryan that forged the action, it was not in truth, Sir Bryan."

"The old warlord wrung his hands. "Yea, I know too well what it is you mean, Robert. Aye, I was witness, too, of that dastardly bewitching power unleashed on you after the battle on the moor, for which I can truly say now that I am ashamed....Return to the king and prince and inform them that the siege is over. I shall withdraw my army in the morn. I see clearly now the fool I've been."

Robert snapped his head in acknowledgment, then asked, "And what of Bennet's forces, including the earl's men—what's left of the latter, that is, after their foolish sacrifice the other day. What should I tell Sir John?"

"To hell with Bennet and his treachery. I doubt that they will have heart after my full force is gone—especially without the crack flag brigade. And even if the witch and Bennet persist, the king can easily rout them; furthermore, I shall remain in reserve if he needs my assistance provided he returns my daughter to me."

"I've been ordered to inform you that such a condition is unacceptable without evidence that you are verily free of the witch."

Kalab grimaced. "I've just told you that I am."

"Aye, that you have, but the king and prince need hard evidence, which would mean that tonight you return the rest of the Mari regiment to your castle where hopefully they will meet up with Lance."

"Aye, hopefully indeed—for I know he is a loyal son." Kalab said contritely. "Now what of my daughter?"

"I shall personally escort her out of Castle City through a secret passage not under siege and take her to meet up with the regiment to take her home safely."

Kalab nodded and extended his hand to Robert. "I know gallant knight that Rhonda will be safe with you." Robert bade farewell and left the tent.

Kalab guzzled down a brimming drink and slammed down his tankard. "So evil, bitchy witch," he murmured to himself as he picked up a sheer red and yellow scarf left by Erinysia, "Bryan was indeed involved, but thankfully, witch, your forecast was not entirely correct. It is apparent, bitch, that your scheming self sees not in your damnable crystal what *is* but what you want it to be!...Could it be, then, that Lance—granted quickly born—is indeed my true son despite those taunting canards so long ago and now the tormenting pictures in that damnable crystal dome of hers?" He poured himself another tankard of ale, and again guzzled it down. He stretched yawned and lay down on his cot.

As Robert, still bearing the white flag, swished through the tall grass of the sloping approach to the moat, he instinctively grabbed his shield when an arrow whizzed by him from behind. Instantly he bridled round his steed to see Bennet and the six riders emerge from a behind a boulder at the bottom of the ravine. Another arrow was unleashed, but he raised his shield to deflect it as he fearlessly spurred his charger toward them, swinging his sword menacingly. Bennet receded behind the riders. With one swoop of Robert's blade one of them was unhorsed and gravely wounded. Two others cowered while the other three tried to attack the brave knight from behind, but Robert immediately bridled round and slew two of them before they could level a parry. The other rider galloped back to the camp. Bennet bridled behind the two remaining and urged them forward. One was immediately beheaded by Robert's swirling sword. The other bridled back and turned to take off, leaving Bennet to face his predicted doom.

Erinysia heard the clatter of swords just as she greeted Maureen at the entrance to her tent. She pushed her inside, looked to the sky. Suddenly Robert was unhorsed by a violent swing of an immense tail from the son of Plateos. Bennet froze in terror. Robert leaped to his feet and deftly plunged his blade into the reptile's ribbed breast. The dragon staggered and let out a hideous wail, then exhaled its fiery breath and Robert became a statue of melted armor.

Later Kalab rose from his nap, disgruntled that he had fallen asleep when he had things to do. Immediately he girded his sword and left hurriedly for Erinysia's tent. Tossing the flap of her tent aside he was aghast to see her in bed with the innocent Maureen. "Is there no shred of decency in you? Release the child at once. See that she is escorted home safely and forever free from the licking likes of you who's prone to engage innocent babes in your zones of war."

Frightened, Maureen squirmed out of Erinysia's arms and jumped out of bed, gathering up her clothes to cover her budding breasts. Erinysia glowered at him and yelled, "You shall pay the price for daring to impose upon my privacy. I need her to soothe my anger toward you for being unable to make decisions and leave me hanging....And just who do you think you are to order my property away from here? This darling child belongs here with me."

She glanced over at Maureen who bewilderingly nodded agreement, saying softly, "Yes, dear Mother." Kalab reached out for the child; Maureen sat back down in the bed, clinging to Erinysia's diaphanous robe-linge.

He countered, "Oh? It's property now for everyone whose misfortune it is to be under your spell, eh? And of course that includes me!...Well, I now declare that you are without property." He turned again to the bewildered girl and ordered, "Make haste. Put on your clothes and go directly to my tent. I shall be there shortly and see to it personally that you are taken home and away from this incestuous debauchery."

Maureen had a puzzled look on her face as though she were trying to recall this man whom she had actually known. She quickly hopped out of bed, dressed and ran out of the tent sniffling.

Erinysia momentarily bewildered over his change of heart, put on a tact of soft pursuit. "What's wrong, my lord?—why this sudden rudeness? Have you been over-indulging in crude ale again? Have you forgotten the finer taste of wine?" He sat down at a table near the cat's eye and nervously flexed his big hands. Throwing back the heavy blanket, she rolled on her hip and posed alluringly bending a knee and parting her diaphanous robe-linge to expose bare her long tawny limb which then crossed over the other and stretched out over the edge of the bed. Then pivoting on her hip she drew the other limb to the edge, crossing the outstretched one over and momentarily displayed a scissor action until she brought up her torso and crossed her leg. Stretching her arms and flexing her fingers, she slowly, gracefully lowered them to up sweep her long black hair and caress the back of her neck while fluttering her eye-lids at him. She uncrossed her legs for a moment to reach over for her slippers which, instead of simply slipping into, she recrossed each long-shapely leg, before putting the slippers on. She leaned back on the bed with arms stretched behind into the soft down to look at him; tantalizingly she smiled and fluttered her lids. He scowled back with a shaking head. Upright she stood for a moment before walking over to him in a slinky manner to kiss his head and slip her hot little hand down under his tunic to his hairy chest.

"Oh, Erinysia, you are in sooth a wicked witch—alas, I fear there is no change of heart when it comes to your sumptuous being. It is rather your ways that hurl me into anger."

"But, my lord, the two are inseparable," she said, running her hot hand further down to his full belly."

"Aye, and that is why as far as I'm concerned I must be strong and put an end to your wily ways." He drew her hand out from under his shirt.

"Oh, and just how do you propose to do that?" she asked coyly, putting her hands on her hips. "Perhaps you plan to take my life and thereby lose my love?"

He nodded absently, then abruptly shook it off, saying sadly, "Yea, the two indeed cannot be separated—would that they could....Oh, Erinysia, how could you lie about such a thing so dear to me?" His eyes rolled up at her inquisitively. "'Twas callous to let me think my dear Rhonda dead."

"What?" She seemed struck by it. "My lord, I swear..."

"Nay, you knew—wishful thinking, eh? Or that your vicious and evil mind was planning to do it by dreadfully charming Bryan—and speaking of whom how did you get hold of him? He's supposed to be with Lance."

"My, but you have some imagination! You are entirely mistaken, my love." She placed a hand gently on the scarfed gem. "My crystal never quite makes it clear whether action taking place is past, present or future."

"Ha, sly witchcraft even within this glazed, distant power, eh?" He chuckled putting his hand on top of hers that still rested on the covered cabochon. "Its demon inside enjoys deceiving you, too, eh?" He laughed and patted her hand.

She laughed too. "How very perceptive—yea, I admit that there is petty envy within my institution of witchery, like everything else. But surely, my lord, you don't believe that I could possibly harm a hair on Rhonda's pretty head?" she begged innocently, moving her hand from the tiger gem to his shoulder, but he flicked it off.

He bent forward, lifting his elbow from the table, and put his chin on his fist as if in thought, but then with his other hand he absently ran his finger along her thigh so delicious looking under the sheer robe. "I'd like to think that were the case, but I know you better than that. Still, even you wouldn't, if you had not seen her as a threat. How in the world could you perceive that darling child as anyone other than one in need of a mother? You know how much she misses her, yet you have done nothing to ease her loss."

She snarled above him but moved closer and pressed her ribs to his face. "I tried but she made it obvious from the start that there was no replacing her mother." Then she twittered. "But I shall not give up; I promise." She took his bearded cheeks between her hands and said, "My, my, such a glum look. You should be happy she's alive and well. That news makes me happy, so why not you?"

He pulled her down enough for him to tongue her breast for a moment, then said, "Methinks your deception being discovered begets but another device to keep me confused." He pushed her away. "And have you already forgotten? What of the other child in bed with you? To molest is evil enough—but to assail such upon your other stepdaughter is beyond description!"

"Have you forgotten the earl's children wanted no part of me—practically threw me out of their keep?" she asked with mild vexation, wishing she had then the powers she now had.

"Then why bother with her at all?" He pawed his forehead. "Oh, you are in truth a confusing female."

"Why confusing? Why, I adore the child—in my own way—is it not better than to hold a grudge against the little dear"

"Aye, the latter is preferred. With the truth of hatred in her heart she'll mature without any help from you."

She stepped forward and pressed up against him again and chortled. "Oh, you're just an old warhorse—how you whinny on! You know nothing of a young girl's fantasies!"

Hesitantly, reluctantly he edged her away and whined, "Maybe not—and even less of yours! Why, Erinysia, my love..." He reached for her hips and pressed her against him and in a playful motion pushed a finger into her nipple. "Why the need for this young girl when here I am literally insane over you?"

She edged away from him and teasingly circled him while saying, "Oh, now am I still? Since you claim to be taking your leave of me, it sounds rather strange."

His eyes followed her round. "You know what I mean. Dregs in your chalice! Just before our first assault on Henry, I made love to you! What need is there for this perversity?"

"A mere harmless diversion with the child Maureen, my pet. Think no more of it." She giggled, pulling on his chair to sit in his lap and fondled his beard. "My love, I need you always—like *now*." She ran her hand over his head and kissed him on the lips. He responded by crowding her in his powerful arms and with a sigh receiving her busy tongue. Then she slipped away from his mouth and asked, "Have I not revitalized you sufficiently? Would you like me to mix another potion?"

"Nay, your presence is enough." Yet precipitously he disengaged her arms from around his neck to push her away, his hand went on his hilt, then hesitated and looked warmly into her eyes. Before letting her slide off his knees while he stood up, he smothered her hand with kisses.

On her knees she gripped him about his thighs. "See, my love? You really do want me, need me. So why this silly talk of giving up our plans, our royal future together?"

He waved an arm and shook his head and protested, "Too great a cost—my family. I wager Rhonda doesn't even know she's a hostage. I can't trust Henry to return Rhonda to me if I continue with this rebellion....Nor can I trust you and that damnable tiger eye-ball of yours," gesturing to the pulsating gem. "It is wrong, I tell you; for now I feel it in my loins that Lance is truly my son."

She released him and fell back on her haunches and laughed derisively before raising her voice, "Oh, spare my ears of your male mirages! You, once a soldier of fortune and a stranger to the Mari, and yet Lord Mari rushes you into marriage of his daughter and you in turn become the commander of the his regiment—and to boot a father at the blink of an eye!...Nay, my cat's eye does not give false images!—and verily not of past events."

He had covered his ears while she ranted and when she stopped, he grinned. "Oh, the damn fickle crystal dome of yours picks and chooses, eh? Nonetheless, I care less of your imaginary invocations. Perhaps I just don't want to believe this disruptive stuff. Besides, Lance has been a good son—even if I wasn't the siring agent."

Erinysia knitted her marvelously curved brows and countered, "Oh, but someday he'll find out the truth that he is the king's son and rightful heir to the throne. I trust you are not foolish enough to think that he will deny his right to power."

"Frankly I don't care anymore. Life was good to me without you."

She squinted at him and said in a rasping tone, "Ah, but it was not without humiliation in that the Mari family stripped you of manhood....And without love, don't forget."

He leaned over and drew her body up to his and caressed the oily ringlets framing her face, then his hand slid down to her throat and he applied light pressure. "Not entirely without love, but, alas, nothing can compare with the excitement you have given me. Still, I do not care to pursue your goal—let's just say I am too old." He grunted, growled, released her and plopped back in the chair.

"But not too old to give *me* a son!" she snapped back bitterly. "And need I remind you that as king you will have an heir to the throne of a great, new and ambitious kingdom—a *legitimate* son, I may add."

Frowning, the old warlord growled, "Bah, gazing into that preposterous, cracked crystal again to come up with more unfounded speculation, eh?" He leaned over and buried his face in his hands.

"What manner of man are you?—willing to give up this promising future—why, you would go down in history's scrolls as a masterful king who set fire to an emasculated charter so a country could be great under a masterful hand."

He grumbled, "Whose hand?—*yours*, to be sure."

Erinysia went over and ran a finger along the back of his neck, and went on, "Oh, my lord, surely, you have not turned to common flab of an agéd man. Brace up your loins and fight for what can be. Do not let Lance rob you of greatness. Excel your son's fame that was handed to him by his grandfather. You've ripped the Mari banner to shreds and replaced it with your own. Are you now going to patch it up?...My lord, you must fight for what is yours—and your true son-to-be."

"Why do you persist with this myth? Even if in fact you were with child..."

"*Were!*" she repeated indignantly, then held his head to her stomach and softened her tone. "My dear lord,..." she took a hand to his beard and lifted his face upward to gaze softly into his tired eyes. "Do you not see the happy, proud glow to my face? Should I instead show rage and resentment that I carry the future king?"

Kalab smirked up at her. "Erinysia, is there nothing you wouldn't do? You crown that which lies in your womb before the father himself can smelt one crown to forge another. Besides, you lie!"

She took his hand and pressed it to her stomach. "No, my lord, he is there."

Violently he shook his head and broke away from her, stood up, pressed his hand to his forehead and paced the browning sod, murmuring, "You make me dizzy—first Rhonda, Bryan, Lance—there is no end to your threads." He paused before her and asserted, "Just another cruel weave to your wild tapestry!"

"What am I to do to convince you?" She fondled her lower stomach and stepped toward him.

He bruskly turned away and threw up his arms and mewled, "Oh that it were true!" From behind she wrapped her arms round him and pressed her stomach into his buttocks. He felt a slight quivering and said, "It's probably Bennet's, you whore." He turned round to her and gripped her throat, glancing to the tent top. "Oh, God, why do I not have the strength to kill this demon?" And he relaxed his grip which turned to light strokes of her long narrow neck.

"You are just overwrought, my love, from the dastardly hovering round this damnable siege. "You need your rest." She urged him toward the bed. "Come lie with me, I shall caress you to sleep away your speculative perplexities." She sat him down on the edge of the bed to remove his boots.

He stared at her beautiful black shiny hair and said, "Oh, Erinysia, why am I so helplessly bewitched? I used to take pride in my cold detachment. Never would I allow sentiment to rear its sweet face."

She looked up with an arched brow and spewed, "Verily, these past moments, you have proven that sweet sentiment is called for. Instead you spew out rubbish about Lance and Rhonda, both of whom have no use for you now that you have bestowed affection to the only one who has ever shown you love."

"There are many kinds of affection over the years that I've been blest with from my family," he corrected her by tapping her nose. "Nor am I sure that this is truly I who want you so passionately—how do I know that you have not made me an imposter unto myself?"

She chortled, while removing his tunic and kissed his hairy teats. Then teased, as she fondled his lower parts, "Does this belong to another?" He let out a long sigh and fell back on the bed while she lifted the small of his back to ungird his sword. She swiveled to put it on the table, but he sat up and grabbed her arm.

"No, leave it here by the bed."

Suspiciously she glanced at him with raised brows. "As you wish," she said blandly, and complied, then finished undressing him. She climbed upon him and tried to maneuver his heavy body to the other side of the bed but; he rolled her back and he remained on the outside within reach of the sword. He then rolled on top of her and with a kind of vengeance cruelly took her, but she loved it all the more. He rolled back and vented a grunt and a sigh, then reached down for his sword. Alas, too late, she slipped her arm under the pillow, then with swift adeptness plunged a dagger into his back. He jerked up to reach back to remove it, but she already had drawn it out and stuck him in the heart. He gasped, then exhaled gurgling blood, staring at her, moaning, "I really loved you, my wondrous witch." Then he exhaled the last infinitesimal second of his life.

She removed the dagger and gingerly wiped it in the hair of his bloody chest. "Yea, my lord, I know—as I strangely did love you." She licked the blood from his mortal wound.

31. Lucia & Lance Join the King

Lem had no recent news for Lance when Lucia's forces camped at the Mari castle for an evening, except that Bryan and Tracy had also mysteriously disappeared. Lance had not the heart to tell Lem of Tracy's fate from sorcery. He worried now that perhaps Bryan and Rhonda had met some similar fate of diabolical witchcraft. Lance, of course, was disappointed that his father had indeed marched on Castle City. He was sure now that Erinysia was his father's driving force.

He led Lucia's band round the outskirts of the king's castle, bypassing the siege force at a strategic distance to avoid a clash and bring Erinysia's perfidious horde down on them. Lance had estimated that the main force of the rebels far out-numbered the king's as well. The hardy Lodestonians continued on some two miles east of the castle until safely out of sight in a peat trough. Tonight the princess gave in to her royal up-bringing. Lucia was exhausted from this ten day journey. She ordered her traveling tent to be set up so she could rest comfortably and besides the weather was threatening. Like her men, Lucia—except for the hospitality of the baroness and Lem—had been sleeping under the stars, clouds and rain, covered only by a hide-skin cover. She ordered some of her archers to hunt for boar and fowl on the fringe of the forest another two miles away so they could relax by campfire and eat heartily for a change. The princess was served a solid meal and had invited Lance to join her. There were two candles on a small collapsible table at which she was kneeling and holding a goblet high.

Lance felt, in spite of her fatigue of travel, that she was more beautiful than ever. It was not that she had unpinned her hair, though it was glowing magnificently by candlelight, nor was it that she had shed her mail coat and was wearing a heavy, but feminine robe. No, it was his perception of her indomitable spirit that he had witnessed increasing from the moment she slew the Plateos, as though she had been motivated beyond the simple loyalty of aiding him. It grew dramatically now when he disclosed his plan that he would alone try to penetrate the castle to reach the king and hopefully to find out the fate of his sister. She objected strongly.

His jaw dropped and he asked, "But why, my love?—surely, you realize that if not for my country, I still must save my sister—and my father too if possible to wrench him from Erinysia's claws."

Her light brows unknit and she answered softly, "I know, Lance; I, too, heard old Lem's beseeching priority for Rhonda. I simply meant that you will not go alone. I must be with you. Don't you realize what's happening?—first Rhonda, then that poor girl Tracy, and still no word from Bryan."

"Aye, I have blundered."

"You mustn't think that. Even a lord-protector cannot be ubiquitous. You deserve better than this harsh treatment of yourself."

"Nor should you take the world on your little shoulders," he countered. "Nay, Lucia, you have done enough already. I'll not jeopardize you and your men by leading you into a castle under siege. Besides, there's a better chance if only one sneaks through the siege line."

She smiled. "Yes, I know that; I meant you and me."

He gaped at her in shock. "Why, that's insufferable and too dangerous!"

She frowned, then smiled. "Ah, all the more reason, then, we are together on this."

He shook his head; his face grimaced. "But why? This is not your fight. I feel guilty enough that your troops might be committed soon."

Lucia squinted and shook her head a little. "It is *our* fight now. If it is any comfort to you, I see clearly that it is my country's battle as well."

He rubbed his beard, while his squint turned to widening eyes, then asked, "What do you mean?"

"The entire land is unsafe with this mad woman. She will not be content with just the conquest here....Don't ask me why; for I am not sure myself why it is that these ominous events are glints in my mind's eye. Somehow I feel she is actually more interested in the northern lands than she is of the lowlands."

He gaped at her again. "What has come over you, Lucia? Lately you have been wonderfully mysterious!"

"Honestly, Lance, I don't know. But if I don't accompany you it is certain, I shall never see you again. You must trust me on this."

"But our love goes stronger everyday!" he protested with a quiver in his voice.

"Mark me; I know of what I speak. I've come this far; I'm not going to lose you now," she said sternly. "Do not cross me, Lance; otherwise, I shall have to put you in chains and I shall go alone."

He stared at her in awe. "What wonder have I fallen in love with! First my father is bewitched. Now, I swear, I'm under *your* spell!"

She laughed, then took a few sips of wine. "Perhaps, but the spell is *not* —lest I be under yours— that you stay the night in my tent, my love. So eat and drink, then be off with you to tell the captain of our plan, else my marksmen will fill us with arrows when we leave the camp before dawn."

It was still dark when the twosome left camp. They pulled up their cantering steeds to a cautious trot a thousand feet from the scattered campfires on the line of siege. About half way, Lance motioned to a tree where they could tie their horses. He slipped a coil of rope with a grapnel over his shoulder.

Lucia grinned and said, "I see you have the means to scale the castle wall but, since the bridge is drawn how do you propose to cross the moat?"

He chuckled. "What's this, my lady? I thought you were in command and had the answers to everything. Surely, you can part the waters."

She smiled. "I'm a novice at this power. I fear I don't have the right incantation for it."

"Well, then, without the jargon, we'll have to swim," he said.

"Ugh, moats have slimy, crawly things!"

He smiled over at her shadowy face. "Verily, but nowhere as bad as what was in the witches' cauldron back on the moor."

"Very funny." She shivered as they continued on foot. Lance led the way, veering well to the right of the drawn bridge. Unbeknown to him, Lucia had stumbled over a rock, turning her ankle. In stoic silence she removed her boot to massage her ankle. Then she hobbled after him. As Lance was nearing the moat, a tall shadow appeared in front of him.

"Who goes there?" A grumbly voice cried out.

"Baron Bennet, my vigil soldier," Lance answered calmly.

The guard griped, "By the Lord's bloody wounds, brave baron, I could've crossbowed you at this dark early hour! Inspecting the guards, are you? Well, this is one you won't find asleep," he added with a chuckle.

"Aye, unfortunately for you!" Lance said menacingly as he quickly drew his sword.

The guard groaned, "But hold! The voice is not of the Baron's!"

Lance lunged, but the figure already had slumped forward with a startled murmur from Lucia's arrow in his stomach. Before the shocked guard could cry out alarm, Lance dealt him a final blow.

Lance looked back at her limping approach. "What did you do—shoot yourself in the foot first?"

She snarled. "My, you are just filled with dry humor this morning."

"Not dry for long once we wade into the moat!"

She laughed softly. "Again you deftly draw the jester out of you!"

In approaching the moat and watching Lance slide down the mud embankment where it curved round a rear corner of the castle, she said, "Ooh, I'm glad I wore my boots!" She followed him into the smelly slime and they paddled across. "Ugh, this *is* almost as bad as the witches' cauldron!"

"Aye, but at least this muck isn't boiling," Lance quipped back, then helped her up onto the dry strip. They rested against the wall. While she shivered in her wet clothes, he uncoiled the rope. "This part of the wall is scarcely guarded by the king's men. I'll be surprised if there's a guard in the vicinity."

Her voice shaking from the cold, quivered, "So what?—we're among friends now."

"Aye, but they won't know that when they see the grapnel flying up. I can't very well yell up to them for fear Bennet's men circling the wall will hear. Besides, they wouldn't believe us, anyway—unless, like the angel you are, you fly up to convince them."

"Oh, another quip, eh? I'm in no mood for jokes—I'm freezing," she wailed.

He heaved up the cleat—padded with skins to reduce noise—the rope of which curved round a merlon and the grapnel clung to the edge of a crenel. Tugging on the grapnel to be sure it held, he began the ascent, Lucia following. He squirmed into the crenel and then assisted Lucia through it. Suddenly he felt a powerful arm pressing his throat and he gagged. Lucia quickly circled the interloper and threatened, "Release him or this dagger at your back will be tickling your lungs. This is hardly the manner of greeting each other inasmuch as we are allies."

The guard relaxed his grip and cried, "My God, a woman's voice!"

"My God," cried Lance, rubbing his throat and turning round to get a glimpse of the stocky man in the dark, "Sir John!"

Sir John laughed in disbelief. "Lance!...By God, are you a sight for sorry eyes and depressive heart!" The two warriors clutched each other's forearm. With great relief and enthusiasm John led them to the Mari officers.

Later, escorted, along with Lucia, to his sister's room, Lance sighed in thanksgiving for the sight of her. Rhonda shrilled with surprised happiness and literally jumped into her brother's arms, clinging to his neck.

"Thank the Lord you're safe!" Lance exclaimed, managing to add between her kisses all over his face and beard, "My darling baby!" He held her tight for several moments in silence as she sobbed convulsively, snuggling closer to his strong presence, and indifferent to the smell of his moat-soaked clothes. Finally, gently he tried to let loose, but she only clung to him more. He smiled over at Lucia who herself seemed tear-filled.

At last Rhonda extracted her face from his chest, looked up with watery, but happy eyes, and he let her down. With mild curiosity, she looked over at the beautiful woman then turned to her brother quizzically. Lance introduced them, and Rhonda curtsied, saying, "My, a princess and so beautiful like the tales of yore!"

Lucia beamed a smile and said, "You're very kind, Rhonda, especially coming from one as ravishing as yourself—and here I am in ghastly mud-soaked battle wear." She added a chuckle.

Lance placed his hands on each woman's shoulder and said, "Never have I seen such double beauty, regardless of the moat stench and tearful red eyes," and glancing at his sister, added, "Speaking of beauty, Lucia sent you a beautiful red-chestnut mare to match your hair." Then he hesitated. "Bryan picked it out for you."

Rhonda hugged the princess. "How darling of you, Lucia." Then she looked up at her brother, horrified, and brought her hands to her face and cried, "Oh, my brother, I hesitate to speak of Bryan—so horrible was our meeting!"

"Then he did arrive!...But what on earth..."

Rhonda rejoined, "No, nothing on earth, rather hell." She then told him the story. Lance was so stunned he wavered on his feet and had to sit down.

He looked up at Lucia, "Is there no hope in face of Erinysia's powers?...At this moment I feel so powerless. I am cautious enough not to storm into her camp and lop her head off. But if she could do this to poor Bryan—no finer than he—I fear she has the power to trick me to betrayal."

Lucia went to him and put her hand on his shoulder. "It is good to hear you have no sense of heroics for now. For indeed you would be defeated.

Thank God, we have arrived in time."

"Why do you say that?" he asked, arching his brows.

She pressed the back of her hand to her forehead. "It is ordained that she indeed shall have invaded the castle,...and all would be lost."

Rhonda reacted with surprise. "I too see clearly, your highness, that somehow you are the answer to our prayers. Are you a magician?"

The princess laughed.

The king had been impatiently awaiting their arrival, having sent Sir John to summon them. Personally and emotionally he was anxious to gaze upon the daughter of Lady Margaret. Politically he was hoping Lance would have a solution to the siege and defense of the city. King Henry was well aware of the throne's dependence on his leading knight. Though a king of material means, he had not the wherewithal to coördinate a state and to lead men into battle. Up to this time, having the confidence of an enduring peace after Lance put down the last resistance of feudalism, he felt secure in that he could delegate to young Henry the administration of an up and coming nation and the defense thereof to Lance. In fact, he had even been planning to again visit the queen mother Margaret to ask for her hand in marriage, thus joining the northern mountains to the kingdom.

Now that the couple stood before him, he could think of nothing beyond cordial greetings, so mesmerized was he by Lucia's beauty—now refreshed—which replayed out his youth with the mother. Lucia was embarrassed by the king's suspended state and blushingly turned to Lance. Fortunately, the young Henry entered the throne room and stationed himself by his father's side and broke the silence. "Your arrival is most welcome, Lance." Turning to Lucia he added, "Of course, your highness, I wish the reception could be under more favorable circumstance befitting your station."

Lucia beamed a smile. "You're so very kind, good prince, but my accommodations are very satisfactory. Lady Rita has been a warm hostess. Besides, I was aware of the rebellion and why I am here to offer my service."

The king snapped out of his internal reminiscing and asked, "Was it your gracious mother's idea to journey here?"

"Oh, no, your majesty,...quite the contrary, rather, I wished to be here at Lance's side. In spite of his impressive war record, I trust he will be in need of my band of warriors."

With a dumb-founded grin, the king resounded, "What? You mean to say a girl, scarcely older than the child Rhonda, has come to do battle!"

Lucia blushed. "Presumptuous, I know, but there is brewing within me, and as yet unfathomable phenomena, a destiny truly beyond appearance."

The king stared at her. "Hmm, I know of destiny and for the time our young nation's is in jeopardy." He turned to Lance. "Well, my most capable general, what do you intend to about this—specifically your father's out-rageous disloyalty?"

"Would that it were as simple as dealing with my father, your majesty."

The king leaned over wide-eyed. "What do you mean? Surely, it is only your father that questions my right."

"But not seriously; it is not my father who is solely responsible for this turmoil. It is rather a serious question of divine right from elsewhere."

Glancing at his father, young Henry broke in, "Why surprised, father? I told you of the fate of brave Bryan."

The father scowled, saying angrily, "Bah, he was just an envious lover!"

"I beg to differ, good king," Lance interjected.

The prince reinforced Lance: "Yea, father, he loved sweet Rhonda and had no cause for jealousy. I tell you he was bewitched....Why, you know yourself of Erinysia's charms."

"Aye, beautiful, wily, but hardly a witch!" the king maintained.

"If you think that, King Henry," Lucia said, "then she has already cast a spell upon you."

Lance left the king and Lucia who remained to answer the many inquiries he had about her mother. Though Lance knew Lady Margaret was a native of the south, he did not realize that the king knew her and clearly had been fond of her. Lance traversed the keep's inner ward to meet Sir John on the ramparts and together inspected the guards of the huge parapet, almost a mile in circumference. Lance wondered if the ancient at the fire pit had anything to do with the power Lucia apparently felt stirring in her bosom.

Sir John greeted him. "I tell you, Lance, with you here and the band of longbow marksmen from the princess, I know we can take them."

Lance shook his head. "You underestimate the witch. I've seen what she can do—why you yourself have witnessed the fate of loyal Bryan."

"Aye, I know, though only heard of it." He nodded absently, then offered, "But that's not all—I dispatched brave Robert two days ago to meet with your father in the hope old Bal would come to his senses and withdraw. Robert has not returned. I fear the worst."

"My God! Witchcraft has no chivalry," Lance concluded grievously.

"Aye, and I'm sure your father would have honored the flag of truce. It's obvious that he is not in control of the forces."

"Nor of himself obviously," Lance inserted, then he heaved, "Brave Robert—our finest captain."

"No argument there....I regret not accompanying him." John bit his lip, then said, "Lance, oh, how he fought on the moor—and so undermanned!..."

Lance put his hand on John's shoulder and said grimly. "Aye, on the way down, I saw the graves of our brave men."

John nodded absently. "I wish I had been with him there too...but I was so concerned for Rhonda."

"I know, friend, and I'm indebted to you for that."

A crossbowmen ahead took aim through a crenel and a cry was heard below. John looked down to see a stray member of the siege force topple over, and roll down the moat's embankment. "Well targeted, my man, he said to the grinning bowman.

Lance smiled at the soldier. "Aye, accurate sentry, continue like-discharges and the siege will be over in no time." He gripped the sentry's shoulder as he passed.

As they continued along, John said, "The fact is, Lance, we cannot weather a siege through winter. We might just as well counterattack now while the weather is clement."

"We are outnumbered three to one—even with Lucia's forces," Lance reminded him.

Sir John smirked and pawed his red beard. "That never would hold you back before."

"I know; but this isn't a battle between mere mortals, you know."

John tugged on his beard again and conjectured, "Granted, yet Erinysia evidently needs mortal troops to suit her ends. So why not reduce those numbers?"

"Aye, and we shall; ultimately, though, it is Erinysia and Lucia's war. The kingdom teeters on this. Lucia must put Erinysia's black soul to rest. Therefore it is Lucia's decision, not ours."

Momentarily astonished, John, plucking his beard, remarked, "And if she is incapable of defeating Erinysia?...Then what?"

"Alas, we will have to retreat to the northern mountains and defend ourselves against the witch's further ambitions," Lance said solemnly, but added, "Nevertheless, I have implicit faith in Lucia's intuitive powers."

John shook his fist and growled, "Bah, women's intuition!...All the more reason to take a squad and try to reach the Mari renegades and swing them back over to us."

"Foolhardy," Lance rebuked him, shaking his head. "Had Robert succeeded the regiment would be here now. They are thoroughly under her spell, I suspect, along with a mix of loyalty to my father."

"I'm a doubting Thomas. I refuse to believe she is that powerful."

"Tell that to Bryan and Robert, if you could," Lance reminded him.

"Maybe they let their guard down," John speculated.

"Bryan perhaps, but Robert, never. You are a courageous warrior — but bullheaded "

John stroked his graying beard while nodding and said solemnly, "Aye, and why I've got to know what happened to Robert. I feel responsible."

"Go, then—against my better judgment—to clear your mind. But be overly cautious and steer clear of Erinysia —believe me, she is dangerous. I would go with you but I dare not chance leaving the castle to its own defense."

"Aye, sorely needed here," John reaffirmed.

John and his squad, all on foot, took the secret passage where lay a hidden boat. The men quietly boarded and paddled across the moat. They stealthily outflanked the western siege force and headed for the enemy camp. In the ravine between the western moat and the camp there shone a green flamed torch that had been stuck in the ground. The eerie light illuminated the melted armor of the rigid remains of Sir Robert. The men gasped and moaned. John cautioned, "Get hold of yourselves, men...." In a feeble attempt to muster confidence, he said, "It's nothing more than a damnable vision. Push on. I'm sure gallant Robert is with the regiment by now."

However, Erinysia, still skeptical of Lance's men, encamped the regiment way back in reserve, even further back of the skeletal force of the earl's. After fifteen minutes of crawling between the lines without a trace of the regiment's camp and keeping in mind Lance's caution, John aborted the task, deciding it too risky to penetrate so deeply. Heading back, he noticed an unusual tent emanating another strange green glow that accentuated a silhouette of a dragon across the top. He could not resist—ignoring Lance's specific order—deploying his men to circle the tent which he surmised was Erinysia's. A few crack raiders quickly and stealthily slew the guards at the entrance. John slit open the back and slipped into a flood of vaporous light from the crystal at which Erinysia, thinly dressed, stood with a calm expression as though expecting the intruder.

"I was wondering when you would finally come to your senses and the wisdom of my ways," she said haughtily.

He raised his sword and rumbled, "Sleet in hell first!...before enslaving myself to your dastardly evil." He lunged for her.

She laughed and suspended him in his tracks with a fiery glare that beamed a ray of red light and burned his hand, the sword falling to the satin covered floor. Out of the shadows pounced the cat that metamorphosed to a panther in flight, knocking the cataclysmic knight onto his haunches. John howled in pain when the panther ripped off his sword hand and dropped the dripping extremity at its mistress' bare feet. She continued to laugh hideously as the knight groveled, as if desperately trying to retrieve his hand. She snapped a finger, and the panther, while returning to the dark corner, devolved into its original form.

"Stop squirming like a brat in a tantrum, Sir John; it is unbecoming a knight of your reputation," she commanded as she picked up the hand and gazed upon it fondly while directing it to fondle her breasts. She looked down at him. "It is a pity you are cut off from the sensuous feel of these glorious breasts. Why, were it not severed you would find pleasure never before equaled in your lifetime. It has been said that these voluptuous beauties," taking a deep breath to accentuate them, "of which I am so proud, would make Venus's seem like hanging squash." She took the busy hand away and lowered it to John's prone body. "I really don't want you to bleed to death, dear John: let's say in return for this powerful but loving hand, you give me something."

John, quivering from shock, groaned, "Anything!...Aye, anything,... *everything* you wish."

"Capital! Spoken like all the rest of Lance's renegades!"

"But how am I to know you can rejoin my hand to this bloody wrist?" he croaked out.

"A disbeliever such as you will not know if and when I do."

"Trickstress!" He yelled raising his bloody stump. "Finish your deed and kill me now!"

She shook her head. "Too easy—my ego compels me to spare you just to see you serve me by killing Lord Lance."

He crawled to her feet and with his one whole hand tugged the hem of her light silk chemise. "Not for three hands would I betray him!"

She bent down and spread two long slender fingers and poised the claw-like nails before his eyes. "Not even for two eyes?"

He cowered and pleaded, "Spare me! You are now my queen! But to do the deed I shall need two good hands to fell so mighty an opponent."

"Ah, yes, not friend but opponent! Good! You are progressing!" She swayed the hand and then dropped it and it miraculously locked onto its wrist and sealed itself, not a scar showing. "Now, you have the weapon to do my deed."

He smiled with elation and stood up. "Ah, to be whole again regardless of my ignoble future."

"Soon you will learn to rise above such classification," she said blandly. "Nobility as you see it will be no more. Everyone will be in the service of the one and only noble being."

"Aye, I see—just you, eh?" He cocked his ear to the entrance flap. "What is that ruckus I hear outside?...Why, I believe I hear my men!"

She grinned. "Not for long—my pet dragon will make short work of them."

"You cannot—else I'll not do the vile deed!"

She smiled warmly. "Half only will I spare. Ask no more." She then glared at him and warned, "More stipulations and I'll close the deal and send you to Lilith's pit this instant!"

He bowed his head. "Aye, your majesty's will be done."

She waved him off, pointing to the entrance. "Go now and put an end to my Nemesis."

Sir John left and strode right into the decimation of his men. Sufficient vestige of the knight's code was resident in his bosom. With sword high, he stalked the fiery dragon. The lime vertical eyes turned to scarlet as the monster glared at John's slashing sword. Then it unleashed a tongue of fire. John a mass of flames continued to slash away. The giant son of Plateos roared out a white hot flame and John was reduced to cinders.

Erinysia rushed out of the tent just as John was in flames. "That stupid, most disgustingly loyal, fool!"

Meanwhile Lucia, a guest in Rita's apartments in the keep, was sitting on Rhonda's bed holding the young girl in her arms trying to comfort her over the loss of Bryan. "There is little one can say at a time like this;...still, you did say in his final moment he had returned to his loving self."

Rhonda looked up with a fleeting sparkle. "Oh, yes, Lucia, thank God for that....But, oh, my dear, it is horrible enough to have lost him, but not even to have his body to bury him in proper knight's ceremony, tears at the last remnant of my heart."

"I have a strange inkling that all may not be lost....An ancient sage back home, I recall, said that body's that vanish from witchcraft are really present but suspended somewhere in another time and some are not always dead because they were the actions of the body only at the time of possession and not of the mind's doing."

"Oh, dear princess, do you really believe that?...could it really be that he is still alive?"

"We can only tell if he resides in the immediate future; if in the past then we shall never see him again. Yet the sage did say that if the spirit of love is strong enough that even the past, too, might be traversed."

"Oh, it is!" Rhonda said, pulling herself away and bouncing on the mattress. "In spite of the terror of that moment, I love him dearly....Yes, yes!...And even though young Henry saved my life twice, I do not feel much more than gratitude toward him."

Lucia spread a modest smile. "Oh, that could change, you know....You are so very young."

Rhonda stared at her absently then finally nodded. "Yes, I suppose, if Bryan is really gone, the prince could grow on me. He's really very nice. Still, it will never be the same."

Lucia squinted for a moment, then reflected, "Might it not be even better?...After all, you never would have experienced such feelings but for your having grown up with Bryan."

"Yea," Rhonda said dreamily, "and that's what makes it so special—so pure, unvarnished by courtly grace and custom."

Lucia laughed. "My, I should be having you verse me in this love business! I'm just a novice at it."

"Ah, but then you too have but pure feelings for my brother! We are therefore much alike."

That evening Lucia joined Lance on the turret tower whence he secured vigil for Sir John's return. Her back against a merlon she gazed at him who was bent over the crenel as though in wary thought. She asked, "What is it, Lance, that fixes you to the tower all day and evening...expecting another attack?"

He leaned back and said, turning to her, "That as sure as monks go to heaven is the attack coming,...but no, I fear that I have foregone a leader's discipline by weakening and granting Sir John leave to steal into the enemy camp last night. There has been no word of him, nor of any of his men."

"Good grief, Lance, you didn't!"

"Aye, and I wish I hadn't. I'm afraid I sealed their fate in permitting John's last desperate encounter with whom he stubbornly felt was a fraudulent witch."

"Nay, Erinysia is all too real," she muttered solemnly. "For it is clear now the meaning of my dream last night."

"Oh?" he uttered gutturally.

"Sir John is dead. Done in by the wayward Erinysia," she reported with bowed head.

"Oh, no!...First Bryan, then Robert, now this....Oh, Lucia, such a loyal warrior who fought not only with my father but grandfather as well." He stroked his beard and looked out over the field. "How so this time?...If what you dream is true."

She reached over and touched his back. "How? Too horrible to describe....Alas, of late my dreams are unlike any other—tactile they are, like I was there not simply as an impartial witness but very much alive within, feeling the sorrow of bloody scenes yet powerless to interfere."

Lucia felt even more intensely the supernatural powers growing within mind and body. On reflection, she felt she was not ready for the daughter of Lilith; besides, Henry and his son had not, of course, anticipated this crisis and thus few provisions to weather a long siege, though the city was well-provided for a month longer. The ever-cunning Lance, derived a plan of strategy to exit the entire population of Castle City at night and onto the Lodeston camp, then ultimately head for the black forest.

Come nightfall, Lucia and Lance went through the secret passage that tunneled through the outer parapet but because the boat was now on the other side had to again wade through the moat. Only this time Lance, in spite of her coat of mail, carried her. "Hardly as romantic as being carried over a threshold." she quipped.

"Aye, and soon I hope will come that day," he said.

"Yea, Lance, and an added incentive for me to grasp my powers quickly."

"Faith I have that you shall," he said letting her down on the dry embankment of the other side.

Chuckling nervously, she uttered, "In a few minutes we shall know."

They continued along a trough beside the moat's slope to the rear gate to accost the siege-platoons responsible for guarding the east end of the city. The officer in charge, in seeing their shadows approach, reached for his sword and was about to alert his men. Lucia waved her amulet of the tree of knowledge that burst with a golden glow as she continued walking toward him. Immediately his eyes became glazed and his mouth agape. When Lucia confronted, but a few paces in front of him, his hand lost its grip and the sword fell to the ground. Lance, with drawn sword stood ground, spinning on his heels, with a snarled expression at anyone of the troops who rushed to surround them dared to do harm. The small gathering, however, seemed as arrested as the lieutenant.

Lucia pressed the amulet onto the lieutenant's forehead. Mobility returned to him; he kissed her hand and kneeled before her simultaneously. Then he rose up, turned to his men and ordered, "Stout guardsmen, ye see for yourselves, our new glorious queen. Rise, then to dismantle Bennet's eastern bivouac and follow her to glory!" The men of the Late Earl Hunter's ranks quickly followed orders.

It was not till the bivouac's mules were packed and carts loaded that Sir Charles had ordered the bridge down. Scores of troops deluged onto the wide cobblestone apron and split ranks to flank the bridge where Sir Charles appeared towering over the massive influx of people, animals and carts swarming over the bridge. Lucia guided them down the road to a detachment of Lodeston archers. As she returned, Lance's northern flank was engaged in a skirmish with a small band from the northern siege line, which was quickly subdued without bloodshed. The lieutenant of the siege bivouac went over to them and had each of his troops bow and swear allegiance to the new queen. One soldier braved a question: "Has the king remarried, lieutenant?"

Lucia approached to review the new ranks and smiled down upon them. "No, my new warrior, the king is still a faithful widower. I'm afraid our lieutenant exaggerates somewhat since I am still but a princess. For now let it suffice that I and the great Lord Protector are your commanders."

The young soldier reached out and kissed her hand. "We are honored to serve you and the great Lord Lance."

"Aye," said the lieutenant, still under the spell of the amulet, "but mark me, the princess is truly a queen over all the land."

Once the king and his entourage and main body of troops guarding the rear crossed the bridge, the trek to the black forest was in full motion lighted by trails of hundreds of torches. Lance, Lucia and Rhonda were at the point guarded by the Lodeston archers. Charles and his troops guarded the civilian flanks while Arnold commanded the King's soldiers at the rear. Deep within the black forest, the march came to an end by the next afternoon. The Lodeston main force greeted them.

The princess was so exhausted from the long trek and in exercising her new powers that she apologized to Lance and retired early to her tent. Though she fell asleep in an instant, she tossed and turned half the night. Suddenly she was wakened by a soft voice calling her name. She opened her eyes and the tent was softly illuminated by a golden light dancing on the tinkling sound of a harp.

"Lucia, daughter of humanity, by now thou hast a glimmer of thy purpose; for humanity is at the crossroad as it was five thousand years ago." Lucia sat up and wide-eyed the beautiful blonde woman draped in a white garment trimmed in gold. Across the breast was embroidered a tree whose blossoms were the Hebraic alphabet. The lady gracefully moved toward the cot and put her hands on Lucia's shoulders. "On these delicate shoulders rests the fate of our world as only we know it."

So entranced, Lucia rested her cheek on the lady's slender hand and finally uttered, "Five thousand years,...so you must be the much maligned Eve....This crossroad I face,...I suspect, Erinysia already awaits there?" The lady nodded with grim mien. Lucia looked into the crystal clear hazel eyes of this celestial image and said, "Yes, I have had premonitions of late. But what precisely was the motive of your action so long ago? And how is the crossroad I face similar?"

Eve smiled affectionately. "Thou inferred that I have been maligned. That perception has been juxtaposed unjustly with the myth of Pandora, who unleashed misery onto the world. Nay, the loss of innocence is not the same. I made a choice; the alternative was to remain in the darkness of no choice at all. Yea, I made the decision to bring forth humanity."

Lucia knit her brows momentarily as she stared into the proud sparkle of Eve's eyes. "Excuse me, great lady, but is that not putting it rather strongly?...It seems to imply that God created you as less than human."

Eve laughed unassumingly. "Not quite, Lucia, else I would not have possessed the potential of decision. However, had I chosen not to choose, we would have slipped back into the darkness of the animal kingdom or the subhuman species that still roams parts of the earth and have for millions of years."

Lucia smiled. "I could not imagine one as beautiful as you belonging to savages I have heard existed before biblical time."

Eve chuckled. "No, my dear, God still has his preferences and would have granted us godlike beauty, but without meaningful thinking."

Lucia lightly rubbed the bridge of her nose. "My mother, you know, has great sympathy for Lilith who she believed might have foreseen clearly and patiently the ultimate aim of humanity, whereas you may have been headstrong. It is said that you defied God. Is it possible that He had seen value in the creation of you that you did not see?"

Eve laughed off the ripple of criticism—she knew she was being tested—and answered, "Precisely the problem, Lucia, neither Adam nor I could see! We were kept in awful darkness; only Lilith was granted the gift of divine intuition. Oh, to be sure, Adam had a glimpse of divination; otherwise, he could not have created me, knowing that something in his life was lacking. You see, Lilith was the superior one. When I awakened to the world, God, too, granted me a glimmer and I seized the opportunity to become free."

Lucia, however much impressed with the image before her, still probed, lest it be trickery from Erinysia or Lilith herself. "But why, dear Eve? How is it in spite of being granted everything you were dissatisfied?"

Fleetingly chafed at the remark from one she herself had a hand in creating, she scoffed, "Everything?...No, my child, there is nothing without free will and choice. God, I believe, was ambivalent about this. For he knew it was an awesome power that could do harm as well."

Lucia nodded emphatically. "Yea, as indeed it has....My mother's theory notwithstanding, how is it Lilith developed into a demon?"

Eve said sadly, "Because God in His notorious wrath denied her divination because she lost control over us—of course, not completely as you by now well know, but left her with divine power of the worst kind. She through Erinysia is unleashing a power of vengeance. Once more, she wants to crush us into dumb brutes. If permitted to go unchecked, she will drive us like herds into the pastures of darkness and ignorance. She must reduce us to unquestioning pawns in order to move us by command."

Lucia's jaw dropped. "My,...do you suppose that was God's intent all along. That we be mere unthinking, oafish things?"

"Sadly, yes," Eve asserted; "As I said those who came before me millions of years ago wandered the face of the earth without a trace of advancement under Lilith's rule."

Lucia knit her brows again. "But I thought Lilith and Adam were created together? Yet you say she dominated poor creatures for millions of years!"

"But not simultaneously were they created," Eve said. "Who knows in the mind of God that a second or two could not be even billions of years? In truth, Adam sensed he had not been created equally—or first for that matter—by virtue of not having the power of intuition and understanding."

Lucia chuckled. "Ah, till you came along, wise Eve, and snared the apple!"

"Yea, and I might immodestly add, for the good fate of humanity. That is why I have called upon you to protect the human race. It is only through you, my chosen one. You *only* are capable of resisting the scourge of Erinysia. I am forbidden to directly interfere."

"Oh?" Lucia perked. "And what of Lilith—is she too forbidden to engage?"

"Of that I cannot be sure — she is more wily than I. Nevertheless, you must chance it or the mountain's oracle that you shall be queen to further enlighten our species will not come to pass. This, then, is your destiny, but because of your heritage stemming from me, you do have a choice....Erinysia, on the other hand, does not: Lilith drives her to succeed or fail." She looked at Lucia quizzically. "That is why I say we are again at the crossroad, for in that split second long ago I had a choice as you do now."

Lucia sensed a sadness in Eve's face which she reached out to caress. "No, my lady, there is no choice. I shall take up arms against darkness....I gather, this will displease God?"

Eve laughed. "Oh, I believe He's coming around. Though we have disappointed Him innumerable times, He seems to be enjoying us more."

Lucia sighed. "Well, how nice to hear!"

32. Erinysia's New Castle

Without even consulting Bennet, Erinysia had the respective legion and regiment of the Late Kalab and the Earl of Hunterland, together with Bennet's company, assembled in full war gear at dawn. She appeared before them on a splendid, sleek black gelding adorned in a red blanket crested with a gold L and the same red and gold for the bridle and saddle. She too was splendidly garbed in a red tunic flaunting the same golden crest, and a bright yellow robe trailed down her back and partially to the animal's haunches. The shield hanging from the saddle was so polished that it looked silvery to enhance the gold embossed 'L' at the center. She wore a crown of gold with inlay of rubies.

The troops looked curiously at the riderless horse with Kalab's crest and also struck by her crown which they had not seen before. She trotted her horse in a regal gait closer to the sprawl of men. Her eyes rolled, blazing dawn's fiery light and her head swayed slowly along the long line. The men seemed apocalyptic by the straight regal posture and that she straddled a manly saddle as she drew out her sword, gleaming red in the morning light and held it high as she announced:

"Men of destiny—yea, I mean all of you—are now about to embark on a mission long overdue. I know you look puzzled; for your true history has been denied you for thousands of years. I am the rightful descendant of the first and only queen of this your holy land. Many millennia of unwritten history, before the Romans invaded our idyllic land, this nation was ruled by benevolent queens."

She lowered her sword and set it into her scabbard. She swept her eyes across the columns and could see they were struck dumb.

"You have been duped to believe that the first woman was Eve. In fact, it was Lilith. my ancestral mother. And because Adam was cruel to her, our great God swept her out of Eden and placed her gently here to begin a new and greater race. Only this time the *new* Adam would be subservient to her. Thus was the beginning of queenly rule whence this nation of ours flourished in its grand simplicity.

"Alas, the dreaded gods-ridden but unGodly Romans, descendants of the evil Eve came to break the divine chain of peaceful rule. Good men, King Henry springs from the Roman race to perpetuate the blockade of the nation's destiny set by God in behalf of Lilith.

"Thus, my men of destiny regained, it rests on your broad shoulders to put an end to these false and unlawful origins and to rebuild what is pure, not in the eyes of the false gods of the Romans that now call themselves Catholic, but in the gleaming spirit of our true God and our true mother, LILITH."

Again she unsheathed her sword and held it up. Commandingly she ordered, "Swordsmen, raise your weapon and bow your heads to the hilt, spearsmen, hold proud and high your craft and all vow allegiance to the daughter of Lilith, the one and only ruler of this holy land!"

Thunderously, miraculously they vowed in unison the very same words, *"Allegiance to Erinysia, our true queen and ruler of our holy land!"*

Regally she spurred her horse into a trot down the first long line abreast, smiling and nodding to the thoroughly bewitched soldiers who spontaneously smiled back. Not one soul among this enormous fighting force stirred: so taken in by her commanding presence and stunning beauty. She rode back to the center of them where Bennet awaited, equally stunned and confused as the rest. All he was able to do was gape at her in wonder with not a question on his mind. However, one of the lieutenants of the late earl's command did ride up to inquire, though hesitantly, "My queen, may

I inquire as to why Warlord Kalab is absent?"

She looked at him kindly and answered, "Oh, but he is with us, rest assure." She waved an arm toward the warlord's steed. Then she jerked her horse round to the men. "My soldiers of destiny, you all do recognize the handsome destrier of the warlord's by my side. You may wonder why Lord Kalab is not mounted. Well, in spirit he is. Yea, his dying wish was that I lead you with his mount at my side so in spirit he could reap the reward of regaining our autonomy." She scanned their faces and smiled. "Yea, it is good that you seem shocked but not dispirited. For on this glorious day—the morning after he left this world—we shall give him a crown for his *daughter* that grows within me."

They all cheered and rattled their shields. Then she signaled them to advance, and they quietly with utmost discipline deployed into combat readiness. As the main force advanced with the self-proclaimed queen at the lead, a small band of riders rode the flanks to meet up with the siege linemen to tighten the circle of the siege-infantry. Suddenly Erinysia held up her hand and reined in her horse; the massive wedge behind held up. She turned to Bennet at her side. "What do you make of this, Bennet?" she asked, motioning to the drawbridge down. "Nor do I see any sacrificial peasant activity with pikes and stones stranded on the ramparts."

He nodded. ".'Aye, strange, and there are no archers in the peeps or on the battlements either. And though indeed the bridge is down the portcullis was not raised. I suspect a trap. They might be expecting us to roll our turrets across so they can unleash a rain of fire. This is completely contrary to the stiff resistance to our attacks these past days."

"Unless," she said confidently, "they have been overwhelmed by our superior numbers and determination."

He shook his head. "Nay, rather I smell the blood of Lance. He's reached them, forsooth, with his damnable strategies."

She snarled. "Lance, Lance—all I ever hear! I tell you he's kept busy in the high country....There's one way to find out. We cannot dally here. Forget the turret and send a vanguard to scale the wall to raise the gate. We'll soon learn if they're still there; we shall force them to crawl out of their cowardly holes."

"I wouldn't count on their cowering, my...queen," he cautioned.

"If not, they soon will," she smiled at him. Growling, he rode off to assign a dozen men.

Midway on the bridge she sat calmly in her saddle observing the courageous vanguard, which had not found on the other side of the moat any trace of soldiers hiding in ambush along the rocky outer parapet that circled the moat's inner rim. Unmolested they stacked their ladders and tossed their grapnels to the fifty foot battlement behind the outer parapet. Each man carefully slipped through a merlon and lay low on the castle wall until all twelve were in position. All were amazed in popping their heads over the low inner wall of the ramp in seeing not a soul stirring in the spacious ward and bailey's marketplace below—not even a domestic animal could be seen. The leader of the small band leaned between two merlons and waved all clear; then sent a team to winch up the portcullis.

Erinysia turned to signal an advance, and she crossed the bridge well ahead of the file of troops. Bennet at quick gait pulled up to her and said, "No, my queen, you must stay back until we are absolutely sure."

"Never! I'll not have my courageous force think that I would send them into danger without leading them." Then she winked at him. "Anyway, what harm would come my way?" She spurred her horse ahead and she turned back to him and offered, "Come join me, my love, in triumphant entrance," presuming there would be citizens inside the bailey to hail her.

Hundreds of troops passed under the arch and filled the marketplace. Bennet deployed his regiment round nearly a half league masonry parapet. Others were assigned the task of scouring every nook and cranny of the peasant ward and shops. Still others scaled the bailey walls of the nobility's wards to hunt out any officers and nobles in adjacent buildings to the keep. Bennet and a detachment investigated the castle and its keep. Except for ample hogshead of wine and ale, no provisions were left in the storehouses. Nor were there any signs of stragglers. The city had been completely abandoned.

Bennet was worried and angered. He mounted his steed and galloped a quarter league through the rear portcullis arch to find the lieutenant of the rear siege guard. There was but one befuddled guard, helmetless, rubbing his shock of hair while sitting on the rim of the moat. "Where is your bloody outfit, sentry?"

The sentry snapped up and said perplexedly, "So help me, Baron, 'tis a mystery to me. Last night I walked off to nature's calling; when I returned they were gone! Nary a trace—swallowed up by night demons, they were."

"Bah, desertion, you mean! I never should have trusted Hunter's men!" He spurred round the moat to the northern side and approached one of his knights assigned to oversee the siege unit. "How could you possibly allow the entire city population to exit from its walls?" Bennet inquired with a raucous voice and fire in his eyes.

"No such thing could happen—unless somehow we were bewitched." The officer put a hand upon his tunic across which was the crest of Baron Bennet's line. "I swear, baron, until now we had no inkling they were not within the walls."

"Bah!" growled the baron. "Sick I am of witchcraft talk! Why, would our queen induce a spell to let them escape? Why it's utter nonsense."

"Oh, but I'm not suggesting it. Somehow vaguely in my mind lurks another one, I swear I did feel banging in my head!" The officer said in bewilderment.

"Sounds to me like an alibi for not being alert, did I not know you to be a trusted knight, unlike those treacherous dogs from Hunter's ranks " the baron countered, then reflected: "I know we had to spread the line thin—but where are the rest of them?. You were not at the rear-gate all the time—are you sure the men were alert?"

The knight looked surprised. "Well, no, I wasn't, but I can assure you that the men would have noticed thousands leaving even if they had been asleep!...As for the rest," he scratched under his helmet, "perhaps the Hunter commandant reassigned them."

Bennet rapped his gauntlet. "Zounds, has everyone gone berserk? Assigned where? To another castle!" He rubbed his beard. Has a head count been taken of the siege unit?"

Again surprised, the knight replied, "Nay, why?"

"I think you'd better find the siege-commandant—probably still sleeping—and tell him that I order a counting." Bennet commanded as he spurred his horse back to the castle.

Bennet sent squads to search the peasant fields and villages within a radius of a half a mile round the castle's north and south flanks. When they returned, he was not surprised when they reported not a soul stirring. He ordered the rear-guard to roll in huge catapults to position strategically within the castle wards. When the commandant of the siege unit rode in to report that the forty men assigned to the rear portcullis were indeed missing, Bennet promptly pulled him from his horse and ran a dagger through his heart, saying, "Soon those deserters will join you in the nether world designed for cowardly and incompetent men of war!"

For several days and nights the rebel forces were vigilant and wary. Rumors flew that the king had his own powerful witch who had been responsible for the mysterious death of Kalab and turned the king's men invisible. Gradually nervous alertness grew to restlessness in questioning the occupation of a city that was uninhabited and lacked loot; thereby many yearned to return home to their families. One evening, a week afterwards, a knight who captained the parapet guard climbed up to inspect the vigil. He was not surprised to see many sleeping and others with their backs to the wall in conversation. He shook his head but said nothing. Along the way he had to poke a few on watch to regain their vigilance. The further along he noticed greater gaps of those on watch at the battlements. When he completed his rounds, he paused at a merlon, squinted into the cold night and cocked his ear. He could not see, nor hear anything but for the hooting of an owl. He swung round to a few men, who now feigned alertness, and said, "Men, it seems our witch has bewitched the whole kingdom....What is it the Lord Jesus said, 'What good is it to reap the rewards of flesh if we lose our minds?' Well, it seems that we have gained neither booty nor spirit. Why, at least the king could've done was to leave us some women, eh, men?" The men guffawed with emphatic nods. "Still, I caution you, to keep your bowstrings taut and eyes wide. The fierce Lance is on the loose, I'll wager, and I wouldn't be surprised if this lull is his tricky doing." He smiled to himself as he descended the ladder in that the men snapped back to alertness, lest the mighty knight under whom they once fought and now their enemy would descend upon them, smiting their bodies and cursing their souls. All along the ramp the men were jarred to vigilance with the fear of Lord Lance wreaking vengeance.

In the meantime Erinysia budged her ladies to housekeeping and in the redecorating of the king's stark apartments. Artifacts of witchcraft abounded along with fine silks and satin. She had the dark, aged oak throne painted red, edged with gold. Though the ladies were anxious over the mysterious abandonment of the city, Erinysia was confident and persuaded them to engage in private orgies of a gentle nature among themselves—including Maureen and David. Within a fortnight the orgies were stepped up by opening them up to selected knights.

Before this, Bennet had met with Erinysia in the throne room to question her rather indolent attitude. "My lady, this is total madness. As you in strange behavior wile your time in the castle as though subjects were outside engaged in toil for the kingdom, your troops are restive out of the uncertainty of pending action. Moreover, some of them think it is a fiasco, thinking they victorious and wish to return to their loved ones."

Her snarl turned to a smile and replied, "Why, of course, how thoughtless of me! Send a task party to round up their families and bring them here to celebrate—indeed, victorious we are and need civilians to join in this great victory. Verily a queen should have subjects toiling on behalf of her crown and bestowing adulation for her presence Moreover, a migration of civilians will prod the peasants and city dwellers out of hiding."

"My ears deceive me! Surely, you don't mean...why, it's impossible to move thousands! Even if they were willing it would take months."

"Impossible!...If impossible, how then was the city emptied out? Is your treasured Lance the only one capable of doing the impossible?" And, pray, what do you mean 'willing'?—certainly they would be willing!...But I speak of merely a hundred for select troops."

"But you're asking people to pull up roots of hundreds of years to trek to the city and its farming strips for no purpose and surely no permanence."

"Their roots are in *my* soil now," she reminded him with a glare.

"Aye, but without a harvest. I tell you it would be chaos, particularly when the city-dwellers and strip serfs do return—they're bound to, you know."

"Yea, surely, and my anticipatory purpose, they will return to be guided by their queen—we shall expand the space. But my loyal knight, I suppose, to a degree you are right. So if you're worried about morale, allow some men to return to their homes for a spell. That will raise the expectations of the others."

"Never, we cannot spare them—what with Henry and possibly Lance lurking about."

"Bah," she growled, "All you ever speak of is Lance. I tell you he has turned to mush by that bitch of the north, if he is not already dead by the fired tongue of Plateos. Speak of him no more," she added, scowling. "As far as Henry is concerned, he's probably aboard a ship heading for his Roman roots."

"Even so, what of the king's people and his troops?" he asked shaking his head. "Truly, they did not go abroad with him. And granting there is not Lance to worry about, there is still that sly Sir John to contend with and the Mari regiment. He will never accept this without a fight. Moreover, since you were so bent in declaring yourself queen, what satisfaction is it to have a crown without subjects?"

"You underestimate me, dear Bennet, if you think I would not launch a reign of torture if soon there is no compliance. Relax, as I said, they will return and bend before their queen. And as for Sir John, he is up to no more mischief now since he is but a cinder in a dragon's eye." She laughed proudly. "But if you wish, take a battalion and rout the king's forces, though I doubt those quaint castle guards of Henry's are still a unit, much less a fighting one."

"A battalion! Why, Lance's loyalists would have all the king's men behind him! And fighting men they would be under the flag of Mari knights!" Have you forgotten their fierceness at the border? What is a battalion against a royal army? — particularly ensconsed, I wager, in a dense forest."

She laughed. "You forget;...we are the royal army now. But believe me, that hearty band you speak of is in disoriented weakness....An army once, perhaps, but never strong. By now they have lost heart—especially if the king indeed has abandoned them."

"You say if?" He knit his brows and tugged on his beard. "Why doesn't your green, bloodshot eye-ball show you for sure?"

She smiled coyly. "Methinks it has gone fickle on me."

"Oh, it too has abandoned you, eh?...Could it be the work of the bitch from the north you referred to earlier?"

She glowered at him. "Why if a witch, she has the mere powers of a novice!"

"Hmm," Bennet muttered, "I wonder."

33. Bennet's Dilemma

Erinysia having several times been unsuccessful in her bid to conjure images on her dimming cabochon, tried again to track Bennet's progress, but again met up with the same frustration. She shrilled, "Damn you, Eve!" and wildly hurled the balking domed crystal, but it caught in the bed curtain and bounced on the bed. With a sigh of relief, she lovingly picked it up and placed it back on the table.

Had she been able to bring up an image, she would have seen Bennet and some of his officers drinking at a table in an inn on the north fringe of the black forest to the east. Bennet just finished guzzling a tankard of ale and said, "Well, my drinking mates, you heard the innkeeper say that the heart of the black forest has been uninhabited for a century and not even penetrated by hardy hunters because of its witchcraft." He swung round with his tankard held high, motioning to the innkeeper at the bench bar for replenishment.

An older officer and captain of the best fighting unit in Bennet's battalion, said seriously, "You know as well as I, baron, that it is pure superstition. Just because a small band of settlers mysteriously disappeared from there a hundred years ago doesn't mean its populated with sorcerers, witches and demons. No one knows for sure the wherefores of a century ago."

Calling for another tankard, Bennet replied, "How else is history born?"

A heavy set knight who still had on his coat of mail to hide the flaccid gravitation of a once powerful figure, laughed heartily, then comforted them in jest. "What do we care of demoniac apparitions when we have the protection of the greatest witch of all—our newly self-anointed queen!" He held up his tankard and bade, "Drink, men, to our witchy, bitchy queen!"

"Aye," said another, raising a mug, "and by the way who on earth is Lilith?" Several shrugged; no one else lifted his tankard; so the two men guzzled alone; then each had a good laugh.

The heavy set knight added, "Who is Lilith?—why not, refer to Bennet's faith in history!" He chuckled, then burst with laughter.

A young officer snarled at the heavy toastmaster, then turned to the elder captain, "But, captain, the innkeeper said that the tale is still prevalent today. And why wouldn't it be? My God, it is not everyday that scores of people are boiled alive as supper for cannibalistic witches!"

The captain laughed. "I'll excuse you because of your youth. It's poppycock to believe such a story. People are ignorant and will believe anything—not unlike this Lilith creation. Adam's first woman—in an elf's eye!"

The heavy set one rattled his coat of mail with a growling chortle and interspersed, "Aye, just as you, captain, believe in the queen's witchcraft, eh?...Why, she' s no more than a harlot and has the power to arouse us all only because we fools think we will be the next to bed with her." He glanced over at Bennet whose nerve was touched but merely winced.

The young officer grimaced at the crude remark. "How dare you, Sir Harold! Why, that's treason!" He stood up and drew his sword.

Bennet said to the young man, "Put away your sword, Donald." Glancing at Sir Harold, he added, "Regardless, she has the spellbound power to dupe us right or wrong, and exemplifies the power of those possessed of witchery. We shouldn't treat it lightly," he added as though to himself, "apparently old Kalab did—and to boot it seems young Bryan."

Donald raised his drink, then made the sign of the cross as if it were a holy chalice. "May the old warlord and the once loyal squire now rest in peace." The rest joined in the solemn toast.

Then the captain pressed his theme, "Because of the incredibly thick interior is the only reason the black forest has never been penetrated. Besides, what's the need since there are miles of hunting game round the accessible perimeters. But a cowardly king running for his life would surely escape into it."

"I tend to agree with the captain," said Bennet. "There is no other explanation for the disappearance of the king's regiment,...and who knows how many citizens and villagers."

The young Sir Donald, gulped down his ale, then said, "Surely, my lord, you're not suggesting we root them out!"

"I hope not," said Harold. "Let them rot there."

"Ah, would that I could agree," replied Bennet; "But I still feel deeply that this mystifying strategy is Lance's doing. He's playing the waiting game and the longer we do nothing the stronger he will become."

Harold slapped his tankard against his coat of mail and said, "But why didn't he simply—assuming Lance *is* behind it—wait out the siege? What's the point of abandoning the city?"

The elder captain rejoined, "They were probably low on provisions and went to the forest where it is rich in game."

Harold peered over the rim of his tankard. "How rich is rich? To be sure not rich enough to feed a fighting force along with thousands of citizens and serfs."

Bennet conjectured, "Oh, I'm sure the peasantry is scattered all over the countryside by now, absorbed by countless manors and villages unfriendly to our cause. And those that didn't, I suppose, are supporting the troops. Henry, you know, is badly undermanned compared to us—despite our horrendous losses at the border."

"Don't remind us," the captain inserted, "of that humiliating day."

Donald bit his lip and uttered, "I wish I could be sure of that. How can we be certain the king did not conscript from other manor lords?"

"Time, lad," the captain said.

Bennet laughed. "Aye, we beat him to it."

"The king, don't forget, was totally taken by surprise, thinking Lance was in control," the captain rejoined.

Donald again bit his lip. "Speaking of whom, I can't imagine him avoiding a battle."

Bennet nodded. "True, still, he is no stranger to delaying strategy either."

"I can't fathom his objective," Harold said, tugging on his bushy moustache. "Besides, you're just presuming Lance is with the king. There's no evidence of that."

"Granted," said Bennet, "but the mere fact that the queen cannot track him on her damnable cabochon, which seems resistant now to show her the way, is good enough for me that somehow he has thwarted her for a time."

The captain asked, "Then what is it you intend for us to do?"

The innkeeper returned with Bennet's refill. He took a drink, then looked in each one's eyes. "We must enter the forest and see for ourselves."

"That's suicide!" Sir Donald whined.

"Hold on, youthful one; I'm not committing the entire regiment. I shall lead a squad to scout the interior to return hopefully with a layout of their camps and decide whether it is feasible for us to attack them by night."

"With just a battalion?" Harold was quick to ask.

Bennet took another drink. "I'm not sure—we'll have to measure their strength."

"I don't like this," Harold said, nervously rubbing one wing of his moustache with his thumb and forefinger. "I still say let them rot it out in there. After all, we control the city."

"Still, with the possibility of Lance—and Sir Charles and the crafty John, don't forget—we won't have control for long. We've got to find out," Bennet concluded.

"But Sir John is dead," the young knight reminded him. "Done in hideously by a dragon."

Bennet choked on his ale. "Saint George, that's right. I guess I wanted to forget that. John was my friend."

"What?...Then it's really true!" Harold yelped.

"Aye, though dragons are not supposed to exist, I was witness to John's gruesome death," the captain rejoined, "not to mention the gallant Robert."

"Hmm,...Robert too, you say?" Harold, twisting his moustache again and looking to Bennet, uttered somewhat unnerved, "I see,...so that's why you see our new queen as a legitimate power."

Bennet indeed led a squad of men into the forest. Not able to penetrate it deeply to determine the actual presence of the king's troops, he nevertheless could presume their presence from fresh tracks and trails and though cleverly covered over, his training with the Mari taught him to look for decoys and cover-ups. Having returned to the castle, still covered in travel dust, he went directly to the keep to report to the new queen. The guard at the entrance to her suite extended his spear, denying Bennet access. Bennet drew his sword, scowled and warned, "Step aside, pretense of a soldier, or suffer the anger of my point!"

The guard protested mildly, "But, my lord Baron, the queen gave strict orders not to be disturbed."

"Granted, but not with respect to the general of her army." He pushed the distraught guard and flung open the door.

Erinysia was in the king's huge bed with Maureen. Bennet, though stunned, momentarily observed with prurient curiosity the tender love-making between woman and girl. Had he not felt so unclean from his long journey he would have stripped to join them. Finally he approached the busy bed as envy displaced his wonder. He tugged on Erinysia's long raven hair until her face wet with lubricant and saliva emerged from between the girl's petite thighs.

"How now you dare invade my inmost pleasures!" Erinysia carped as her hand continued to fondle the girl's thigh.

"If you wanted privacy you should've chosen another hour—the afternoon for a queen especially is hardly the time to engage in this fantasy, incorrigible witch," he groused with a trail of rancor.

Maureen did not even blush on his entrance. She skidded her buttocks to the edge of the bed and threw on a flimsy chemise. Erinysia kissed the girl on the mouth and dismissed her kindly.

"Oh, dear Queen Mother, do not send me away to your ladies' chambers where they demand so much of me when my heart feeling the pang of perfidy tells me that there is only you," she whined with a pout.

"Oh, my darling stepdaughter, you have much to learn in this art. They will teach you well so that you will further please me."

Maureen protruded her lower lip. "But why is it not you who teaches me. Verily, learning, should be a heartfelt joy."

Erinysia twittered and hugged the girl. "My sweetest, you will find that with them as well. The secret is in acceptance. Do not think you are being unfaithful. On the contrary, in your hours with them, think of it as a path to love me even more." She tweaked Maureen's nose. "Now away with you, sweetheart, and learn your lessons." Maureen ran off, sniffling.

Bennet grinned and offered, "Such delicious secrets you women keep. I see now why you are also a queen in bed and oft take the initiative."

"I have little choice with men who are fitted with weak loins that do early spend themselves into limp oblivion," she said with snideness, then rolled her nude body to the head of the bed and lay back, propped by pillows. "But wider purpose is the issue now. What news from your prowling escapades in the countryside? Did the cowardly king flee abroad?"

He shook his head. "Not as long as the crafty Lord-Protector is by his side."

She frowned and sat up. "What!...He lives?"

"I'm sure of it and as fearless and cunning as ever with the Mari loyalist bivouacked in the black forest. And, I trust with demons of their own."

"Hardly fearless if ensconced in the shades of protection like common animals," she vented, chuckling derisively.

"I wouldn't stake my life on that. He's up to something assuredly."

"But what evidence have you that he is in fact alive and holds up there? And if so, what can he do without his combat-experienced troops?...Why, Henry's troops are nothing more than dressing for kingly pomp. "

"You forget the detachment that whipped us. Furthermore, it cannot be said that his archers are mere dressing. And Lance will shape the infantry in a hurry," he said with a trace of anxiety.

She slid to the edge of the bed. "Archers you say?"

"Aye, bold ones with deadly accuracy. They sent a rain of fire down on us, smoking us out of the forest....Odd, though..."

"Oh?" she perked.

"Not a crossbow in the bunch as at the castle. Longbowmen they were—only a handful in this country that I know of."

"Oh, no!" She quickly dressed. "Well, if fire is their weaponry. Fire they shall have more of!"

At the forest camp in a small tent shared by Lady Rita and Rhonda, the two women were sitting in light folding chairs at a small table, supping. "You really must try to eat, my dear," Rita suggested, "in spite of these indelicate meals in this frightful camp."

Rhonda lackadaisically picked up a fork while mustering a smile. "Oh, the food is substantial, under the circumstance, though granted peasant-like."

"Substantial!...Your brother sees to it that his fighting men are fed well while we are served the leftovers!" Rita mocked a scowl, then chuckled. "Why, if I didn't know better, I'd swear that was the cause of your weight loss....Oh, my darling, I know it is difficult for you, but you must not grieve so for Bryan and think more of your health—at your age the body is still growing."

Rhonda sniffled, released the fork and mewled, "Oh, Lady Rita, the awful event is still so horribly singular and pulsating within me. It is one thing to accept the awful news of a knight killed in battle...but this...so bedeviled was he to attempt to take my life that Bryan—or more accurately that wicked witch—did take away my spirit!"

Rita reached over and gently squeezed Rhonda's hand. "Yes, grossly real—yet not! Bewitchment is not reality in its instrument but rather in the mover that lurks behind. Try to comfort yourself in that Bryan was not Bryan but an unthinking tool."

Rhonda sighed. "Oh, I know, I know....Still, the apparition I did find all too real!"

Rita reached over again and picked up the girl's fork. "Find this instrument real and that which is on the plate." She rose up and added, "I must now tend to the king. He, too, is much depressed of late. This camp life does not agree with his constitution. And though at the moment the food may not agree with that which you are accustomed, when I return I expect to see that plate scraped clean."

Rhonda smiled. "I promise...to reconstitute the food in a new, delectable light." She put a morsel in her mouth.

"Good," Rita said at the entrance and left, not having the heart to spring on her the news from Lance's scouts of the death of her father. Rhonda ate another bit on the tip of the fork and dropped the utensil when she heard a subdued wail from outside the tent. She bent her ear but the sound went away. She pushed back the little chair and lay down on the bunk, staring at the low lying tent top that rippled with shadows from the flickering candlelight. She closed her eyes, but feeling a strangeness, quickly opened them. Green and yellow crystals hovered and sparkled overhead. She blinked her eyes and the crystals disappeared. She rolled over and pulled a coverlet over her head. She dozed off, only to be wakened by boot steps and a gush of wind from the entrance flap opening. She threw off the coverlet and quickly sat up, sighing with relief in seeing young Henry.

"Forgive me, my lady for startling you," he said, approaching the bunk and draping the coverlet onto her shoulders. "You have for so long kept to yourself that, having missed you so, I just had to intrude upon you."

Rhonda blushed, then said, "Please, Prince, don't apologize. I am glad to see you. It is I who should apologize for having been so inconsiderate to one who saved my life."

"No such thought, please," he pleaded, taking her hand. "I understand how much you miss Sir Bryan. Still, you live for more, I trust, than grief."

"Yes, yes, I know, but it takes time."

"Of course, especially with the death of your father barely a breath behind."

"What's this?" Rhonda gasped . "Oh, prince, so cruel a jest can only be that you still harbor resentment for my rejection back at the castle."

He grimaced a mixture of sorrow and anger. "Fie, don't *you* cruelly jest that such resentment would linger in face of your sorrow!...Oh, dear Rhonda, forgive me for my bluntness, but I thought Lady Rita had told you of your father's death."

She drew the coverlet to her dampened cheeks. "Cruel jest from fate, then, is this news." She looked into his eyes. "Pray, am I dreaming this?...My mother not six months buried and now my father!...Oh, is there no finale other than the death of us all by the deadly hand of this horrid Erinysia?...For surely, just as sweet Maureen's father, this evil witch killed my father."

"Aye, of that there is little doubt." He grimaced and held her hand in his.

"Oh, God, forgive me. As upset as this makes me, I, in unspeakable terms, do feel relief that his soul—in essence good despite the siege of an evil spell—is now at peace with my mother's."

"Yea, my sweet, in this you must believe," he comforted. Then hesitantly he squeezed her hand, "Forgive me, Rhonda, for this I know is not the time, but please do not be a stranger to me. In spite of these sorry affairs of state, I can think of nothing but you."

She touched his face and smiled gratefully. Suddenly the moan she had heard before returned and then a piercing caterwaul. She flung her arms round Henry's neck. Suddenly a huge paw tore through the tent, narrowly missing Rhonda's back. Henry pulled her off the bunk to the sparsely grassy floor and threw his body over her just as the panther leaped through the tent and attacked the prince who rolled off Rhonda who squirmed back against the cot. Henry drew out his dagger as the panther clawed at his chest. He plunged the dagger into the animal's side but it had no effect. The panther sank saber-like teeth into the prince's throat. Rhonda screamed.

Back at the castle, Erinysia, with an eerie smile, bent over the crystal that had revitalized its light: she flicked her fingers at the frightened image of Rhonda, cringing from the giant cat, which, nevertheless and curiously seemed to ignore Rhonda as it feasted on its prey. Rhonda back at the tent cried out, "Oh, good God, what is happening!" as she saw herself melting down to where her stature was barely above the prince's writhing face. A bat flew through the torn opening and bit into her hair, which webbed in its claws. It flew away with the diminutive figure who fainted from the imposing horror.

A guard rushed in, and with swinging sword lashed out at the panther, which quickly bolted through the torn tent and into the night. The guard bent down over the bleeding prince who was gurgling from the tear at his throat. Suddenly his eyes glassed over and he gasped, uttering virtually inaudibly, "Our love wasn't meant to be." He tried to close his eyes but they bulged with the stare of death.

The king was devastated by the news of his son. He summoned Lance, accompanied by Lucia, and ordered him to armor up in pursuit on behalf of his sister and royal revenge. Lucia, however, calmed down the king and pleaded that he be patient.

"Our time has not arrived," she said mysteriously to the king while glancing over at Lance who was pacing and clutching the hilt.

"The time is now!" asserted Lance. "I cannot wait for your spiritual strategy while my sister is in claws of the devil! 'Twas bad enough you called up my patience for revenge on news of Bryan, John, and my father's death!"

"Believe me, Lance, no harm will come to her. Erinysia is using her as hostage. Rhonda would be useless to her dead."

"Bah, what of the tortures in the meantime?" he growled.

"Please, Lance, do not betray me now. I know, I feel what must be done. Have faith in me."

"Aye, that I have, but in our garrison I haven't! How could Erinysia's men steal away with my poor sister?"

"We know only of the stealth of a panther," she replied. "For all we know Erinysia has the power to kidnap by some sordid metempsychosis of the living."

"Oh, fie on the cryptic workings of witches! I long for the day of honest chivalric battle!" he moaned and left for his tent.

Bennet, superseding his own objection, led his cavalry of knights and the earl's diminished infantry into the forest before dawn. "Young Donald is right. This is totally suicidal," he growled.

The formidable heavy set knight riding next to him agreed with a hearty laugh, "Aye, my liege, it seems the queen is under her own spell."

"Be on the lookout for those damnable archers," Bennet ordered. "Trail the orders for shields high and to spread out."

Harold jerked his horse round and trotted along the line, yelling, "Stomp your way through the brush and spread out, my hearties, and keep your shields high. Those archers are sure to be in the trees."

No sooner had the infantry fallen into squad-abreast formation, than they were parrying arrows from high and behind trees. The uncanny accuracy of the archers were not frustrated by mere shields as those high in the trees with their powerful longbow were able to penetrate the helmets and those below went for the lower limbs. The knights because of the dense undergrowth were forced to dismount but thought their heavy armor would protect them. They bewailed fearful surprise more so than pain in feeling the powerful arrows penetrate their heavy coats of mail and armor.

Bennet, still on horseback, dodged and parried close aims until a direct hit tore his shoulder and unhorsed him. Bravely he got to his feet and cunningly ordered the men to take cover and not to advance. But from a deep trench a hundred yards in front, archers hailed flaming arrows, forcing the men to withdraw.

Meanwhile Erinysia focused on her cabochon until the mayhem in the forest appeared. She snarled and waved her hand across the polished dome and suddenly three great sinuous dragons appeared in the lead of Bennet's men. Rapidly the giant apparitions thundered toward the entrenched archers, unleashing hot tongues of flame and alternately gnashing saw-like teeth. Archers scrambled out of the trench and ran for their mounts. One, however, was hooked onto a giant tooth, cooked by hot flames mid his hideous screams and swallowed—perhaps mercifully. Bennet ordered his cavalry in pursuit of the archers.

Harold objected, "My lord, surely you do not mean for us to ride through that raging fire!"

"Especially with our troops so far behind, and archers still in trees and behind." cried Donald .

Erinysia waved her hand again and the dragons spewed a green slimy mist and the immense fires were reduced to green smoke. "What fire?" Bennet grinned and mounted his steed. "Pursue those pin-cushion cowards, brave knights!" The skilled horsemen wove in and out of the charred trees in hot pursuit. But the archers most exposed that had mounted skirted away into the shadowy density. The knights held up in amazement at the incredible swiftness of the archers' horses. The big knight yelped, "Forsooth, they must have wings!"

Bennet said, "And who knows what awaits us in that thicket."

"Couldn't we just follow the dragons in?" one of the lieutenants nervously offered.

Bennet shook his head. "What and burn us all to a crisp?"

"Then let the dragons go in alone," Harold suggested.

"Oh, no, and burn the camp and all the innocent women and children there?" Sir Donald shook his head violently and bit his lip: "We might be bewitched, but I have enough of my honor in tact."

"But we don't know for a fact that the city dwellers are with them," the big knight persisted.

"If not then where? We combed the countryside for them—I tell you it's too risky," Donald said warily.

Harold turned to Bennet. "It's your decision."

"To hell with the women and children," Bennet barked. "It's the real estate I'm thinking of. It's too rich in game and timber to burn out. We will withdraw and see if Lance who surely must be seething with revenge has to be anxious to meet us in open ground."

"Aye," agreed Harold, "Lance, in truth, will never hide forever."

"I hope he does," inserted Donald meekly.

The knights returned to the infantry still under a barrage of arrows. The dragons aimed their fire power to the trees and lapped as far as seventy-five feet above. Archers began to fall like balls of fire adding to the inferno below. The troops, fearful of the dragons as well, withdrew, but the brave archers in the tallest trees continued their harassment. The knights galloped through the scrambling troops to lead them out of the forest. Having emerged into the open field, Bennet shook his head in despair, estimating the heavy casualties. "'Tis foolhardy, men! Retreat!"

"Fools!" screamed Erinysia as she in disgust waved away the dragons and the green light dissolved. She stormed out of her apartments to double the watch on the battlements and to alert them to Bennet's disgraceful return. She went back to her chambers and had Maureen summoned to ease her tension. Yet after having made love and now bored with Maureen's tireless fawning, she dismissed the spellbound child and turned her attention to the titillating amusement across the face of the crystal which focused on the guarded room where Rhonda, restored to natural size, at the moment was fighting off the sexual advances of Erinysia's ladies. At every kick, resistant squirm and shrill screams of Rhonda's, Erinysia, gazing into the crystal, tongued her lips and fondled her breasts with hot sighs, yearning for the time when she would be in bed with her other, and more ravishing, stepdaughter. Alas, she had to turn from this entertainment and went back to the battlements.

Earlier the same day the king's men, led by Lance, had left the camp from the opposite direction while the fighting was going on in the interior. Lucia also led her force but for the fifty archers left to guard the rear opening to the forest. Once out on the plain both forces split to fringe the forest from opposite flanks. Lucia held her amulet to the sun as she intuited that its reflection would divert Erinysia from tracking them. By early morning, she and her men had reached the other end of the forest first and ensconced her forces along a huge horseshoe rim a half mile beyond. A half hour later Lance reached a rocky mound jutting out from the forest just as Bennet's unsuspecting men appeared from a lower hill a short distance away. Lance ordered a cavalry charge upon the retreating enemy. Fifty knights, lightly clad on fifty of steeds borrowed from Lucia's archers, swarmed down on Bennet's knights heavily armed. They veered to head off Lance's knights until they saw a thousand troops had lined the ridge. They changed course, trying to reach cover of the forest, but the pursuing knights easily overtook them. Harold yelped, "God's Wound! The knights' mounts too have wings!"

Though they slightly outnumbered the king's knights, they were quickly subdued, so out-maneuvered by the lightly armed knights upon the fleeting horses. Observing the debacle the infantry dashed madly for cover behind the horseshoe rim only to be decimated by Lucia's archers and horsemen, together with Henry's detachment of infantry.

Bennet cried out to the sky for his queen's help and when none came, he abandoned his few gallant knights who were haplessly trying to govern their large horses in face of the fleet horses of the north. Lance galloped after him and caught up quickly, knocking him to the ground with the broadside of his sword. Lance dismounted to face the knight scrambling to his feet. "I could've lopped off your head while you were mounted but it would have denied me this pleasure of eye to eye combat with a treacherous scoundrel."

"My dear Lance, surely you don't hold me accountable. I, just like your father and Bryan, am bewitched!"

"Nay, under your own free will you entered into contract with Erinysia. But even that I might have forgiven, but not your dastardly assault on my helpless sister who would not be alive were it not for my faithful steed Stars that foiled your evil attempt."

Bennet fell to his knees. "I tell you Erinysia cast a spell for me to do what she herself had wanted to do. She felt she could not control your father with Rhonda alive."

"And what have you done with my dear sister now?"

Bennet arched his brows. "What's this? Why, I thought she was safe with the king?"

"Don't lie to me!" Lance scowled. "You sent your ignoble knights into our camp, killed the prince and absconded with Rhonda."

The bewildered baron bent his body and groveled at Lance's boots. "I swear by Jesus and the Holy Rood, I know nothing about this! Erinysia, verily! She seldom confides in me anymore."

"Aye, you are no use to her anymore just as you with your treachery are no use to me. On your boots and die like a knight," Lance ordered with a snarl.

"What chance have I against the mightiest warrior of the land?"

"None, but at least you will have died with a sword in your hand."

Bennet crossed his arms and refused to draw his sword. Lance turned in disgust and signaled to a fellow knight. "Execute him with your axe."

33. The King Mourns

King Henry was left undisturbed in his tent for several days while he mourned his son. Lady Rita, though rattled herself over the event but her fears for Rhonda took precedence, finally insisted on an audience so she could hopefully bring solace to him—and perhaps to herself. He was propped up in a modest traveling bunk, languidly examining his dagger. Though she formally curtsied, Rita sat on the bedside.

He looked up from the dagger and said in a heavy voice, "What is this world of flesh, dear Rita?" He reached for her hand and sighed. "All those years....how did you survive the loss of your gallant husband?"

She touched his hand, thinking she would like to wrest the dagger from it, and responded, "Yes, good king, it seems at times the only purpose is for the living flesh to rot as well," then she yielded a sigh: "yet while it remains, it is time to give it better purpose. That's how we both endured the death of our spouses," she added, though she knew he barely mourned the passing of the queen.

He cleared his throat. "Aye," nodding slightly, "callous self-survival does trick the heart....But now a son gone...I don't know...." He went back to involuntarily toying with the dagger.

Rita looked at the small table by the bed. Her finger flexed to a small portrait propped against the candlestick and next to the physician's potion. She stared for a moment at the Prince's likeness, then sighed. "Loss of dear ones, especially so young, is terrifying because of the guilt imposed upon the living who feel they should join those who matter most."

The king grunted. "Yea, what difference now or later?" he asked himself as he stared at the dagger. "Why not now?" He tensed his fingers over the dagger. "Stick my heart and end the haunting memories."

Calmly she grasped his knuckles firmly. "Oh?...But are they so haunting? It would seem to the contrary that without memories of love there would be little to edge us on."

Lacking true will, he but mildly tried to wrench her hand away, but she retained her grip. "Bah,...egregious!...." he growled, "to edge us onto the use of this!" Despite her hand round his, he urged the dagger under his breastbone. "To eat, drink,...sleep and stuff ourselves, too, with ambition leading nowhere....How now, without the stuff of true meaning to share the life's deadly drive and thus inspire us to change the view of it....Oh, Rita, had I the courage to plunge this blade to stop the beastly pumping of my heart!" He loosened his grip; she, too, and the dagger fell to his lap.

She exhaled relief and distanced her vigil hand. "Shush, now, Henry; clear up the sickness in your head to allow the blood to pump revenge in behalf of your son and Rhonda."

He nodded absently. "Aye, the dear girl...perhaps she still lives. Yet I feel nothing."

"But you must. She is your subject. You cannot forget you are king of a young nation in need of you. You started it."

"Barely,...more like the Mari legacy."

She took note: "Even so, you must maintain it and see to its growth by putting down the fractious contenders who will not yield up the horrendous manor system of erratic lawlessness in lieu of the Great Document's Law."

He looked at her askance and slid down under and drew up a coverlet. "Small comfort without a son with whom to share this ambition as you perceive it."

Rita smiled. "Yea, you need sleep, my lord, but first...." She reached for the potion. "You take me lightly, but at least do as your physician ordered to rid Old Nod of his depressing dreams and breathe in the night with restful sleep." He sat up again and drank it down. She smiled again and tucked him in and blew out the candle.

Later into the evening, he opened his eyes to a bright light at the foot of the bunk. The likeness of Margaret materialized bedecked in a similar gown of Eve's and blazoned across her breast was the tree. He gaped at the apparition that seemed not to look upon him kindly; he bolted upright. He gasped and issued a jittery voice. "My physician has made me drunk; for I swear it is the lovely Queen Margaret that scowls before me!"

"Indeed, I do frown upon the one whom I once loved," Margaret countered. "Here among women and children, you shelter yourself in self-pity while the army is off to fight your battle."

"Oh, God, please tell me my ears and eyes deceive me! For indeed the shame would be insufferable in knowing my childhood love is witness to my shameful state!"

Margaret shook her head. "Though in body I am not here, there's no deception as far as I myself stand before you. Yea, shamelessly deceitful indeed are you!"

Momentarily he pulled the coverlet over his head and groaned a muffled tone, "I cannot bear your look into my coward's eyes!"

Her eyes and temper softened. "A coward you aren't—incompetent, perhaps....Surely a father in grief. But you are more than a father, my once outspoken courtier. You are now a king and must act like one."

He jerked his head from the coverlet. "In title only!...O truly I am ashamed that I am not at the head of my troops and at the side of Lord Lance."

"And need I remind you—at my daughter's side?" she said sarcastically. "Your dear departed son, notwithstanding, how could you send *her* into battle while you wallow in fears unbecoming a king?"

"True, all true, but I fear I am no king in spite of our great document!"

She nodded emphatically. "Yea, not worth the parchment it is inscribed on if you continue this pathetic, aimless path."

"Agreed! A wretch like me can no longer subscribe to divine right!"

She burst into laughter, then blurted, "Yea, a wretch and wretched am I for once loving you."

"Ah, but then I was not king, which was furthest from my mind!" He jumped out of the bunk and kneeled before her. He reached to kiss her hand but only his hand grew bright as it pierced the aura. "What's this? poetic justice that now I find there is no substance to my love?"

She laughed. "Yea, you've proved that more than once."

"Oh, my love, to regain your faith in me, I swear I shall in the morn take my score of personal guards and ride swiftly to join my army. Then you will see a king of action. And because I now know of your daughter's great powers, I shall gladly abdicate the throne to her and Lance if you but show again affection toward me."

"You cannot abdicate that which is already the true divine right of my daughter's," she jibed acrimoniously.

He rose to his feet and stared through the apparition. "What do you mean?"

"The great document is a forgery," she said.

"Preposterous!" he sputtered, "My, you really are revolted by me."

"No, simply a historical fact. "The true divine right is in the rock of the North."

He rubbed his chin. "You jog me!... Aye, now I remember the legend."

"It is real—and probably why you were thinking of proposing to me," she said, eying him suspiciously. "Father like son, eh? Long ago your father reduced love to crass acquisition."

He shook his head and reached for her; though disappointed again in not touching flesh, he felt a warmth running through his body from her displacement of light. "Believe me, my love, the only motive is to be with you, to share in your loving presence."

"This is not the time to talk of love; but I shall reconsider if you ride out of this dark retreat and restore your nobility. Yet you must keep in mind that you can never fully replace my dear departed husband, whose relationship I see clearly now was destiny." She placed her ethereal hand into his and giggled. "Why, I might even entertain your fantasy of royalty—for a while, that is—until my daughter marries."

"But, my dear Margaret, why should I ride out now if you have so little faith in my divine right to be king?"

"For your own sense of dignity that keeps eluding you. And if not for that, at least for me to regain my respect for you should be reason enough. But there is another...."

"Oh?" He raised a brow.

"Oh, don't look surprised, you old fox," she said, wagging a finger. "The other more important reason is to rise up for your true love, the mother of Rhonda....Surely for her you cannot indulge in self-pity while her child is at death's door."

He rapped his fist. Then by George's dragon, I shall ride to rid the kingdom of Erinysia's sorcery!"

35. Assault

Erinysia was dismayed when a mere handful of Bennet's battalion returned. Not a single knight was among them. Infuriated, she ran from the battlements to her cabochon and focused into its crystalline depths to observe Lucia and Lance several miles away leading the long column of fighting men on the way to the castle. Further back she saw the king on a gray horse in fast gait, leading his mounted guards and closing the gap. She grinned and muttered, "The old fool! What does he know about combat?" She ignored this helpless interloper and brought up close into focus the vanguard led by Lance. She glided her palm across the face of the crystal dome and laughed triumphantly in seeing her conjured dragon strike fear into the marching column as it exhaled its flames. Lucia shot a silver arrow into the throat of but another of the endless lineage of Plateos. The monster's fire power turned to vapor leakage through the open wound. Triumph turned to frustration in seeing Lucia rise *literally* to the occasion as her mount soared high to meet the dragon head on while Lucia, shield raised, with one swoop of her gleaming golden sword beheaded the reptile. Erinysia groaned, rapped her fist on the table and flipped the cover over the tiger's eye. "Enough of your deceptive eye that dazzles with fairy tales!"

She stormed out of her chambers and out of the keep to cross the inner ward toward the northern battlement tower where she redeployed the guards to the palisades. Looking to the azure of the northern sky, she raised her arms and repeatedly shrilled, "Mother Lilith!" and then pressed and rolled her forehead against the cylindrical wall, then continued moaning for Lilith as she nervously twitched the emerald at her breast. After a moment her eyes lowered and she became conscious of the stolen gem, which had been willed to Rhonda. She caressed it as though it were her cabochon and spoke to it, her head still pressed to the wall: "Do you, slumbering green, subtly pulsate Eve's bustling green earth or do you softly glimmer for the more perfect natural state of Lilith's rugged mountains and caves?" Finally she pushed herself away from the wall and held out the emerald to the extent of its chain. Refocusing on it she asked herself, "Why, Lilith, why this abandonment?...Have I not done your bidding since you tore me from a contented gypsy home and from the arms of my adoring earthly mother?"...Oh, dear Lilith, at this very moment I wish for the happy camp life of a simple dancing girl!....Why should I care about your silly biblical battle?...Verily, God, does not if he still confines your spirit to that damnable eternal fire hole, so why should I?"....How without you can I match the works of Eve through this bold flaxen hussy from the north?" She broke the emerald's chain. "Away, sick gem of Kalab green! For without Eve's untiring industry you would still be embedded in a peaceful mountain side!" She threw it down into the turret below, then walled up her eyes stoking fire to the sky turned a quivering gray. She heaved out a hideous howl, more of a caterwaul, and then lightning burst through, networking the sky and large twilight clouds rolled north and south.

Ethan at the cave was in deep meditation trying to control the raging, heaving energy in the pit. He could hear the piercing shrills of Erinysia; and when they subsided, he heard wails from the deep within the pit. He moved to the edge and looked down at a huge bulge in the center of the restive lava. Slowly it stretched to a pillar of white hot flame within which the figure of Lilith writhed. He fell to his knees and clasped his hands. As his lips quivered in prayer, the figure in the flames began to descend back into the bulge. Lilith half immersed, squirmed and raised her arms, screaming, "My daughter, my daughter!"

At the tower, Erinysia heard the cry and pressed her temples into deep concentration. Lilith re-emerged; to greater heights, her arm stretched up as though to grab a stalactite. Ethan reached for an apple and held it high, pleading, "Stay, noble but ill-spirited Lilith! The world has no need of you! Human knowledge now reigns!"

She fell back, whimpering, sizzling into the pit. From the dark heights of the volcanic aperture shrilled down the voice of Erinysia: "But I have desperate need of you, Mother! For Eve once more does disrupt the rightness of your fate!"

Suddenly Lilith was thrust from the boiling liquid; the bough from Life's stump grew strong. She reached up for it, it bent momentarily from her weight, then hurled her up among the stalactites. High up into the shadows of the vault she crystallized in all the splendor of her godliness. The shadows were displaced by a blinding light as Lilith rocketed upward and out of the mountain and high into the clouds, gliding along the lightning toward the south.

Ethan cringed but for a moment, then dropped to his knees and beseeched, "This changes the rules of combat....I have no recourse, what with Eve prohibited, to go outside the frame of things." He looked to a golden spear hanging on the cavern wall and chanted:

"Shake loose from Olympic slumber, O Mars!

Lean to the underdog as you had at Troy

Take up your spear in behalf of dear Lucia."

His eyes remained fixed to the spear, hoping for a sign. Suddenly the spear quivered and unhooked from the wall and fell to the hard rock. Then it glowed and rose upright while shaking furiously. A handsome but wrathful looking woman transformed while the spear fell to ashes. She was adorned in ancient war garb and a silver helmet with red and white plumage, together with her own gleaming spear tip of diamond, atop a pole of sturdy oak.

Ethan fell back on his haunches and cowered.

She spoke, "Why, if thou art so wise, old man, dost thou call for Mars? It is known in Olympus that you are skeptical of our existence."

"Oh, sadly true, fearsome lady....Still, I did hope that there exists another layer of assistance in my hour of need. In seeing you, I have hope that perhaps indeed the God of War exists and you could beseech him in my behalf."

"But this fracas is not his. Mars, actually Ares, scoffs at women. He is tolerant of me only because I am his sister Enyo and have bailed him out of innumerable skirmishes—especially with his arch enemy Athena, whom you call Minerva."

"Alas," cried Ethan, "then all is lost if he despises a goddess so in love with wisdom and justice—or so the myth goes."

Enyo looked up, extended her arm and in instant a glorious spear of ivory and gold shaft topped by a gleaming bronze head with a silver tip was in her hand. "Myth?...Has thou not thyself spent a hundred lifetimes trapped in a myth?"

"Oh, but grand lady in my long life I have seen the wrath of the pit; I have touched the golden hem of the gracious Eve."

"Need thee, then, to feel this spear in thine heart?" she said with a curious smile as she leveled the tip at him.

He crossed his arms over his breast. "No, No, lady warrior, I accept your imposing presence....And may I trust that you can do something to help my darling princess?"

"Perhaps, if thou dost something for me."

"Oh, anything, my lady warrior; but pray tell what could I possibly do for such a great goddess as you?"

"Great?...Hah, there are no temples in my true name....What is my name?" she asked bluntly.

"Your name...oh, my,...I'm afraid...I...don't know."

"I just did'st give it to thee."

"Oh, my, you did, didn't you?...Oh, forgive me I beseech you!"

"Humph,...you mortals are all alike. Why, half the time Homer forgot my name!" she rattled her spear.

"Oh, wait, dear lady,...yes, yes, you did just tell me....Ah, yes, and such a sweet sounding name it is!....Ir...no,...Ju...ah,...of course, Bello..."

"If thou valuest thy long life, do not utter that name! The Romans mocked me by making me the goddess of the declaration of war! Verily, I engage in war, but I do not seek it out as my brother doth."

"I see,...yea, yea, in the softening of your countenance you go not by that other name. Of course, you are Enyo, the heralded sister to Ares!...Oh, my, Enyo, the great goddess of war in behalf of peace, in her own right that needs no sibling to establish her place in legendary history!"

Her sternness completely waned and emitted a radiant beauty as she smiled and giggled. "Oh, my darling man, let me hear it again!"

"Enyo, Enyo, the dearest goddess in all Olympia!" he sang. "For Enyo has appeared before a tired old man and took pity on him. She, Enyo, is not only the most powerful but the kindest, sweetest and now I see most beautiful of all the goddesses—aye, including Venus—uh, forgive the slip,...Aphrodite!"

She chortled, danced around her spear, and smiled up at Olympus and cried out, "Yea, a most discerning man!" She put down her spear and ran to him, drew him up from his knees and kissed him. "Promise now, that always thou wilt remember?"

He touched her raven tresses peeping out from her helmet. "Aye, sweet and gracious Enyo...the name Enyo shall be always on the tip of my tongue. Why, instead of coughing agéd mucous when I rise in the morn, I shall cough out the famous name and then let while away on the tip of my tongue with refrains of Enyo!"

She giggled and hugged him. "Still, thou art old and wilt forget."

"No, never!" he protested. "But what is it I must do for you?"

"Why, that's it! Simply to believe in me and remember my name!"

"Oh, but I shall, why, your immortality so filled with humanity has converted me! O how like Eve you are!"

"Memory is important to sustain immortality. At your age Mnemosyne plays taunting tricks. Therefore,...." she went to the pile of cinders that was once her brother's spear and reshaped it then heaved it into the fiery pit. She then tossed her own spear against the same spot her brother's was and its diamond tip miraculously scratched out on the igneous rock *Enyo, Defender of Lucia.*

Ethan's eyes popped and he clapped his hands. "Bravo! Sweet, kind Enyo!...Yea, unto, defender...nay, unto aggressor!"

"Yea, indeed, I shall defend thy precious princess of Promethean life!...And search out she who affronts by laying claim to divine existence even beyond Olympus." she promised as the spear softly returned to her hand. In a puff of her brother's red smoke she disappeared.

A lightning bolt in the image of Lilith struck the city's northwest tower and merged into Erinysia and the ensuing phosphorescence fired Erinysia's body with renewed energy. She immediately alerted her archers and swordsmen on the parapets and her infantry guarding the gates of the bailey wards. Her army was struck dumb when she stationed a three-headed dragon at each of the drawbridges, east and west. The men then gasped, "giant bats!" when seeing a cloud of thousands of crepuscular bats split off and then merge clusters to forge a dozen pterodactyl hovering the watchtowers.

Night fell and campfires flared up as Erinysia observed the King's forces camped along the same ridge that her units had before their triumphant march on the city. She returned to her chambers in order to see the camp clearly through her crystal eye. Focusing on the king's tent, she grinned devilry and looked down at the black cat purring at her feet. "My, how poetic, Mephistopheles, yea, yea, I get your drift: why not after all have the king exit in the manner of his son?"

Lucia slept deeply through the night by campfire while Lance kept vigil. He wakened her when dawn's light stretched round the city's walls. Her hand, he thought, was clutching the familiar gold amulet. When she stretched, he was stunned in seeing that the horseshoe was replaced by a wooden charm shaped as a tree, on which was carved in relief a human eye and an arrowhead imbedded in the eye of a snake. He was already so mystified by her and his childhood vision, that he decided not to inquire. Handing her a bowl of steaming pottage, he said, "I trust you've had sufficient rest, my love; for it seems we have a mighty challenge ahead of us. He swayed his head to the western bridge. "Apparently Erinysia is fond of dragons."

Lucia had just swallowed a spoonful of pottage and almost choked when she looked over the ravine. "Oh, no, not another! I exhausted myself in challenging yesterday's ugly, scaly thing—and I despise looking into those evil vertical eyes—no windows to the soul there." She chuckled. "And that one had only one head!—ugh, three pairs of those despicable yellow slits!"

Suddenly there was a scream from the king's tent. "The King is dead! The king is dead!" A young attendant emerged from the tent. "Our nation is cursed! The king's throat is gorged just as our dear Prince met his death."

Lucia bowed her head and sobbed. "Oh, Lance, I shouldn't have slept! It was my duty to watch over him."

"Nonsense, how much are you expected to do?...He shouldn't have joined us anyway."

"Alas, that was my mother's doing."

"Your mother?"

"Yea, we both apparently are moving in strange ways of late."

Two of the king's most trusted knights, Gideon and James, approached. Lord Gideon scowled and demanded, "There's no point now in going on, Lance. Where's the point?—to save a nation without a king."

Sir James shook his head, glancing at Gideon. "Don't be rash, Gideon. Let us first hear from Lance." He put his hand on Lance's shoulder. "What say you, Lord Lance? Do we give up the ghost of the sacred Document?"

Lance did not hesitate, though he looked askance at Lucia. "The point of being here is indeed to save a nation—with or without a king. We cannot be subjugated to the likes of Erinysia who will enslave us all."

"My sentiments exactly," chimed Sir James with a grin; then he pointed to the castle across the ravine. "That monstrosity at the bridge notwithstanding."

Gideon paced and looked to the castle gate. "This is totally foreign to a knight's challenge: despite the fantastic legends of old, we are supposed to face men of war!" He turned back to them. "How can we expect to face up to such black magic as this?"

Sir James laughed. "My, my, memory has escaped you quickly! Are you forgetting the incredible heroics of this lovely princess just yesterday in facing up to such a challenge?"

With mild embarrassment Gideon looked at Lucia. "Forgive me, princess, I am not minimizing your great accomplishments; but it is ignoble for us knights to anticipate your continual engagement with these monsters of Erinysia's frenzied imagination."

Lucia smiled kindly and said softly, "Goodly knight, be not concerned with feelings of helpless pride at this crucial hour. I do what I must do just as you must indeed face thousands of warring men. It is destined that I defend humanity from Erinysia; you are destined to defend your country from rebellious men."

Gideon asked, "But by the Rood, even if we are successful, what will become of the country with both Henrys dead? "Where is the nation's destiny?"

Lance interjected, "The document is the destiny, not flesh and blood. We can always find a king."

Unconvinced, Gideon swayed his head and rubbed his beard. "Where then lies the divine right?"

Sir James laughed. "Excuse me for saying this—why, the king has not yet turned cold—nonetheless, not a decade ago did any of us see divinity in Henry?"

Lucia said firmly, "At the moment this is not our concern; rather we must pay our respects to the King and see to his interment with befitting honor. Then we turn to defeat the demon at her game."

Erinysia with morbid curiosity and an eerie grin watched from the battlement the early morning ceremony on the ridge for the king. Yet her thoughts of Rhonda, having been repressed by preparation for battle, reared up, and she could not resist the temptation to go to her. She returned to the keep, passed by the landing of her own suite and walked another flight to where she had her imprisoned. Erinysia unlocked the door and entered.

Still in bed, Rhonda was startled and groaned, pulling the blanket over her head. Erinysia giggled and sat down on the bed and with a quick jerk removed the blanket. The girl gaped in fear and cowered into the pillow. Erinysia feigned mild disappointment and bent over and kissed the girl's bare shoulder. Erinysia rose up and removed the baldric, her coat of armor, and boots. "Hardly a suitable costume for such a tender scene," she muttered. "But there will be other times. Meanwhile, I shall idle the time while the enemy gives its respect to the dead."

Rhonda rolled her body round and with a frightened look, inquired, "Pray, you evil undertaker, whose death now?"

The witch laughed. "Oh, fear not. I shall save your brother till last." She sat back down on the bed to reach for her.

Rhonda fell back and sobbed into the pillow. "Is there nothing in heaven that can stop you? Woe is me to think you are to rule! And if so, why must you end my brother's life? I'd rather he be under your spell than under six feet of earth, and thereby never to see his kindliness again! Oh, spare him and I shall do your bidding."

Erinysia fondled the long red hair down the back of Rhonda's chemise. Lifting the hair up to the girl's nape, Erinysia bent over and kissed her gently, then laid her cheek on Rhonda's shoulder and sighed. "Hmm, you offer me a challenge, little one. Lance, I doubt can be charmed. Still, a willing prize like you is worth the effort....We shall see, my sweet. Yet, mark, either way you shall be mine." She swept up the lithe body and held it close to her full breasts. Rhonda stiffened, then squirmed, maneuvering her elbows to push away, but Erinysia only squeezed her tighter and placed a hand under Rhonda's chin, forcing their eyes to meet. Rhonda's eye-lids drooped, she swooned and became limp. Erinysia hungrily salivated over the tiny breasts, then released her. She got back into her military gear, muttering, "Yea, I do love this child—why, I believe, that was the motive for my marriage to her father!" She giggled, "My, such motherly instincts!—And why not since I have two mothers!"

36. Eve's Thrust

The coalition of the late king, Lucia and Lance loyalists assembled along the ridge. The princess on her wondrous steed faced the thousand strong. She pointed toward the banner bearer of the white and gold crest of Lodeston—a scroll and scale of justice hanging from a tree—and explained, "Brave men of the south and north, you see before you the symbol of rightful royalty of this land. We have indeed buried a king who left no heirs; but I am compelled to reveal at this painful moment that King Henry did not possess the divine right to be king. He was instead a prophet of the ultimate destiny of a preordained united land for the celestially appointed leader thousands of years ago. It is for this reason that we now must climb the motte and storm the castle, ridding the land of the rebellious witch, the daughter of the befallen Lilith who has resurrected her ambition of revenge against self-rule naturally embedded in human destiny. It remains with you and me to defend ourselves and all of humanity against her rude efforts to strip from us our precious right to free-will."

Suddenly a great shadow blocked the morning light; the ranks cowered and wailed in unison. A huge pterodactyl swooped down on Lucia and with its ten foot beak wrenched her from the saddle. Her horse reared up and grew out wings and flew after them, but the immense beast swatted its webbed wing at the comparatively diminutive horse, dashing it to the ground. Lance urged the steed to its hoofs and attempted to mount, but it bucked to soar once again toward the prehistoric beasts. Despite its extraordinary speed it was no match for the pterosaur which slapped the horse again to earth. In triumph the pterosaur blared hideously and circled high above the castle as its mates perched on the cone caps of the towers seemed to flap their wings in approval. Instantly their wings abruptly halted as the resistant princess continually pricked the point of her dagger at the thick-skinned claws.

High above in a fleecy cloud was Eve kneeling in prayer as another cloud bumped against it and thundered with the appearance of Enyo who held the diamond tip to her lips, then without having to release the spear, aimed it toward the flying monster. The beast was jarred momentarily by the invisible force. Lucia slid out of its hold and dropped some fifty feet until Enyo rubbed the diamond tip, transforming the princess into a huge white eagle that soared back up toward the prehistoric bird and clawed at its thin filmy wings. The beast shrilled and began to fight back but the eagle out-maneuvered it and continued to jibe at the weakening wings. The other pterosaurs took invasive flight to converge on the air battle, but already Lucia's assailant in flight spiraled heavily and fell into the castle ward, crushing and smothering many scattering troops who fell under its weight and wings. The superior speed of the eagle angled in and out, clawing and biting the wings of the squadron of pterosaurs. Then suddenly the great white bird soared high into the fleecy clouds, tipping a wing to Eve and Enyo as it passed. The flying monsters zoomed up in pursuit. High above in the blazing sun above the fleecy clouds, one by one the great pterosaurs' membrane- wings erupted in flames from the rays unimpeded from the density of the atmosphere. The eagle descended and as it approached the ridge it transformed into Lucia and she triumphantly settled back into her saddle to the cheers of the army. They began to chant "Long Live Lucia, the queen goddess of all the land."

She beamed a smile across the sea of faces, then looked askance at Lance. "That was good of you to help my steed, my love."

He blushed. "Nay, I felt rather stupid—especially since it threw me off."

She laughed. "Well, you are surely of use now. Lead the charge on the castle, my good knight."

"Oh?" He gestured across the ravine to the gate. "And what of that three headed thing?"

She laughed again. It seems I'm well equipped to handle such matters."

He laughed. "Indeed!...What will you be this time?"

Erinysia went into a frenzy on the battlement in seeing the immense carcass of the pterosaur stretching across the bailey and above her prehistoric turret guards tumbling down from the sky in balls of fire. Spreading her arms to the sky in beseeching help from Lilith brought no results. "Fie, deserted again!" Turning to see the approaching enemy with Lance and Lucia at the lead, she leaned over through a crenel to the dragon below and screamed, "Dumb beast, cross the moat and lay fire across their path!" The great beast, though not as large and heavy as Plateos line but more nimble, slid into the deep muck and crossed to the other side. Its three heads sprayed fire across a field of tall grass growing on the lower side of the ravine. The invaders' march came to a halt.

In spite of Lucia's protest, Lance bridled his horse along the path of flame trying desperately to find an opening to gallop or leap through, but concluded the swath of flame was too thick to leap. He returned to the princess and eyed her with puzzlement. She looked to the sky, then closed her eyes in concentration her little hand clutching the amulet. Thunder rolled and lightning bolted and a heavy cloud burst ensued. Within seconds the fiery field was an array of rising steam as the fire was quickly doused by the sudden downpour. The dragon continued exhaling flames, only to end in a cloud of steam. Lucia's steed spread wings again and with sword swinging overhead, Lucia charged under the flames of Erinysia's monstrosity and in tandem deftly lopped off its heads which toppled into the moat, instantly boiling from their dying, flaming breaths. Simultaneously at the eastern drawbridge, the other dragon imploded into its nether world.

The troops at the main drawbridge hailed her wondrous powers and all gaped in greater wonderment when Lance latched onto her steed while it flew over the moat to approach the gate. Lance quickly swung his roped grapnel through a crenel. The gatekeeper ran to release the tackle, but in looking down where Lucia's golden arrow aimed at him he backed away as Lance climbed up to release the bridge. A half dozen troops challenged him but the mighty Lord-Protector quickly out-dueled three of them while Lucia climbed up, straddled the wall and cast a spell of immobility on the others by simply grasping her gold hilt. Lance reached the winch and the bridge lowered while Lucia stood guard holding at bay another dozen under her spell.

From the highest watchtower Erinysia screamed in frustration as the king's horsemen converged and sped over the bridge under the watchful marksmanship of Lucia's archers. Erinysia looked down and snapped her fingers: a huge black stallion mounted by the stiff black armored body of Bennet with a fixed lance appeared on the bridge. The foot soldiers halted abruptly. Then a brave officer bolted from the ranks to challenge the black apparition. He yelled, "Men, do not fear the dead. We all did see Baron Bennet's execution. Look again; see ye his head is tilted as though hastily sewed back on!" As the knight raised his sword to strike, the black stallion reared up; the knight backed away to avoid getting kicked. As the horse landed, the knight gasped at a green glow crystallizing into a squirming, screaming Rhonda in the arms of the Bennet apparition. Try as she might she could not break the dead man's hold.

Lance raised the portcullis for the horsemen's charge. He looked down in horror to see his sister struggling. He yelled to Lucia in search of Erinysia who now cowered against the tower support trying to summon up more powers, "Princess! My God! Rhonda is in danger! I must defend her!"

Lucia ran back to him along the parapet. "Nay, Lance make no attempt! This is not your battle!"

"It is when my sister is in jeopardy!"

"Think, Lance, you cannot fight a dead man!"

"Surely, I can at least cut him away to release my sister from death's grip!"

"The dead must undo the dead!" She momentarily clasped the wooden amulet, then pressed it to her forehead, invoking an incantation: "Look into the soul and merge the body." Suddenly on the bridge facing the black horseman was a pale rider in gleaming armor upon the great red mare Bryan had tamed in the north.

Lance stared in amazement. "My God! You've brought him back!"

The pale rider's glossy eyes met those of the black rider. Both steeds reared up in unison and engaged in a biting match. Suddenly a faint glimmer came into Bryan's eyes and he bridled his steed to the side, drew his silvery sword and struck a blow several inches above Rhonda to Bennet's neck and the lifeless head tilted to the other side. Bennet released his hold on Rhonda; simultaneously Erinysia summoned a great condor that swooped up Rhonda by its giant claws. Despite his tilted head, Bennet, discovering a mace in his hand, began to attack by rote in pummeling the shield of the white rider who fell from his horse. The great red steed reared up and thrust its fore hoofs, dismounting the black rider. Bennet landed on his feet and wielded the heavy club over Bryan who, still on his back, quickly held up a wooden cross. Bennet's glossy eyes flared in amber; his expressionless face suddenly grimaced, and he began to melt down to green slime, spilling into the moat and onto the floating carcass of the dragon.

The Forces of Free Will rushed across the bridge; the brave but helpless knight who had before challenged the black rider, stopped to help up the near lifeless champion. A squadron of longbowmen followed with arrows high to pick off the defending bowmen on the parapet. The rest of Lucia's archers formed a horseshoe virtually unmolested round the western walls to continue their deadly marksmanship. Erinysia screamed for her spiritual mother and suddenly she had the power to reincarnate from the cinders her fleet of pterosaurs to swoop down on the bowmen. She shook her fist to the sky when Lucia launched an overwhelming number of brown eagles that pecked away at the pellicular wings until each reptile helplessly fell with a thud.

Lucia saw overhead the giant condor circling the castle; Rhonda screaming and kicking her legs, and squirming in desperation between the massive talons. Quickly Lucia metamorphosed into the great white eagle, which quickly soared toward the condor and clawed at the condor's snapping beak and then crushed its head in its powerful talons. The condor immobilized, opened up its claws and Rhonda went into a screaming free-fall. The eagle instantly followed and snared her in its talons and gently dropped her on the bridge at Bryan's feet. The eagle dissolved into a shining light and Lucia reappeared. She knelt beside the champion, gently removed his helm and pressed her amulet to Bryan's forehead. Life shone through his eyes and he smiled as they cast new life onto Rhonda who squealed in delight. Rhonda would have hugged him were it not for his heavy armor. Instead, she leaped up to hang on him while she kissed him on lips, once cold blue, now turned to warm pink. Lucia's archers quickly formed a circle of defense and escorted the couple into the castle where already the vast western bailey up to the twenty foot wall of the keep's middle ward was in the main captured but for much of the rampart leading to segments of the parapet where Lucia's archers continued to rain down their fatal arrows upon Erinysia's dwindling forces.

Erinysia growing restive from defeat, wailed to the sky and the sun suddenly set and from the darkened sky to the north thousands more of the bats from Lodeston's cave arrived and swooped in on Lucia's archers and the rest of the Forces of Free Will fighting on the bailey ramparts. Howls of pain permeated the battle scene as the nipping bats bloodied the bodies of those who defied the daughter of the spirit with whom these creatures dwelled for thousands of years. The longbowmen, despite the fluttering, swooping bats tried desperately to shoot them down but the echolocation mechanism of these busy intruders proved too effective for the arrowheads to pick them off. Suddenly out of the mêlée, towered Sir Charles with his heavy sword battering down dozens of bats at a time. Quickly, as though in communication with one another, a half dozen bats swooped under his sword and plunged through his opened visor and into his shaggy beard. Horrified, Charles let out a hideous cry as the bats, though snared in the beard nipped at his chin. He fell like an aged oak.

Lance, leaped from the battlement onto the rampart, retrieved a gauntlet on the way and hastened to Charles's side, waving the gauntlet and battering the busy bats round his head. Sir Arnold ran to help and guarded his comrades from the onslaught of the bats by broadsiding them in flight. Lance slid off Charles's helmet and with his gauntlet picked off the snared rodents one by one from his shaggy beard. Each time Charles howled, and looked up with untold fright. Never had Lance witnessed fear in this brave knight. He tried to comfort him with humor by asking, "Would you rather I cut off your beard, Charles!"

Charles chortled, "Don't you dare!" Arnold laughed.

Lance removed the last from his friend's beard and put the helmet back on and helped him to his feet. He looked at Arnold. "Search for the medic—these bites are nasty." Arnold led Charles to the makeshift apothecary while his busy sword swung at the bats hovering over them.

Lucia, in the meantime, waved her hand to the firmament blackened by the bats, and down swooped a giant cloud of immense owls—their crescendo of hooting, orchestrated by Enyo, drowned out the hideous squealing of their prey. They swallowed in flight many of the flying rodents while clutching several at once in their claws and flying away with them. Within minutes the skies were clear of busy flight and the sun peeped out in full again. Erinysia butted her head against the tower wall in frustration, yet yelled down to her fighting men, "Fight on, children of Lilith! Rid the land of the evil of these misled know it alls—these bearers of biblical falsehoods!" She descended the parapet by the inner ward and crossed over to the keep where she ascended the stairs to her chambers.

Lance, having removed his heavy armor, climbed the secondary wall to the keep and met up with Lucia from where they bounded the spiral steps in pursuit of Erinysia. Lance broke down the door to Erinysia's chambers where he was immediately pounced on by the panther once more transmogrified. The once invincible Lord-Protector was driven back through the doorway past Lucia and tumbled down the steps. The panther pursued, but Lucia immediately altered it to a purring, harmless kitten, but not before its sabre-like teeth had pierced the shoulder plate, and Lance, stunned from the fall, lay sprawled on the steps in a pool of blood. Lucia, whimpering, bent down to tend to his wound.

Erinysia charged through the doorway and down the steps with a battle-axe she had telekinetically torn from the wall. Lucia lithely held up her shield of divine antiquity and the blow glanced off. Erinysia tried again, but Lucia held her at bay with her great golden sword and edged her back up the stairs. Erinysia hurled the axe at her and peddled up to the crystal in her room. Lucia, stunned for a moment by the axe she parried with her shield; then, oblivious to Lance, pursued the witch who was now conjuring up more blood-thirsty bats, but Lucia's sword and shield hacked and battered them down to the floor where she ground her boot into them. "Since you wish to continue this game of weird and ugly forms, then face up to this and dance away if you can!" Lucia warned. A giant wolf spider rapidly attacked and wound its web round its prey as it edged closer to the startled witch. Erinysia tensed herself and knitted her brows in concentration; she metamorphosed into a snake that slid along the web and swallowed the spider. The snake squirmed itself perpendicularly and snaked out Erinysia's angry self who yet laughed triumphantly. "'Twas a mere insect, my dear novice, hardly worth the effort."

Lucia, so swiftly did she draw her golden sword that her motion was invisible, and with a deft arc beheaded the witch. Suddenly crashing the balcony portal was a swirling mass of white hot molten lava hovering over Erinysia. It quickly cooled spewing fragments round the room forcing Lucia to hug the floor. The great mother figure of Lilith appeared and gently picked up the head of her daughter and fused it back with laser-like eyes onto the body. Mother and daughter glanced at each other with loving smiles, then proceeded to rush Lucia who speedily rolled away to avoid them.

Lance recovered his senses, struggling to his feet, and charged up the steps into the chamber and lunged his sword into Lilith who laughed and immediately drew it out of her body and threw it back like a dagger. Lucia quickly protected him with her shield. Lilith advanced toward Lance, and with her fist, smashed him on his mail headpiece; he dropped like lead to the floor. Erinysia snapped her finger at the kitten and it leaped out of its helpless form back into the ferocious black leopard. Larger and more powerful than ever the animal leaped at Lucia who nonetheless smashed the beast with her heavy shield, but not before it tore at her shoulder and its claws snagged her hair. Lance jumped up and pulled the beast from his love, but the brave knight was no match for the immortal combatant, Lilith, who pushed him away from the panther and princess like a rag doll. Lucia grimaced in pain as she tried to stop the shoulder's bleeding. Lilith then stepped in and pulled Lucia up by her golden hair and held her high. Lucia squealed and squirmed in suspension trying to loosen Lilith's grip. Erinysia pulled down a whip from the wall. "Yea, spank the life and spirit out of her!— 'tis fitting for a bratty usurper!" Lilith growled. Then Lilith saw Lucia's amulet. "Wait, my daughter, do you see what she wears?...The eyes of Eve!" Take your sword of ancient bronze and run it through her; that is the only weapon that will harm her!"

Erinysia scowled. "Can't I at least have the thrill of lashing her a hundred times?"

"Do it after she's dead. Now, mark, draw your sword!"

"What you even deny me the pleasure of defeating her in a duel?"

"Don't be headstrong, Erinysia! Your gypsy ways are unbecoming. With one swoop of her golden blade and you'll be in the pit with me!"

"But before she did just that and I am here!"

"Yea, but I was not incarnate at the moment. Now that I am in body, Eve now drives her."

Erinysia pouted. "Then I'll remove it, Mother!" Erinysia reached for Lucia's golden hilt.

"No, never! Anyone who grips that hilt or tries to unbuckle her will be under her spell!" cried Lilith who abruptly turned to stop her daughter and in so doing loosened her grip on Lucia's hair. Lucia, oblivious to the blood streaming from her shoulder now pried open Lilith's grip and dropped to the floor. She rolled over several times and got to her feet and placed her hand on her hilt. Both adversaries momentarily slipped into a stupor as Lucia drew her sword.

Surprisingly Erinysia snapped out of it in raising her sword of bronze menacingly at Lucia. "So, only by the sword, eh? Then a sword it shall be!"

Lucia laughed. "Have you forgotten that I lopped off your beautiful head once already."

She lunged at the princess who deftly parried and plunged the golden blade into Erinysia's free arm. She howled in pain but lunged again only to be wounded again in the dueling arm. Falling to her knees, Erinysia dropped the sword and whimpered. Fatally, Lucia turned from her when Lance groaned into consciousness. She hastened to his side and helped him up. Suddenly both froze as Lilith stood before them with sword in hand.

"Well, this is the end of Eve at long last. Just a prick from this sword will bring it all to an end. Foolish of her to leave you so vulnerable as to run to the aid of a mere mortal."

Lance stepped in front of Lucia. "Verily, the end is here, but for you, ancient queen," he said and drew his mighty sword.

"Oh, no, Lance, please don't—she is too dangerous!"

"Exactly!" he countered. "Therefore, stay back." Swiftly he wielded his sword and Lilith's was swept from her hand."

Lilith laughed. "Very good, skilled knight, but there's more to opposites than sword play." Her eyes went ablaze, targeting his sword overhead as he was about to split her skull. The hilt burned hot in his hand and the great blade melted and wiggled like a snake. He dropped it but immediately drew a dirk and stabbed her in the heart.

She laughed and pulled it out. He was dumbstruck in seeing not a trace of blood. Lucia urged, "My love, it is no use. Please desist, I must deal with her alone."

"Wisely put," Lilith said; then rubbed her square jaw. "'Dear,' is it? If you want him spared then face the sword's point."

"Don't, Lucia,...what use if you are dead?" he pleaded. "Rather I die in the effort of saving you."

"Hush, Lance, fate spins its thread in ever mystifying lines. What must be mysteriously—*is*." Lucia raised her sword. Lilith picked up Lance's heavy sword and bent it back, perfectly straight.

A bulbous incandescence radiated between Lucia and Lilith. Margaret evolved out of the light and ripped the sword from Lilith's hand. She then with the hilt smashed her in the face, and Lilith fell back, toppling over wounded Erinysia. "That is a message from Eve!" Margaret reported.

Erinysia endured her wounds and steadied her mother who yammered, "Don't dare utter the name of that imposter!" Thus renewed, Lilith took in a deep breath and grew to seven feet tall. Reaching out with enormous arms, she hurled Lucia's mother through the balcony window and over the railing. Lucia dashed to the balcony, leaned over with down-stretched arm. Suddenly Margaret was suspended in flight and swept up, landing on the balcony. She managed a grateful smile, then slumped to the floor, dazed as red and white feathers swirled about her as though sentinels. Lilith pursued Lucia who narrowly escaped a sword's thrust. They dueled fiercely on the balcony. Often, in spite of Lilith's gargantuan size, Lucia found the mark but just as before the wounds immediately sealed without a drop of blood. But each wound dwindled her size. By the seventh thrust into her body she was of normal stature. Lilith could not believe the dexterity of Lucia's sword play.

Meanwhile inside, Erinysia was regaining her strength as the wounds in her arms were rapidly healing. She crawled over to her sword to assist Lilith. When she reached for it, Lance stepped on her arm. She shrilled, "Mephistopheles!"

Out of its daze the great panther crouched before Lance who quickly, as the giant cat flew toward the hapless knight, picked up Erinysia's sword, ducked the claws and ripped the black magic sword into the cat's belly. The panther ignited in flames and dropped its ashes. Lance thought aloud, "Ah, dear Tracy, how fitting the revenge for thee!" Outraged, Erinysia picked up her whip and snapped it round Lance's tabard and rolled him toward her; whereupon she burned her coal-like green-black eyes into his and he froze in catalepsy.

Impatience and frustration grew in Lilith in not being able to so much as scratch Lucia. "Daughter!" she called into the room, "this is an unfriendly sword—bring the bronze; it seems fate has it that you must strike the blow." She threw down the sword, ducked under Lucia's thrust as Erinysia bounded to the balcony, swinging the bronze sword wildly, broadsiding Lucia over the balcony wall. Both women leaned over to see the satisfaction of their foe at least battered by the fall, if not killed, and for all in the court to see the consequence of denying the power of life and repressed will. Lucia let out a piercing scream, that echoed off the watch tower bells. The shrill and subsequent bells reverberated the castle combatants in the bailey and on the parapet. Lucia's Forces of Free Will gasped in horror from the scream of their destined queen in fatal descent. The echo traveled to the sky which became clouded and parted by an immense iron hand in which Enyo braced herself to catch the one she etched to protect. Suddenly a gargantuan iron, rusted foot stepped into and covered the bailey, scattering the troops who eyed in wonder the superstructure of an iron knight a hundred feet tall, brushing off and raining down flakes of rust upon them.

Even Lilith was stunned by the spectacle and extremely disgusted in seeing the immense wonder of the world catch the princess descent from the high keep. Along with Erinysia, both cowered back into the room. Gently the immense iron hand returned the princess safely to the balcony. She thanked Enyo and smiled up—the iron warrior was a head taller than the keep—at the brittle mask-like face, then ran into the room. She clapped her hands in glee as the hand brushed past her to reach in and wrap its chain-mail fingers round both Erinysia and Lilith—both screaming helplessly. He wrenched the squirming, kicking women up from the balcony, turned and stepped over the bailey wall to the cheers of the Forces of Free Will whose eyes all followed its giant steps which within minutes had taken it to the northern moor and he disappeared beyond the horizon.

Margaret self-administered her healing powers and she was quickly on her feet. Lucia rushed to embrace her. "Oh, Mother, I was so frightened. I thought for sure we had lost the cause." She ran over to Lance and pressed the wooden charm to him to revive him.

Her mother laughed. "Ah, my dear, you had one last remaining king in the deck. Your call for Colossus was the draw that ended the game."

"But Mother I didn't...I thought it was you!" Lucia said with wrinkled brow.

"Oh, my, you don't suppose Eve, though forbidden, would again defy God?" Margaret's eyes twinkled.

"I doubt she has a connection with mythology!" Lucia analyzed humorously.

"Nevertheless, she's a crafty one."

"So is your ancient sentinel at the cave," Lucia reminded her.

Margaret tapped her forehead. "Why, of course! — that old fox!"

They, along with Lance, still groggy, parted for the bailey.

The great giant knight of antiquity at the northern foothills kicked up a cloud of peat as it spun like a top hurling the screaming women toward the volcano to the north whereupon they rocketed through the torn cap and submerged into molting lava that erupted some fifty feet into the dark shadows, then subsided. The Colossus dissolved into an immense mushroom cloud of Ares' blood-like light and vaporized into the firmament.

Ethan emerged from the tunnel and kneeled in prayer of thanks; then he rose up and walked round the rim to check on the progress of the burning stump he had the guards set fire to. Twigs from the bough left strewn from their chopping, he kicked them into the lava. He went to the inscription. "Ah, dear Enyo, indeed, you have made a believer of me with your ingenious and wily defense!" He ran his hand over the inscription and then kissed it.

The last remaining resistance of the rebel forces had stopped in its tracks in seeing the awesome Colossus. There had been dead silence in and round the castle when the great mobile structure strode off with thunderous steps carrying the two women beyond the horizon toward the mountains. And when he had spun the women round and unleashed them, his centrifugal force had sent furious gusts toward the castle, wafting red and white plumage onto the bailey ward.

Rhonda at the center of the bailey, still clinging to Bryan, hailed, "Long live Queen Lucia!" This catalyzed the fighting men of both sides to chant the same and soon it traveled through the entire bailey to the east end.

"Aye, my darling," Lance said as they stepped out into the wards to mingle with the throng, "long live my love."

"Oh, I shall, my king!"

"King!" he echoed. "But I have no rights to it."

"No, it is fitting to be Henry's successor ." Lucia winked over at her mother. "Besides, since he had no divine right and I have, it is my wish."

He chuckled. "How embarrassing to be king and have a queen for his champion!"

"Ah, but you were a great champion for Lucia in Lodeston valley," Margaret reminded him, "And you shall be again."

"Oh?...And just how is that?" he asked. "In face of that rusted thing she called upon there is no use of chivalry and knights to preserve the peace."

"Well, with Erinysia and Lilith no longer a threat," Margaret explained, "events shall return to the normal ways of mankind."

"Yea, and in addition," Lucia piped, "apparently through good will—cunning Ethan's, no doubt—we only borrowed the Colossus from the Romans, more accurately the Greek's stunning Enyo. So, dear Lance, there will still be much use of you."

"Ah, my daughter" yelped Margaret, "then the force isn't as mystifying to you as had let on." Lucia winked and smiled.

Lance laughed. "My love, I have never met anyone like you who could mix myths, legends and religion in one fell swoop!"

"Oh, now, who's to say they don't all come from the same pot?"

"Lord, not the witches' cauldron, I trust!" Lance roared, then laughed.

She giggled and observed, "Nevertheless, you are indeed my knight in battered armor." Lucia further tweaked, "And my champion;" she looked up at him coquettishly, "That is, if you still want to be."

He laughed. "You might just as well ask the rooster if it wants to greet the dawn or the owl to hoot the night." He kissed her, and the infantry and knights circling round the three cheered. Then Lance inquired, "Well, my queen by apparent acclamation, and since you've anointed me king, just how are we to govern?"

"Why, justly, of course."

"But where?"

"Why from here, at least for a while, and Rhonda, since she is now a princess, shall rule Lodeston and with Bryan as *her* champion." She frowned playfully. "And what do you mean, by acclamation? It is more than that, you know. It is scrolled indelibly in everlasting stone back home."

"Back home?...Then you will miss it?"

"Oh, yes, it shall always be thought of as my home," she said reflectively as she eyed a red and white feather wafting in the yard. She smiled. "Ethan will make certain."

"As indeed for both of us; but now the vast low and highlands are in truth your home now, my queen."

"And, remember, Lucia," Margaret intervened, "Quandron here is my home from earlier years!" Just then Margaret spotted Rita coming through the gate with the forest throng that received news of the victory over the baron's forces the day before and folded camp. She ran to greet her.

Rhonda, standing next to the no longer spellbound David and Maureen, broke through the throng and ran to her brother to hug him. "Oh, darling Lance, isn't it wonderful? My Bryan is alive and is the same loving self, cleansed of that wicked witch's darkened spell!"

"Verily, if only to see you happy again, but I too am thrilled to see my old squire a worthy knight again!" Lance turned and greeted Bryan who extended his hand. "Alive or half dead, you have proven your knighthood, good Bryan!"

"Thank you, my lord," Bryan said; "but I rather suspect it was my love for Rhonda that was certified today."

"Ah, yea, sweet love!...It seems, Bryan, you were right. I have been enchanted by Lucia and finally found my love."

Bryan grinned, then guffawed, "A double wedding perhaps?" He glanced over at Rhonda.

"Ah, yes, yes, I should like that!...despite my one haunting sorrow is that my darling Tracy is no more to share the moment." Rhonda wiped a tear drop, then lifted her spirit to hug Lucia. "Do we have permission, your majesty, to intrude upon yours?"

Lucia laughed. "Hardly an intrusion! I'd be delighted!"

Rhonda and Bryan traipsed off to be alone. Lance said to Lucia, "Ah, so good to see Bryan again. I trust this is no magical deception—that he is here to stay?"

"No fear, my mother saw to that."

He scratched his forehead. "What do you mean?"

"As you know she took a liking to Bryan from the start. The son she never had, I suspect. Before he left us for Quandron, my mother blest him with a reserve of life that not even Erinysia could penetrate fully."

Margaret returned, and Lance rubbed his chin, asking, "How is it, Lady Margaret, that you yourself interceded and directly confronted Lilith?...Why, of course, it was from your Eve's bidding, wasn't it?"

"Not *your* Eve, eh?" Margaret stabbed.

"Verily, *ours*!" He corrected himself.

Margaret squealed in delight, "You underestimate Lucia and me.... Thinking us unable to cope with a divine, but demoniac force, eh?" She giggled as she caressed her cheek with one of Enyo's feathers. "I think that this time we had God on our side."

"*And* Colossus." He chuckled, then reflected, "This time?...Hmm, aye, I see."

Lady Margaret grinned. "Yes, Eve had a premonition that God was beginning to favor her."

"Enough of this ironic small talk of giants and divine matters," Lucia intervened with a laugh. "Excuse us, Mother, but Lance and I must rid ourselves of this battle gear— then bathe and dissolve the grime of war."

"Yes, my daughter, for what is conquest leading to royalty without the consummation of an immaculate love to epitomize your love of humanity—and thus help Eve in her quest for absolution?"

"Yes, dear Mother, I trust the Tree of Life and the Tree of Knowledge are at long last one and the same."

The End